~~Choice~~ Award, a Cata~~lon~~... ~~Award~~,
and she's a double recipient of the Book~~sellers'~~ Best
Award. She belongs to the Orange County chapter and
the Los Angeles chapter of RWA.

Charlene writes "hunky heroes with heart." She knows a
little something about true romance—she married her
high school sweetheart! When not writing, Charlene
enjoys sunny Pacific beaches, great coffee, reading books
from her favorite authors and spending time with her
family. You can find her on Facebook and Twitter.
Charlene loves to hear from her readers! You can write
her at PO Box 4883, West Hills, CA 91308, USA, or sign
up for her newsletter for fun blogs and ongoing contests
at www.charlenesands.com.

Moonlight Beach Bachelors

CHARLENE SANDS

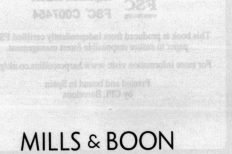

MILLS & BOON

First Published in Great Britain 2018
by Mills & Boon, an imprint of HarperCollins*Publishers*
1 London Bridge Street, London, SE1 9GF

MOONLIGHT BEACH BACHELORS © 2018 Harlequin Books S. A.

Her Forbidden Cowboy © 2015 Charlene Swink
The Billionaire's Daddy Test © 2015 Charlene Swink
One Secret Night, One Secret Baby © 2016 Charlene Swink

ISBN: 978-0-263-26711-2

05-0418

HER FORBIDDEN COWBOY

CHARLENE SANDS

To our own Zane William (Pettis), the bright little light
in our family. And to his mommy, Angi,
and daddy, Kent, with love to all!

One

The heels of Jessica's boots beat against the redwood of Zane Williams's sun-drenched deck overlooking the Pacific Ocean. Shielded by the shade of an overhang, he didn't miss a move his new houseguest made as he leaned forward on his chaise longue. His sister-in-law had officially arrived.

Was he still allowed to call her that?

Gusty breezes lifted her caramel hair, loosening the knot at the back of her head. A few wayward tendrils whipped across her eyes and, as she followed behind his assistant Mariah, her hand came up to brush them away. Late afternoon winds were strong on Moonlight Beach, swirling up from the shore as the sun lowered on the horizon. It was the time most sunbathers packed up their gear and went home and the locals came out. Shirt-billowing weather and one of the few things he'd come to like about California beach living.

He removed his sunglasses to get a better look at her. She wore a snowdrift-white blouse tucked into washed-to-the-millionth-degree jeans and a wide brown belt. Tortoiseshell-rimmed eyeglasses delicately in place didn't hide the pain and distress in her eyes.

Sweet Jess. Seeing her bro͞————————...memories, and the frigidness in his heart thawed a bit.

She looked like...*home.*

It hurt to think about Beckon, Texas. About his ranch

and the life he'd had there once. It hurt to think about how he'd met Jessica's sister, Janie, and the way their small-town lives had entwined. In one respect, the tragedy that occurred more than two years ago might've been a lifetime ago. In another, it seemed as if time was standing still. Either way, his wife, Janie, and their unborn child were gone. They were never coming back. His mouth began to twitch. An ache in the pit of his stomach spread like wildfire and scorched him from the inside out.

He focused on Jessica. She carried a large tapestry suitcase woven in muted tones of gray and mauve and peach. He'd given Janie and Jessica matching luggage three years ago on their birthdays. It had been a fluke that both girls, the only two offspring of Mae and Harold Holcomb, were born on the same day, seven years apart.

Grabbing at the crutches propped beside his lounge chair, Zane slowly lifted himself up, careful not to fall and break his other foot. Mariah would have his head if he got hurt again. His casted wrist ached like the devil, but he refused to have his assistant come running every damn time he wanted to get up. It was bad enough she'd taken on the extra role of nursemaid. He reminded himself to have his business manager give Mariah a big fat bonus.

She halted midway on the deck, her disapproving gaze dropping to his busted wrist and crutches before she shot him a silent warning. "Here he is, Jessica." Mariah's peach-pie voice was sweet as ever for his houseguest. "I'll leave you two alone now."

"Thanks, Mariah," he said.

Her mouth pursed tight, she about-faced and marched off, none too pleased with him.

Jessica came forward. "Still such a gentleman, Zane," she said. "Even on crutches."

He'd forgotten how much she sounded like Janie. Hearing her sultry tone stirred him up inside. But that's about all Janie and Jessica had in common. The two sisters were different in most other ways. Jess wasn't as tall as her sister. Her eyes were a light shade of green instead of the deep emerald that had sparkled from Janie's eyes. Jess was brunette, Janie blonde. And their personalities were miles apart. Janie had been a risk-taker, a strong woman who could hold her own against Zane's country-star fame, which might've intimidated a less confident woman. From what he remembered about Jess, she was quieter, more subtle, a schoolteacher who loved her profession, a real sweetheart.

"Sorry about your accident."

Zane nodded. "Wasn't much of an accident. More like stupidity. I lost focus and fell off the stage. Broke my foot in three places." He'd been at the Los Angeles Amphitheater, singing a silly tune about chasing ducks on the farm, all the while thinking about Janie. A video of his fall went viral on the internet. Everyone in country music and then some had witnessed his loss of concentration. "My tour's postponed for the duration. Can't strum a guitar with a broken wrist."

"Don't suppose you can."

She put down her luggage and gazed over the railing to the shore below. Sunlight glossed over deep steely-blue water as whitecaps foamed over wet sand, the tide rising. "I suppose Mama must've strong-armed you into doing this."

"Your mama couldn't strong-arm a puppy."

She whipped around to face him, her eyes sharp. "You know what I mean."

He did. Fact was, he wouldn't refuse Mae Holcomb anything. And she'd asked him this favor. *It's huge,* she'd said to him. *My Jess is hurtin' and needs to clear her head. I'm asking you to let her stay with you a week, maybe two. Please, Zane, watch out for her.*

He'd given his word. He'd take care of Jess and make sure she had time to heal. Mae was counting on him, and there wasn't anything he wouldn't do for Janie's mother. She deserved that much from him.

"You can stay as long as you like, Jess. You've got to know that."

Her mouth began to tremble. "Th-thanks. You heard what happened?"

"I did."

"I—I couldn't stay in town. I had to get out of Texas. The farther, the better."

"Well, Jess, you're as far west as you could possibly go." Five miles north of Malibu by way of the Pacific Coast Highway.

Her shoulders slumped. "I feel like such a fool."

Reaching out, he cupped her chin, forcing her eyes to his, the darn crutch under his arm falling to rest on the railing. "Don't."

"I won't be very good company," she whispered, dang near breathless.

His body swayed, not allowing him another unassisted moment. He released her and grabbed for his crutch just in time. He tucked it under his arm and righted his position. "That makes two of us."

Her soft laughter carried on the breeze. Probably the first bit of amusement she'd felt in days.

He smiled.

"I just need a week, Zane."

"Like I said, take as long as you need."

"Thanks." She blinked, and her eyes drifted down to his injuries. "Uh, are you in a lot of pain?"

"More like, I'm being a pain. Mariah's getting the brunt of my sour mood."

"Now I can share it with her." Her eyes twinkled for a second.

He'd forgotten what it was like having Jess around. She was ten years younger than him, and he'd always called her his little sis. He hadn't seen much of her since Janie's death. Cursed by guilt and anguish, he'd deliberately removed himself from the Holcombs' lives. He'd done enough damage to them.

"Hand up your luggage to me," he told her. With his good hand, he tucked his crutches under his armpits and propped himself, then wiggled his fingers. If he could get a grip on the bag...

Jessica rolled her eyes and hoisted her valise. "I appreciate it, Zane. But I've got this. Really, it's not heavy. I packed light. You know, summer-at-the-beach kind of clothes."

She let him off the hook. He would've tried, but fooling with her luggage wouldn't have been pretty. The doggone crutches made him clumsy as a drunken sailor, and he wasn't supposed to put any weight on his foot yet. "Fine, then. Why don't you settle in and rest up a bit? I'm bunking on this level. You've got an entire wing of rooms to yourself upstairs. Take your pick and spread out."

He followed behind as she made her way inside the wide set of light oak French doors leading to the living room. "Feel free to look around. I can have Mariah give you a tour."

"No, that's not necessary." She scanned over what she could see of the house, taking in the expanse—vaulted ceilings, textured walls, art deco interior and sleek contemporary furniture. He caught her vibe, sensing her confusion. What was Zane Williams, a country-western artist and a born and bred Texan, doing living on a California beach? When he'd leased this place with the option to buy, he told himself it was because he wanted a change. He was building Zane's on the Beach, his second restaurant in as many years, and he'd been offered roles in several Hollywood movies. He didn't know if he was cut out for acting, so the pending offers were still on the table.

She sent him an over-the-shoulder glance. "It's...a beautiful house, Zane."

His crutches supporting him, he sidled up next to her, seeing the house from her perspective. "But not *me*?"

"I guess I don't know what that is anymore."

"It's just a house. A place to hang my hat."

She gave his hatless head a glance. "It's a palace on the sea."

He chuckled. So much for his attempt at humble. The house was a masterpiece. One of three designed by the architect who lived next door. "Okay, you got me there. Mariah found the house and leased it on the spot. She said it would shake the cobwebs from my head. Had it awhile, but this is my first summer here." He leaned back, darting a glance around. "At least the humidity is bearable and it never seems to rain, so no threat of thunderstorms. The neighbors are nice."

"A good place to rest up."

"I suppose, if that's what I'm doing."

"Isn't it?"

He shrugged, fearing he'd opened up a can of worms. Why was he revealing his innermost thoughts to her? They weren't close anymore. He hardly knew Jessica as an adult, and yet they shared a deeply powerful connection. "Sure it is. Are you hungry? I can have my housekeeper make you—"

"Oh, uh…no. I'm not hungry right now. Just a bit tired from the trip. I'd better go upstairs before I collapse right here on your floor. Thanks for having a limo pick me up. And, well, thanks for everything, Zane."

She rose on her tiptoes, and the soft brush of her lips on his cheek squeezed something tight in his chest. Her hair smelled of summer strawberries, and the fresh scent lingered in his nose as she backed away.

"Welcome." The crutches dug into his armpits as they supported his weight. He hated the damn things. Couldn't wait to be free of them. "Just a suggestion, but the room to the right of the stairs and farthest down the hall has the best view of the ocean. Sunsets here are pretty glorious."

"I'll keep that in mind." Her quick smile was probably

meant to fake him out. She could pretend she wasn't hurting all that badly if she wanted to, but dark circles under her eyes and the pallor of her skin told the real story. He understood. He'd been there. He knew how pain could strangle a person until all the breath was sucked out. Hell, he'd lived it. Was still living it. And he knew something about Holcomb family pride, too.

What kind of jerk would leave any Holcomb woman standing at the altar?

Only a damn fool.

Jessica took Zane's advice and chose the guest room at the end of the hallway. Not for the amazing sunsets as Zane had suggested, but to keep out of his hair. Privacy was a precious commodity. He valued it, and so did she now. A powerful urge summoned her to slump down on the bed and cry her eyes out, but she managed to fight through the sensation. She was done with self-pity. She wasn't the first woman to be dumped at the altar. She'd been duped by a man she'd loved and trusted. She'd been so sure and missed all of the telling signs. Now she saw them through crystal clear eyes.

She busied herself unpacking her one suitcase, layering her clothes into a long, stylish light wood dresser. Carefully she set her jeans, shorts, swimsuits and undies into two of the nine drawers. She plucked out a few sleeveless sundresses and walked over the closet. With a slight tug, the double doors opened in a whoosh. The scents of cedar and freshness filled her nostrils as she gazed into a girl cave almost the size of her first-grade classroom back in Beckon. Cedar drawers, shoe racks and silken hangers were a far cry from the tiny drywalled closet in her one-bedroom apartment.

Deftly she scooped the delicate hangers under the straps of her dresses and hung them up. Next she laid her tennis shoes, flip-flops and two pairs of boots, one flat, one high-heeled, onto the floor just under her clothes. Her meager collection barely made a dent in the closet space. She closed the double doors and leaned against them. Then she took her first real glimpse at the view from her second-story bedroom.

"Wow." Breath tunneled from her chest.

Aqua seas and the sun-glazed sky made for a spectacular vista from the wide windows facing the horizon. She swallowed in a gulp of awe. Then suddenly, a strange bone-rattling feeling of loss hit her. She shivered as if assailed by a winter storm.

Why now? Why wasn't she reveling in the beauty surrounding her?

Nothing's beautiful. You lost your sister, her unborn baby and your fiancé.

"Would you like to go out onto the balcony?"

She whirled around, surprised to find Mariah, Zane's fortyish blonde assistant standing in the doorway. She'd worked for him since before he had married Janie. Jessica and Mariah's paths had crossed a few times since then. "Oh, hi." She glanced at the narrow glass door at the far end of the wall that led to the balcony. It was obviously situated there to keep from detracting from the room's sweeping view of the Pacific. "Thanks, but maybe later."

"Sure, you must be tired from the flight. Is there anything I can do for you?"

"I don't think so. I've unpacked. A shower and a nap and I'll be good to go."

Mariah smiled. "I'll be leaving for the day. Mrs. Lopez, Zane's housekeeper, is here. If you need anything, just ask her."

"Thank you... I'll be fine."

"Zane will want to have dinner with you. He eats dinner just before sunset. But he'd make an exception if you're hungry earlier."

"Sunset is fine."

Mariah studied her, her eyes unflinching and kind. "You look a little like Janie."

"I doubt that. Janie was beautiful."

"I see a resemblance. If you don't mind me saying, you have the same soulful eyes and lovely complexion."

She was pale as a ghost, and ten freckles dotted her nose. Yep, she'd counted them. Though, she'd never had acne or even a full-fledged zit to speak of in her teens. She supposed her complexion wasn't half-bad. "Thank you. I, uh, don't want to cause Zane or you any trouble. I'm basically here because it would've been harder to convince my mother otherwise, and I didn't want her to worry about me off in some deserted location to search my soul. Mama's had enough on her plate. She doesn't need to fret over me."

"I get it. Actually, you might be exactly what Zane needs to get his head out of the sand."

That was an odd statement. She narrowed her eyes, trying to make sense of it.

"He's not been himself for a while now," Mariah explained without spelling it out. Jessica gave her credit for the delicate way she put it.

"I figured. He lost his family. We all did," Jess said. She missed Janie something awful. Sometimes life was cruel.

Mariah nodded. "But having family around might be good for both of you."

She doubted that. She'd be a thorn in Zane's side. A kink in his plans. She would bide her time here, soak up some fresh sea air and then return home to face the music. Humiliation and desperate hurt had made her flee Texas. But she'd have to go back eventually. Her face pulled tight. She didn't want to think about that right now.

"Maybe," she said to Mariah.

"Well, have a good evening."

"Thanks. You, too."

After Mariah left, Jessica plucked up her shampoo and entered the bathroom. Oh, boy, and she'd thought the closet

was something. The guest bathroom came equipped with a
television, a huge oval Jacuzzi tub and an intricately tiled
spacious shower that was digitized for each of the three
shower heads looming above. She peered closer to read the
monitor. She could program the time, temperature and force
of the shower and heaven knew what else.

After she punched in a few commands, the shower
spurted to life, and water rained down. Jess smiled. A new
toy. Peeling off her clothes, she opened the clear glass door
and stepped inside. Steamy spray hit her from three sides,
with two heads spewing softly and one pulsing like the
pumping of her heart. She turned around and around, using
the fragrant liquid soap from a dispenser in the wall. She
lingered there, lost in the mist and jet stream as pent-up
tension seeped out of her bones, her limbs loose and free.
Eventually, she got down to business and worked shampoo
into her hair. Much too early, the shower turned off automatically. As she stepped out, the steam followed her. She
dried herself with a cushy white towel. How nice.

She dressed in a pair of tan midthigh shorts and a cocoa-
brown tank top. She hoped dinner with Zane wasn't a formal
thing. She hadn't brought anything remotely fashionable.

After blow-drying her hair, she lifted the long strands up
in a ponytail, leaving bangs to rest on her forehead. A little
nap had sounded wonderful minutes ago, but now she was
too keyed up to sleep. The time change would probably hit
her like a ton of bricks later, but right now, the sandy wind-
blown beach below beckoned her. She slipped her feet into
flip-flops and headed downstairs.

Lured by the scent of spices and sauce wafting to her
nose, she headed in that direction. Inside a magnificent
granite-and-stone kitchen, she came face to face with an
older woman, a little hefty in the hips, wearing an apron
and humming to herself.

The woman turned around. "*Hola*, Miss Holcomb?"

"Yes, I'm Jessica."

"*Hola*, Jessica." She nodded. "I'm Mrs. Lopez. Do you like enchiladas?"

She was Texan. She loved everything Mexican. "Yes. Smells yummy."

Mrs. Lopez lowered the oven door, and a stainless-steel rack automatically pushed forward.

"They will be ready in half an hour. Can I get you a drink? Or a snack?"

"No, thank you. I'll wait for Zane. Well, it's nice to meet you," she said, retreating from the kitchen. "I'll be back in—"

A boom sounded. "Double damn you!" Zane's loud curse echoed throughout the house.

Jessica froze in place.

Mrs. Lopez grinned and shook her head. "He cannot dress himself too well. He will not let anyone help him. He is not such a good patient."

They shared a smile. "I see." But when she'd first arrived, he was wearing jeans and a casual cotton shirt. Was he dressing up now? "Do I need to change my clothes for dinner?"

"No, no. Mr. Zane spilled iced tea on his shirt. You are dressed nice."

"Thank you." Okay, great. She felt better now. When she'd packed her clothes, she hadn't given much thought to her wardrobe. All she hoped for was to clear her head a little while here. "I thought I'd go for a walk on the beach. I'll be back in plenty of time for dinner. See you later."

Mrs. Lopez nodded and focused on the stove. Jess's stomach grumbled as she left the spicy smells of the kitchen and walked out the double doors to the deck. From there, she climbed a few more stairs down, until warm sand crept onto her flip-flops.

There were no lakes or rivers back home that compared with the balmy breezes whipping at her hair, the briny taste on her lips or the glistening golden hues reflecting off the ocean. Her steps fell lightly, making a slight impression in the packed wet sand until the next wave inched up the shore and carried her footprints out to sea. Even with the sun low over the water's edge, her skin warmed as she walked along the beach. To her right, beachfront mansions overlooking the sea filled her line of vision, each one different in design and structure. She was so intent on gauging the houses, she didn't notice a jogger approaching until he'd stopped right in front of her.

"Hi," he said, his breaths heaving.

"Hello." A swift glance at his face made her gasp silently. He was stunning and tanned and one of the most famous movie stars in the world. Dylan McKay.

He hunched over, hands on knees, catching his breath. "Give me a sec."

For what? She wanted to ask, yet she stood there, feet implanted in the sand, waiting. He was easy on the eyes, and she tried not to stare at his bare chest and the dip of his jogging shorts below a trim waist.

He righted his posture, and blood drained from her body as he aimed a heart-melting smile her way. "Thank you."

Puzzled, she stared at him. "For?"

"Being here. For giving me an excuse to stop running." He chuckled, and white teeth flashed. Was the sun-gleaming twinkle from his smile real? Could've been. Dylan McKay was every red-blooded woman's idea of the perfect man.

Except hers. She knew there was no such thing.

"Okay. But...you could've just stopped on your own, couldn't you?"

He shook his head. "No, I'm supposed to run ten miles a day. It's a work thing. I'm preparing for a role as a Navy SEAL."

No kidding? She wasn't going to pretend she didn't know who he was. Or that his bronzed body wasn't already honed and ripped. "Gotcha. How many did you do?"

His lips twisted with self-loathing. "Eight."

"That's not bad." Judging by the pained look on his face, he was a man who expected perfection of himself. "There aren't too many people who can run eight miles."

His expression lightened and he seemed to appreciate her encouragement. "I'm Dylan, by the way." He put out his hand.

"Jessica." It was a one-pump handshake.

"Are we neighbors?" he asked, his brows gathering. "I live over there." He pointed to a trilevel mansion looming close by.

She shook her head. "Not really. I'm staying with Zane Williams for a short time."

When his brows lifted ever so slightly and his eyes flashed, she read his mind. "He's...he's *family*."

He nodded. "I know Zane. Good guy."

"He is. My sister...well, he was married to Janie."

A moment passed as he put two and two together. "I'm sorry about what happened."

"Thank you."

"Well, I think I've gotten my second wind. Thanks to you. Only two miles to go. Nice meeting you, Jessica. Say hi to Zane for me."

He about-faced, trotted down the beach in the opposite direction and soon picked up his pace to a full-out jog.

She headed back to the house, a smile on her lips, a song humming in her heart. Maybe coming here wasn't such a bad idea after all.

She spotted Zane braced against the patio railing and waved. Had he been watching her? She was hit with a surge of self-consciousness. She wasn't a beach babe. Her curvy figure didn't allow two-piece bathing suits, and her pale skin tone could be compared only with the bark of a birch tree or the peel of a honeydew melon.

As she climbed the stairs, her gaze hit upon his shirt, a Hawaiian print with repeating palm trees. She'd never seen

Zane look more casual and yet appear so ill at ease in his surroundings.

"Nice walk?" he asked, removing his sunglasses.

"It beats a stroll to Beckon's Cinema Palace."

Zane laughed, a knowing glint in his eyes. "You got that right. I haven't thought about the Palace in a long time." His voice sounded gruff as if he'd go back to those days in a heartbeat.

There wasn't a whole lot to do in Beckon, Texas, so on Saturday night the parking lot at the Palace swarmed with kids from the high school. Hanging out and hooking up. It's where Jessica had had her first awkward kiss. With Miles Bernardy. Gosh, he was such a geek. But then, so was she.

It was also where Janie and Zane had fallen in love.

"I met one of your neighbors."

"Judging by the glow on your face, must've been Dylan. He runs this time of day."

"My face is not glowing." She blinked.

"Nothing to worry over. Happens all the time with women."

"I'm not a wom—I mean, I am not gawking over a movie star, for heaven's sake."

He should talk. Former brother-in-law or not, Zane Williams was a country superstar hunk. Dark-haired, six foot two, a chiseled-jawed Grammy winner, Zane wasn't hard on the eyes, either. The tabloids painted him as an eligible widower who needed love in his life. So far, they'd been kind to him, a rare thing for a superstar.

He picked up his crutches and lifted one to gesture to a table. "This okay with you?"

Two adjacent places were set along a rectangular glass table large enough for ten. Votive candles and a spray of flowers accented the place settings facing the sunset. "It's nice, Zane. I hope you didn't go to too much trouble. I don't expect you to entertain me."

"Not going to any trouble, Jess. Fact is, I eat out here

most days. I hate being cooped up inside the house. Just another week and I'll be out of these dang confinements." He raised his wrapped wrist.

"That's good news. Then what will you do?"

Inclining his head, he considered her question. "Some rehab, I'm told. And continue working out details on the restaurant." He frowned, and the light dimmed in his eyes. "My tour's not due to pick up until September sometime. *Maybe.*"

She wouldn't pry about the maybe. He hobbled to the table. Leaning a crutch against the table's edge, he managed to pull out her chair—such chivalry—and she took her seat. Then he scooted his butt into his own chair. Plop. Poor Zane. His injuries put him completely out of his element.

Mrs. Lopez appeared with platters of food. She set them on the table with efficient haste and nodded to him. "I made a pitcher of margaritas to go with the enchiladas and rice. Or maybe some iced tea or soda?"

"Jessica?" he asked.

"A margarita sounds like heaven."

He glanced at the housekeeper. "Bring the pitcher, please."

She nodded. Within a minute, a pitcher appeared along with two bottle-green wide-rimmed margarita glasses. "Thanks," he said. Zane leaned forward and gripped the pitcher with his wrapped hand. His face pinched tight as he struggled to upend the weighty pitcher. He sighed, and she sensed his frustration over not being able to perform the simple task of pouring a drink with his right hand.

"Let me help," she said softly.

She slipped her hand under the pitcher and helped guide the slushy concoction into the glasses. She gave him credit for clamping his mouth shut and not complaining about his limitations.

"Thanks," he said. He reached out, and the slide of his rough fingers over hers sent warm tingles to her heart. They were still connected through Janie, and she valued his friendship now. She'd made the right decision in coming here.

The food was delicious. She inhaled the meal, emptying her plate within minutes. "I guess I didn't know how hungry I was. Or thirsty."

She reached for her second margarita and took a long sip. Tart icy goodness slid down her throat. "Mmm."

The sun had set with a parfait of swirling color, and now half the moon lit the night. The beach was quiet and calm. The roar of the waves had given way to an occasional lulling swish.

Zane sipped his third margarita. She remembered that about him. He could hold his liquor.

"So what are your plans now, Jess?" he asked.

"Hit the beach, work on my tan and stay out of your way. Shouldn't be too hard. The place is huge."

Tiny lines crinkled around his eyes, and he chuckled. "You don't need to stay out of my way. But feel free to do whatever you want. There are two cars parked in the garage, fueled and ready to go. I can't drive them."

"So how do you get around?"

"Mariah, usually. When I'm needed at the restaurant site or somewhere, she's drives me or I hire a car. She's been a trouper, going above and beyond since my accident."

Mrs. Lopez picked up the empty dishes, leaving the margarita pitcher. A smart woman.

"Thank you, Mrs. Lopez. Have a good night," Zane said. "See you tomorrow."

"Good night," she said to both of them.

"Thanks for the delicious enchiladas."

On a humble nod and smile, she exited the patio.

Zane pointed to her half-empty glass. "How many of those can you handle, darlin'?"

"Oh, uh…I don't know. Why?"

"'Cause if you fall flat on your face, I won't be able to pick you up and carry you to your room."

He winked, and a sudden vision of Zane carrying her to the bedroom burst into her mind. It wasn't as weird a notion as she might've thought. She felt safe with Zane. She truly liked him and didn't buy into his guilt over Janie's death. He wasn't to blame. He couldn't have known about faulty wiring in the house or the fire that would claim her life. Janie had loved Zane for the man that he was, had always been. She wouldn't want Zane's guilt to follow him into old age.

"Well, then, we're even. If you got pie-eyed, I wouldn't be able to pick you up, either." She took another long sip of her drink. Darn, but it tasted good. Her spirits lifted. Let the healing begin.

Zane cocked a crooked smile. "I like your style, *Miss Holcomb.*"

"Ugh. To think I would've been Mrs. Monahan by now. Thank God I'm not."

"The guy's an ass."

"Thanks for saying that. He sure had me fooled. Up until the minute I was having my bridal veil pinned in my hair, I thought I knew what the future had in store for me. I saw myself married to a man I had a common bond with. He was a high school principal. I was a grade-school teacher. We both loved education. But I was too blind to see that Steven had commitment phobia. He'd had one broken relationship after another before we started dating. I invested three years of my life in the guy, and I thought surely he'd gotten over it. I thought I was the one. But he was fooling himself as well as me." A pent-up breath whooshed out of her. A little bit of tequila loosened her tongue, and out poured her heart. The unburdening was liberating. "My friend Sally said Steven looked up his old girlfriend seeking sympathy after the wedding that never happened. Can you imagine?"

Zane stared at her. "No. He should be on his knees begging you for forgiveness. He did one thing right. He didn't marry you and make your life miserable. I hate to say it, darlin', but you're better off without him. The man doesn't deserve you. But you're hurt right now, and I get that. You probably still love him."

"I don't," she said, hoisting her glass and swallowing a big gulp. "I pretty much hate him."

Zane leaned back in his seat, his gaze soft on her. "Okay. You hate him. He's out of your life."

She braced folded elbows on the table and rested her chin on her hands. The sea was black as pitch now, the sky lit only with a few stars and clouded moonlight. "I just wanted…I wanted what you and Janie had. I wanted that kind of love."

Her fuzzy brain cleared. Oh, no. She hadn't just said that? She whipped her head around. Zane's expression of sympathy didn't change. He didn't flinch. He simply stared out to sea. "We had something pretty special."

"You did. I'm sorry for bringing it up."

"Don't be." His tone held no malice. "You're Janie's sister. You have as much right to talk about her as I do."

Tears misted in her eyes. "I miss her."

"I miss her, too."

She sighed. She didn't mean to put such a somber mood on the evening. Zane was gracious enough to allow her to stay here. She didn't want to bring him down. It was definitely time to call it a night. She put on a cheery face. "Well, this has been nice."

She rose, and her head immediately clouded up. The table, the railing, the ocean blurred before her. She batted her eyes over and over, trying to focus. Two Zanes popped into her line of vision. She reached for the tabletop, struggling to remain upright on her own steam. She swayed back and forth, unable to keep her body still. "Zane?"

"It just hit you, didn't it?"

"Oh, yeah. I think so." She giggled.

"Don't move for a second."

"I'll…try." A tornado swirled in her head. "Why?"

He rose and hobbled over to her. Using one crutch, he

tucked it under his left arm. "I'm going to help you get inside."

"But, you said…you c-couldn't. Uh…" She giggled again.

Zane wrapped his right arm around her shoulder. "Okay, now, darlin', I've got you. Your body will be my other crutch. We'll help each other. Move slowly."

"W-where are we g-going?"

"I've got to get you to bed."

Her head fell to his shoulder. Somewhere in the back of her mind, she thought how nice it felt to have him hold her. He smelled good. He would take care of her.

"Focus on putting one foot in front of the other."

She tried.

"That's good, honey."

Hobble-hopping, they moved together. It seemed to take forever to go a short distance in the dark shadows of the night. Keeping her eyes down, she watched her feet move. Then blinding light appeared in a burst. She squinted. "What's that?"

"We're inside the house now," Zane was saying.

"That's g-good, right? I'll be in b-bed soon." A warm buzz spread through her like soft, sweet jelly.

"Not upstairs. You'll never make it. We're going to my room."

She couldn't wait to lay her head down someplace. She didn't care where. More careful steps later, they entered a room. A ray of moonlight beamed like an arrow, aiming straight at the bed.

"Okay, we made it," Zane said. He sounded weird and out of breath. "You'll sleep here tonight."

He guided her down. The bed hit her bottom quickly and cushioned around her. She swayed sideways and was immediately set to right. Zane held her steady as the mattress dipped again and he sat next to her. Dizzying waves bombarded her head. She'd sat too quickly.

"Think you can take it from here?" he whispered.

No. Aware of Zane's eyes on her, she waited until the twister in her head calmed. "Yeah, I think so."

"Good."

Her giddiness fading, her lighthearted high dropped to a pitiful low. It hadn't taken her long to become a burden to Zane. If only she hadn't sucked down that second margarita. Zane had warned her to go slowly. Expensive tequila and jet lag had done her in. Man, chalk another mistake up to her lousy intuition.

"I'm sorry."

"Nothing to be sorry for," he said.

But she was, and an urge to thank him wiggled through the fog in her head. Pursing her lips, she leaned forward toward his cheek. Her aim off, she missed and caught the corner of his mouth instead. As she brushed a soft kiss there, he tasted of tequila and the sea. So good. Inside, a warm sprinkling of something wonderful spread through her body. "Thank you," she whispered, not sure if her words slurred.

Then his arms wrapped around her and gently lowered her down. Her head was enveloped in a large, fluffy pillow, and a silky sheet came to rest over her body.

She heard a whispered, "Welcome," right before the world finally stopped spinning.

Two

Jessica gazed at the digital clock on the nightstand. Eight-thirty! She flashed back to last night and drinking those two giant margaritas, then slowly looked around. She was in an unfamiliar bed.

She'd finally let go and given herself permission to have a good time, and where had that gotten her? She'd made a fool of herself. Zane had hobbled her inside the house and slept heaven only knew where. Was there another bedroom on this floor? Maybe a servant's quarters? She'd seen an office, a screening room and a game room. No beds, just couches. "Oh, man," she mumbled.

She scanned the stark but stylish bedroom where she'd slept. A flat-screen TV, a dresser and a low fabric sofa were the only other furniture in the room. If it wasn't for a shelf that housed Zane's five Grammys, as well as a couple of CMA and ACM awards, she wouldn't have guessed it was his master suite. There was nothing personal, warm and cozy about the space.

Hitching her body forward, she waited for signs of pain, but there was nothing. Thank goodness—no hangover. She grabbed her glasses from the nightstand, tossed off the covers and rose. Seeing she was still dressed in her shorts and tank top, she emitted a low groan from her throat as she slipped her feet into her flip-flops. How reckless of her. She'd abused Zane's hospitality already.

She entered the bathroom, another ode to magnificence, and glanced at herself in the mirror. Smudged mascara and rumpled hair reflected back at her. She washed her face and finger-combed her long wayward tresses. She'd take care of the rest once she reached her own room.

Exiting Zane's room, she made her way down a short hallway. Voices coming from the kitchen perked up her ears.

Mrs. Lopez spotted her and waved her inside. "Just in time for breakfast."

Mariah and Zane sat at the kitchen table, coffee mugs piping hot in front of them. Upon the housekeeper's announcement, both heads lifted her way. Blood rushed up her neck, and her face flamed.

"Morning," Zane said, peering into her eyes and not at her wrinkled mess of clothes. "You ready for some breakfast?"

"Good morning, Jessica," Mariah said. They'd obviously been deep in concentration, poring over a stack of papers.

"Yes, yes. Sit down," Mrs. Lopez insisted.

"Oh, uh…good morning. I don't want to intrude. You look busy."

"Just same old, same old," Mariah said. "We're going over plans for Zane's new restaurant. We could use your input."

She'd given Zane her input last night. God. She'd kissed him. Remembering that kiss sent a warm rash of heat through her body. She'd missed his cheek and gotten hold of his lips. Was it the alcohol, or had her heart strummed from that kiss? The alcohol. Had to be. He must have known it was a genuine miscalculation on her part. She hadn't meant to kiss him that way.

"Yes, have a seat, Jess," he said casually. "You need to eat. And we sure need a fresh perspective."

Before her shower? Luckily Zane hadn't mentioned anything about her lack of discretion last night or her state of dress today. She'd overslept, that much was a given. Back home, she rose before six every morning. She loved to go through the morning newspaper, take a walk in the back-woods and then eat a light breakfast before heading to her classroom.

There were a platter of bagels with cream cheese, a scrambled egg jalapeno dish and cereal boxes on the table. The eggs smelled heavenly, and her stomach grumbled. See-ing no other option, she sat down and reached for the eggs as Mrs. Lopez provided her with a bowl and a cup of coffee.

"Bien." She gave a satisfied nod.

Jessica smiled at her.

As Zane and his assistant finished up their breakfast, she ate, too, complimenting Mrs. Lopez on the food she'd prepared.

Zane told Mariah, "Janie and Jessica worked at their folks' café in Beckon. They served the best fried chicken in all of Texas."

"That's what most folks said," she agreed. She couldn't claim modesty. Her parents *did* make the best fried chicken in the state. "My parents opened Holcomb House when I was young. They worked hard to make a go of it. It wasn't anything as grand as what you're probably planning, but in Beckon, the Holcomb House was known for good eats and a friendly atmosphere. When Dad died five years ago, my mom couldn't make a go of it by herself. I think she lost the will, so she sold the restaurant. I'm no expert, but if I can help in any way, I'll give it a try."

"Great," Mariah said.

"Appreciate it," Zane added. "This restaurant will be a little different than the one in Reno, in cuisine and atmo-sphere. The beach is a big draw for tourists, and we want it to be a great experience."

Zane probably had half a dozen financial advisors, but if he needed her help in any way, she'd oblige. How could she not? She cringed thinking that Zane slept on a sofa last night. A quick glance at his less than crisp clothes, the same clothes he'd worn last night, meant that he probably hadn't got to shower this morning, either. Because of her.

Once the dishes were cleared, Mariah pushed a few papers over to her. "If you don't mind, could you tell us what you think of the menu? Are the prices fair? Do the titles of the dishes make sense? We're working with a few chefs and want to get it just right. These are renderings of what Zane's on the Beach will look like once all done, exterior and interior."

For the next hour, Jessica worked with the two of them, giving her opinion, voicing her concerns when they probed and offering praise honestly if not sparingly. Zane's on the Beach had everything a restaurant could offer. Outside, patio tables facing the beach included a sand bar for summer nights of drinking under the moonlight. Inside, window tables were premium, with the next row of tables raised to gain a view of the ocean, as well. It wasn't posh, but it wasn't family dining, either. "I like that you've made it accessible to a younger crowd. The prices are fair. Have you thought about putting a little stage in the bar? Invite in local entertainment to perform?"

Mariah shot a look at Zane. "We discussed it. I think it's a great idea. Zane isn't so sure."

Zane scrubbed his chin, deep in thought. "I've got to get a handle on what I want from this restaurant. My name and reputation are at stake. Do I want ocean views and great food or a hot spot for a younger crowd?"

"Why can't you have both?" Jessica asked. "Quality is quality. Diners will come for the cuisine and ambiance. After hours, the place can transform into a nightspot for the millennials."

Amused, Zane's dark eyes sparked. "Millennials? Are you one?"

"I guess so."

His head tilted, and his mouth quirked up. "Why do I suddenly feel old?"

"Because you are," Mariah jabbed. "You're cranking toward forty."

"Thirty-five is a far shot from forty, and that's all I'm saying."

"You're wise to stop there," Mariah said playfully, yet with a note of warning. Jessica could tell that Mariah Jacobellis wasn't a woman who put up with age jokes. Although Mariah was physically lovely, she seemed to take no prisoners when it came to business or her personal life. Jessica admired that about her. Maybe she could take a lesson from her rule book.

Zane leaned way back in his seat. "You got that right."

Mariah stacked the papers on the table and rose, hugging them to her chest. "Well, I'm off to make some phone calls. Zane, think about when you want to resume your tour. I've got to let the event coordinators know. They're on my back about it. Oh, and be sure to read through that contract that Bernie sent over the other day."

Zane's lips pursed. "I'll do my best."

"Jessica, have a nice morning. And if you're around Zane today, please give him a hand. He may look like a superhero, but he's really not Superman."

Could've fooled her. Last night, he'd been super *heroic*.

Mariah pivoted on her heels and strode out the door.

Zane chuckled.

"What?"

"The look on your face."

"I'm mortified about last night. Where on earth did you sleep, and does Mariah know what happened?"

"First off, don't be upset. It's our little secret. Mariah doesn't know that you're a margarita lightweight." He smiled. "That woman's been babying me for weeks. Doesn't do a man a bit of good being so dang useless. For the first time in a month of Sundays, I was able to help out and do something useful with this banged-up body."

"I took your bed."

"Glad to give it up."

"Where did you sleep?"

"The office sofa is the most comfortable place in the whole house."

"Oh, boy. I'm sorry. The first night I'm here, I give you trouble."

He smiled again, a stunning heart-melter. "If livening up my life some is trouble, then bring it on. Fact is, I'm glad you're here. You bring a bit of home with you. I miss that."

She needed to believe him. She'd been afraid coming here would remind him of Janie and all that he'd lost. To have him say he was glad she'd come made a big difference. "Okay."

He put his palms on her cheeks and leaned forward. Her heart stopped. Was he going to kiss her? His touch sent tingles parading up and down her chest. Oh, wow. It wasn't alcohol this time. Probably wasn't the alcohol last night, either. She'd been dumped by a scoundrel, and now a man she had no right responding to made her feel giddy inside. How screwed up was that?

She gazed into his eyes. He was looking somewhere above her eyeglasses. Then he lowered his mouth—she stilled—and he brushed a brotherly kiss across her forehead. Breath eased from her chest, and her foolish heart tumbled. Of course, Zane wasn't going to kiss her *that* way.

"And thanks for the input about the restaurant," he said. "I respect your honesty and what you have to offer."

She swallowed hard. Tamping down her silly emotions, she offered a quick smile. "Anytime."

Beaming sunshine simmered over Jessica's body, the invading heat soaking into her bones. Salty air, a cushion of sand beneath her and the soothing sounds of waves crashing upon the shore gave her good reason to forget her disastrous relationship with Steven Monahan. He didn't deserve any more of her time. But the sting of his rejection stayed with her, leaving her hollowed out inside, afraid to trust, questioning her intuition. She feared she'd never fully recover the innocence of her first love. Good thing she didn't have to make any decisions here on Moonlight Beach. She could just be.

Drenched in sunscreen, she lay on a beach blanket in a modest one-piece bathing suit, a folded towel under her head. Slight breezes just outside Zane's beachfront home deposited flecks of sand onto her arms and legs. Children's giggles and adult conversations drifted to her ears. For the first time in days, her nerves were completely calm.

She promised herself to keep out of Zane's hair, and she had for the most part these past three days. He spent hours inside his office working with Mariah, and occasionally they would ask for her input on the restaurant. She figured it was just a way for him to keep her entertained and make her feel welcome. Each morning, under an overcast sky that would burn off before noon, she walked a three-mile stretch of beach, loosening up her limbs and clearing her head. At night, she'd dine with Zane on the patio facing the ocean, and except for having an occasional glass of white wine or a cold beer, she kept her alcohol consumption to a bare minimum. The Pacific Ocean and fresh air were her balm. She didn't need to rely on anything else.

She wiggled her tush into the sand, carving out a more comfy spot on her blanket, and closed her eyes. The flapping of wings and piercing squawk of a seagull overhead made her smile.

"Glad to see you've taken to Moonlight Beach."

Blocking rays of sunlight with a hand salute, she opened her eyes. The handsome face of Dylan McKay came into view.

"Hi, Jessica." He stared at her with his million-dollar smile. "Don't let me disturb you."

Gosh, he remembered her name.

Wearing plaid board shorts and a muscle-hugging white

T-shirt, and fitting into beach society with the casualness of a megastar, he sort of did disturb her. Yet he did so in such a friendly way, she didn't mind the intrusion. As she sat up on her elbows, his gaze dipped to her chest. To his credit, his eyes didn't linger on her breasts, and that was more than she could say about most men.

"Hello, and I am enjoying the beach. When in Rome, as they say." She chuckled at the cliché. It was Mama's favorite saying, and she'd used it a zillion times over the years. The most recent was last night when they'd talked on the phone. Did others in her generation get that phrase?

Her eyes fell on a black portfolio tucked under his arm. It looked odd there, as if he should be wearing a three-piece suit while carrying that austere leather case. Instead of moving on, he squatted down beside her, his tanned knees nearly in her face. Obviously, he wanted to chat.

"I see you sometimes in the morning, walking along the beach."

"You've inspired me," she said. "Of course, I only do three miles. How are your runs going?"

"Killing me, but I'm getting in the ten miles."

His legs were taut, like those of a natural runner, and the rest of his body, well…it would be hard not to notice his muscles and the way his T-shirt nearly split at the seams around his shoulders and upper arms. "Good for you."

"So, how's it going?" he asked. "Other than sunbathing and taking long walks, are you having a good time?"

"Yes. It's nice here. I'm working on some new lesson plans for my class. I teach first grade back home."

"Ah…a teacher. Such an honorable profession."

She waggled her brows. Was he poking fun at her? Or was he being genuine?

"My mother taught school for thirty-five years," he added, his smile wistful, pride filling his voice. "She was loved by her students, but she wasn't a pushover. It wasn't easy pulling my antics on her. She was too savvy. She knew when kids were up to no good."

"I bet you gave her a run for her money."

He laughed, the gleam of his lake-blue eyes touching her. "I did."

"What grade did she teach?"

"All grades, but she preferred fourth and fifth. Then, later on, she became dean of a middle school, and eventually, the principal of the high school."

She nodded. She didn't have much else to add to the conversation. Not that Dylan McKay wasn't easy to talk to. He was. And she loved talking about education to anyone who would listen. It was just that he was fabulous, famous Dylan McKay. And he kept smiling at her.

"Hey, I'm having a party on Saturday night. If you're still here, I'd love for you to come. Maybe you can get Zane to get out and have a little fun."

"Oh, thanks." He'd caught her off guard. Wasn't that what she needed right now, to be a wallflower at an A-list party? "I'm…uh, I'm not the partying type. Especially now."

"Now?"

She shrugged. "I'm going through something and need a little R and R."

"Ah…a breakup?"

She nodded. Her pride aside, she opened up a little to make her point. "Broken engagement as the wedding guests were taking their seats in church."

"Ah…gotcha. I've been there once, a long time ago, when I was too young to know better. It turned out for the best, so believe me, I understand. Listen, I promise you, the party is low-key. Just a few friends and neighbors for a barbecue on the beach. I'd love to see you there."

"Thanks."

He smiled, and she smiled back. Then he pointed to her upper thigh, on the right side, closest to him. "Uh-oh. Looks like you missed a spot. You're starting to burn."

Grabbing the sunscreen tube from the blanket, his long fingers brushed the soft underside of her hand as he set the sunscreen into her palm. "Better lather up and—"

"Stop corrupting my little sis, McKay."

Jessica whipped her head around. Zane stood on the sundeck railing, staring at Dylan. His voice was a far cry from menacing, but the cool look he shot Dylan made her wonder what was up.

Dylan winked at her. "Maybe she wants to be corrupted."

"And maybe you want to turn tail and go home. I don't have to read that script, you know."

"Whoops," he said, flashing a charming smile. "He's got me there. Maybe you can help me convince him to take this role. Wanna try? Since you're about to turn into a fried tomato out here."

Under normal circumstances, she was probably the least starstruck person in Beckon, Texas, but how could she not take Dylan up on his offer to go over a movie script? The notion got her juices flowing, and excitement buzzed around her like a busy little bee.

She glanced down at her legs. Oh, wow. Dylan was right. There were more than a few splotchy patches on her body. Time to get out of the sun. "Sure, why not?"

"Great." He swiveled his head in Zane's direction. "We're coming up right now."

Gallantly, he offered her his hand. She couldn't very well refuse the gesture. She slipped one hand into his and simultaneously clutched her cover-up with the other as they rose together. He was too close for comfort, his eyes smiling on her, their hands entwined. Gently she pulled away, making herself busy zipping herself into a white cotton cover up and ignoring his rapt attention. He was a charmer, but thankfully his touch hadn't elicited a jolt of any kind. She glanced at Zane, leaning by the railing, his sharp gaze fixed on her.

Something hot and unruly sizzled in the pit of her belly.

She ignored it and pushed on, climbing the steps with Dylan McKay following behind.

"Did he ask you out?" Zane probed the minute Dylan McKay exited the house. Looming over her, Zane was a bit foreboding, as if he was her white knight protecting her from the wicked prince of darkness. Geesh.

"Wh-what?"

"The guy couldn't take his eyes off you down on the beach."

She shrugged and picked up three empty glasses, reminiscent of her waitress days at Holcomb House.

After coming back into the house she'd left the two men to take a quick shower and slip on a sundress. She'd listened to Dylan's script proposal to Zane with keen interest in a spacious light oak–paneled office on the main level of the house. The meeting took almost an hour. Then they'd had drinks in the cool shade of the patio. Iced tea for her. The men were content to knock back whiskey and soda.

Dylan was a charming lady's man to the millionth degree, and she knew enough to steer clear. The idea that he'd be interested in a little ol' school teacher from Beckon, Texas, was ridiculous. She had no illusions of anything else going on between them, and Zane should know that.

Her mama's image flashed before her eyes. That was it. She bet her mother put Zane up to watching out for her, making sure her tender heart didn't get broken again. Well, heck. She'd let him off the hook, but not without giving him some grief. Her chin up, she said, "He invited me to his beach party Saturday night. It was just a friendly invitation."

Zane's mouth tightened into a snarl and he snorted. "Doubtful."

"I told him I probably wouldn't go."

"Good." Zane nodded, satisfied. "You don't need to get involved with him. He's—"

"Out of my league?"

His eyes widened. "Hell, no."

"Well, he is. And I know it all too well. Heck, my life is messy enough right now. There's no room for romance, though it's absurd to think of Dylan McKay actually being into me."

Zane immediately reached out to grab her arm. Surprised, she jerked from his touch, and the glasses she held nearly slipped from her hand. "Don't put yourself down, Jess."

A jolt sprang to life, spiraling out of control where the strong fingers of his bandaged hand pressed into her skin. Sharpness left Zane's dark eyes, and he gave her a bone-melting look. "I was going to say, he would never appreciate you. You're special, Jess. You always have been."

Because she was Janie's sister.

Zane held dear her sister's memory, closing his heart around it and not allowing anyone else into his life. He was a sought-after hunky bachelor, but he'd been true to Janie's love even now, years later. Jessica understood she was only here because Zane was too nice a guy to refuse her mama a favor. "Thank you."

He nodded and released her to go lean against the railing.

Free of his touch, she marched the glasses into the kitchen, handing them to Mrs. Lopez one at a time. She had to do something to quell her pounding heart. What the heck was wrong with her?

"*Dios*, you do not do the work around here. That's my job, no?"

"Yes. But I like to help."

It was the same conversation she'd had with Mrs. Lopez since she'd arrived here. Jessica saw nothing wrong with putting clothes in the washer and turning the thing on, or clearing the dishes, or helping slice potatoes for a meal. Today, especially, she needed to do something with her hands.

"*Sí*, okay." A relenting sigh echoed in the kitchen.

She picked up dirty dishes on the counter, loaded them in the dishwasher and put things back in the refrigerator. A few chores later, after scanning the clean kitchen they'd both worked on, she gave Mrs. Lopez a bright smile. The woman was shaking her head, but with a twinkle in her eyes. Progress.

Jessica strode out the kitchen door and was immediately knocked against the doorjamb. Pain shot to her shoulder. The jarring bump brought Mariah's face into view. "Oh, sorry."

Mariah was equally shocked from the collision. "I didn't see you."

"My fault. I should learn how to slow down."

She chuckled. "I'm the same way. I've got to get where I'm going fast, no matter if it's just to sip coffee and read the newspaper." Mariah, always impeccably dressed, rubbed her shoulder through her cognac-colored silk blouse. "Guess we're alike in that regard. Where were you going in such a hurry?"

"Nowhere. Just outside. I left Zane hanging and I wanted to go back to talk to him."

"Good luck with that. I just left him, and he's a bear right now."

"Oh, really? Why?" It couldn't be the Dylan McKay thing, could it?

"I don't know exactly what set him off other than he hates being confined. He feels like a caged animal. Though he doesn't make an effort to go anywhere, other than for business."

"I can see how that would make him restless."

Mariah smiled. "That's the perfect way to describe it. He's restless. But I'm afraid that came on well before his fall. I think a change of pace is good for him. I've helped him make the decision to open this second restaurant, and now he's thinking about movie roles. It might be just what he needs."

Or maybe he was running away from his past, the same way she was. Zane loved music. He loved writing lyrics and composing songs. He was meant to entertain. His sexy, deep baritone voice made his fans swoon. That's the only Zane she'd known.

"Dylan invited you in to hear his pitch, I understand. What did you think of the movie?"

"Me? Well, I, uh…to be honest, I think the idea of Zane and Dylan being estranged brothers coming home after the death of their father might work. If Zane can act, he'd be great in the role. The only issue I see is the love triangle about the girl back home. I saw Zane's reaction to Dylan's description of the romantic scenes he'd have to do. Zane instantly shut down. I'm not sure if Zane's up to that."

"That's exactly what I think, too. Zane's not going to do something he's not comfortable with. Believe me, I know. I've had plenty of discussions with him about his recent decisions. He bounces things off me. He asks me a question, and I tell him the truth."

"Which is?"

"I will say this. Zane can act. He's been doing so for over two years now. His public persona is far different than the real Zane." Mariah was ready to say more and then clamped shut. Her eyes downcast, she shook her head. "Forgive me. I keep forgetting who you are."

Jessica drew her brows together. "It's because of Janie. He's still hurting."

Mariah nodded. "I'm afraid so."

Mariah's eyes fell on her softly, her genuine warmth shining through. "Please forget I said anything. It's none of my business."

The idea that after two years, Zane was still making decisions based on the love he had for Janie, nestled deep into her heart. It was beautiful in a way, but also incredibly sad. "You're Zane's personal assistant. You spend a lot of time together. I can see that you care about him as a friend, too, so maybe it's more your business than mine."

"Zane thinks of you as family. He's said so a dozen times since you've come here."

"I'm the little sis he never had." Wasn't that the term he'd used this afternoon with Dylan McKay?

Stop corrupting my little sis.

Zane's loyalty to her family was very sweet. She didn't take it lightly, but she also didn't want him to think of her as a pity case. From the moment her shocked guests walked out of the church on her wedding day, weeks ago now, something harsh and cold seeped into her soul. Trust would be a long time coming, if ever again. So Zane didn't have to worry over her. She wasn't a woman looking for love. She wasn't on the rebound. He could sleep well at night.

"So, what are you up to today?" she asked Mariah. She was learning the ins and outs of Zane's superstardom. Mariah sifted through a dozen offers a day for special appearances, television interviews and charity events on Zane's behalf. She'd learned that Zane was a generous contributor to children and military charities, but lately, he'd declined any personal appearances. Mariah worked with his fan club president on occasion and took care of any personal business, such as setting up medical appointments or shopping trips. It was a different world, one that her sister, Janie, had resigned herself to because she'd been with Zane from the launch of his career. They'd grown into this life together.

"More restaurant business to do today. We've got a decorator working on the interior design, but Zane's not sure about the motif." Mariah's cell phone rang, and she excused herself.

Jessica walked over to the French door leading out to the deck. Zane was sprawled out on a lounge chair, shaded from the sun, his booted foot elevated, reading the script Dylan had brought over. Keen on the subject matter, he seemed deep in thought. As her gaze lingered, she watched him close the binder and stare out to sea, his expression incredibly wistful.

She followed the direction of his gaze and honed in on the vast view of the ocean. The sounds of the sea lulled her into a soothing state of mind. It was a place to find infinite peace, if there ever was such a thing. Her nerves no longer throbbed against her skin. These past few days, she'd been much calmer. Were time and distance all she'd needed to get over Steven Monahan? Geesh, Jessica felt at one with nature and started to believe. A chuckle rose from her throat at the notion. She was beginning to sound like a true Californian.

"Crap! Damn things."

Out of the corner of her eye, she witnessed Zane's crutches fall to the ground. The slap echoed against the wood deck. Zane was off the chair, bending to pick them up and trying to keep weight off his bad foot. It looked like a yoga move gone bad. She moved quickly, her legs eating up the length of the deck to get to him.

"Zane, hang on."

He stumbled and fell over, landing on his bad hand. "Ow!"

By the time she reached him, he was on his butt, cursing like the devil, shaking out his wrist. She kneeled beside him. "Are you okay?" she asked softly.

He tilted his head toward her. "You mean other than my pride?"

She smiled. "Yes, we'll deal with that later. How's the hand?"

"I managed to catch the fall on the tips of my fingers, so the wrist should be fine."

He moved his fingers one by one as if he was playing keys on a piano. So much for keeping his hand immobilized. "Maybe your doctor would be a better judge of that."

"Now you sound like Mariah."

"I knew an old goat like you once," she said, putting his right arm over her shoulder. "Let me help you up."

"I knew the same goat," he bounced back. "Smart critter."

"Pleeeze. Okay, are you ready? On three." She swung her arm around his waist. "One. Two. Three."

His weight drew her toward him, the side of her face against his chest, her hair brushing his shirt. He smelled like soap and lime shaving lotion. His heart pounded in her ear as she strained to help lift him.

Zane did most of the work, his brawny strength a blessing. Together, they managed to stand steady, Zane keeping weight off his foot by using her as his right crutch. Once again, just like the other night, she was wrapped tight in his arms. Ridiculous warmth flowed through her body. She couldn't explain it except she felt safe with him, which was silly because this time she'd done the rescuing. "There," she said, satisfied she'd gotten him upright. "Now, we're even."

His arm over her shoulder, he turned to her with eyes flickering. "Is that so?"

Well, maybe not. She was getting drunk on him, minus the alcohol. "Yes, that's so."

"I could've gotten up on my own, you know."

"It wouldn't have been pretty."

He laughed. "True."

"So, I'm glad I was here to help. Show a little gratitude."

He wasn't a man who liked taking help. That was part of the problem. His gaze roamed over the deck where he'd spent most of his day, and she sensed his frustration.

"Wanna get out of here?" he asked.

"Sure. Where would you like to go?" Mariah said he didn't like to go out, so she couldn't let this opportunity pass by. If he needed some breathing room, away from his gorgeous house and his familiar surroundings, who was she to deny him?

"Anywhere. I don't care. Are you up to driving my car?"

"I can manage that. I'm going to get your crutches now, okay?" She didn't wait for an answer.

She released him and he stood there, balancing himself for the two seconds it took her to pick up both of his crutches and hand them over. Tucking one under each arm, he pointed a crutch toward the door. "After you."

Three

To her surprise, Zane picked his silver convertible sports car for her to drive over the black SUV sitting in his three-car garage. The other car, a little blue sedan, had to be Mariah's car. Jessica helped him get into his seat, taking his crutches and setting them into the narrow backseat before closing his door.

As soon as she climbed behind the steering wheel, she understood why Zane didn't venture out much. Sitting in the passenger seat, he was encumbered by his foot, broken in three places, which required him to be extremely careful. He also put on a disguise. Well, a Dodgers baseball cap instead of his signature Stetson and sunglasses wasn't much of a disguise, but she knew where he was coming from. He couldn't afford to be recognized and surrounded by fans or paparazzi. In his condition, he couldn't make a fast getaway. "Why am I driving this car?"

"More fun for you."

"You mean more scary, don't you? How much is this car worth, just in case I wreck it, or—heaven forbid—put a scratch on it?"

He smiled. "Don't worry. It's insured."

Stalling for time, she fidgeted with her glasses and took several deep breaths before she turned to Zane. He was still smiling at her. At the moment, she didn't enjoy being his source of amusement.

"Here goes." With the press of a button, the engine purred to life. Zane showed her how to adjust her seat and mirrors using the control buttons. Once set, she supposed she was as ready as she would ever be. She pumped the gas pedal and gripped the steering wheel. She'd never driven anything but a sedan, a boring four-door family car with no bells and whistles. This car had it all. A thrill shimmied up her legs…all that power under her control.

She backed the car out of the garage and made the turn into a long driveway that reached the front gate. Upon Zane's voice command, the gate slid open, and she pulled forward and onto the highway. She drove along the shoreline, keeping her eyes trained on the road and her speed under thirty miles per hour.

His back was angled against the passenger door and his seat. She sensed him watching her. He'd opted to keep the top up on the convertible, for anonymity, she supposed. Even though he'd not had a hint of scandal to his name, every time Zane went out, he risked being photographed. Putting the top down on his car in the light of day would be like asking for trouble.

She didn't dare shoot him a glance, keeping her focus on the road.

"What?" she asked finally. "Your grandmother drives faster than me?"

"I didn't say a word." His Texas drawl seeped into her bones. "But now that you mention it, I think my great-grandmother drove her horse and buggy a mite faster than you."

"Ha. Ha. Very funny. Maybe I'd drive faster if I knew where I was going."

He sighed. "I've learned that sometimes, it's better not to know where you're going. Sometimes, planning isn't all it's cracked up to be. Some roads are better not mapped out."

After that cryptic statement, she did look his way and found him resting his head against the window. His sunglasses hid his eyes and his true expression. The mood in the car grew heavy, and she didn't know how to answer him, so she buttoned her lips and continued to drive.

After five minutes of silence, Zane shifted in his seat. "Wanna see the site of the restaurant? The framework is up."

"I'd love to."

He directed her down a side road that wound around a cove. Then the beach opened up again to a street that faced the ocean. Unique shops and a few other small restaurants sparsely dotted the shoreline before she came upon the skeletal frame of a building.

"There it is. You can park along the side of the road here." He gestured to a space, and she swung the car into the spot.

"This is a great location."

"I think so, too. On a clear day, there's visibility for miles going in either direction."

The beach was wide where the restaurant would sit, far enough from the water to avoid high tides. A rock embankment jutted out to the left, where pelicans rested, scoping out their next meal. Above them and across the road, far up on the cliffs sat zillion-dollar homes overlooking the coastline.

"Do you want to get out?" she asked.

"Yep."

"Hold on," she said, killing the engine and climbing out. She reached into the backseat and grabbed his crutches, then strolled to his side of the car. He was lifting himself out of his seat by the time she got there. "Here you go."

"Thanks."

She waited for him to get his bearings, and they moved through the sand until they reached the beach side of the restaurant. "So this is Zane's on the Beach."

"Yep. Gonna be."

"I suppose it's good that you're branching out. You've become a regular entrepreneur."

"Can't sing forever."

Why not? Willie Nelson, George Strait and Dolly Parton weren't having career problems. And neither was Zane. "Why do I get the feeling you're not eager to go back to doing what you love to do?"

It was a personal question. Maybe too personal, given that Zane didn't react to it at all. He simply stared at the ocean, thinking.

"I'm sorry. It's none of my business."

"Don't apologize, Jess," he rasped with a note of irritation. "You can ask me anything you want."

Okay, she'd take him up on that. "So, then, why are you searching for something else when you've established yourself as a superstar and you have fans all over the world waiting for your return?"

He closed his eyes briefly. "I don't know. Maybe I'm tired of being in my own skin."

It was the most honest answer he could've given her. Zane was hurting. Still. And he didn't know how to deal with it. "I get that. After my disastrous breakup with Steven, I felt totally out of options. I didn't know who to trust, what to believe. I couldn't make a decision to save my life. That's why when I had to get out of Dodge, I let my mother take over and make arrangements. After she did, I didn't have the gumption to argue with her. No offense, but visiting you wasn't even on my radar."

He chuckled. "Should I be insulted?"

She softened her voice. "You made a point of keeping away from the entire family after Janie…"

He winced at her honesty. Maybe she shouldn't have been so blunt. "It's not for the reasons you think."

"I know why you did it, Zane."

He put his head down. "I was having a hard time."

"I know." He'd been swallowed up with guilt. Janie was five months pregnant when she lost her life. Zane was touring in London, and Janie wanted desperately to travel with him. Zane had given her a flat-out no. He didn't want her away from her doctors, on a whirlwind schedule that would sap her energy. They'd argued until Zane had gotten his way. He'd loved Janie so much, trying to protect her and keep her safe. It was a tragic irony that she'd died in her own home on the night Zane had performed for Prince Charles and the royal family. Momentary grief swept over his features. He'd probably feel the guilt of his decision until his dying day. But there was no one to blame. No one could've known that Janie would've been safer in London than resting in her own sprawling, comfortable ranch house while Zane was gone. Her mother had recognized that. Jessica recognized that, but Zane wouldn't let himself off the hook.

Braced by the crutches under his arms, Zane let go of one handle and took her right hand. Lacing their fingers, he applied slight pressure there, squeezing her hand as they stared at the ocean. "I'm glad you're here, Jess."

Peace and pain mingled together, a bittersweet and odd combination of emotions that she was certain Zane was experiencing, too. They'd both lost so much and shared a profound connection.

Afternoon winds blew her hair onto her cheek and Zane touched her face, removing the wayward strands, tucking them behind her ear. "It's good to have someone who understands," he whispered.

She nodded.

"You can trust me," he said.

"I do." Strangely, she did trust Zane. He wasn't a threat to her, not the way every other man in the universe might be. She had learned some harsh lessons about men and about herself. She'd never overlook the obvious the way she had with Steven. She'd never allow herself to be fooled into believing a relationship would work when there were three strikes against it from the get-go.

"This is nice," she murmured.

"Mmm," he replied.

Zane released her hand, and they fell into comfortable silence, watching wave upon wave hit the shore. After a minute, he turned her way. "Do you want to see the inside of the restaurant?"

Her gaze was drawn to the framed, unroofed, sandy-floored structure behind her. "I sure do!"

He laughed. "Follow me, if you can keep up." He hobbled ahead of her. "I'll give you the grand tour."

Zane folded his arms and leaned back in the booth of Amigos del Sol—friends of the sun—watching Jess pore over the menu items of his favorite off-the-beaten-path Mexican restaurant. It was a small hacienda-style place known for making the most delicious, fresh guacamole right at the table. "Everything is great here, but the tamales are out of this world."

And the guacamole was on its way.

Jessica's head was down, and her glasses dropped to the tip of her nose. With her index finger, she pushed them up to the bridge of her nose. He grinned. It was a habit of hers that he found adorable.

"Tamales it is. I will bow to your vast culinary taste. But I'm even more impressed at how you managed to sneak us in the back way and get this corner booth."

"I shouldn't give away my secrets, but while you were navigating turns and learning how to gun the engine on my car, I texted Mariah to call the owner and let him know we needed a quiet spot and we'd appreciate coming in through the back door."

"Ah…Mariah. Your secret weapon."

"She makes things happen."

"I've noticed. She anticipates your every move and watches out for you."

"Yeah, like a mother hen," he said. "Not that I'm ungrateful. She's like my second right arm." He lifted his broken wrist. "And in my condition, that's important."

A uniformed waiter pushed a food cart to their table. Zane practically salivated. He'd been craving the homemade guacamole since earlier in the day. The waiter set out a *molcajete* and *tejolote*, a mortar and pestle carved from volcanic rock, to begin preparations. Squeezing lime juice into the bowl first, he added cilantro, bits of tomato, garlic and other spices. Next he used the pestle to grind all the flavors together and scooped out three perfectly ripe avocados. The aroma of the blended spices and avocados flavored the air. Once done, the guacamole and warm tortilla chips were placed on the table.

After the waiter took their dinner order, he walked off with his cart. Zane grabbed a tortilla chip and dipped it into the fresh green mixture, offering it to Jess first. "Taste this and tell me it's not heaven."

She leaned in close enough for him to place the chip into her mouth. As she chewed, a beautiful smile emerged, and her eyes closed. She sighed. "Oh, this is so good."

Drawn to the sublime expression on her face, he forgot about his craving for a few seconds. Eyeing her reaction distracted him in ways that might've been worrisome, if it hadn't been Jess. As soon as she finished chewing, she snapped her eyes open. "You didn't have one yet?"

"No…it was too much fun watching you."

"I seem to be a source of your amusement lately."

That much was true. Jess being here brightened up his solemn mood. That wasn't a bad thing, was it? He dipped a chip in and came up with a large chunk of guacamole. He shoved it into his mouth and chewed. On a swallow, he said. "Oh, man. That's good."

Jess's eyes darted past him, focusing on something happening behind his back.

"Uh…oh. Don't turn around, Zane," she whispered.

As soon as her words were out, two twentysomething girls approached the table, giddy and bumping shoulders with each other. "Hello. Excuse me," one of them said. "But we're big fans of yours."

"Thank you," he said.

"Would you mind signing a napkin for us?"

He glanced at Jessica and she nodded.

"Sure will."

They produced two white napkins and a pen, which made things a little less awkward. Zane hated waiting around while fans scrambled for something for him to autograph. They gave him their names, and he signed the napkins and handed them back.

"Thank you. Thank you. You're our favorite country singer. I just can't believe we've met you. Your last ballad was amazing. You have the best voice. I saw you in concert five years ago, when I was living in Abilene with my folks."

Zane kept a smile on his face. The girls were clueless that they were interrupting his meal with Jessica. "Well, that's nice to hear."

They stared at him, hovering close.

Jessica stood up then. Bracing her hands on the table, she smiled at the girls. "Hello. I'm Jessica, Zane's sister-in-law." The girls seemed baffled when she shook both of their hands. "We were having a little family talk, and we're limited on time. Otherwise I'm sure Zane would love to speak to you. If you give me your names and addresses, I'll see that you get a signed CD of his latest album. And please be discreet when you leave here," she whispered. "Zane loves meeting his fans, but we really need a few private moments during our meal tonight."

"Oh, okay. Sure," one of them said congenially.

The other girl wrote their addresses on the napkin Jessica provided before she wished them well. Giggling quietly, the two women walked away.

Zane stared at Jessica. "I'm impressed."

"I've been listening to how Mariah deals with your fan club members. I hope it's okay that I offered them a CD."

"It's fine. Happens all the time. I wish I'd have thought of it myself."

"They were persistent."

Zane shook his head. "I could tell you stories." But he wouldn't. Some of the things that had happened to him while touring on the road weren't worth repeating. "Actually, these two were a little subtle compared with some of the people who approach me."

"You mean, compared with the *women* who approach you."

He scrubbed his chin, his fingers brushing over prickly stubble. "I suppose."

Jessica snorted. "You don't have to be modest on my account. I know you're in demand."

He tossed his head back and laughed. "In demand? What are you getting at?"

"You're single, available, successful and handsome. Those two women who left here would probably describe you as a hottie, a hunk, a heartthrob and a hero. You're in the 4-H club of men."

His smile broadened. "The 4-H club of men? You just made that up."

"Maybe," she said, taking a big scoop of guacamole and downing the chip in one big swallow. "Maybe not."

"You constantly surprise me," he said, sipping water. He could use something stronger. "I like that about you."

"And I like that you're decent to folks who admire you."

Their eyes met, and something warm zipped through his gut. Jessica's compliments meant more to him than ten thousand wide-eyed, giddy fans. He admired her, too. "Ah, shucks, ma'am. Now you're gonna make me blush."

Another unladylike snort escaped through her mouth. Zane grinned and leaned way back in his seat just as his cell phone rang. Dang, he didn't want to speak to anyone now, but only a few close friends and family knew his number. He fished the phone out of his pocket. "It's Mariah," he said to Jessica. He turned his wrist to glance at his watch. It was after eight. "That's odd. She usually texts me if she needs me for something after hours. Excuse me a second."

"Hi," he said. "What's up?"

"Zane, s-something terrible's h-happened." Sobs came through the phone, Mariah's voice frantic and unsteady. Zane froze, those words instilling fear and flashing a bad memory. "My mother had a stroke. It's pretty b-bad."

"Oh, man. Sorry to hear that, Mariah."

"I have to fly home right away. Th-they don't know… oh, Zane…she's so young. Only sixty-four. She never had health problems before. Oh, God."

"Mariah, you just do what you have to do. Don't worry about a thing." Her voice broke down, her sobs growing louder. "Where are you?"

"At Patty's h-house in Santa Monica." She shared a place temporarily with an old college roommate. The situation was perfect while he was staying on Moonlight Beach. She was close by without living under his roof.

"Pack up a few things and try to stay calm. Do you have a flight?"

"Patty got me on a midnight flight to Miami."

"Okay…I'll send a car for you in an hour. Hang in there, Mariah."

"It's okay, Zane. I a-appreciate it, but Patty offered to d-drive me. I'll be fine." A deep, sorrowful sigh whispered through the phone. "Are you going to be all right? I don't know how long I'll be gone."

"Don't worry about me." He stared at Jessica. Her eyes were softly sympathetic and kind. "Take all the time you need. And call if there's any way I can help, okay?"

"Okay. Thanks. Goodbye, Zane."

Zane hung up the phone. "Man, that's rough. Mariah's mother had a stroke. She's on her way to Florida now."

"Gosh, I'm sorry to hear that. Is it serious?"

"Seems that way." He ran a hand down his face, pulling the skin taut. "I've never heard her so unraveled before. She may be gone a long time."

"I would think so. Will you find a replacement for her?"

Zane wasn't thinking along those lines. Not yet. He kept hearing the disbelief and pain in Mariah's voice and understood it all too well.

Your wife didn't make it, Zane.

Didn't make what? he'd asked the doctor over and over, screaming into the phone. Then, all the way home from London, he kept thinking, hoping, praying it had been a mistake. A horrible, sick mistake. It wasn't until he saw the desolate ruins of his once proud home in Beckon that it finally sank in Janie was gone. Forever.

The meal was served, and as his gaze landed on the plate of saucy cheese-topped tamales, blood drained from his face, and his gut rebelled. For Jessica's sake, he pushed his haunting memories aside. He didn't want to ruin her meal.

Jessica reached for him across the table, her fingertips feathering over his good hand gently, comforting him with the slightest touch. When he lifted his lids, he gazed into her knowing, sensitive eyes, and she smiled. "Let's have them pack up this food. We'll eat it later on."

"Do you mind?" he asked.

"Not at all. I'm ready to go anytime you are."

He felt at peace suddenly, a glowing warmth usurping the dread inside his gut.

And then it hit him. Sweet Jess. She was good for him. She understood him, perhaps better than anyone else on this earth. She was a true friend, an authentic reminder of home, and he needed her here.

"You asked me before if I'd find a replacement for Mariah."

"Yes, I did. Hard shoes to fill, I would imagine."

"Yeah, I agree." He looked her squarely in the eyes. "Except I've already found someone, and I'm looking straight at her."

Four

Jessica woke to a glorious sunrise, the stream of light cutting through early morning haze and clouds in a host of color. Every morning brought something new from the view outside her bedroom window, and she was beginning to enjoy the variance from fog to haze to brilliance that took place before her eyes.

She stretched her arms above her head, working out the kinks, not so much in her shoulders and neck, but the ones baffling her brain. Last night, Zane told her to keep an open mind and sleep on his suggestion of replacing Mariah as his personal assistant. Her mouth had dropped open, and she thought him insane for a few seconds, but then he pointed out that he wasn't working, he had no gigs lined up, and he wasn't doing interviews right now. Most of what she had to do was hold off the press and postpone anything pending to future dates.

She wouldn't go into it cold. Mariah would be in touch to give her the guidance she needed to get her through anything remotely difficult.

"You're an intelligent woman, Jess. I'm convinced you'd have no problem, and I'm right here to help you," he'd said.

Zane's assurances last night gave her the push over the edge she'd needed this morning. Her head was clear now, and she valued the challenge and even looked forward to it. She wasn't ready to return to Texas anyway. Zane wanted freedom from his agent and manager's constant urging to get back on the horse. Zane wasn't ready yet and she could understand that. He needed more time, just as she did.

The new, bronzer Jessica no longer had freckles on her nose, thanks to a wonderful suntan that had connected those freckly dots and browned up her light skin. How many more hours could she feasibly sunbathe her day away? Staying on for a few weeks and helping Zane out would give her a new sense of purpose.

Jessica showered and dressed quickly. Putting on a pair of khaki shorts and a loose mocha-brown blouse, she slipped her feet into flip-flops and strode toward the kitchen. There were no wickedly delicious aromas drifting from the kitchen this morning. Mrs. Lopez had yet to arrive.

"Sonofabitch!"

A string of Zane's profanities carried to her ears. She grinned. Poor guy. He hated being confined.

She ventured into his bedroom. "Zane?"

"In here!"

She followed the sound of his cursing. He was standing over the bathroom sink, and their eyes met in the mirror. A scowl marred his handsome face, and three blood dots covered with bits of tissue spotted his cheeks and chin. Remnants of lime-scented shaving cream covered the rest of his face. "Damn hand. It's impossible to get a good shave."

"Whoops." With her index finger, she caught a drop of blood dripping from his chin before it landed on his white ribbed tank. "Got it."

He peered at her in the mirror and handed her a tissue. "Thanks."

"Thank me later, after I shave you. We'll see if I can't do a better job."

"You?"

"I used to lather up my dad and shave him when I was a kid." She hoisted herself up onto the marble counter to face him and picked up his razor. "It used to be a game, but darn it, I did an excellent job. Dad was surprised. Seems I'm pretty good with one of these."

Doubtful eyes peered at the razor in her hand.

"What? You don't trust me? It's a guarantee I'd do a better job than what I see on your face now. Or, I can drive you to the local barbershop. Since I'm going to be your new personal assistant and all."

The scowl left his face immediately, and her heart warmed at seeing approval in his eyes. "You've decided, then?"

"Yes, I'm on the clock now. So what will it be? A shave by your PA or a drive to the barber?"

"Try not to cut me," he said.

"You've already done a good job of that." She handed him a towel. "Wipe your face clean. We'll start from scratch."

Zane's eyes widened.

She chuckled at her bad choice of words. "You know what I mean." Pressing down on the canister, she released a mound of shave cream in her hand and leaned forward to rub it over his cheeks, chin and throat.

Zane leaned a little closer, his body braced by the counter. Her heart did a little dance in her chest. His nearness, the refreshing heady lime scent, her position sitting on the counter, *touching him*—suddenly she was all too aware of the intimate act she was performing on her brother-in-law.

What on earth was she doing?

Zane needed help and she'd rushed to his aid. But she hadn't thought this through.

He still towered over her, but only by a few inches now. She lifted her eyes and found him, waiting and watching her through the mirror.

Her hand wasn't so steady anymore.

She couldn't fall down on her first official act as Zane's personal assistant, intimate as it was.

"Okay, are you ready?"

He kept perfectly still. "Hmm."

Her legs were near his hip, and she angled her body to get closer to his face. Bracing her left hand on his shoulder to steady herself, she was taken by the strong rock-hard feel of him under her fingertips. She stroked his face, and the razor met with stubble and gently scraped it away. Carefully she proceeded, gliding the razor over his skin in the smoothest strokes she could manage.

His breath drifted her way as heat from his body radiated out, surrounding her. Cocooned in Zane's warmth, she fought an unwelcome attraction to him by thinking of Steven, the man who'd shattered her faith. And that reminder worked. Thoughts of Steven could destroy any thrilling moment in her life. She dipped the razor into the sink and shook it off. Zane's gaze left the mirror, and as she lifted her eyes to his, there in that moment, a sudden surprising sizzle passed between them.

One, two, three seconds went by.

And then he focused his attention back on the mirror, keeping a silent vigil on her reflection.

"How are you holding up?" she asked, breaking the quiet tension.

"Am I bleeding?"

Her lips hitched at his intense tone. "No."

"Then, I'm good."

Yes. Yes, he was.

"Okay, now for your throat. Chin up, please."

He obeyed without quarrel. Gosh, he really did trust her. Something warm slid into her belly, and the feeling clung to her as she finished up his shave.

"All done," she said after another minute. "Not a nick on you, I might add." At least one of them had come out of this unscathed.

"I think I hear Mrs. Lopez tinkering in the kitchen now." She handed him his razor and jumped down from the counter. "Do you want breakfast? Coffee?"

She was partway out the door when Zane caught her arm

just above the elbow. He looked gorgeous in his white ribbed tank, his face and throat shaved clean but for the last traces of shave cream. "Just a sec. I haven't thanked you. And you don't have to worry about breakfast for me."

"I don't?"

"No. That's not part of your job description."

Well, duh. She knew that. Mariah hadn't served him his meals, but Jessica couldn't very well tell him she'd run her mouth in order to get away from him as quickly as possible.

"We'll go over what I expect of you as my assistant this morning. Thanks for the shave." He slid his hands down his smooth face, and his eyes filled with admiration. "Feels great. You're pretty good."

She swallowed. Did this mean she'd have to shave him every day?

Gosh, she really didn't think this through thoroughly enough.

"Thanks. Well, I'll see you at breakfast."

"Oh, and Jess?"

"Yeah?"

He released her arm. "I'm glad you'll be staying on. I do need your help. And I think you'll enjoy it, but whenever you're ready to head home, I'll…understand."

"Thanks, Zane. I'll do my best."

Four hours later, Jessica sat behind the desk in Zane's office, satisfied she had things under control. It had been a little scary at first. What did she really know about Zane's celebrity life? But Mariah had been acutely efficient, keeping good records and documenting things, which made it easier for Jess to slide into the role of personal assistant. She seemed to live by a detailed calendar, and Zane's appointments, events and meetings were clearly labeled. *Thank you, Mariah, for not being a slouch.* In the day planner she came to regard as The Book, Mariah had jotted down phone numbers next to names and brief reminders of what needed to be said or done.

No to the *People* magazine interview.

Yes to donating twenty thousand dollars to the Children's Hospital charity. Zane would make an appearance in the future.

No to an appearance on *The Ellen DeGeneres Show*.

And so on.

With a little help from Zane earlier this morning, she was able to field a few phone calls and make the necessary arrangements for him. It was clear Zane was in a state of celebrity hibernation. Other than opening a new restaurant, Zane was pretty much in a deep freeze. Maybe he needed the break away from the limelight, or maybe he wasn't through running away from his demons.

In a sense, she was doing the same thing by being here, afraid to go home, afraid to face the pitfalls in her own life. She, too, was hiding out, so she had no right to judge him or try to fix the situation. It wasn't any of her business. That was for sure.

"How're you doing?" he asked.

She glanced up from The Book to find him standing at the office threshold, leaning on his crutches. She flashed back to shaving him this morning and the baffling emotions that followed her into breakfast. Her heart tumbled a little.

"Good, I think."

He smiled. "Anything I can help you with?"

"No, not at the moment."

He didn't leave. He didn't enter the room.

"Is there anything I can do for you?" she asked.

"Sort of." His lips twisted back and forth. "You see, Dylan's bugging me about this script. Fact is, I don't know if acting is right for me. I never had an acting lesson in my life. So I want to say no to him. But…"

She braced her elbows on the desk and leaned forward. "But, just maybe it's something you want to do?"

He stared at her. "Hell, I don't know, Jess. I guess I need a reason to say no."

"And how can I help you with that?"

"Dylan's got this idea that if I had someone run lines with me, I'd feel better about accepting the role. Or not. I didn't ask Mariah, well…because she works for me and I'm not sure she would be—"

"Honest?"

"Objective. She tends to encourage me to try new things, so she might not be the person to ask."

"So you're saying I'd have no problem telling you 'you suck'?"

He chuckled. "Would you?"

"No, no problem at all."

His brows gathered. "I'm not sure how to take that."

"I'd have only your best interests at heart. But honestly, Zane, what do I know about acting? What if my instincts aren't dead-on? What if I get it wrong?"

"Bad acting is bad acting. You can tell if someone sings off-key, can't you?"

"Sometimes, but my ear for music isn't as good as yours."

"But you're *real*, Jess. You would know when something is authentic. That's all I'm asking you to do."

His faith in her was a heady thing. She couldn't deny she was flattered. And as his personal assistant, she couldn't really tell him she didn't want to do it.

"Okay. What did you have in mind?"

"We read through some scenes. See if I can grasp the character."

"Where?"

He pointed to the long beige leather sofa—the most comfortable place to sleep in Zane's world. "Right here." He hobbled into the room on his crutches and sank down, resting the crutches on the floor. "The script is behind you on the bookcase. If you could get it and bring it over…"

"Sure." She turned and found it quickly. *"Wildflower?"*

"That's the one. You know most of the story."

She did. She was there when Dylan explained the premise of the romantic mystery to both of them the other day. It was about a man who comes home to his family's ranch after a long estrangement and finds his brother romantically involved with the woman he'd left behind. There's a mystery surrounding their father's death and a whole cast of characters who are implicated, including both brothers. "I think it's a good story, Zane."

"Well, let's see if I can do it justice."

"Sure."

She walked over to the couch and took a seat one cushion away from him.

"I don't think that's going to work," Zane said. "You have to sit next to me." He waved the script in the air. "There's only one of these."

"Right." As she scooted closer to him, Zane's eyes flicked over her legs and lingered for half a second. Oh, boy. The back of her neck prickled with heat. In a subtle move, she adjusted her position and lowered the shorts riding up her legs to midthigh. Zane didn't seem to notice. He'd focused back on the script and was busy flipping through story pages.

"Okay, here's a scene we can do together. It's where Josh and Bridget meet for the first time since his return."

She peered at the pages and read the lines silently. It was easy enough to follow. There were one or two sentences of description to set up the scene and action taking place. The rest was dialogue, and each character's part was designated by a name printed in bold letters.

"You start first," he said, pointing to the top of the page. "Where Josh speaks to Bridget in front of her house."

"Okay, here goes." She glanced at him and smiled.

He didn't smile back. He was taking this very seriously. She cleared her throat and concentrated on the lines before her. "Josh? You're home? When did you get back? I…I didn't know you'd come."

"My father is dead. You thought I wouldn't return for his burial?"

"No. I mean…it's just that you've been gone so long."

"So you wrote me off?"

A note of anger came through in Zane's voice. It was perfect.

"That's not how it happened. You left me, remember? You said you couldn't take living here anymore."

"I gave you a choice, Bridget. You didn't choose me."

"That wasn't a choice. You asked me to leave everything behind. My family, my friends, my job and a town I love. I don't hate the way you do."

"You think I hate this place?"

"Don't you?"

"Once, I loved everything about this place. Including you."

Jessica stared at him. The way he dropped his voice to a gravelly tone and spoke his lines was so real, so genuine, it impressed the hell out of her.

"But you've moved on." Now Zane's voice turned cold. He had a definite knack for dialogue. "With my brother."

They read the next three pages, bantering back and forth, learning the characters and living them. The scene was intense, and Zane held his own. He had a lot of angst inside him and found his release using the screenwriter's words on the page.

The scene was almost finished. Just a few more lines to go.

"Don't come back here, Josh," she said, meeting Zane's eyes. "I don't want to see you again."

Zane was really into the character now. "That's too bad, Bridget." The depth of his emotion had her believing. "I'm back to stay."

"I'm going to marry your brother."

"Like hell you are," Zane said fiercely, leaning toward Jessica, his face inches from hers.

"Don't...Josh...don't mess with my life again."

"This is where he grabs her and kisses her," Zane whispered. His breath swept over her mouth, and she found herself wanting to be kissed. By Zane. Heat crept up her throat and burned her cheeks.

Zane glanced at her mouth. Was he thinking the same thing? Did he want to kiss her?

He was a man she trusted. He was a man she truly liked. "Do you want to, uh, bypass the kiss?"

He shook his head, his gaze dropping to her mouth. "No," he rasped. "I don't."

Her pulse pounded as he took her head in his hands and caressed the sides of her overheated cheeks with his long, slender fingers. Her head was tilted slightly to the left, and then his mouth lowered to hers. He touched her lips gently, and she felt the beautiful connection from the depths of her soul. Was she supposed to stay in character? How would she accomplish that? Everything inside her was spinning like crazy.

The script called for a brutal, crushing kiss, but this kiss was nothing like that. His lips were firm and giving and generous...pure heaven.

"I'm not through messing with your life, Bridget." The gravel in his voice convinced her. He did *harsh* perfectly. "I might never be through."

As Zane backed away, his gaze remained on her. He blinked a few times, as if coming to his senses, and then cleared his throat.

The air sizzled around her. Was Zane feeling it, too? She didn't know where to look, what to say.

"It's your line," Zane whispered.

Oh! She glanced at the page and read her last line. "I—I can't do this again, Josh."

Zane paused for a second, glaring at her for a beat. "I'm not gonna give you a choice this time."

There. They'd made it through the entire scene. Zane flipped the script closed, and as he braced his elbows on his knees, he leaned forward.

Her heart was zipping along. She needed space, a few inches of separation from Zane. She flopped back against the sofa and silently sighed.

"Thank you," Zane said quietly.

"Hmm."

"Now for the hard part. I respect your opinion. No hard feelings either way, so lay it on me."

He'd convinced her he could act. Aside from the kiss that still had her reeling, she was completely enthralled with his character. He'd stepped into Josh's shoes without a bit of awkwardness. "I'm no expert, but I know when something's good. I'd say you were a natural, Zane."

He leaned back and looked into her eyes. Oh, God. She didn't want him to notice how nervous she was. "You really think so?"

"I do. You dove into that character and had me believing."

He stroked his jaw and sighed.

"I'm sorry if you wanted to hear you stink at acting. But I don't think so."

A crooked smile lifted the corner of his mouth. "I admit, I was hoping that was the case. Makes my decision harder now."

"Sorry?" she squeaked.

He released a noisy breath. "Don't be. I asked for your opinion. I appreciate you, Jess," he said. "I trust your judgment. I, uh…sort of got caught up in the scene. Hope you didn't mind about the little kiss I gave you."

Little kiss? If that was his little kiss, what would a real, genuine, from-the-heart kiss feel like from her one time brother-in-law? He didn't know the kiss had sent her senses soaring, and it would have to stay that way.

She'd never admit she'd wanted to kiss him. He was her brother-in-law, for heaven's sake. He was her employer now. And he was a good, decent man who'd never take advantage of her situation. She knew all that about Zane.

Of course he'd wanted to stay true to the script. He'd delved so deeply into character that he didn't want to lose the momentum of the scene. But, oh…for that brief moment when he'd looked into her eyes and her heartbeat soared, she believed he, Zane Williams, really wanted to kiss her.

And it had been a wow moment. "No, I didn't mind at all."

Her cell phone on the desk rang and she jumped up to answer it. "Oh, uh, excuse me, Zane. It's Mama."

"Sure."

He began to rise, and she put up her hand. She wasn't going to have him leave his own office. "No, don't get up. I'll take it in my room." Her mother's timing couldn't have been better. She needed to get away from Zane and the silly notions entering her head.

She walked out of the office and climbed the stairs. "Hi, Mama."

"Hi, honey. How're you doing this afternoon? Oh, I guess it's still morning there."

"Yes, it's just before noon. I'm doing fine." Her heart-beat had finally slinked down to normal since Zane's kiss a few minutes ago.

"Really?"

"Yes, I'm fine." It was weird how distance and the new surroundings made her see things differently. She wasn't thrilled with the way her life was turning out—she'd invested a lot of time on Steven Monahan—but she didn't need to worry her mother over it. Right now, she was taking it one day at a time. "Actually, I'm glad you called this morning. I have news. Zane's personal assistant, Mariah, had to take a leave of absence. Her mother's very ill and, well, since I'm here and Zane needs help, he's asked me to take over the position. It's temporary, but I won't be coming home this week or the next, probably. I might be here longer than that."

"Oh, that's good, honey."

"It is?" There was something in her mother's too-cheerful tone that raised her suspicions. She entered her bedroom wondering what was up? "What I mean to say is, I'm sorry Mariah's mother is ill. Bless her heart. I'll be sure to say a prayer for her. But you staying there for a little longer might be best for you, after all."

Really? Her overprotective mother—the woman who had set her alarm at 3 a.m. every night to get up and check on her two sleeping little girls when they were young, the woman who'd worried and fretted during their teen years, and the woman who, after Jessica's disastrous nonwedding, arranged for her to move into Zane's house just so he could keep an eye on her—*that mother* was actually glad that she wasn't coming home anytime soon?

Now she knew something was going on.

She lowered herself onto the bed. "Why, Mom? What's happened?"

"I hate to tell you this, honey. But better it come from me than you hear about it another way."

Her heart nearly stopped. Was her mother ill? Was it something severe? She flashed back to Janie's death. How the news had seemed unreal. She'd gotten physically sick, acid drenching her stomach and her breaths coming in short, uneven bursts. Now she held her breath. "Please, just tell me."

"Okay, honey. I'm sorry…but I just found out that your Steven eloped with Judy McGinnis. They just up and left town two nights ago. Went to Vegas, I hear. The whole town's crackling about it."

"W-with Judy?"

"I'm afraid so. I never expected that from Judy. Honey, are you okay?"

She might never be okay again. She'd just learned that the man she'd banked on for three full years, the man who had sworn up and down in her dressing room on their wedding day that he wasn't ready for marriage and that it wasn't anything she'd done, had just gotten married. The fault was all his for not recognizing his problem sooner, he'd told her. She'd believed he had commitment issues. But now she knew the truth. He wasn't ready for marriage to *her*. Instead, he chose one of her bridesmaids to speak vows with.

Judy had been her friend since grade school. Oh, God. She'd accepted losing Steven and any future they might've had together, but losing Judy's friendship, too? That was a double blow to her self-esteem. They'd both betrayed her. Made a fool out of her. She hadn't seen the signs. How long had Judy and Steven been hooking up behind her back?

Her eyes burned with unshed tears.

Being here and having a new sense of purpose in helping Zane, she was beginning to feel better and gain control of her emotions. But now, fresh new pain seared her from the inside out. What an idiot she'd been. That was the worst part of all, this hopeless sense of loss of *herself*. Her heart ached in a way it never had before. She felt herself slipping away.

She couldn't give in to it. If she did, she'd be totally lost. She couldn't dwell. She wouldn't let their betrayal dictate her life. She wouldn't curl into a pitiful ball and let the world spin without her.

"Jessica?"

"I'm going to be fine, Mama. I just need some time to digest this."

"I'm here if you need me, honey. I'm so, so sorry."

"I know. I love you. I'll call you tonight. Bye for now."

Jessica pushed End on her cell phone and faced the mirror. Her mousy-brown-haired reflection stared back at her through tortoiseshell-rimmed glasses. "What's happened to you, Jess?" she muttered.

She was tired of feeling like crap. Being a victim didn't suit her. She wasn't going to put up with it another second. The old Jessica had to go.

It was time for her to take hold of her life.

Afternoon breezes whispered through Zane's hair as he sat on his deck, gazing out to sea. Dylan McKay sat beside him, sipping a glass of iced tea. He didn't mind Dylan's company as long as he wasn't pressuring him about taking on an acting role.

"How soon before you're all healed up and ready to start living again?" Dylan asked.

Not soon enough for him. The confinement was getting to him. The only good thing about being temporarily disabled was that he didn't have to make any decisions right away. And he was milking that for all it was worth.

"The blasted boot comes off on Monday."

"And how's the wrist doing?"

His wrist? He flashed to trying to shave himself this morning. He'd been hopeless. Mariah usually took him to the barber twice a week. He hated being so damn helpless, and Jess had rescued him. She'd given him a clean, smooth shave and for a second there, as she leaned in close to him, her honeyed breath mingled with his and his body zinged to life. Electricity stifled his breathing for those few moments.

Jess?

He'd written it off as nothing and gone about his business.

Then he'd asked Jess to read lines with him. He'd gotten so caught up in the scene that when it came time to kiss her…he didn't want to deny himself the opportunity. Had it been only because the scene demanded a kiss? Or had it been something more?

A tick worked his jaw. It damn well couldn't be something more.

Though kissing her soft giving mouth packed a wallop. He'd forgotten what it felt like to have a sweet woman respond to him. He'd backed off immediately and didn't dare take it any further. The complication was the last thing either of them needed.

"My wrist should be healed soon, too…with any luck." He wiggled the tips of his fingers unencumbered by the cast. "I can't do a damn thing left-handed. You have no idea how uncoordinated you really are until you lose the use of your right hand."

"I hear you. How long will Mariah be gone?"

"Not sure. I spoke with her this morning. Her mom might have some permanent paralysis. Mariah's pretty torn up about it."

"So it's just you and Jessica now, living in this itty-bitty ole house?"

Zane rolled his eyes. The house was enormous, much more than he needed. He was hardly bumping into her in the hallway in the middle of the night.

Now, there was a thought. He struck that from his mind.

"She's taken on Mariah's duties here."

"You hired her?"

Zane nodded. Dylan didn't need to know that having Jessica around made him feel closer to Janie. She, above everyone else, understood the loss he felt. They shared that horrific pain together. Jess was *home* to him, without him having to return to Beckon. He liked that about her. So maybe it was selfish of him to ask her to stay on, but he hadn't pressured her. Much. He'd like to think she wanted to stay.

"I did. I didn't have a backup for Mariah. You know as well as I do it's hard to find a replacement for a trusted employee. I trust Jess. She'll do her best."

Dylan eyed him carefully. "You sure sing her praises."

"She's bright and learns quickly." He shrugged. "She's family."

"You keep saying that."

"It's true. Why wouldn't I say it?"

Dylan flashed a wry smile and then shook his head. "No real reason, I guess. Any chance I can convince you to be my costar before you head back on tour?"

"I haven't made up my mind yet, McKay. I told you I'm not making you any promises."

"Yeah, yeah. So I've heard. Remember what they say about people who drag their feet."

"No, what the hell do they say?"

"They risk getting them cut off at the ankles."

He laughed. "I should be flattered you're so persistent. Honestly, if I lose the role to someone else, so be it. I'm not sure." About anything, he wanted to add.

"Buddy, you're not going to lose the role to someone else. I'm the executive producer, and I see you doing this character."

"You want my fan base."

"That, too. I'd be a fool not to want to reel in your fans. I know they'd turn out for you. But I have no doubt in my mind you'd be—"

"Zane?" A sultry voice carried to the deck. His heart stopped for a second. Sometimes, when he was least expecting it, Jess would call out his name and he'd swear it was Janie asking for him.

"Out here," he called to her.

Jessica popped her head out the doorway. "Oh, sorry. I didn't realize you had a guest."

"Hi," Dylan said. "How're you doing, Jess?" Dylan sent her a brilliant smile. The guy could charm a billy goat out of a field of alfalfa.

"Hi, Dylan."

"Come on out here, Jess." Zane hadn't seen much of her since they'd run lines and *kissed* earlier in the day. He'd heard her working in the office, but she hadn't asked for his help, and he'd let her be. "Have a cool drink with us?"

"Uh, no thanks," she said, taking a few steps toward them. She wore a loose-fitting flowery sundress. Her hair was up in a ponytail, and a straw satchel hung from her shoulder. "Actually, I finished up what I could this afternoon. I was hoping to go shopping now. I wanted to see if you needed anything while I was out."

"Oh, yeah? What are you shopping for?" Was he so dang bored that he had to nose into Jessica's private business?

"I, uh, didn't bring enough clothes with me. I thought I'd pick up a few things."

"Hey, I know a great little boutique in the canyon," Dylan said. "I'd be happy to drive you there."

Zane swiveled his head toward Dylan. Was he kidding?

Jessica chuckled. "Thanks, that's a kind offer, but I'm good. I'm anxious to explore and see what I can find."

"Gotcha," Dylan said. "A little me time. I hope Zane hasn't been working you too hard."

"Not at all. I'm enjoying the work." With her finger, she pushed her sunglasses up her nose. She did that when she was nervous, and obviously, Dylan McKay made her nervous. Zane wasn't sure that was a good thing. He inhaled deep into his chest. Jessica was vulnerable right now, and she didn't need Dylan hitting on her.

"But you're both coming to the party tomorrow night, right?" Another charming smile creased his neighbor's face.

"Nope, sorry," Zane said. "We're not available."

Jessica faced him a second and blinked, then shifted her focus to Dylan. "Actually, I've changed my mind. I'd love to come. What time?"

Dylan's grin seemed to spread wider than the ocean view. "Six o'clock."

"I'll be there."

"You will?" Zane asked. They'd both decided on not going.

She nodded. "Sure, why not? Sounds like fun."

Zane couldn't argue the point. If she wanted to go to Dylan's little party, he had no right to stop her. "Well, then... I guess we're coming."

"We?" Jessica asked. A genuine spark of delight lit her expression. "You're going now? That's great, Zane."

He shrugged it off but couldn't stop his chest from puffing out. Why did it make him so doggone happy that Jessica wanted him around?

"Well, I'd better be off. Zane, is it still okay that I take one of your cars?"

"Yep. You know where the keys are in the office."

"Okay, thanks. I'll take the SUV. Bye for now," she said. She pivoted and walked back into the house.

"She's nice," Dylan said.

"Very nice. "

"Too nice for me? Are you warning me off?"

"Damn straight I am." Zane eyed him. "You know darn well Jessica isn't your type. So stay away. I'm serious. She's had it rough lately."

The patio chair creaked as Dylan leaned over the arm and focused on him. "You like her?"

"Of course I like her. She's like my..." But this time Zane couldn't finish his thought. He couldn't say she was like a sister to him. An image of taking her mouth in a daring kiss burst through his mind again. In that moment, he'd forgotten she was Janie's sister. All that filled his mind was how sweet and soft her lips were. How much he wanted to go on kissing her. He'd felt at peace with Jess, yet electrified at the same time.

He'd had women in the past to satisfy his physical needs. He hadn't been a total saint after Janie died, but he hadn't had a real relationship, either, and he sure as hell wasn't going in headfirst with Jessica. So why in hell was the memory of kissing her earlier torturing him?

"I meant you want her for yourself."

Zane snorted. "Are you not hearing what I'm saying? She's off-limits. To everyone. She has a lot of healing to do. Until then, no one gets near her." He'd promised her mother he'd protect her and make sure she didn't get hurt again.

"Okay, okay. I get it, Papa Bear. Now, let's get back to the script. I think Josh's character is perfect for you, like it was written with you in mind."

For once, Zane was grateful the subject changed to his possible acting career.

Five

Thank goodness for credit cards. They gave Jessica the freedom to spend, spend, spend at the boutique Mariah had once raved about. She scoured the golden wardrobe racks at Misty Blue, and every time something struck her as daring and unlike her small-town schoolmarm image, she handed it to Misty Blue's *attire concierge* to put aside for her to try on. Sybil, the thirtysomething saleswoman, was dogging her, making suggestions and flattering her at every turn.

"Oh, you must have that," and "you'll never find a better fit," and "you'll be the envy of every woman on Moonlight Beach," were her mantras.

Jessica ate up her compliments. Why not? She needed them as much as she needed to buy a whole new wardrobe. The old Jessica was put to rest the minute she'd heard about her so-called good friend eloping with her fiancé. So be it. Jessica would return to Beckon a new woman.

Her clothes would be stylish. Her attitude would brook no pity. And she'd have a few thousand dollars less in her very tidy bankroll.

Saving money wasn't everything.

"I'll just put these items in your dressing room," Sybil announced. "Take your time looking around. When you're ready, you'll be in the Waves room."

Jessica blinked. Even the dressing rooms had names. "Okay, thank you."

She moved around the boutique slowly, taking her time perusing the shelves and racks. She picked out a two-piece bathing suit, a few hip-hugging dresses, two pairs of designer slim-cut jeans, and four blouses in varying colors and styles.

Sybil came racing forward. "Let me take those off your hands, too. I'll put them in the dressing room."

She transferred the clothes into Sybil's outstretched arms. "Thanks."

"Would you like to keep shopping?"

Jessica eyed several pairs of shoes on top of a lovely glass display case. "Yes, I'll need some shoes, too."

"I'll have Carmine, our shoe attendant, help you with that."

Thirty minutes later, Jessica glanced around the Waves dressing room. Clothes hung on every pretty golden hook, and shoes dotted the floor around her feet. She'd gone a bit hog-wild in her choices and needed guidance from someone who knew her well. She punched the speed dial on her cell phone and was relieved when her best friend, Sally, answered.

"Help me, Sally. I need your honest opinion," she whispered. "I texted you pictures of five of the dresses I've tried on. Did you get them?"

"Sure did. I'm looking at them now."

"Good." The inventor of cell phone technology was a genius. It made shopping a whole lot easier. "Which ones do you like?"

"Gosh, none of them look bad on you. You have a great figure," Sally said, almost in disbelief. "You've been hiding it."

"I guess I have." She'd never been comfortable with her busty appearance and had always chosen clothes to hide rather than highlight her figure. Now, all bets were off.

"Did you like the red one?"

"Definitely the red. That's a given," Sally said. "Whose eyeballs are you trying to ruin?"

"What do you mean?"

"That dress is an eye-popper."

She pictured Zane. Why had he come to mind so easily? It was ridiculous and yet, something had hummed in her heart when he'd kissed her today. He'd been caught up in the scene. She shouldn't make a darn thing out of it. But she was having a hard time forgetting the feel of his lips claiming hers. As short as the kiss was, it had been potent enough to shoot endorphins through her body. That wasn't necessarily a good thing.

"Do you think maybe I shouldn't be doing this?" she asked Sally, her bravado fading.

"Doing what? Pampering yourself? Spending some of your hard-earned money on yourself? Indulging a little? I'm only sorry I'm not there to help you with your TLC gone wild. Believe me, if I could swing it, I'd hop on a plane today."

She chuckled. "TLC gone wild? That's a new one, Sal."

"I'm clever. What can I say? Buy the clothes, Jess. I'll let you decide on the shoes, but those red stiletto heels will kick some major butt. Oh, and while you're at it, lose the eyeglasses. You brought your contacts, didn't you?"

"Yes, I have them."

"Well, use them. If you're going to do it, do it right."

Of course, Sally was dead-on. If she was going to invest in these clothes, she had to go all the way. She'd already decided to ditch her tortoiseshell glasses. Her hair could use some highlights, and her California tan was coming along nicely. Already she felt better about herself.

"And Sal, I wish you could come out here. It's really… nice."

"I bet. Zane's place sounds like heaven. Right on the beach. I bet you don't even have any swamp heat and humidity."

"Nope, not like home."

"Tell me you haven't met any big movie stars and I swear I won't be jealous."

"I, uh, well," her voice squeaked.

"Who? Tell me or I'll haunt you into forever."

"Would you believe Dylan McKay lives two doors down?" Jessica squeezed her eyes shut, anticipating the bombardment. No one was a bigger fan of the Hollywood heartthrob than her bestie Sally.

"You've met him?"

"Yes, I sort of ran into him on the beach." Or rather, the other way around—he'd run into her. "He's a friend of Zane's."

"No way! I can't believe it. Tell me everything."

A knock on the dressing-room door startled her, and she jumped. She'd forgotten where she was.

"Miss Holcomb, can I help you with anything?" Sybil asked.

"Whoops, gotta go," she said in a low voice. "I've got to get dressed. I'll call you later."

"You better!"

Jessica smiled as she ended the call and answered the saleswoman. "No thanks. I'm doing great.

"I'll be out in one minute."

"You sound happy. Find anything to your liking?"

"Just about everything," she answered.

She imagined the attire concierge who worked on commission smiling on the other side of the door.

Her purchases today would make both of them happy.

Zane had received a text message from Jessica half an hour ago telling him not to wait for her to have his meal. She was going to be late. But he didn't feel much like eating without her. It had taken Jessica living here for him to realize he'd eaten too many meals alone.

She must've gotten carried away on her little shopping spree.

When Jessica finally pulled through the gates, driving toward the garage, Zane made his way to the living room and, with the grace of an ox, plunked down onto the sofa.

A minute later the door opened into the back foyer, and he heard the crunch of bags and footsteps approaching. He picked up a magazine and flipped through the pages.

"Hi, Zane," Jessica said. Her voice sounded breezy and carefree. "Sorry I'm so late."

When he lifted his head, he found her loaded down with shopping bags. "Did you buy out the store?"

She chuckled from a warm and deep place in her throat. "Let's just say the store manager couldn't do enough for me. They offered me a vanilla latte and a chocolate mini croissant, and the shoe salesman almost gave me a foot massage."

His brows gathered. "A foot massage?"

"I told him no. I didn't have time. Is that done here?"

"I don't know if it's done *anywhere*," Zane said. For heaven's sake, she was buying shoes, not asking for a damn foot rub. His nerves started to sizzle. He studied the assortment of shiny teal-blue bags she held. "Where did you go?"

"Misty Blue. Mariah recommended the shop to me. It's just up the coast."

"Leave it to Mariah," Zane muttered. She had impeccable taste, but she could be indulgent at times.

"Speaking of Mariah, have you heard from her today?"

"Yes, we spoke earlier this morning. Do you need to talk to her about anything in particular?"

She shook her head and lowered her packages to the floor, releasing the handles. "I'm managing for right now." She walked over to lean her elbows on the back of his angular sofa. From his spot on the couch, he had a clear view of her face. "How is her mother doing?"

Zane shook his head. "Not great." He was lucky his mother and father were in their seventies and still quite active living in a retirement community in Arizona. He saw them several times a year. And when something like this happened, he thought about spending more time with them. "Mariah said her mom might have some permanent damage from the stroke, but it's too soon to tell. She spends most of her day at the hospital or meeting with doctors."

"I'm sorry to hear that."

"Yeah, me, too. And with all that, she asked about you. She made me promise to have you call her with any questions."

Jessica sent him a rigid look. "Unless it's an emergency, I'm not going to call her, Zane. You and I both know what it's like having to deal with a family crisis."

A lump formed in his throat. "Yeah. I agree, and I told her as much. There's nothing so important that it can't wait. Between the two of us, we'll figure out what needs figuring from this end."

"Right. Hey, I almost forgot. I bought you a present."

His heavy heart lightened. "You did?"

She bent to forage in one of the bags and came up holding a long, shiny black box. It wasn't a gift from Misty Blue, that was for sure. She stretched as far as her arms could reach, eyeing the box carefully one last time, before handing it over. "I, uh, hope this doesn't upset you, but I know how much you loved the one Janie got you, and, well…this one is from me."

Her fingers gently brushed over his hand, and her caring touch seized his heart for a moment. With his good hand, he managed to lift the lid and gaze at his gift. He found himself momentarily speechless. It was an almost identical replica of a bolo tie with a turquoise stone set on a stamped silver backing that Janie had given him on the anniversary of their first date. It had been lost in the fire, and he'd never replaced it. It wouldn't have had the same sentimental meaning. But the fact that Jessica gave it to him meant something. He lifted the rope tie out of the box and shifted his gaze to her. "It's a thoughtful gift, Jess."

"I know you treasured the first one. I helped Janie pick it out, so I remember exactly what it looked like."

"You didn't have to do this." But he was glad she had.

"You're putting a roof over my head and feeding me, but more importantly, being here is helping me heal. It's the least I could do for you. And I wanted it to be…something special."

"It is. Very special."

He rose from the sofa, found his footing and, using his crutches, shuffled over to her. He gazed through the lenses of her glasses to dewy, softly speckled green eyes. They were warm and friendly and genuine. He bent to kiss her forehead the way a brother would a sister, but then awareness flickered in her eyes, and he felt it, too. He lowered his mouth, heady in his need to taste the giving warmth of her lips again. When he touched his mouth to hers, he savored her sweetness and assigned this moment to memory for safekeeping. He backed away just in time to keep the kiss to one of thanks. "Thank you."

"You're welcome." Her deep, sultry voice thrilled him and churned his stomach at the same time. She sounded so much like Janie.

"I haven't had dinner yet. I waited for you. Mrs. Lopez put our meal in the oven to keep warm. Are you hungry?"

"Starving," she said. "Shopping is tough. I worked up an appetite."

He laughed. The women he knew loved to shop and spend endlessly. He'd never heard one remark about hard work.

"I'll put the bags away in my room. Meet you in the kitchen?"

He nodded. He hated that he couldn't offer to help her. He watched her climb the stairway holding three maxed-out shopping bags in one hand and two in the other. The next time she wanted to shop, he'd be damn ready to take the packages off her hands and carry them upstairs for her.

Zane made his way into the kitchen. Mrs. Lopez had left chicken and dumplings warming in the oven. Zane lifted a periwinkle-striped kitchen towel tucked over a basket and eyed cheesy biscuits, still warm. He dipped into the basket and sank his teeth into a biscuit. Warmth spread throughout his mouth and reminded him he was ready for a hearty meal.

"Wow, smells good in here." Jessica entered the kitchen.

"Mrs. Lopez made one of my favorites tonight."

"In that case, I'm surprised you waited for me."

"I figured a Southern girl like you would appreciate sharing chicken and dumplings. It's my mother's recipe."

"You figured right. Well, then. Have a seat." She gestured to the table. "I'll dish it up. Unless you want to eat outside?"

He shook his head. The sun had already set, and winds howled over the shoreline, spraying sand everywhere. "Here is just fine."

Before he knew it, the table was set, plates were dished up and he had the company of one of his favorite people sitting across from him.

The chicken was tender, the dumplings melted in his mouth and Zane spent the next few minutes quietly diving into his meal. He liked that he could sit in silence with Jess without feeling as though he had to entertain her. She was as comfortable with the quiet as he was.

"Mmm, this was so good." Jess took a last bite of food, and as she wiped her mouth, his gaze drifted down to where the napkin touched her lips. "I'll have to steal the recipe from Mrs. Lopez and make it for my mother when I get home."

"No problem." He shouldn't be noticing the things he was noticing about Jess. Like the cute way she pushed her glasses up her nose, or the way she smelled right after a shower, or how her light skin had burnished to a golden tone from days of sunbathing. The sound of her voice dug deep into his gut. Janie and Jess were the only two women he knew that had a low, raspy yet very feminine voice. Janie had been sultry, sexy, alluring, but...Jess?

"Zane?"

He lifted his gaze to her meadow-green eyes.

"You went someplace just now."

"I'm sorry."

"No need to be sorry. Are you okay?"

He nodded and cleared his throat. "So, did you have fun shopping today?"

"Fun?" Her head tilted as a slow, easy smile spread across her face. "I had an attire concierge help me. That was weirdly entertaining. She dogged my every step but was nice as can be. Actually my best friend, Sally, helped me make the right choices. Sally was my maid of honor in the wedding that never was."

"Is your friend in town?"

She laughed and shook her head. "No, not at all. I texted her pictures of the clothes I tried on, and she helped me decide. I'm *so* not a shopper."

"Ah, the power of technology."

"Yeah, ain't it great?"

It beat having Dylan McKay help her shop. Zane wasn't about to allow that to happen.

A heartbreaking ladies' man was the last thing sweet Jess needed in her life right now.

"Actually, it is pretty great. I'm glad you had a good day."

"I plan to have a lot of good days from now on." A glint of something resolute beamed in her eyes, her face an open expression of hope.

Jess was healing, and that was a good thing. He liked seeing her feeling better. That was the whole point of her coming here. But it seemed too soon. And she seemed a little too happy for a woman who'd been betrayed and heartbroken. Right now, Jessica Holcomb looked ready to conquer the world, or at least Moonlight Beach. Instincts that rarely failed him told him something else was going on with Jess.

And he didn't know if he was going to like it.

"Hi, Zane." Jessica stepped into the living room, dressed and ready for Dylan's party.

Zane turned from the window… His hair was combed back, shiny and straight, the stubble on his face a reflection of not having a shave in two days. He looked gorgeous in a white billowy shirt and light khaki trousers. When his gaze fell on the *new* her, his lips parted and his eyes popped as he took in her appearance from the top of her head to her sandaled toes. Pain entered his eyes, and he blinked several times as if trying to make it go away. Relying on the two crutches under his arms, he straightened to his full height and sighed heavily.

"Zane?" Her lips began to quiver. What was wrong with him? "Are you all right?"

He stared at her, his expression unreadable. "I'm fine."

"Are you? Have I done something? Don't you like the dress?" Her mind rushed back to the clothes she'd laid out on the bed. She'd chosen the cornflower-blue sundress that accented her slender waist in a scoop-neck design that, granted, revealed more cleavage that she was comfortable with, but wasn't indecent by any means.

His mouth opened partly, but no words tumbled forth, and then he gulped as if swallowing his words.

"What is it?" she pressed.

"You look like Janie," he rushed out, as though once pressured, he couldn't stop himself from saying it.

"I…do?"

How could she possibly look like Janie? Janie was stunning. She had natural beauty, a perfectly symmetrical face. She wore stylish clothes, had the prettiest long, silken hair, and oh…now she understood. Of course she and Janie resembled each other—they were sisters—but Jessica had always stood in Janie's shadow where beauty was concerned. Her blonde-from-a-bottle hair color had turned out a little less dark honey and much more sweet wheat, similar to Janie's hair color. Jessica didn't usually wear her contacts, but she imagined her eyes looked more vibrant green than ever before. Like Janie's brilliant gemstone eyes. Did Zane think he was seeing a ghost of his former wife? She didn't believe she looked enough like Janie for that and never thought about how it might appear. "I, um, wasn't trying to, but I take that as a compliment." She shrugged, compelled to explain. "I guess I needed a change."

An awkward moment passed between them, which was weird. They didn't do awkward. Usually they were completely at peace with each other.

"You didn't need to change a thing," he said firmly.

Was he trying to make her feel better? Even she had to admit, after looking at herself in the mirror today, that her new look made her appear revitalized and well, better than she had in years. Zane had no idea what she was really going through right now, the pain, rejection, anger. He didn't know, because she hadn't told him. He wasn't her shrink, her sounding board. And call it pride, but she wasn't ready to talk about Steven's quick marriage to her once-friend/bridesmaid to anyone, much less him. "I'm sorry if I upset you. Obviously you don't approve. I don't have to go tonight."

The last thing she wanted to do was cause Zane any upheaval in his life. He was still in love with Janie. She got that. No one knew what a special person her sister was better than she did.

She was staying here thanks to Zane's generosity. He was her employer now, too, and she had to remember that, yet underlying hurt simmered inside her. He had no idea how hard this was for her. She'd come into this room hoping for some sort of approval. She'd made a change in her appearance, but it was more than that. She looked upon this makeover as a fresh start, a way to say "screw you" to all the Stevens in the world. She'd come into this room with newfound confidence, and Zane's dismal attitude had caused her heart to plummet. Why did it matter so much to her what Zane thought?

She pivoted on her heels, taking a step toward the staircase, and Zane's voice boomed across the room. "Damn it, Jess. Don't leave."

She whirled around and stared at him. A dark storm raged in his eyes.

Was he angry with her? Maybe she should be angry with him. Maybe she'd had enough of men dictating what they wanted from her. "Is that an order from the boss?"

"Hell, no." His head thumped against the window behind him once, twice, and then he lowered his voice. "It wasn't an order."

"Then what was it?"

Zane's gaze scoured over her body again, and as he took in her appearance, approval, desire and *heat* entered his eyes. Her bones could have just about melted from that look. Then, with a quick shake of his head, he said, "Nothing, I guess. Jess, you don't need my approval for anything. Fact is, you look beautiful tonight. You surprised me and, well…I don't like surprises."

She didn't move. She was torn with indecision.

From the depth of his eyes, his sincerity came through. "I'm a jerk."

Her lips almost lifted. She fought it tooth and nail, but Zane could be charming when he had to be.

"Blond hair looks great on you."

She drew breath into her lungs.

"The dress is killer. You're a real knockout in it."

His compliments went straight to her head. He'd finally gotten to her. "Okay, Zane. Enough said." She'd been touchy with him, maybe because she'd hoped to impress him a little. Maybe because, in the back of her mind, she'd wanted to please Zane or at least win his approval. "Let's forget about this." She didn't like confrontation, not one bit.

"You'll go to the party?"

She nodded. "Yes. I'm ready."

They'd had their first real argument. Granted, it wasn't much of one. A few minutes of tension was all. But she'd stood her ground, and she could feel good about that. One thing that loving Steven had taught her was never to turn a blind eye. From now on, she wanted to deal in absolute truth.

"You mind driving?" he asked.

"I should make you trudge through the sand all the way to Dylan's place."

"I'd do it if it would put a smile back on your face."

"It's tempting. But I'm not that cruel."

Amused, Zane's mouth lifted, and they seemed back on even footing again.

Whatever that was.

Six

Zane stood outside in the shadows, his shoulder braced against the wall of Dylan's home. The setting sun cast pastel colors across the cobalt sky, and waves pounded the shoreline. The Pacific breezes had died down and no longer lifted Jessica's blond locks into a flowing silky sheet in the wind. She stood in front of a circular fire pit on the deck. Her flowery summer dress had been a victim of the wind, too, and hell if he hadn't noticed her hem billow up, *every single time*. And every single time, something powerful zinged inside him.

He couldn't figure why Jessica had made such a drastic turnabout in her appearance. He wouldn't have called her an ugly duckling before—she'd been perfect in her own natural way—but tonight, she'd bloomed into a beautiful swan and he feared he was in deep trouble.

He liked her. A lot. And he knew damn well she was as off-limits to him as any woman would ever be. The old Jess he could deal with. She was like his kid sister. But now, as he watched the predusk light filter through her hair and heard the sound of her sultry laughter carry to him as she spoke with Dylan and his friends, she seemed like a different woman.

Sweet Jess was a knockout, and every man here had noticed.

Dylan popped his head up from the group and gestured to him. "Come on over and join the party."

Well, damn. He couldn't very well stay in the shadows the entire night. He'd have to shelve his confused thoughts about Jessica and join them. He pushed off from the wall using his crutches for balance and made his way over to the fire pit.

"I thought Adam was the only recluse on the beach," Dylan said.

"There's a difference between savoring one's privacy as opposed to hiding out from the world," Adam said.

Adam Chase was his next-door neighbor, the architect of many of the homes on the beachfront and a man who didn't give much away about himself. He'd been featured in *Architectural Digest* and agreed to a rare magazine interview, but mostly the man's astonishing work spoke for itself. The one thing he'd learned about Adam in the time he'd known him was that he shied away from attention.

"He's got you there, Dylan. Being someone who craves attention, you wouldn't understand." Zane zinged him because he knew Dylan was a good sport and could handle the teasing.

Dylan took Jess's hand, entwining their fingers. "They're ganging up on me, Jess. I need someone in my corner."

Jess's giggles swept over Zane, and he eyed the half-empty blended mojito she held in her other hand. She freed her hand and inched away from Dylan. It was hardly a noticeable move, except maybe to Zane, who was eyeballing her every step. "You boys are on your own. I'm staying out of this."

Dylan slammed his hand to his chest. "Oh, you're breaking my heart, Jess."

Adam's eyes flickered over Jess and touched on the valley between her breasts in the revealing sundress she wore. She was dazzling tonight, and Zane had a hard time keeping his eyes off her, too. He shouldn't fault the guys for flirting, yet every inappropriate glance at her boiled his blood.

"You're a smart woman, Jessica," Adam said.

"The smartest," Zane added. "She's going home with me tonight."

All eyes turned his way. Ah, hell. He'd shocked them, but no more than he'd shocked himself. He spared Dylan a glance, and the guy's smug grin was bright enough to light the night sky. Adam's face was unreadable, and the four others around the fire pit became awkwardly silent. "She's my houseguest and she's…"

"I think what Zane meant," Jess chimed in, "was that I've had a tough time lately. I'm getting over a broken engagement and, well, he's sweet enough to want to protect me." Her eyes scanned the seven people sitting around the fire pit. "Not that I'd need protecting from anyone here. You've all been so nice and welcoming."

They had. And now Zane felt like an ass for staking his claim when he had no right and for putting her in an awkward position.

"But I do make my own decisions. And I'd love to get to know each of you better."

"You *are* a smart woman." Dylan turned to Zane with genuine understanding. He and Dylan had had this conversation before. "And we all knew what Zane was getting at."

Zane clamped his mouth shut for the moment. He'd said enough, and he had a feeling that Jessica wasn't too thrilled with him right now. His big brother act had probably started to wear thin on her. He didn't say boo when she walked down to the water deep in conversation with Adam Chase for a few minutes. He didn't register an inkling of irritation when Dylan offered to give her a tour of his house. But darn if he wasn't keenly relieved when Jessica made friends with three of the women at the party. She'd spent a good deal of time with them. He recognized one woman as an actress recently cast in a film about a Southern girl. She'd gobbled up a good deal of time asking Jess questions about Texas.

"You look like you could use a beer." Adam handed him one of the two longnecks he clasped between his fingers.

"You read my mind. That sounds good." Adam's mouth twitched. The man didn't often smile, but obviously Zane had amused him. "Right. How's the restaurant coming?"

Zane had asked Adam for a recommendation of someone whose specialty was designing shoreline commercial establishments since Adam didn't work with small restaurants. "We've broken ground. The framework is up, and we should open our doors in a few months. I'm hoping for Labor Day."

"Glad things are going smoothly."

He nodded. Last year, he'd opened a restaurant in Reno, and his friend and CEO of Sentinel Construction had overseen the building. But Casey's business didn't reach the west coast, and Adam had connections all over the world. He wound up hiring a builder Adam said was top-notch. "They seem to be."

Adam sipped his beer. "Jessica seems like a nice girl. She said she's indirectly related to you."

Indirectly? Though those were true words, it still stung hearing them coming from her mouth secondhand that way. There was something painful in the truth, and if he was being gut-honest with himself, it was liberating, as well. "Uh, yeah. She was my wife's little sis. She's staying in Moonlight Beach for a while."

"With you. Yes, you made that clear earlier." Adam's mouth hitched again. It was more animation than Zane had seen in the guy practically since he'd met him. "I'm going out on a limb here, but either you're hooked on her, or you've got a bad case of Big Brother syndrome."

Zane peered over Adam's shoulder and caught a glimpse of Jessica speaking with a man who looked enough like Dylan to be his twin. "Who the hell is that?"

Adam swiveled his head and gave the guy a once-over.

"Dylan introduced him to me before you arrived. That's Roy. He's Dylan's stunt double."

Roy and Jessica stood in the sand under the light of a tiki torch and away from the crowd of people beginning to swarm the barbecue pit, where a chef prepared food on the grill. Zane didn't like it, but he couldn't very well pull her away from every guy who approached her.

"So, which is it?" Adam asked.

"Which is what?" He watched Jessica laugh at something Roy said.

"Are you playing big brother? Cause if you're not, I think you have to amp up your game, neighbor. Or you're going to lose something special, before you know what hit you."

Zane stared at Adam. The guy had no clue what he was talking about. Adam had no idea how hard he'd loved Janie. He had no idea how he couldn't get past what happened. He'd tried over and over to put his emotions to lyrics, to gain some sort of closure in a song meant to honor his love for Janie, but the words wouldn't come. "I've already lost—"

Adam began shaking his head. "I'm not talking about the past, Zane. I'm talking about the future."

"Spoken by a man who rarely steps foot out of his house."

Now Adam did laugh. "I'm here now, aren't I?"

"Yeah, that surprises me. Why are you?"

He shrugged. "I've got a temperamental artist painting a wall in my gallery. It's going to be fantastic when he's through, and he insists on complete privacy. I'm staying at Dylan's for a few days."

"Well, damn. You're sorta here by default, then."

"It's not so bad. At least I got to meet Jessica and all her Southern charm."

"Why, that's very nice of you to say, Adam."

A sweet strawberry scent wafted to his nostrils, announcing Jessica's presence even before she'd uttered a word.

He'd come to recognize her scent, and every time she approached, a little bitty buzz would rush through his belly. She took a place by his side, and he refrained from puffing out his chest.

"Just speaking the truth," Adam said.

"Hey, Jess," Zane said.

"Hey, yourself," she said to him. He wasn't sure if she'd been deliberately avoiding him since his dopey remark earlier, or if she was flitting around like a butterfly to make new friends. Either way, he was glad she'd come over to him.

"Having fun?"

"Sure am. I'm meeting some great people here. It was sweet of Dylan to invite me. Sorry if I abandoned you."

He raised his beer bottle to his lips. "No problem. I spent my time keeping Adam amused."

Jessica shot a questioning glance at Adam.

"He's quite a party animal these days," Adam explained, tucking his free hand into his trouser pockets.

Zane gulped the rest of his beer. He wouldn't be here if Jessica hadn't changed her mind about coming. "C'mon Jess. Looks like the meal's being served. I've got me a hankering for some barbecue chicken."

"Adam, will you join us?" she asked.

Adam shook his head. "I'll see you over at the table later. I'm going to have another drink first."

Zane began moving, and Jessica kept by his side as he headed for a table occupying the far corner of the massive patio. "Chances are we won't see much of Adam tonight. He keeps to himself pretty much."

"Does he?" she asked. "Why?"

"I don't really know. We got friendly when I leased the house from him. And we had some business dealings, but I sensed he's a loner. It's probably why he was standing with me, over against the wall."

"Well, he was cordial to me."

"Yeah, I know." Zane dipped his gaze to the swell of her breasts teasing the top of her frilly sundress. Her skin looked creamy soft and—Lord help him—inviting. With that blond hair flowing down her back and her eyes as green as a grassy meadow, she made his heart ache. "I saw the two of you walking out to the water."

"All I did was ask him about his designs. Architecture has always fascinated me."

"Yeah, that's probably why he spent time with you. He loves talking shop." Lucky for him, Jess didn't notice the sarcasm in his voice. He managed to pull a chair out for her, crutches and all.

Man, he'd be glad to rid himself of them.

It couldn't happen soon enough.

They'd stayed at the party a little too long. Zane was smashed, going over his liquor limit an hour ago, and now she struggled to get him out of the car. He obviously didn't take his own advice. Hadn't he warned her of not drinking too much, because in his handicapped state, he wouldn't be able to help her? Well…now the shoe was on the other foot. "Hang on to me," she said, reaching inside the car.

"Glad to, darlin'."

He slung his arm around her shoulder, nearly pulling her onto his lap.

"Zane!"

An earthy laugh rumbled from his throat.

"Not cute."

"Neither are y-you," he said.

After a few seconds of maneuvering, she managed to get him upright.

"You're b-beautiful."

Oh, boy. She rolled her eyes and ignored his comment.

He swayed to the left. Sure-footed he was not. She leaned him up against the car. "Here." She shoved a crutch under his arm, tucking it carefully but none too gently. "Please, please, try to concentrate."

Maybe she should've taken Dylan up on his offer to drive Zane home. But Zane wouldn't have any of it, insisting he could manage.

Men and their egos.

Now she had two hundred pounds of sheer brawn and muscle to contend with. "Lean against me, Zane. Try not to topple. Ready?"

He nodded forcefully, and his whole body coasted away from her. "Whoa!" She gripped him around the waist and tugged with all of her might to bring him close. Letting him go right now would be a disaster. "Don't make sudden moves like that."

"Mmm."

He sounded happy about something. She was glad someone was enjoying this. When he seemed secure in his stance, she took a step and then another. With his body pressed to hers and one shoulder supporting his arm, she managed to get him through the garage and inside the house. By the time she made it to his bed, her strength was almost sapped. "Here we go. I'm going to let go of you now."

"Don't," he said.

"Why? Are you feeling dizzy?"

He shook his head, and his arm tightened around her shoulder. She was trapped in his warmth, his heat. And as she gazed up into his eyes, they cleared. Just like that. The haze that seemed to keep him in a woozy state was gone. "No. I'm feeling pretty damn good. Because you're here with me. Because I can't get you out of my head."

As if his own weight was too much to bear, he sat down, taking her with him. She plopped on the bed, and the mattress sighed. Streaming moonlight filtered into the room, and their reflection in the window bounced back at her. Two souls, searching for something that they'd lost. Was that what the attraction was?

"Are you drunk?" she asked.

"Not too much anymore." He pushed aside her hair at her nape, his touch as gentle as a Texas breeze. He nipped her there, his teeth scraping around to the top of her throat and the sensation claimed all the breath in her lungs.

"You sobered up fast," she whispered, barely able to form a coherent thought. Having his delicious mouth taking liberties on her neck was pure heaven.

"I know when I want something."

His nips were heady, and she tilted her head to the side, offering him more of her throat. "Wh-what do you want?"

With his good hand under her chin, he turned her head, and then his lips were on hers, pressing firm against her softness, igniting fireworks that started with her brain and rushed all the way down to her belly. She turned to him, roping her arm around his neck, kissing him back. He smelled like pure male animal, his scent mingling with whiskey and heat. Her breasts perked up, and her nipples pebbled against the silky material of her dress.

"I want to kiss you again and again," he rasped over her lips. "I want to touch your body and have you touch mine. I need you, too. So badly, sweetheart."

Oh, wow. Oh, wow. Oh, wow. A fierce physical attraction pulled at her like a giant magnet. She couldn't fight the force or the combustible chemistry between them. And Zane didn't give her time to refuse. With his left hand, he began unbuttoning his shirt and did a lousy job of slipping the buttons free until she came to his rescue.

"Let me." She shoved his hand away and quickly finished for him. With his shirt open now, his chest was a work of art, muscled and bronzed. She itched to touch him, to put her hands exactly where he wanted her to. She inhaled, and as she released a breath, she spread her palms over his hot, moist skin. From the contours of his waist up his torso to where crisp chest hairs tickled the underside of her fingers, she savored each inch of him.

A guttural groan exploded in the room, and she wasn't sure if she'd made that sound, but one look into Zane's eyes darkened by desire and she knew it wasn't her.

He was on fire. His skin sizzled hot and steamy, his breathing hitched and all of that combined was enough to blanket her body with burning heat. "We can't," she said softly.

She had to say it. Because of Janie. Because of Steven. She and Zane were both trying to heal, but none of that resonated right now. None of it seemed powerful enough to derail the sensations whipping them into a frenzied state.

Maybe this was what both of them needed.

One night.

His mouth claimed her again as he lay down on the bed, tugging her along with him. She fell beside him. Promptly he snaked his arm under her waist and flipped her on top of him.

She had his answer. Yes, they could.

His good hand cupped her cheek, and his eyes bored into her. "Don't question this, Jess. Not if it's what you want right now."

That was Zane. The man who didn't plan for the future anymore, the man who'd said it was better sometimes not to know where you were going. And Jessica certainly didn't have a clue what her future held or where the heck she was going from here.

But she knew what she wanted tonight.

How could she not? Her breasts were crushed against Zane's chest, her body trembling and so ready for whatever would come next. Zane was a good, decent man who also happened to be sexy as sin but he had also been her sis— She stopped thinking. Enough. She might talk herself out of this. "It's what I want."

He gave her a serious smile and kissed her again, his lips soft and tender, taking his time with her, making her come apart in small doses.

In the moment, Jessica gave herself permission to let go completely. He pushed the straps down on her dress and her breasts popped free of restraint. Zane caressed her, running his hand over her sensitive skin, lightly touching one wanton crest that seemed made for his touch.

A deep moan rose from her throat. She closed her eyes and enjoyed every second of his tender ministrations. "You have a beautiful body, sweetheart," he said, then rose up to place his mouth over one breast, his tongue flicking the nub, wetting it in a flurry of sweeps. He moved to the other side and did the same, a little more frenzied, faster, rougher. She squealed, the exquisite pain sending shock waves down past her belly.

Zane reacted with a jerk of his hips. "Get naked for me, Jess."

She pulled her dress over her shoulders, and he helped as much as he could to lift it the rest of the way off. She gave it a gentle toss to the floor and straddled him, bare but for her panties, and looking into eyes that seemed distant for a moment. "Are you sure about this?" he rasped, his brows gathering.

He was giving her a way out, but she was in too deep now. Her body hummed from his touch and the promise of the pulsing manhood beneath her. She wanted more…she wanted it all.

She was the *new* Jess.

"I'm sure, Zane."

He nodded and blew out a breath in apparent relief, but there was something else. A part of him seemed undecided. It was only a feeling she had, a vibe that worried her in some small part of her consciousness. Don't think. Don't think. Don't think.

The new Jess wasn't a thinker. She was a doer.

She bent to his mouth, her sensitized nipples reaching his chest first. He bucked under her. "Oh, man, babe." She smiled at him and opened her mouth, coaxing his tongue to play with hers. His strokes made her dizzy, and her desire for him soared. She was almost ready. She reached for his zipper.

"No," he said. He gently rolled her to her side and leaned over her. "There might be something I'm good at with my left hand."

A smile broke out on her face, but Zane wiped the smile away the second his fingers probed inside her panties. He cupped her there, and a melodic sigh escaped her throat. He kissed her, swallowing the rest of her sounds as he stroked her with deft fingers. Her body moved, arched, reached as he became more and more merciless. "Zane," she cried.

She climbed over the top immediately, her limbs shaking, her breathing quickened and labored. A drawn-out, piercing scream rang from her throat. She was cocooned in heat. Zane held her patiently while her tingles ebbed and she came down to earth.

"Reach over to the bed stand, sweetheart," he said as she caught her breath. "Dig deep in the drawer." He nuzzled her ear and said softly, "It's been a while."

Seconds later, with a little of her help, he was sheathed. She reeled from the passion she witnessed in his eyes. It wasn't lust, but something more. Something she could feel good about when she remembered this night. They were connected, always had been, and right now all things powerful in the universe were pulling her toward this man.

"Ready?" he asked.

As she nodded, boldly she lifted her leg over his waist to straddle him. Both of his hands came around her back, encouraging her to lean down. She did, and he pressed a dozen molten kisses to her mouth before he set her onto him.

Instinctively she rose up, and he helped guide her down. The tip of his shaft teased her entrance, and she closed her eyes.

"So beautiful," she heard him say softly as he filled her body.

They moved together as one, his thrusts setting the pace. Her heart beat rapid-fire; she was in the Zane zone now and offered to him everything he wanted to take.

He was all she could ever hope for in a lover. His kiss drove her crazy, and he was more adept with one good hand than the men she'd known in the past who'd had the use of both. He explored her body with tender kisses and bold touches, with harmonious rhythm and unexpected caresses. He was wild and tender, sweet and wicked. And when he pressed her for finality that he seemingly couldn't hold back another second, her release astonished and satisfied her. "Wow," she whimpered, her body still buzzing. She lay sated and spent on the bed.

"Yeah, babe. Wow." Zane sighed heavily, an uncomplicated sound telling her how much pleasure she'd brought him. She wasn't sorry. She had no regrets. But then, she hadn't let her mind wander since she'd entered Zane's bedroom. She didn't want to think. Not now.

Zane wrapped his arm around her, tucking her into him, and soon the sound of his quiet breaths steadied. With all that he'd consumed tonight, there was no reason to hope that he would wake soon.

She closed her eyes, savoring the safety and serenity the night brought to her.

Zane's eyes snapped open to the ceiling above. It was funny how the crater-like texture seemed odd to him this morning. He'd never noticed it before. Back home, solid wood beams supported the house. The rich smell of pines and oaks and cedar lent warmth and gave him a true sense of belonging. He missed home, longed for it actually, but how in hell could he complain? He lived in a rich man's paradise, on a sandy windswept beach with dazzling pastel sunsets and beautiful people surrounding him.

He didn't have to look over to know Jess wasn't beside him on the bed. He'd heard her exit the room in the wee hours of the morning. He should've stopped her. He should've reached out and tugged her back to bed. If he had, she'd be here with him now, and he would nestle into her warmth again.

Sweet Jess. *Sexy Jess.*

Oxygen pushed out of his lungs. He was still feeling the effects of last night. The alcohol, the soft woman—the entire night played back in his mind. He was in deep now.

He hinged his body up and swiveled his feet over the bed to meet with the floor. He made a grab for his crutches that lay against the wall and luckily hung on to them. Rising, still wearing the pants he'd worn last night, he ambled from the bedroom to the living room. From there, he spotted Jess pressed against the deck railing in a pair of sexy shorts and a ruffled blouse, gazing out to sea. It was just after dawn, and the beach was empty but for a few seagulls milling about. Low curling waves splashed against the shore almost silently. It was a beautiful time of day.

Made even more beautiful by his golden-haired houseguest.

As quietly as a man on crutches could, he made his way out the double French doors and headed toward her. Her concentration was intense, and she didn't hear him approach until he was behind her. He put his crutches near the wall and braced his arms on the railing, trapping her in his embrace.

She stood with her back to his chest. Her hair whipped in the breeze and tickled his cheeks as he nibbled on her nape. She tasted like a woman who'd had a delicious night of sex. She smelled like a woman who'd been sated and well loved. He breathed her in. "Mornin', Jess."

"Hmm."

"Wish you hadn't left my bed. Wish you were still in there with me."

As she nodded, she leaned her head against his shoulder.

"I don't know what we're doing," she said softly.

"Helping each other heal, maybe." He nipped the soft skin under her ear. "All I know is, I haven't felt this alive in a long time. And that's because of you."

"It's only because I remind you of—"

"Home." He wouldn't allow her to think for a second she was a replacement for his dead wife. He wasn't certain in his own mind that wasn't the case—her transformation last night had knocked the vinegar out of him, she'd looked so much like Janie—but he didn't want Jess believing it. What kind of a scoundrel would that make him? "But it's more than that. You remind me of the good things in my life."

"You're romanticizing about Beckon. It's really not all that."

In a way, they were both in the same situation. She'd had her heart broken. Of course she wouldn't look upon home with fond memories now. He couldn't go home because it wouldn't be the same. He blamed himself for Janie's death, and the guilt wracked him ten ways to Sunday, each and every day. "Maybe you're right, sweetheart."

Memories being what they were, he couldn't deny he held Beckon close to his heart. But he didn't need to win this round with Jessica today.

"I don't have a single regret about last night. Well, except that I had the damn boot and cast still on."

She turned away from the ocean and captured his attention with her pretty fresh-meadow eyes. "Not one, Zane? Not one regret?"

He blinked at the intensity of her question. This was important to her. "No."

What he had were doubts. He wasn't ready for anything heavy, with her or anyone else. The thought of entering into a relationship gave him hives. He might never be ready. He'd removed himself from any thoughts of the future and lived in the present. He'd shut himself off for two years. It was safe. His haven of sanity.

"Are you regretting what happened last night?" He wasn't sure he wanted to hear her answer.

Her chin lifted as she thought about it for an eternity of seconds. "*Regret* isn't the right word. I think you're right. We both needed each other."

"We don't have to attach any labels to last night," Zane said. "It just happened." He wanted it to happen again. But it wasn't his decision. He was smart enough to know that.

"But where do we go from here?"

Breezes blew her hair off her shoulders, the golden strands dancing in the morning light. Her face was clean of makeup, glowing with a fresh-washed look. All of Zane's impulses heightened.

"First," he said, dipping his head to her mouth, "I give you a good morning kiss." He pressed his lips to hers and kissed her soundly. She made a tiny noise in the back of her throat that made him smile inside. He could kiss her until the sun set and wouldn't tire of it. He inched away from her face as her eyes opened, glowing with warmth. God, she was sweet. "If you're inclined to do some cooking this morning, we have breakfast. Mrs. Lopez doesn't work on Sunday. And then we do whatever comes natural. No pressure, Jess."

He'd had sex with Janie's younger sister. He should be beating himself up about that now, but oddly he wasn't. He couldn't figure the why of it. Why was being with Jess making him feel better about himself instead of worse? He had nothing to offer her but strong arms to hold her and a warm body to comfort her, if she needed them. He couldn't pursue her. It wouldn't be fair to her, but that didn't stop him from wanting her.

A soft, relieved breath blew from her lips. "That sounds good to me, Zane." She gave him a sweet smile and handed him his crutches. "Meet me in the kitchen in half an hour."

His gaze landed on the curvy form of her backside as she strode inside the house. He hung his head. Oh, man. He was in deep.

Life at 211 Moonlight Drive wasn't going to get any easier.

Seven

Two and a half months after his accidental fall off a Los Angeles stage, Zane had gotten a good report from his doctor. His foot had healed nicely and was now out of the cast. His wrist had taken longer than expected to heal, but that, too, was in great shape and cast-free. Jessica was almost as relieved as he was, hearing the news today after driving him to his appointment. Zane had never gotten used to the crutches and now, with a little physical therapy, he'd be back to normal, good as new. And her duties wouldn't be so up close and personal with him any longer. She could concentrate on work and try to forget about making love with him two nights ago.

The new Jess would've let it go by now.

But traces of the old Jess were resurfacing, and she wanted to kick her to the curb. Falling in love with Zane would be a bonehead stupid move. He was still in love with Janie, and nothing much could persuade her otherwise. How could she be sure that the night they'd had sex wasn't more about her resemblance to her sister than any intense affection Zane had for her?

"I feel like celebrating," Zane said as she drove toward the gates of his home.

"I bet you do. But you can't go dancing just yet. You have to get through physical therapy."

From out of the corner of her eye, she spied Zane flexing his hand. "I'm fine. Just dandy. Even wearing my own boots for a change."

She took her eyes off the road for a split second to gaze at his expensive boots. Snakeskin. Gorgeous. Studded black leather. They made her mouth water. "You do know you live on the beach. Sandals are expected. Even admired."

A belly laugh rolled out of his mouth. "I could say the same about you. Lately, you've been wearing those high-falutin heels."

"Me?" Yes, it was true. The new Jess wore pricey heels when she wasn't in her morning walk tennis shoes.

"Yeah, you. Admit it. You're happier in a pair of soft leather boots with flat heels than those skyscrapers you've taken to wearing. Not that I mind. You look hot in those heels."

The compliment lit her up inside, but she couldn't let him see how it affected her. She lowered her sunglasses and gave him a deadpan look.

He grinned.

The man was in a great mood today, happier than she'd seen him in days. It was certainly better than putting up with his sourpuss, like on Sunday afternoon when he'd balked at her going to Dylan's house for the screening of *Time of Her Life*. She'd thought he'd be okay with it. After all, he'd said to do what came natural, and she had promised Dylan she'd be there. When she'd walked in past nine, missing dinner with him, he'd been sullen and distant, none too pleased with her.

Yes, they'd had sex the night before, and it had been amazing. Surely Zane had to know that Dylan McKay, handsome as he was, didn't strike her fancy. She'd gone because she'd promised and because she needed time away from Zane to clear her head, yet that entire afternoon and evening, she'd wondered if she'd made a mistake by going to Dylan's.

"You know what I feel like doing?" Zane asked, breaking into her thoughts.

"I'm afraid to ask."

"I feel like taking a dip."

"In your Jacuzzi? That's a good idea. I bet the warm water—"

"In the ocean, Jess. Tonight, after dinner."

She pulled through the gates and drove along the winding road to his house. "I don't know if that's wise, Zane. You shouldn't push it. You only just—"

"I'm going, Jess." He set his face stubbornly, and she couldn't think of anything to say to change his mind. "I've been confined long enough."

Pulling into the garage, she cut the engine. "I get that, but I won't be—"

Oh, shoot. He wasn't going to like this.

"Won't be what?"

"Home after dinner."

"Another shopping trip?"

A lie could fall from her lips very easily. But she wasn't going to lie to Zane. "No. I'm invited over to your neighbor's house."

Zane's lips thinned. "Dylan again?"

"Adam Chase."

Zane's eyes sharpened on her. "You're going over to Adam's tonight?"

"I kind of didn't give him a choice the other night. He was telling me about his new artwork, and I hinted at wanting to see it. I guess he was just being nice by inviting me over." She'd been a little stunned and humbled when he'd asked her since, according to Zane, invitations from Adam were rare.

Zane closed his eyes briefly. "That's Adam. Mr. Nice Guy."

"You don't think he is?"

Zane snorted. "I think he's a genius. But I don't know much about his personal life."

"I don't want to know about his personal life, either. This isn't anything, Zane." If only she could melt the disapproval off his face with an explanation. "It's just me, being curious. The teacher in me loves learning."

They'd been carefully dancing around what had happened between them. It seemed neither wanted to bring the subject up. So how could she admit that she'd rather be home with him? That after making love with him, it was better that they spend time apart. Too much alone time with him could prove disastrous. One disaster per decade was her limit. One disaster in her entire life would be preferable.

She cared deeply for Zane, thought he was gorgeous and more appealing than any man she'd ever met, but she couldn't be dumb again. And that meant not reading too much into having sex with him, wonderful as it was. She rationalized it was all about healing. Isn't that how Zane passed it off?

"I'm sure Adam wouldn't mind if you joined me."

He reached for the door handle. "I've seen his house, Jess. You go on. Have a nice time," he said through tight lips.

She didn't buy his comment for a second, but she clamped her mouth shut, and as he opened the car door, she rushed around the front end to meet him. Putting his good foot down, he braced his hands on the sides of the car and brought himself up and out.

"Lean on me," she said. "I'm here if you need me."

"I'll make it just fine."

She moved out of his way, and he walked slowly but on his own power, his boots scraping the garage floor as he made his way into the house.

Her shoulders fell, and black emptiness seemed to swallow her up. She wanted Zane to need her.

Or maybe, she just plain wanted Zane. Either way

wasn't an option. She couldn't very well count the days until Mariah returned. Nobody knew when that would be.

But for the first time, she hoped it would be soon.

Zane leaned his elbows over his deck banister, grateful to be on his own two feet now. His gaze focused on Jess as she made her way down the deck steps to the beach. "Bye, Zane. I won't be long."

Her sultry voice hammered inside his brain. It was unique, and he was beginning to hear the slight nuances that differed from her sister's. There was more sugary rasp and a lightness in her tone that made him think of only good things.

She held the straps of her heeled sandals up by two fingers and waved at him once her bare feet hit the sand. In her other hand, she held a flashlight to guide her way over to Adam's house. It wasn't too far, just about one hundred yards from back door to back door, but the half moon's light wasn't enough illumination on the darkened beach, so the flashlight was a good idea.

Her blond hair touched the top of a nipped-at-the-waist snowy white dress that flared out to just above her knees. She looked ethereal in a delicate way that would turn any man's head.

"Bye" he heard himself growl, and lifted his hand up, a semiwave back, watching her trudge through the sand and out of his line of vision.

She was determined to go, yet he'd noted a flicker in her eyes earlier, a moment of doubt as if she waited for him to tell her to stay. He wanted her, and his newly healed body was in a state of arousal around her most of the time now, but he held back. He let her go off to another man's house tonight instead of giving in to his lust.

Was he an idiot or being smart, for her sake?

His cell phone rang, and he plucked it from his pocket. It was probably Mariah. She'd been a saint, checking in and worrying about him when she was the one who needed the support. He'd had Jess send her flowers this morning to cheer her up.

He answered the ring. "Hello?"

"Hello, Zane. This is Mae."

His brows rose. It wasn't Mariah after all, but Jessica's mother. "Hi, Mae. This is a nice surprise."

"I hope so. Zane, how are you feeling these days?"

"Better. I'm out of my cast and healing up real good. And how are you, Mae?"

"I could be better. You know I'm an eternal worrier. And I'm worried about my Jess. I haven't heard from her in three days."

"Is that unusual?"

"Yes, very. She usually checks in with me every day or every other day. We've been playing phone tag over the weekend, and I can't seem to reach her. She didn't answer my call today. I wondered if something was wrong with her phone. Thought it'd be best to check in with you."

"Well…I can assure you, she's doing fine."

"Really?"

"Yes, ma'am."

"That's a relief. I thought after I gave her the news, she'd be crushed. My dear girl has been through a lot this past month. She can't be happy about Steven."

Steven? Just hearing the guy's name made his hand ball into a fist. "What news is that, Mae?"

"I couldn't hide it from my sweet girl. She didn't need to hear it from anyone else but her mama."

"Yes, I think you were right." Zane hadn't a clue what she was getting at, but he knew Mae. She'd eventually get around to telling him what was going on.

"Can you imagine her bridesmaid, Judy, running off with Steven to get married? Why, she'd been like a member of our family when the girls were younger. And Steven? I thought I knew that boy. I'd like to wallop both of them for the hurt they put my daughter through."

His face tightened and he squeezed his eyes shut, wishing like hell he could give that jerk a piece of his mind. And to add to the insult, he'd run away with one of Jess's good friends. A woman who'd vowed to stand up for her at her wedding.

Something clicked in his head. "Wait a minute, Mae. When did you tell Jess about this?"

"Oh, let me see. It must have been on Thursday. Yes, that's right. I remember, because I was getting my hair done at the salon and, well, it was the talk of the entire beauty shop. I felt so bad when I heard, I walked out after my cut with a wet head, didn't bother having my hair styled. All I kept thinking about was my Jess and how she would take the news. But you know, when I told her, I was surprised at her reaction. She seemed calm. I think she was in shock. Have you noticed anything different about her, lately?"

Had he? Hell, yeah. Now he understood her transformation. She'd dyed her hair blond, gotten rid of her eyeglasses, starting wearing provocative clothes. Was it rebellion? Or worse yet, had Jess decided to throw caution to the wind and… No, he wouldn't let his mind go there. She wasn't promiscuous. She was a woman who'd been betrayed by people she trusted. He could only imagine what hearing that news did to her.

And what had he done? She'd come into the room the night of party and he'd shot her down, doing the unthinkable by telling her she looked like Janie in a voice that held nothing but disapproval. He'd been selfish, thinking only about how much it hurt to look at her that way. If he was damn honest with himself, seeing that daring side of Jess had excited him. He hadn't known how to handle his initial reaction to her. She almost didn't go to the party because he'd given her a hard time about the way she looked, gorgeous as she was.

And he'd been jealous because he couldn't have her, and yet he didn't want any other man going after her, either. Wow. What a revelation.

"Zane, I asked if Jessica has been acting differently lately?"

Uh, yeah. But in this case, he saw no reason not to bend the truth a little. "She's been keeping busy, Mae. She tells me she likes the work. And she's made a few friends here, too. She seems to fit in real nice. In fact, she's visiting my neighbor now. When she comes in, I'll be sure to tell her you called."

"I'm happy about that, Zane. I knew coming to stay with you would be good for her."

Zane scrunched his face up. He'd taken Mae's daughter to bed, and if he had his way, he would do so again. His mind muddied up, and he didn't understand any of it other than that Jess was under his roof and getting under his skin. He felt for her and the hurt she'd gone through. Nothing about liking her seemed wrong, even though he could count the bullet points in his mind why he shouldn't.

"I can't thank you enough. You know how much I love my girls."

Her comment dug deep into his heart. Mae would never stop loving Janie. She always spoke of her as if she were still with them. Zane loved that about her. "Yep, I know, Mae."

"So tell me what you've been doing. That's if you have the time."

"I have the time. Let's see, the restaurant is coming along as scheduled and…"

Thirty minutes later, after he'd hung up with Mae, he sat down with his guitar and strummed lightly to reacquaint himself to the feel of the instrument in his hands and the resiliency of the strings. He had words in his head struggling to get out, lyrics that were just beginning to flow, and he jotted them down as he struck chord after chord. The pick in his hand felt awkward at first, but he pressed on.

Thoughts of Jess distracted him. He couldn't stop thinking about her and what Mae had revealed. He wanted to protect her. Yet he desired her. Her heartache scored his heart. He felt sorry for her, but not enough to keep his distance. He was *conflicted*, as Dylan would say. He needed some release.

Only a dunk in the ocean would help clear his mind and cool his body.

And minutes later, dressed in his swim trunks, he made his way to the shoreline and dived straight in, propelling his arms and legs past the shallow waters, pushing his body to the limit.

After enjoying a pleasant visit with Adam and declining his offer to walk her home, she trudged across the beach alone. Cool sand squished between her toes as she made her way to the shoreline, where the moist grains under her feet became smoother, making it much easier to move. She knew this beach; she'd walked it in the mornings many times.

As she entered Zane's home, silence surrounded her. It was too quiet for this time of the evening. Zane never turned in before ten. "Zane? Are you here?"

Nothing.

"Zane?" She stepped into the office, then the kitchen, and peeked into his bedroom.

There was no sign of him.

She sighed wearily and shook her head. He must have gone for a swim in the ocean. Half a dozen worries entered her head about his night swim. Geesh, he'd just gotten his cast off. What was the doggone rush?

Hurrying to her room, she flung off her clothes and put on her bathing suit. In her haste to rid herself of the old Jess, she'd tossed out her one-piece swimsuits she'd brought from Texas, which left her with the daring bikini she'd bought the other day. She slipped into it and then wiggled a T-shirt over her head. Without wasting a second, she strode down the stairs, grabbed her flashlight and ventured out the sliding door.

If she were lucky, she'd find Zane walking toward the house, whistling a happy tune.

Who was she kidding? Luck wasn't with her lately. Zane's towel was on the beach, which meant he was out there somewhere. The crashing waves that usually lulled her to sleep made her wary now. Her flashlight pointed out to sea illuminated only a narrow strip of water at a time. She squinted, trying to make out shapes, searching corridors of ocean, back and forth. "Zane! Zane!"

She couldn't find him. Nibbling her lip, she paced the beach, aiming her flashlight onto the water over and over. She'd never swum in the ocean before coming to California, but she'd quickly learned how the currents could take you away, making you drift in one direction or another. She'd start out in front of Zane's house and wind up hundreds of feet away when it was time to come in. Those currents had to be stronger at night, more powerful and…

She spotted something. A head bobbing in the water? She pointed the flashlight and struggled to focus. Yep, someone was out there. But then the form dropped down as if being swallowed up by the sea. She ran into the surf, targeting that bit of water with the flashlight. "Zane!" she shouted, but her voice was muted by the crash of the waves.

He couldn't hear her. He was out past the shallows. She waited several long seconds for him to reappear. She prayed that he would. She couldn't see much, only what the moonlight and stars and her flashlight allowed, but she'd always had a good sense of direction. She knew the exact spot where she'd seen him go down.

"Oh, God. Zane!"

With no time to waste, she dived in, her arms pumping, her feet kicking, fighting against the tide. She swam as fast as she ever had in her life, her eyes trying to focus on the spot she'd seen him. She was almost there, a little farther, just another few strokes.

A thunderous sound boomed in her ears. She looked up. Oh, no. A monstrous wave was coming toward her like a coiling snake. It was too late to get out of its path. The pounding surf reached her in midstroke. The force slammed her back. She flew in the air and belly-flopped facedown against a sheet of ocean as hard as a slab of granite.

Waves buried her, and she sputtered for breath.

Seconds later, she felt herself being lifted, her head popping above the water. She gasped.

"Jess."

Zane. He'd come for her. How did he get here? As she struggled to catch her breath, he half dragged, half swam her to the shallows by floating on his back and keeping her head above water. Once he got his footing, he stopped and stood upright in the water, then scooped her into his arms, carrying her to the beach.

He laid her down carefully away from high tide. The sand granules scratched at her back, but she was never happier to be on dry land. And Zane was safe. That mattered just as much.

He fell to his knees beside her. Huffing breaths, he shook his head. "You gave me a scare."

He bent to her, pushing aside the locks of hair hiding her face, and his magnificent eyes were soft and concerned. "Are you okay?"

She nodded. "I'm okay. Got the wind knocked out of me."

"You almost drowned, sweetheart. What on earth were you doing?"

She filled her lungs with oxygen, this time without gulping water along with it. "Saving you," she said quietly. "I thought I saw you out there, going under."

Zane's eyes were warm on her face, the heat enough to keep the cool drops on her body from freezing. His hands were working wonders, too, caressing her cheeks and stroking her chin, heating her up in ways no other man ever had. He rasped softly, "You mean you thought I was drowning, and you risked your life to save me?"

She nodded.

"That wasn't me, sweetheart."

"It wasn't? I saw someone go under. I thought for sure you were out there."

"I was. I lasted only ten minutes before I came in. What you saw was probably a school of sea lions. They frequent the shallower waters here at night. I've seen one of them pop a head up and then go under and, yeah…I guess in the dark, it might look like a swimmer out there."

"Then how…how did you find me?"

"After my swim, I took a long walk. Thankfully, I returned just in time to hear you calling my name. Took me only a second to figure out where you were."

He began to rub her arms and legs. She was cold, but that didn't stop her from reacting to his touch. As warmth spread through her body, her gentle cooing seemed to draw Zane's attention to her lips. "That feels good," she said.

"Tell me about it." The corner of his mouth crooked up.

His palms heated her through and through, her skin highly sensitized to his touch. She was overwhelmed with relief that he hadn't drowned and grateful that he'd saved her, but there was more…so much more that she was feeling right now. "Thank you, Zane."

She touched his shoulder and felt his cool skin under her fingertips. His eyes gleamed with a fiery invitation to do more. Bravely, she wound her arms around his neck. It didn't take an ounce of effort to pull him close. His mouth hovered near hers.

It was crazy. They were on the beach under the moonlight and dripping wet after the rescue, and nothing seemed amiss in her world. She wouldn't trade places with another living soul right now.

"I'd give you what-for," he said, "but that will have to wait."

"It will?"

"Yep. Cause I think you're about to kiss me."

"Smart man."

She ran her fingers through his thick wet hair and lowered his head down to her lips. Oh…he tasted warm and inviting and salty. His kiss made her tremble in a good way, and she opened her mouth for him.

He plunged inside and swept her up in one burning kiss after another. What was left of her body when he finished kissing her was a pulsing bundle of need. "Zane," she whispered over his lips.

"I need to get you inside the house…"

He didn't have to finish. She knew. They'd get arrested if they acted on their impulses right here on the beach.

"Can you walk?" he asked.

"Yes, with your help."

"Okay, sweetheart. Seems one of us is always leaning on the other."

She smiled. How true.

He bounded up and then entwined their hands. Gently he helped her to her feet. The world didn't go dizzy on her—well, except for the hot looks Zane was giving her. "I actually feel pretty good."

"Glad to hear it." He kissed her earlobe. "Ready?"

"Ready."

Side by side, bracing each other, they walked through the sand and up the steps that led into the house.

As soon as they entered the house, Zane did an about-face and walked her backward until she was pressed against the living room wall. He trapped her there, his body pulsing near hers, his gaze generating enough heat to burn the building down.

"Are you about to give me what-for?"

A low rumble of laughter rose from his throat. Her senses heightened. He was one sexy man. "You know it, Jess." He glanced down at her dripping wet T-shirt plastered to her body and sighed as if he was in pain. "Do you know how incredibly perfect you are?"

His hands wrapped around her waist, and thrilling warmth penetrated through her shirt to heat her skin. "I'm not."

His mouth grazed her throat. "You are. You can't let what those two did to you change who you are. That guy was about the stupidest man on earth."

She stilled. "What do you mean, 'those two'?"

Zane's lips were doing amazing things to her throat. And his body pressing against hers made it hard to think. Her breasts were ready for his touch. Her nipples pebbled hard and beckoned him through the flimsy T-shirt and bikini.

She had to ignore her body. She needed to know what he meant. "Zane?"

He stopped kissing her and inched away enough to gaze into her eyes. "Oh, uh. Your mama called while you were out. She was worried about you, and well…she told me about Steven running off with a friend of yours."

She'd told him about Judy?

All the wind left her lungs, and a different kind of burn seared through her stomach. She wished Mama hadn't revealed to Zane her latest humiliation. She felt so exposed, so vulnerable. Did she have an ounce of pride left?

"You have every right to feel hurt, Jess. But don't let what he did change the person that you are."

"You think that's what I'm doing?"

"Isn't it? You changed your hair, wear your contacts all the time. You dress differently now. Don't get me wrong. You look beautiful, sweetheart. But you were beautiful before."

She shrugged. She found it hard to believe. It was a platitude, a cliché, a way to make her feel better about herself.

"I need the change." Tears misted in her eyes. She really did. She needed to look at herself in the mirror and see a strong, independent woman who had style and confidence. She needed to see that transformation, more than anything else.

"I get that." Zane took her into his arms and hugged her, as a friend now. She felt safe again, protected. And just being with him made her problems seem trivial. "But promise me one thing?"

"What?"

"Don't try to find what you need with another man. Makes me crazy."

Makes me crazy. Oh, wow. There was no mistaking what he meant. Not from the genuine pain she found in his eyes, or the intensity in his voice. "You mean like Dylan or Adam? I told you, they're not—"

He shushed her with a kiss, right smack on the lips. Her body instantly reacted, and goose bumps rose on her arms.

"*You* make me crazy, too," he rasped and began rolling the hem of her T-shirt up. With his coaxing, she raised her arms as he brought the wet garment over her head and her breasts jiggled back into place. Zane's hot gaze touched her there and lingered, then traveled over the rest her body clad in a skimpy New Jess bikini. He made a loud noise from sucking oxygen into his lungs. "From now on, sweet Jess, I want to be the man you go to when you need something."

"You mean, like my rebound guy?"

"Call it whatever you want, honey."

Jess didn't have to think twice. Zane just abolished all deprecating thoughts she'd had about herself and totally wiped out any pain she'd felt about Steven. Even her pride was restored somewhat. The Steven ship had sailed, and she wasn't going to waste another second thinking of him. Not when she had Zane offering her the moon.

He was a real man.

If she had any doubts before about her feelings for him,

they were banished the second she'd thought he was drowning. She'd rushed in to save him, praying that God wouldn't take him from her. And she wasn't going to feel bad about it or apologize to anyone. Forbidden or not, she wanted him.

"I promise."

He hooked his fingers with hers. "Your room or mine?"

"Neither," she said. Her confidence soaring and her heart melting, she let go of every inhibition she'd ever had. "I think we need a hot, steamy shower to warm up, don't you?"

"As long as I get to peel this bikini off you, you've got yourself a deal."

Eight

The peeling was blissful torture. Jessica lay her head against cool slate, her arms behind her. Steam rose up as the customized shower streams poured down, warming her bones. It was like being tucked inside a large waterfall, cascading water all around her. Zane came to her naked, his sculpted, bronzed beach body equal to that of an ancient god. There was enough room for twelve people in the master shower, but she knew Zane would make good use of the space for the two of them.

"You're beautiful, Jess."

His mouth covered hers as both of his hands came under her bikini top. Weighing her full breasts, he groaned deep in his throat, and his appreciation of her body flowed to her ears. She roped her arms around his neck and continued to kiss him even as he unhooked the back of the bathing suit, releasing her breasts. Warm spray moistened them and he worked magic on her, gliding his hands over her bare, wet skin and arousing her in tortuous increments. His thumb caressed her already pebbled nipples until she muted a cry.

He was amazingly gentle, but brutal in his determination to make it good for her. As he removed the bottom half of her bikini, his hands shaking with need, she'd never felt more desirable and powerful.

Drizzling kisses along her throat, his hands came to the small of her back, and she bowed her body for him. He took one jutted breast in his mouth and suckled her, his tongue swirling and flicking. She screamed then, but the pleasured sounds were drowned out by the thunderous showerheads. He gave the other breast equal treatment, and it was almost too much.

"Are you warm yet?" he asked, nuzzling her throat.

"Just getting there."

"Let me help you with that."

He picked up a bar of soap and lathered her from head to toe, bathing her in a soft and subtle flowery scent that reminded her of a spring afternoon. He didn't miss one inch of her, paying special attention to the crux of her womanhood, stroking, washing, cupping her, making her moan. "Oh, oh, oh."

Jess thought every woman should experience a shower this way, just once.

She smiled, gritted her teeth and savored the pleasure he brought her.

His hands moved to her backside and slid over the rounded halves of her derriere, molding her form, spreading his fingers wide as if savoring the feel of her. His manhood pressed her belly, rock-hard and pulsing. She shuddered, unable to hold back another second. Her body released gently, in beautifully timid waves that nudged her forever toward him. His mouth covered hers, and she enjoyed the sweetly erotic taste of his passion.

Wow.

She'd never had an orgasm like that before.

She clung to him and let the full force of her feelings consume her.

"Did you like that, sweetheart?"

"So much."

She sensed his smile, and it made her heart nearly burst.

She moved down on him, letting her mouth and breasts caress the middle of his chest, his belly, and then she touched his full-fledged erection.

"Oh, man," he uttered. "Jess."

He fisted a handful of her hair and helped move her along the length of him. Water pounded her back, the showerhead pulsing now. It was deliciously sexy, and when she was through, she rose to meet him. The hungry look on his face, teeth gritted, eyes gleaming like a wolf about to devour his prey, would have been almost frightening if it wasn't Zane.

He lifted her, and on instinct she wrapped her legs around his waist. He held her tight and murmured, "Hang on."

She clung to him, and his manhood nudged into her, filling her with gentle force. He was patient and oh, so ready. She moved on him, letting him know she was okay with whatever he wanted to do. The beat, beat, beat of the raining drops set the pace of his thrusts. He arched and drove deeper.

"Oh." She sighed. "So good."

He kissed her throat, her breasts, and continued to thrust into her, hard, harder.

It was pure heaven. She'd never made love like this before. Her heart pounded in her chest, and her body soared. Spasms of tight, sweet pain released, and she cried out softly "Oh, Zane."

His eyes were on her, burning hot. He waited for her to come down off the clouds, and then he began to thrust into her again. He set a fast rhythm, and she gave back equally. She wanted to make it good for him, too.

Guttural groans rose up his throat, and she knew he was close. He impaled her one last, amazing time, his reach touching the very core of her womanhood. And waves of his orgasm struck her, one after the other, until he was spent, sated.

He took her with him as he sat down on the stone shower bench, raining kisses all over her face, cheeks, chin, throat. He pushed her hair away from her face. "Are you okay, sweetheart?"

How could she not be? She was overjoyed. "It was beautiful, Zane."

"It was," he said, leaning way back.

She stroked his face, running her hand over his stubbly cheek. He grabbed her wrist and planted a kiss on her palm.

The shower turned off. Perfect timing. It was a perfect night. Well, except for those few minutes she thought Zane was drowning. He'd taxed his body tonight. "You must be tired," she said.

His eyes darkened, and he hiked a brow. "I'm ready to be in bed with you."

"Sounds good."

She didn't want the night to end. She no longer worried about what tomorrow would bring. She was living in the moment, and these moments had been pretty darn spectacular.

Zane lifted her off him and grabbed two giant towels. He took his time drying her off, sneaking kisses on parts of her body, arousing her. She did the same to him, teasing him with her mouth.

They entered his bedroom clean, dry and exhausted.

She took a few steps toward his door, and his arm snaked around her. "Where do you think you're going?"

"To my room. I need to get my nightie."

"No, you don't. Come to bed. I promise to keep you warm."

"Part of your duties as my rebound guy?"

"You know it, honey. Now get in."

Spooning with Zane in his big, comfortable bed, Jessica's eyes eased open. It was slightly after dawn, and the usual early morning cloud cover allowed a smidgen of struggling sunshine into the room. Zane stroked her hip, lightly, possessively, his touch becoming familiar to her, and she purred like a kitten given a big bowl of cream.

"I'm giving you the day off," he murmured, his breath whispering over her hair.

"Mmm." A lovely thought. "I have work to do today."

"It'll keep, Jess. I want to spend the day with you."

"You already do."

He nipped her earlobe, then planted tiny kisses along her nape. His hand traveled deliciously to her waist, just under her belly. "Not the way I want to."

They'd made love twice last night. It was incredible and frightening at the same time. Every so often, thoughts of her future would break through her steely resolve to live in the moment. She'd shudder, and sudden panic would set in. What was she doing? Where was all this leading? They hadn't used protection in the shower last night, but Jess was on birth control, sort of. She'd skipped a few days during the height of her wedding fiasco, but she'd resumed when she'd arrived here to keep her hormones from getting out of whack.

She turned to Zane, roping her arms around his neck. "What did you have in mind?"

He kissed her quickly and then tugged her closer. "A day of play. We can get out of here. Have fun."

A lock of his thick hair fell to his forehead. In many ways, he looked like a little boy, eager to play hooky. He lived in this dream house on the beach and spoke of getting away, as if he'd been in living in the slums all this time. The irony made her smile, and she toyed with that wayward lock of hair, curling it around her finger, mesmerized by the man she shared a bed with.

"You're the boss," she whispered.

"I'm not your boss," he said softly. "Not when it comes to this."

He began kissing her shoulder, her throat, her chin. And then he stopped suddenly and inched away. He shot her a solid, earnest look. "Would you like to spend the day with me?"

Oh, wow. Like a date? "Yes." She yanked the lock of hair. "Of course, silly."

He gave her backside a gentle squeeze. "Then we'd better get up and get showered. You first. If we share another shower, we'll never make it out of here this morning." He waggled his brows. "On second thought, maybe…"

She laughed and jumped out of bed. "I'm going in first."

Less than an hour later, Zane was sitting behind the wheel of his SUV and pulling out of the gates of his home. "Feels good to be driving again. I hated feeling helpless, having to rely on someone to take me places."

A few days of stubble on his face had led to a short, sexy beard. The new look turned her on. Everything about him seemed to do that. All she had to do was think about making love with him last night and tingles fluttered inside her belly.

He wore a baseball cap instead of his Stetson. The beard and sunglasses also helped disguise him. He'd healed so well, she would've never guessed he'd broken his foot, except for his slight limp as he tried not to put too much pressure on it. She already knew she'd be arguing with him about going to his rehab appointments.

He'd told her to wear her boots, dress in jeans and not question where they were going. He wanted to surprise her. She sat in her comfortable clothes, watching the stunning landscape go by as they left the blue waters behind and drove up a mountain road. The scenery lent itself to light conversation and soft music. Zane sang along with the tune on the radio, his voice deep and rich, her own personal concert. She couldn't help but grin.

Thirty minutes later, they were atop the mountain at a sprawling ranch-style home overlooking the city to the south and the valley to the north. The air was clean up here, the smog of the day blown away by ocean breezes. "Where are we?" she asked.

"My friend Chuck Bowen owns this place with his mother. It's called Ruby Ranch."

She glanced around and spotted white-fenced corrals, vineyards off in the distance and acres and acres of hilly, tree-dotted land. The sound of horses whinnying and snorting reached her ears.

"C'mon."

Zane exited the car and walked around to help her out. He took her hand. That little boy excitement once again lit his expression. "We're going riding."

"Riding?" She hadn't been on a horse since she was a teenager. She'd go riding every weekend with her good friend Jolie Burns when she wasn't working at Holcomb House. Jolie lived on a cattle ranch ten miles outside of Beckon. Jessica had the use of a pretty palomino named Sparkle, and she'd learned how to wash down and groom a horse back then, too. It was expected. If you exercised a horse, got him lathered up, then it was your responsibility to see to his needs after the ride. Jessica had fallen in love with Sparkle. She never minded the hard work that came with him.

She rubbed her hands together. This could be fun. "Oh, boy!"

Zane chuckled and kissed the tip of nose. "That's what I thought."

A fiftysomething woman with hair the color of deep, rich red wine walked out of the house. She was flawless in her appearance, neat and tidy, and her pretty face must have stopped men in their tracks when she was younger. Even now, she was stunning and dressed in Western clothes that looked as if they'd just come off a fashion runway.

"Hi, Ruby," Zane said.

"Zane. It's good to see you again."

Zane took Jessica's hand as he moved toward the house. Ruby tried not to react, but her eyes dipped to their interlocked hands for a second before she gave them both a smile. "Ruby, I'd like you to meet Jessica Holcomb. Jess, this is Ruby Bowen. She and Chuck own this amazing land."

They came to a stop on her veranda. "Hello," Jessica said. "The place is lovely. You have vineyards?"

"Thank you. Yes, we grow grapes and raise horses. It's a rare mix, but it works for Chuck and me. We don't bottle the wine here—we're too small for that—but we do have our own label. It's fun, hectic and keeps us plenty busy."

"I bet," Jessica said.

"I met Ruby and Chuck at a charity auction six months ago," Zane said. "Being original Texans, they've been gracious enough to offer their stables for whenever I wanted to ride."

"Absolutely. We've got over a thousand acres and plenty of horses that need exercising. We figured Zane was like a fish out of water, living at the beach these days. We're happy he took us up on the offer. Chuck's out of town and due back later. He'll be sorry he missed you. But please, make use of the grounds. The stables are just down the hill a ways. Our wrangler, Stewie, is waiting for you. He'll find a good fit for both of you."

"Thanks, Ruby. Would've been by sooner, but it's hard to ride with a broken foot and wrist. Just recently got the dang cast off."

"Well, you're here now, and that's all that matters. Have a good time. Be sure to stop by afterward. Chuck may be home by then."

"Will do, and thanks again," Zane said.

Just minutes later, Jessica rode atop a sweet bay mare named Adobe, and Zane sat a few hands taller on a black gelding named Triumph. In her hometown of Beckon, the terrain was flat as the tires in Jeb's Junkyard. But here at Ruby Ranch, set in the Santa Monica Mountains, the powder-blue sky seemed nearly touchable. They ambled along a path that led away from the house into land that rose high and dipped gently alongside a creek.

"No rain lately," Zane offered. "I bet this creek was a rushing stream at one time."

"It's still pretty awesome up here."

"It is. You miss riding?"

She nodded, holding on to the silver-gray felt hat Ruby's wrangler had offered her. Zane kept his ball cap on his head, but there was no doubt he was a cowboy, through and through. He may have great wealth and live in a contemporary beach house, but you couldn't take Texas out of a Texan. And that was fact. "I do. I love horses."

Zane gave a nod of agreement. "Yeah, me, too."

It was a sore subject and one Jess didn't want to press at the moment. Zane had abandoned his home after the fire that took Janie and their unborn baby's life. The place still stood as it was. Acres and acres of land gated off, going to waste. He hadn't had the heart to demolish what was left of his house or improve upon the land. He'd had an agent sell off the livestock, and that was that.

Heartbroken, Zane had picked up roots, leaving memories he couldn't deal with behind. Losing him had taken a big chunk out the hearts of the fine people of Beckon. Zane was their golden boy, a singer whose talent brought him great fame. The townsfolk were darn proud of their hometown hero. He'd had no more loyal fans in the world.

"I'm glad you brought me up here, Zane."

He eyed her, studying her face as if trying to puzzle something out. "I'd have never come without you. Fact is, Chuck's been after me to ride for months, and I never took him up on it." His voice seemed sort of strange, and then he took a giant swallow. "I didn't want to, until now."

She shouldn't read too much into it, but her heart jumped in her chest anyway. Hope could be just as drastic as despair to her right now. She shoved it away and took a different approach. "You were confined a long time. I bet getting up on a horse and riding is just what you needed. It's freeing."

"Maybe," he said. His index finger pushed at the corner of his mouth, contemplating. He gave his head a shake. "Maybe it's something else. Having to do with you."

Oh, God. Out in the open air, in these beautiful surroundings, anything seemed possible. *Don't hope. Don't hope.* "Me?"

He slowed his horse to a stop.

She did the same.

His dark eyes grazed her face. "Yeah, you," he said, his voice husky.

Her cheeks burned, and she hoped her new suntan along with the brim of her hat hid her emotions. Zane didn't need another groupie. They'd already established he was her rebound guy, whatever that really meant. She was his bed partner, for sure. But after that…she had no clue where she stood with him.

Maybe her crazy heart didn't want to know. Maybe she couldn't survive another disappointment. It was better not knowing, not thinking at all.

She clicked the heels of her boots and took off. "Race you to that plateau up ahead. First one to the oak tree wins!" She was already three lengths ahead of him when she heard his laughter.

"You're on!"

Westerly winds blew cool air at her face, her hair a riotous mess, as she leaned low on her mare and pressed the animal faster. The path was wide enough here for two horses, but branches hung low, and she expertly navigated through a thick patch of trees to reach the innermost edge of the clearing. Another fifty yards to go.

From behind, resounding hooves beat the ground, and she sensed Zane catching up.

"C'mon girl!" The mare was shorter, her legs not quite as long as Triumph's, and of course, Jessica was rusty as a rider.

It was a valiant effort, even if she'd cheated at the starting line, but Zane caught her. His gelding made the pass just five yards out, and yet Adobe wrestled to move faster. Her mare didn't like to lose, it seemed. They reached the oak tree, Triumph just nosing Adobe out.

Jess reined her mare in and circled around to the base of the oak tree. Zane sat atop his horse, grinning wide. His joy seared her heart. He was so dang happy. How could she not join in?

He dismounted and sauntered over to her, his confident strides stealing her breath. His recovery looked damn good on him, the smile on his face, the gleam in his eyes, the breadth of his shoulders…

"I win, Jess."

"Just barely." She gave a good fight.

"Still, a win is a win."

He reached up and helped her off, his large hands handling her with ease as she slid down the length of him. Tucked close, she didn't mind being in his trap. The exhilaration of the race and the handsomest darn face she'd ever seen brought on palpitations. Her heart pounded like crazy.

"So what do I win?" he asked.

"Is this a trick question?"

"Not even close."

"What do you want?"

A soap-opera villain couldn't have produced a more wicked grin. "A kiss, for starters."

"For starters?" Her gaze darted to his beautiful mouth, and a delicious craving began to develop. She didn't think she could play coy. She wanted him to kiss her, more than anything.

He nodded and bent his head. The second his yummy lips met hers, her mind rewound to last night and how his mouth had trailed pleasure all over her body. He'd tasted every inch of her. "Oh," she squeaked.

She sensed his smile from her noisy outburst as he continued to kiss her. Then he plucked the hat from her head and angled his mouth over hers again and again.

Backing up an inch, she gulped air to catch her breath and gazed into his mischievous eyes.

"You cheated in the race, sweetheart. You're gonna have to pay for that."

A dozen illicit notions popped into her head regarding how he'd make her pay, and a hot thrill spread like wildfire in her belly.

He tugged on her hand, and she followed as he led her behind the solid base of the sprawling oak tree. Hidden by drooping branches and fully shaded by overlapping leaves, he sat down, his back to the tree, and spread his legs. "Sit." He gestured to the place between his legs. "Relax."

Hardly a position that would have her relaxing, but she sat down, facing out, and rested her head on his chest. His arms wrapped around her, and he whispered in her ear, "Comfortable?"

She snuggled in deeper, her butt grazing his groin. A groan rose from his throat, and she chuckled. "Very."

His hands splayed across her ribcage. "Close your eyes."

She did.

"Now for your punishment."

He began to kiss the back of her neck, but it was what his hands were doing that made her dizzy. Deftly the tips of his fingers glided just under her breasts. Through the rough plaid material of her shirt, her nipples puckered in anticipation of his next move.

The snaps of her blouse popped open, his doing, and a startled gasp exploded from her lungs. "Zane!"

He brought his head around and kissed the corner of her mouth. "Shh. I'm pretty sure we're alone out here, but just in case, keep your shrieks to a minimum."

"You mean there's going to be more?"

He laughed quietly. Dipping into her bra, he flicked the pads of his thumbs over her responsive nipples. Her mouth opened, and he immediately stymied her next shriek with another kiss. "You are a loud one."

"You didn't mind last night," she breathed. He was doing amazing things to her with his hands.

"I don't mind now, but we're not on my turf anymore."

Damn it. She was his turf. It was becoming clearer and clearer to her. "So, maybe we should stop before someone sees us?"

"No one's out here, Jess. But I'll stop if you want me to. And that would be *my punishment*. I didn't think I could go all day without touching you again."

With a confession like that, how in the world could she tell him to stop? "You won, fair and square, Zane. I'm a big girl. I can take whatever you dish out."

Nine

"I like playing hooky with you," Zane said to Jessica over dinner at an exclusive, out-of-the-way nightspot overlooking the beach. He'd heard about this place from his neighbors, who commended the food, the privacy and the music. He sat beside her in a booth, listening to smooth jazz from a sax player with a powerful set of lungs.

Every time his gaze landed on Jessica tonight, he was reminded of the way she fell apart in his arms under that oak tree this morning. He hadn't planned on taking it as far as he did, but there was something about Jess that made him do wild things.

Maybe it was the sweet, squeaky sounds she sighed when he kissed her.

Or maybe it was the forbidden lust that came over him when she entered a room.

Or maybe it was her vulnerability and her honesty that drew him to her the most.

Those sexy shaves she'd given him didn't hurt, either.

"I like playing hooky with you, too." Her deep, sultry tone fit the atmosphere in the nightclub, reminding him every second he needed to finish what he'd started up on that plateau today.

She wore red tonight, a daring dress with a scoop neckline, the hem hiking up inches above her knees. The dress fit each sumptuous curve of her form to perfection. There were times when he forgot who she was, that he'd been married to Jessica's sister and that she wasn't ready for another relationship. He was her go-to guy, and he'd wanted it that way, but where it led from here, he didn't know. He didn't think past the present these days. He couldn't hope, didn't want to hope for more. He'd been sliced up pretty badly when Janie and his child died. The guilt ate at him every day.

He raised his wineglass and sipped, turning his gaze to the scant number of people dancing. He hadn't disguised himself tonight. He'd relied on the dimly lit surroundings and the back booth to keep his privacy. Sometimes his fame came at too high a price, and tonight he wanted to show Jess a good time. He wanted to hold her again. He roped his arm around her shoulder and spoke into her ear. "Dance with me?"

Her gaze moved to the dance floor and the amber hues focusing on couples sharing the spotlight. Yearning entered her eyes, and he'd be damned not to deliver her this little bit of pleasure.

"Are you sure?"

"Positive."

He rose and grabbed her hand, leading her to the center of the room. As soon as he stepped foot on the wood floor, he turned and tugged her to his chest. She fit him, her curves finding his angles, and they moved as if they were born to dance together.

"How's your foot?" she asked.

"It's floating on air right now. Fact is, both feet aren't touching the ground."

She chuckled. "Sweet, but I'm serious. You rode today, and now you're dancing."

"Thank you for your concern." He kissed her temple. "But I'm fine. Feels darn good doing some normal things again. And with the most beautiful woman in the room."

"How do you know? Have you checked all the other women out?"

"I, uh…not going to answer that one."

"Smart man."

He laughed, wrapping his arms tighter around her slim waist. Her breasts touched his chest, and he imagined her nipples pebbling for him, hardening through the delicate lace of her dress. Her hand wove through his hair, her fingertips playing with the strands as her arm lay on his shoulder, and it was the most intimate thing she'd done to him this entire day. His groin tightened instantly, and he backed away from her, fearing they'd get thrown out for an X-rated dance. Her gaze lifted, and pools of soft pasture green questioned him.

He shrugged, helpless.

She smiled then, and nodded.

He and Jess were on the same wavelength lately. They *got* each other, and everything felt right when he held her in his arms. He wasn't ready to let that feeling go. Luckily, he didn't have to think about that now.

Two dances later, they noticed their meals were being delivered to their table.

"Ready for dinner?"

Jessica nodded. "I think I've worked up an appetite."

"For food?"

"Among other things."

Jessica scooted into the booth, and he took his seat beside her as the waiter set down plates of pasta and petite loaves of garlic bread. Jess had chosen penne with sweet pesto sauce, and he'd ordered linguine with meat sauce. Steam rose up, the air around them flavored with spicy goodness.

"Looks heavenly," Jess said, picking up her fork.

"Yep," he said, staring at her. "Sure does."

He didn't think Jess would blush over such an easy compliment, but color rose to her cheeks, and she blinked and wiggled in her seat. He liked flustering her.

"Hey, you two." A familiar voice sounded from the shadows, and Dylan McKay's smug face came into view. "I hope you don't mind me coming over to say hello. Saw the two of you dancing a minute ago. Didn't have the balls to cut in, Zane. Excuse my language, Jessica, but the two of you looked hot and heavy out there. And Zane, it's good to see you without those crutches."

"Hi, Dylan," she said with enough damn cheerfulness for both of them.

"Hey, you," he said, giving Jess a wink.

Zane kept a smile plastered on his face. He liked Dylan, but damn his keen perception and his untimely interruption. "Dylan."

"So, how do you like this place?" the actor asked.

"Very much," Jess said.

"We were just about to dive into our meal." Zane picked up his fork.

"Yeah, the food's pretty good here. And you can't beat…"

Lights flashed, and cameras snapped, one, two, three clicks a second. Zane caught sight of a trio of paparazzi, kneeling down, angling cameras and snapping pictures of Dylan. Damn it.

Dylan turned, giving them a charming smile as Zane wrangled Jess into his arms, turning away from the cameras. Shielding Jess, his first instinct was to protect her from the intrusive photographers. He hated paparazzi ambushes. But Dylan didn't seem fazed. He posed for a few shots, and then the manager rushed over, shooing the photographers away from his customers.

"So sorry, Mr. McKay. This usually doesn't happen."

"I know, Jeffrey. It's okay. It must be a slow news day. I'm here with some buddies. No hot chicks on my arm tonight."

The manager didn't smile at Dylan's attempt at humor. He took his job seriously. "I apologize to you as well, Mr. Williams," he said.

"No harm done." He had to be gracious. The manager couldn't have prevented this from happening. It happened all the time in every place imaginable, especially to Dylan.

The guy was a walking magnet for the tabloids. He seemed to love the attention.

After the manager walked off, Dylan shrugged. "What can I say? I'm sorry. This place used to be off their radar."

"It's not your fault," Jess was quick to say. "Like Zane said, no harm done."

Dylan stared at Jess for a moment, his eyes smiling, and then focused on Zane. "It's good to see you two together like this."

Like what? Zane was tempted to ask. Instead, he sent him his best mind-your-business look.

"O…kay," Dylan said. "Well, I'll be getting back to my friends now. Have a nice evening. Oh, and Jess, I'll see you on the beach."

Jess smiled.

"Bye, Dylan," Zane said, and the guy walked off. If only Dylan's flirty relationship with Jessica didn't grate so much on his nerves.

She touched his arm. "Are you angry?"

Dylan pissed him off, but that's not what she meant. "No. But I don't like having our time together interrupted like that. You don't need to be exposed to my real world. It's bad enough I have to deal with it."

"It's okay." Her face went gooey soft. "It wasn't so bad."

They'd never set boundaries or labeled what was happening between them, except to say she was on the rebound and he was the guy enjoying the privilege. But he wanted to spend every minute with her while she was here. She would go home soon. And he'd have to deal with it. She was forbidden fruit, and at times, his conscience warred with his desire for her. She was vulnerable right now and had come to live with him to heal her wounds. The last thing he wanted was to add to her pain. He'd never knowingly take advantage of her, but was he leading her on or helping her heal? He had to think it was healing for them to be together.

Right now, things were simple, but when the time came for her to return home, he'd have to let her go.

Her palm caressed his cheek. The touch was gentle, caring, and her eyes simmered with enough warmth to light a fire. When she leaned in and kissed him, something snapped in his heart. He wouldn't name it, didn't want to think about it. The sensations roiling in his gut scared the stuffing out of him. The mistake he'd made had cost his wife her life, and he wasn't going back there again. Falling in love was already checked off his bucket list.

Leaning back in his seat, he gave her a smile. "Our food's getting cold, sweetheart."

She blinked, and the heat in her eyes evaporated.

He hated disappointing her, but he had nothing else to say on the subject.

Jessica loved working for Zane. It gave her a sense of purpose, and she enjoyed gaining a new perspective on life. As a grade-school teacher, her world revolved around children, shaping and molding them into good students and eager learners. But this work had its own rewards. This morning she'd already spoken to Zane's fan club president, made a list of devotees she needed to send autographed photos to, and spoken with Mrs. Elise Woolery, a senior citizen who wrote to Zane every month. Yes, at the age of eighty-four, the woman was a Zane Zealot. She was his Super Fan. Mariah had made a special point to make sure Zane read and answered this woman's letters. Jessica would do no less.

Sitting at the office desk, she was reading her heart-warming letter when her cell phone rang. She glanced at the screen and smiled before answering. "Hi, Mama."

"Hi, honey."

"Is something wrong? Your voice…"

"Honey, I'm fine. It's not that, but how are you?"

She was flying high, happy as a clam, strolling on Moonlight Beach shores and spending time with Zane. Last night had been incredible. Except for the crazy camera goons coming out of the woodwork and some odd moments afterward, it had been a picture-perfect day and night. Riding at Ruby Ranch, dinner, dancing and making love with Zane afterward was up there on her Top Ten List of Best Days. What more could a girl ask for?

A lot, a voice in her head screamed.

She ignored it.

"I'm fine, Mom. What is it? Did Steven make another stupid move? Is Judy pregnant or something? I'm telling you right now I'm over it, whatever it is."

"No, honey. I haven't heard anything more about Steven. It's just that…well, have you read the *Daily Inquiry* this morning?"

"Mama, you know I don't read that stuff. And neither do you. What's this all about?"

"I mean, I was sort of used to it with Janie. Zane protected her mostly, and the press loved them. But you, honey. Well, there's a picture of you and Zane, and it's quite shocking."

"There's a picture of me and Zane?"

"On the front page. My neighbor Esther showed it to me this morning. And after that, my phone hasn't stopped ringing."

"It hasn't?" It was noon in Texas. Damn those photographers. She'd thought they were only after Dylan. She should've known better, not that she had any way of stopping the invasion of privacy. "Mama, it's nothing, really. You know the life Zane leads. We were dining out and were ambushed by the Hollywood nut jobs. That's all."

"You changed your hair. You're blonde now. And the dress you were wearing…well, it was quite revealing. Zane had you in his arms, baby girl, and it looked to me as if—"

"He was protecting me from the cameras, that's all."

"Is that *all*, honey?"

She nibbled her lip. What could she say to her mother?

That she'd been sleeping with Zane and they'd been helping each other come to terms with their own personal demons? Could she honestly tell her mother that? No. Her mother would worry like crazy. She didn't know that the new and improved Jessica could handle anything that came her way. God, she only hoped she wasn't wrong about that.

"Jessica, that picture of you…well, do you know how much you look like Janie now?"

Something powerful stung her heart. The subtle implication wasn't anything she hadn't already thought of a hundred times in her head. Was that the attraction Zane had to her? She looked enough like Janie for him to gravitate her way.

"I don't want you to get hurt again."

"I know, Mama. I don't plan to."

Swinging her chair toward the computer, she keyed into the *Daily Inquiry* site on the internet. The front-page picture came up, and there she was, her neckline plunging and Zane's arms around her shoulders possessively, his body half covering hers in a proprietary way. But the headline was what grabbed her the most. "Zane Williams Dating Wife Look-alike." The subtitle wasn't much better. "Who Is His Mystery Love?"

"Holy moly, Mama. I just looked it up." Good thing the paparazzi didn't do much investigating. She could only imagine the headline if they knew she was Janie's younger sister.

"See what I mean?"

"I do. But this will pass. Tomorrow someone else will be their fodder."

"I know that. I'm not worried about the picture or the headline. I'm only worried about you and what you're feeling right now."

"Mama, just know I'm happy. Zane has been incredible, and I'm making friends, enjoying the work I'm doing here."

"Is Zane there now?"

"No, he's having physical therapy." She gasped as a

thought struck her. "Mama, you're not going to call him about this, are you?"

Her mother paused long enough to worry her. "Mother?"

"No, not if you don't want me to."

"I definitely don't want you to. Promise me you won't."

Gosh, the last thing she needed was her mother intervening in her love life. She was the one who had insisted Jessica come here. The damage was already done. Her mama could only make things worse. She hung up on a cheery note, convincing her mother she was fine, and resumed her work.

An hour later, she heard Zane's car pull up. Giddiness stirred inside her, and her heart warmed. She was becoming a lovesick puppy dog where he was concerned. She heard him enter the house, and his footsteps grew louder on the slate flooring as he approached. Seconds later, he was standing in front of her, a newspaper in his hand. He tossed it onto the desk, and she gave it a glance. "Sorry, sweetheart. I've got my manager doing some repair on this. Ideally, he can keep your name out of it." He studied her a second. "You don't look surprised."

"Oh, I was very surprised when my mama called to tell me about it," she said softly.

"Your mama saw this?" he nearly shrieked.

She nodded. "Just about all of Beckon has seen it by now."

He ran a hand down his face, pulling his skin tight. "Oh, man."

"Zane? What are you worried about?" Looking into his pained eyes frightened her.

He came around the desk and, taking her arms, pulled her up against him. "You. I'm worried about you," his said softly into her ear. He tucked her into an embrace while his breath warmed her skin and her spine got all tingly.

"Don't. I'm okay."

"Your mama must think I'm a jerk, subjecting you to this.

You have to go back to Beckon one day. I don't want it to be harder on you than it has to be. I'm so sorry, sweetheart."

You have to go back to Beckon one day.

He was right, she would have to return to her hometown one day. Her mind rebelled at the thought. He kissed her again and eased the battle going on inside her head. Oh, boy.

She gazed at him and was floored by the genuine look of concern on his face.

"How was your appointment?"

He pulled away from her and shrugged. "Fine. I don't think I needed it, but—"

"You need it. So you did okay. It wasn't too hard?"

"I've been swimming, riding and dancing on this foot. Seems I'm doing my own rehab."

"You're lucky you haven't reinjured yourself, babe."

He grinned.

"It's not funny."

"I'm not laughing at that. I like it when you call me 'babe.'"

"Well, if you like that, I have an idea I think you might enjoy."

"Does it involve a bed and soft sheets?"

"No, it involves being poolside with some beautiful hot chicks."

One week later, at the Ventura Women's Senior Center, an hour's ride from Moonlight Beach, Jessica sat poolside in the audience of geriatric hot chicks. The scent of chorine was heavy in the air of the enclosed pool area that opened into the center's recreation center. Zane had his butt in a chair, facing his eager fans with guitar in hand—he'd been brushing up at home—and it sounded to her as if he hadn't lost his touch. Playing guitar was probably like riding a bicycle. Once you mastered it, you never forgot.

Zane's Super Fan Elise Woolery, was all smiles today. She sat in the front row next to her friends, all of whom she'd coaxed into becoming great fans of Zane's, as well. As smokin' hot as Zane appeared to his younger audience, he had the wholesome good looks and Southern charm that any of these women would admire in a son.

Zane had balked at the idea of coming here, not because he wasn't charitable. Nothing was further from the truth. But he didn't know if he had the chops or the will to get back onstage and entertain the masses anymore. It had taken only one little ole note from Elise, saying she'd had a bad week physically, her arthritis so painful she couldn't get out of bed in the mornings, and listening to Zane's songs had helped her get by. That letter and Jessica's urgings had convinced him to play this private concert. He insisted on no press, and Jessica agreed. This wasn't a photo op. It wasn't done for his public image, either. He'd agreed because basically he'd been humbled by her letter and wanted to help.

Zane faced his audience. "Well, now. It's nice to be in such fine company. I guess you all are stuck with me for the next hour or two, so let's start things off." He nodded for Jessica to bring Elise up front and center. There was an empty chair beside him.

"Elise?" She helped the woman sit down next to him. The older woman waved her hand over her chest as the silvery-blue in her eyes gleamed.

"How are you this afternoon?" he asked.

Giddy as a school girl, she nodded and spoke softly. "I'm just fine."

"Yes, you are," Zane said. "Ready for a song?"

She gazed out at the envious women in the audience, her friends in the front fidgeting in their seats, too excited to sit still.

"I am, Mr. Williams."

"Zane," he corrected her, taking her hand. "May I call you Elise?"

"Oh, my, yes."

Zane performed for over an hour, and he'd never sounded

better. Just Zane and his guitar, without all the usual fanfare, lights or band to back him up. His voice was clear and honest and mesmerizing.

After the performance, one by one the seniors said their goodbyes and thanked him, often offering kisses on the cheek before leaving the facility. Elise stayed until the end and chatted with Zane. Jessica didn't contribute much to the conversation. It seemed as though through her letters, Elise and Zane knew each other pretty well, but Jessica did take a number of photos, promising Elise she'd send them to her home address as soon as she could.

"You can thank Jessica here for arranging this," Zane was saying.

"Thank you, Jessica. This made my whole year. I swear today, my arthritis just vanished. I think I'll go home, put on one of Zane's records and dance a jig."

And later, sitting in the backseat of a limo, Zane reached for Jessica's hand as they headed down the highway. He didn't say much as he stared out the window, and every once in a while, he'd give her hand a squeeze.

If she could put a name on this sense of peace and total belonging, she'd call it bliss.

The sea glistened in the moonlight, calm tonight, the placid waves grazing the shore. It was a night like many she'd shared with Zane these past weeks, walking the shore in the dark, holding hands, enjoying the beach after the locals went home.

"You're quiet tonight," Zane said as they strolled along.

She wasn't a complainer. She didn't want to mar the perfection they'd seemed to achieve lately.

"I think I ate something that didn't agree with me."

Zane squeezed her hand lightly. "We can head back. We're only half a mile from the house."

"No, it's okay. The fresh air is doing me good."

"You sure?"

"I'm sure."

"'Cause you know, now that my rehab is done, I could pick you up and carry you all the way."

She chuckled, and the movement caused her stomach to curl. "Oh."

She wanted desperately to put her hand to her belly, but she didn't want to draw his attention there. They were having such a wonderful evening. She managed a small smile instead. "That won't be necessary."

"Could be fun."

"I don't doubt it. You'd probably dunk me into the ocean first or deliver me into your shower, like you did the other night."

"And you enjoyed every second. But I wouldn't do that to you tonight, sweetheart. I can see on your face that you're exhausted." He pivoted, taking her with him. "C'mon. You should get to bed."

"Okay, maybe you're right."

She didn't have the strength to argue with him. Zane had a charity event at the children's hospital in the city tomorrow, and she didn't want to miss it. It wasn't an extravaganza by any means, just an artist making the rounds and singing songs with the kids She hadn't had any difficulty convincing Zane to do it. When it came to making children feel better, Zane was all in.

"Excuse me? You said I was right about something?"

"Very funny." Gosh, her voice sounded suddenly weak. Whatever strength she had left seemed to seep right out of her. Her limbs lost all their juice. "Zane, I'm, uh, really tired." A wave of fatigue stopped her steps in the sand.

Zane halted and gave her a quick once-over, his eyes dark with concern. He lifted her effortlessly, and she wound her arms around his neck. "I've got you. Hang on, honey."

"I don't know what hit me all of a sudden."

"Just rest against me and close your eyes. I'll have you home in no time."

And minutes later, they entered the house. She insisted Zane deposit her in her own bedroom. He balked at first. He said he wanted to keep an eye on her tonight. "Are you sure?"

She needed a place to crash. And if she had a bug or the flu, she could be contagious. Zane didn't need to get sick on her account. "I'm sure. Thanks for the lift." Literally. She smiled, and his eyes grew sympathetic in response.

"Anytime."

"I just need to sleep this off."

"Can I help you get ready for bed?" he asked.

"I'll manage, Zane. Thanks for the thought."

"Okay if I come in to check on you later? I won't wake you."

She could see it meant a lot to him by the protective look in his eyes. "Yes, I'd like that."

"If you need anything during the night, just call for me."

When she'd had the flu during spring break last year, Steven hadn't so much as offered to bring her a bowl of soup. He'd told her he'd keep his distance so she could rest up and get better. He couldn't afford to get sick. She'd received a total of one phone call from him during her recuperation. What a fool she'd been. The signs were all there, but she'd refused to see them.

"Thank you, Zane."

He smiled, but the worry in his eyes touched her deeply. "Good night, sweet Jess." He placed a kiss on her forehead, tossed the sheets back on the bed and gave her a lingering smile before he walked out of the room and closed the door.

Her hands trembled as she put on her nightie and tucked herself into bed. She hadn't lasted but a minute when her belly rattled and the turmoil reached up into her throat, gagging her. Her stomach recoiled, and she covered her mouth, clamping it shut as she raced to the toilet.

It wasn't a pretty sight, but she emptied her stomach in just about thirty seconds.

Sitting back on the floor, she closed her eyes and took big breaths of air in order to calm her stomach. Whatever it was, she hoped it was gone.

Bye. Bye.

Arrivederci.

Good riddance.

She rose slowly and leaned against the marble counter. One look at her chalky face in the mirror told her to wash up and get her butt back into bed. She splashed water on her cheeks, chin, throat and arms, cooling and cleansing herself, and then headed back to bed on wobbly jelly legs. Her eyes closed to the distant serenade of Zane's beautiful voice coming from downstairs as he rehearsed his music for tomorrow's event.

In the morning, her weakened body felt bulldozed. Her head was propped by the pillow and her limbs lay flaccid on the bed as she absorbed the comfort of the luxurious mattress. She missed having Zane's arms around her, but she needed these hours of privacy to rest up.

A soft knock at her door snapped her eyes open. "Jess, are you awake?"

She sat taller in the bed, ran her fingers through her hair and pinched her cheeks, hoping she still didn't look like death warmed over. "Yes, come in."

Zane entered the room, assessing her from top to bottom, and took a seat on the side of the bed. "Morning. Are you feeling any better today?"

"Yes. Just a little tired still. But I'm sure once I get up and eat something, I'll perk right up."

He looked like a zillion bucks. Dressed in crisp new jeans, his signature sterling silver Z belt buckle and a Western shirt the color of sea coral decorated tastefully with rhinestones that outlined a horse and rider, Zane resembled the superstar that he was. His concert shirts were custom-made by a trusty tailor, and this one was perfect for a day with children. "Glad to hear it. Mrs. Lopez has breakfast ready whenever you are."

The mention of food riled her stomach. And blood drained from her face. Her eyes drifted toward the digital clock inside a wall unit near her bed. It was almost ten! "Zane! I had no idea how late I slept. Give me a few minutes to get dressed and I'll—"

As she hinged her body forward, Zane's arms were on her shoulders, pressing her back down. "Whoa, Jess. Slow down."

Dizziness followed her as her head hit the pillow. The world spun for a second, and when it stopped, a soft sigh escaped her. "But I'm supposed to go with you today." It was her job, her duty as Zane's personal assistant. Zane wasn't used to making appearances on his own. He always had an assistant to usher him through the process.

"I didn't have the heart to wake you. I'm leaving in just a few minutes. What I want you to do is take the day off and relax. I'll be back in a few hours."

"I don't want to miss it."

He took hold of her hand. "I wish you could come, too."

"I'm sorry."

"Don't be. I'm sorry you're not feeling well."

"I'll be sure to call Mrs. Russo this morning. She's in charge at Children's Hospital, and I made all the arrangements through her. I'll tell her the situation."

"Don't go to any trouble. I'm sure I'll be fine."

"No trouble." She picked up her cell phone. "I've got the number right here."

Zane's gaze swept over her rumpled sheets and the spot where she'd conjured up her phone. "You sleep with your cell phone?" His incredulous voice tickled the funny bone inside her head.

"When I'm not sleeping with you."

He grinned and kissed the top of her head. "Feel better."

"Thanks."

As soon as Zane left, she made the call and was relieved that Mrs. Russo was amenable to sticking by Zane's side today, keeping him on schedule. She was a fan and was looking forward to the day, as well. Jessica hung up, convinced Zane would enjoy himself, doing what he loved to do. He'd be fine on his own. He liked being around children. Singing to them and with them would be second nature to a guy who'd lived and breathed country music as a boy.

A short time later, ringing blasted in her ear, and she lifted her eyelids. When had she drifted off? How long had she been in sleep land? She squinted to ward off the sunshine blazing into her window. The last thing she remembered was speaking with the director at the hospital regarding Zane's appearance. She took a few seconds to awaken fully, blinking and stretching. Gosh, she felt better, her stomach didn't ache and her head cleared of all the fuzz.

All systems go.

She grabbed her phone and greeted her caller on the third ring. "Hello, Mariah. It's good to hear from you."

Mariah had been calling in at least once a week to make sure things were going smoothly for her and checking in on Zane. Jessica appreciated her diligence and thoughtfulness, but she'd already spoken with Mariah earlier in the week. "Is everything alright?"

"Everything is actually better than I hoped." Enthusiasm that had been vacant in Mariah's voice since her mother's ordeal was making a sparkling comeback. "The last time I spoke with Zane, I told him my mother was being re-evaluated by the doctors. Well, the good news is that even though Mom has something of a long road ahead of her, she's recovered enough to come home from the transitional facility. My sister plans on taking over from now on. She'll have the help of a caregiver during the week. And I'll come home on the weekends whenever I can to help out. I tried to reach Zane to tell him I'll be coming back to work starting Monday morning, but I think he shut his phone off."

Mariah was coming back in five days? The news pounded Jessica's skull. Five days. She'd known this day would come, but she'd been too busy living in the moment to worry about it. "Oh, uh…yes. He's not here. He's doing a show at the children's hospital."

"That's where he really shines," Mariah was saying. "Anyway, you don't have to pinch-hit for me anymore. You, my savior, are off the hook."

She was off the hook? But she liked being on the hook. She *was* hooked on Zane.

Wow. Just like that, her life was about to change again. Mariah would return to work, and things would go back to the status quo. No more sunset dinners with Zane or moonlit strolls or making love on his big bed during the night. The happy place in her heart deflated. Like when the air inside a balloon was released, she fizzled.

"I'm happy to hear your mother's doing well, Mariah." She really was. It was good news, and she focused on that and what Mariah had gone through to get to this point. "And I'll be sure to tell Zane."

"Thanks, hon. I know you've done a great job in my absence. Zane sings your praises and tells me not to worry about a thing."

"Well, there wasn't all that much to do." Except to fall for the boss. "And you left impeccable notes."

"It's a flaw of mine. I'm a detail person. Makes most people crazy, but it comes in handy for the kind of work that I do. I'm happy Zane had you these past weeks. And I'm eager to come back to work. What about you, Jessica? How's your summer going?"

The summer was more than half-over. If she stayed, nothing would be the same. She wouldn't be working alongside Zane, and she couldn't very well carry on with him right under Mariah's nose. She had no name for her relationship with Zane. She wasn't his girlfriend. He hadn't made a commitment to her in any way. Did he look at her as a forbidden fling? He wanted to be her rebound guy, and he'd accomplished that and more. He got an A for effort.

"My coming back doesn't mean you have to leave, you know. Please don't on my account," Mariah was saying. But in fact, her coming back meant that very thing. Zane hadn't spoken about the future with Jessica. He wasn't one to plan anymore. He took things as they came now. Hadn't he encouraged her to do the same? "I would love to get to know you better."

"I feel the same way, Mariah. But unfortunately, I can't promise you that. I...should be getting home soon. There are things I have to do."

Prepare her lesson plans for the new school year.

Avoid Steven at all costs.

Fall back in step with single life in Beckon.

Try not to think about Zane.

"I understand. When home is calling, you must go."

"When Beckon beckons."

Mariah chuckled.

"Sorry. It's a dumb joke the locals think is clever. Small-town humor."

"Sounds kinda sweet. Will you tell Zane I'm sorry I missed him? It was nice talking to you, Jess."

"Sure, I'll tell Zane as soon as he gets back, and same here. Good talking to you."

Bittersweet emotions snagged her heart. She was thankful Mariah's mother was on the mend, but the thought of leaving Zane to return to Beckon was killing her. He'd be home soon.

And she'd have to tell him the news.

Ten

"You're staying," Zane said resolutely. His handsome face was inches from hers as she lay on a beach blanket on the sand right outside his back door, her head propped by a towel. She'd needed some sun to put color on her sickly cheeks while she tried to figure out where in heck her life was headed.

"How can you say that so easily?"

He'd plopped down beside her just minutes ago, wearing shorts and an aqua Hawaiian shirt. He'd been in a good mood since coming back from the children's hospital, and she'd had to spoil it by giving him the news that she'd be returning home.

"It is easy. You're my summer guest. What's so hard about that?"

He made it seem so simple, and he'd brought along his arsenal of secret weapons to convince her. His ripped chest grazed her breasts, teasing and tormenting her. Powerful arms braced on either side of her head surrounded her with strength, and that amazing mouth of his hovered so close she could almost taste it. His presence surrounded her, sucking oxygen from her rational brain.

"It'll be awkward. These past weeks it's been just us, and now that Mariah will be here most of the time, it won't be the same. She'll guess what's going on."

As he cupped her head with both hands, she had nowhere

to look but deep into his eyes. "She probably already knows, Jess. Mariah keeps up on everything, and I'm sure she's seen that tabloid photo of us. But if it makes you feel any better, I'll be up-front with her and explain the situation." Zane lowered his head and brushed his lips over hers. "It won't matter if she knows, as long as you stay."

Yes, yes. His kiss was a potent persuader. Oh, how she wanted to agree with him. She shouldn't care what people thought. But darn it, she did, and her heart was at stake, too. "I'm not... I don't do... Never mind."

"Jess," he said softly, his finger outlining the lips he'd just kissed. His touch seeped into her skin as he curved his fingertips around and around the rim of her mouth as if he'd never touched anything so fascinating. She'd hoped he'd ask her to stay, but she wanted more. She wanted the happily-ever-after that wasn't bound to happen.

He claimed her lips and took her into another world. When he was through kissing her, his deep, dark eyes were hot, heavy and filled with desire. "You can't go yet. This is new and real, and right now I can't offer you more than that." His words were raw with emotion. "But I'm asking you to stay."

New and real? Those were promising words. Hope began to build in her, but she warned herself not to be a fool. She couldn't get blindsided again. She had to face the truth head-on. She didn't know if Zane had the capacity to love again. He was and always would be devoted to her sister. Could she live with that? Could she spend the next five weeks with him and enjoy herself? The new Jess said yes. *Go for it, you idiot!* But the old Jess buried deep down wasn't quite so fearless, and she rose up occasionally to plant dire warnings in her ear. "I want to...but—"

"Sweetheart, you don't have to make up your mind right this minute. Take time to think it over."

Her shoulders relaxed as she blew breath from her lungs. "Okay, I can do that," she said softly.

"Good." He rose and offered her his hand.

"Where are we going?"

"One guess." He waggled his brows. He was six feet two inches of gorgeous, rugged, tan and aroused.

"You don't play fair, Zane Williams."

"*You* don't play fair. That bikini does things to my head and…" He looked down past his waistband. "If I don't get inside soon, I'll be arrested for indecent exposure."

She took his hand, and he yanked her up. She fell against him, her hands landing on his broad, bronzed chest. He smelled of sunshine and sand and sunscreen, and at this moment, she couldn't imagine not being with him.

"What would the residents of the Ventura Women's Senior Center say to that?"

A smile spread wide across his face. "They'd probably invite me back with an engraved invitation."

She laughed along with him, and her day brightened.

Jessica gave her body and soul to Zane, and the past three days had been magical. They rode horses, had moonlight swims, dined and danced together. Zane took her to the new restaurant, and they'd surveyed the progress, sharing ideas. He helped her answer fan mail, giving attention to questions and signing the letters personally. At night their lovemaking was intense, the heat level rising above anything she'd ever experienced before, but it was more than that. Emotions were involved now, their time together precious. Each night before they drifted off to sleep, Zane would hold her close and whisper in her ear, "Stay." In the morning, they'd rise at the crack of dawn to walk along the beach before the world woke up.

Except for a growing suspicion she might be pregnant, everything was perfect.

The idea of carrying Zane's baby made her glow inside, the beaming light of hope strong. It wasn't an ideal situation, but how could she not embrace the new life she might be carrying? She'd been queasy in the mornings ever since her bout of illness, but she managed to hide it from Zane for the most part. She ate little in the mornings, to his raised eyebrows, claiming she put on weight fast and needed to be disciplined. "You haven't got an ounce of fat on you," he'd said.

"And I want to keep it that way." Not entirely true. She wasn't a big believer in stick-thin female bodies, especially since she might be described as voluptuous. But most men bought that explanation, and for now, feminine vanity was a white lie that was necessary.

She'd been overly tired, too, but when Zane noticed, she attributed her fatigue to the energetic pace they'd been keeping in and out of bed. And she was overdue on her monthly cycle.

Locked inside her bathroom, she held the pregnancy test in her hand, waiting those precious few minutes that might change the course of her life. Zane was out shopping—which was bizarre since the man would rather break his other foot than step into a store—and she would use this time alone to deal with whatever came her way. Admittedly, it had taken her half an hour to muster the courage to break open the package and pee on the stick. And now that she had, her pulse pounded in anticipation.

Seconds ticked by, and then she glanced down and got the news.

She leaned against the sink and pressed her eyelids closed.

"Okay." She took a breath.

The new Jess was strong. She could do this.

Tears stung behind her eyes.

"Jess?"

Oh, no. Zane was home. What was he doing back so soon?

"I'll just be a minute." Her voice wobbled from behind the bathroom door.

"Okay, mind if I wait for you in here?"

"Uh, no. It's okay." Shaking, she scrambled to toss all signs of the pregnancy test away. She wrapped everything in toilet paper and shoved it into the bottom of her trash container. She took another few seconds to wash her face and straighten herself out mentally. Then she opened the door.

Zane was lying across her bed, staring out the window. He sat up the minute he saw her and smiled, a winning, charming, loving smile that seared straight into her heart.

"Everything okay, sweetheart?"

She nodded and bit her lip to keep herself from saying more.

Zane studied her face. Did he see the truth in her expression? She lowered her eyes, and that's when she saw a small, square, sapphire-blue velvet box on the spot next to him.

"Sit with me?" He picked up the box and patted that same spot for her to take a seat.

She did and turned his way. He had something to say, and she was all ears.

"Recently, you gave me a gift that was especially meaningful. And now, it's my turn to give you something. Not in reciprocation but because, well, you deserve this. I had this made for you."

His eyes contained a genuine spark of excitement as he placed the box in her hand. Whatever it was, Zane was eager for her to see it. She didn't make him wait. Gently she opened the lid and lifted out a unique charm bracelet. She'd never seen one made with diamonds before. "Oh, Zane." She was truly swept away. "This is…" A lump in her throat blocked her next words. She was speechless.

The silver-and-diamond bracelet held three charms and glittered brightly enough to light all of Moonlight Beach. The charms were well thought-out and special to the person that she was. The first charm was a teacher's apple that reminded her of her students, the second was a schoolbook with opened pages and the third was a pair of eyeglasses, which, up until a few weeks ago, were her mainstay. Every charm was exquisitely outlined by small diamonds. A tiny heart hung from the clasp, engraved with one word in italic script: *Stay.*

"Let me try it on you," Zane said, and she put out her hand.

"Thank you," she said finally. She couldn't have been more surprised. Zane fastened the clasp around her wrist. The fit was perfect, and there was something about a personalized gift, no matter what it was, that made her feel cared for. There were no words to express how meaningful this gift was to her. Zane had outdone himself. "It's very special."

"Just like you. I'm glad you like it," he said.

"I do. You don't play fair, Zane." It was getting to be his signature move. Make her want him even more than she already did.

"I swear to you, I had this bracelet ordered weeks ago, and then, well, the heart was just added on this week. You can't fault a guy for trying."

She put her hand to his cheek and gazed into his eyes. "That's sweet." And then she kissed him, quickly and passionately, before she pulled away, her heart in her throat.

She loved this man with all of her heart.

And she *wasn't* carrying his child.

Sadness blanketed her body, a shallow sliver of sorrow of what wasn't to be.

"Are you sure you're okay, Jess?" Zane studied her movements as she approached his bed. He lifted his sheets and welcomed her. He wanted her with him tonight, sex or no sex. She was special to him, and he didn't want to press her if she needed more rest.

After he returned to the house today, he couldn't wait to see her. His gift was burning a hole in his pocket, so he'd waited for her on her bed. When she'd stepped out of the bathroom and he'd looked at her, he'd seen a haunted expression on her face, and she'd been overly quiet. He worried over her health, but he sensed it was something more than her having an upset stomach. She'd looked sad, and a transparent sheen of despair seemed to cover her eyes.

She'd liked the gift—he could tell that much—and that brightened her mood, but her eyes never really returned to the Jess sparkle he was used to. She'd kept the bracelet on during the day, and there were moments when he'd catch her touching the links, tracing her fingertips over the charms tenderly. After what she'd been through this year, if the gift told her she was appreciated, she was worthy of beautiful things and she was desirable as a woman, then mission accomplished. Zane wanted her to feel all of those things. He'd wanted her to know what she had come to mean to him.

"I'm feeling better tonight," she said. She climbed in and scooted close to him. His arms tightened around her automatically, and he rolled so that her back was up against his chest.

Like it or not, Mae Holcomb put him in charge of her daughter. His first responsibility was to see to her health. Precious little else mattered. He'd failed where Janie was concerned, and he certainly wasn't going to let something happen to Jess while she was here with him. Not on his watch.

"Glad to hear it."

She still looked weary, as if a burden weighed her down. Was she deliberating about staying with him for the rest of the summer? Right now, breathing in the sweet scent of her hair and having her body cuddled up against him, he couldn't imagine her leaving in two days, but he wouldn't pressure her. She needed to come to the conclusion that they were good together, on her own. He'd done everything he could do, short of begging, to convince her to stay, but ultimately it was her decision.

Pushing silken strands away from her face, he kissed her earlobe. "If you need to sleep, I can just hold you tonight, babe. Or…"

She turned around in his arms, her features softening and her eyes tender and liquid. "Or," she said. "Definitely or."

Zane made slow, easy love to her, and she fell in sync with his body movements. He savored every inch of her with gentle strokes and touches. And she did the same to him. He loved the feel of her hands on him, exploring, probing and possessing him in small doses. Little by little, hour by hour, minute by minute, Jess was filling his life.

He cared about her. Worried when she was sick. Praised her accomplishments. Was impressed by her feisty spirit. Wanted to see her happy.

She mattered to him.

And after the explosion that burst before his eyes in warm colors, Jessica's sighs of contentment, completion and satisfaction settled peacefully in his heart. He never remembered being so in tune with another person before. *Except with Janie.*

A wave of guilt blindsided him. Up until now, he'd been able to separate the two, but was he disparaging his deceased wife's memory by finding comfort and some joy with her sister? Was he hurting Jessica and dishonoring his wife?

Zane carefully removed himself from a sleeping Jess and padded away from the bed. Words he hadn't found before came rushing forth, pounding inside his head. He had a song to finish, and the lyrics blasted in his ears now. The song that had haunted him for months would finally see the light of day.

Jessica just put on the finishing touches on her makeup, a hint of pale-green eye shadow and toner under her eyes to conceal the dark shadows from the ungodly remnants of whatever bug she'd had. Her appetite was coming back, thankfully, and she put on a lemon-yellow sundress decorated with tiny white daisies to make her feel human again. She looked at her reflection in the mirror. The dress did the trick. She had a dash of color in her face now, and wearing something fun perked up her spirits.

As she walked into the kitchen, Mrs. Lopez was just setting out her morning meal.

"Thank you," she said, taking a seat. She could definitely handle hard-boiled eggs, toast and a cup of tea. "You always know exactly what I want to eat. How do you do that?"

"I am like a little mouse, observing, watching. I can see you are feeling better, but the stomach needs time to rest. Today, you eat a little. Tomorrow, a little bit more. If you want something more, you just need to tell me."

"No, no. This is perfect. Exactly what I feel like having. It's...late."

"*Sí.* You've been waking late."

"The bug I had wore me out."

Minutes later, just as she was finishing up her last bite of toast and sip of tea, a knock on the deck door brought her head up.

Mrs. Lopez was there before Jessica pushed her chair out to rise. "Hello, Mr. McKay," she said politely, her olive face blossoming. Even Zane's housekeeper was starstruck. Dylan McKay had the same effect on all women, young and old, happily married or not.

"Hello, Mrs. Lopez. I took a walk down the beach to see if Zane could spare a few minutes for me this morning."

"He is not here."

"But I am." Jessica walked over to the door. "Dylan, hi! Is there something I can help you with?"

Dylan had a briefcase tucked under his arm, yet dressed in plaid board shorts and a teal-blue muscle shirt, he looked like a walking advertisement for sunscreen or surfboards. Hardly businessman attire, but that was Dylan.

"Hey, Jess."

"Thanks, Mrs. Lopez," she said, and the woman backed away.

"What's up?"

He brushed past her and stepped into the kitchen. "Looking beautiful as always," Dylan said. It wasn't a line with Dylan. He had a genuine appreciation for women, and he seemed to love to compliment them.

"You're looking fit yourself," she said. "Still running?"

He scrunched up his face. "Yeah. It's getting old."

"Why don't you break it up? Do five miles in the morning, five miles at night?"

His brows rose. "Wow, smart and beautiful. Does Zane know what a treasure you are?"

"I don't know. Why don't you ask him?" She grinned.

"Well, I like your idea, Little Miss Smarty Pants. I might just try breaking up the run and see how it goes."

Mrs. Lopez stood by the oven with a coffee pot in hand, reminding Jess of her manners.

"Would you like a cup of coffee? Water? Juice? Anything?" How comfortable she felt in the role of hostess to Zane's friends. It was something she didn't want to end.

"No, thanks. I'm good right now. Actually, I brought a revised script for Zane to look over. The screenwriter made some adjustments that I think really enhance the story. I've highlighted the parts that would affect Zane. Would you like to see them?"

"Of course!" It sounded better than watching her nails dry, and she was still on the clock as far as work went, even if it was Saturday. "I'd love to. Why don't you come into the office?"

He followed her, and as she entered the office, she went to the wood shutters first, opening them and allowing eastern light to enter the room. "Have a seat."

"Wow, looks like Zane's doing some writing."

Dylan was eyeing Zane's desk littered with sheet music

crumpled into tight balls. Ready to clear away the mess, she noticed the waste basket was full to the brim with the same. Mrs. Lopez worked her way through the rooms every morning. It was evident she hadn't made it to this room yet. "Yeah, I guess he is."

"That's good, right? As far as I know, he hasn't written a song for years."

Since Janie's death.

"I suppose so."

Dylan sat down on the sofa and opened his portfolio. "Do you know where he keeps the original script I gave him? We can compare the two. I'm eager to see if you think the changes work as well as I do."

"Sure. I think Zane locked it up in his desk for safekeeping. Just give me a second to get the key."

"No problem. I'm a patient man."

She doubted that. She moved quickly to retrieve the key from a set Zane kept in his bedroom dresser drawer. She came back to find Dylan with head down, making notes on the script. "Okay, here we go."

She unlocked the bottom drawer, and sure enough, there was the script. She made a grab for it and did a rapid double take at the folder that lay beneath it. In black lettering and handwritten by Zane, the title was spelled out. "Janie's Song. Final."

Zane never mentioned he was writing a song about Janie.

All that sheet music? She had to guess that Zane had been working on this recently. As recently as last night, maybe? She'd woken in the middle of the night and opened her eyes to an empty pillow beside her. She'd heard distant strumming and figured Zane was practicing his guitar again. She thought nothing of it and had fallen right back to sleep. But now, as she glanced at all the rejected papers strewn across his desk and bubbling up from his trash, she knew it had to be true.

It was and always had been all about Janie.

How could she be jealous of her dead sister?

Tears welled in her eyes. She felt sick to her stomach again.

She handed Dylan the first version of the script and went back to the drawer to lock it up. Instead, her profound sense of curiosity had her giving Dylan her back. She opened the manila folder and slipped out the first page of new, unwrinkled sheet music.

She shouldn't be prying. It wasn't her business. Yet she had to know. It was killing her not to know. Her hands trembling, she scanned the lyrics. "I will always love you, Janie girl." She'd forgotten he used to call her that. His Janie Girl. "Without you here, my road is bleak, my path unclear. My heart is yours without a doubt…"

Dylan cleared his throat. The innocent sound reminded her she wasn't alone. She slapped the folder shut. She'd seen enough. She didn't need to see more. What good would it do to torture herself? She was already torn up inside.

She locked the drawer before Dylan grew suspicious and turned to give him a smile. His head was still buried in the script. Then she heard the familiar sound of boots clicking down the hallway.

"Jess?"

She didn't answer. Dylan gave her a look and then called out. "We're in here, Zane. Your office."

Zane popped his head inside the doorway before entering. He shot Jess a questioning stare. She averted her eyes. She couldn't look at him right now, and he was probably wondering why she hadn't answered him. Was Zane jealous of Dylan? Did he think something was going on behind his back? It would serve him right, but that was a small consolation for her.

"Hey, Dylan. What's up?" Zane asked.

She had to get her mental bearings. She needed out of this room, pronto.

Dylan rose to shake his hand. "Hi, buddy. I came by looking for you with a new and improved version of the script. Jess invited me inside, and I was just about to go over it with her to get her opinion."

"Looks like you two don't need me now," she said. "Dylan, you can go over it with Zane. I just remembered I've got some urgent phone calls to make. See you, later."

"Sure. Later," Dylan said, distracted. He turned to his friend. "Zane, is this a good time?"

She dashed away before Zane could get any words out to the contrary. But his completely baffled expression rattled her already tightly strung nerves.

Jessica refused to shed a tear. She refused to cave to her riotous emotions. What good would it do? She'd wasted a lifetime of tears on Steven. Her well was dry. But her heart physically hurt, the kind of pain that no tears or aspirin or alcohol could cure. She marched into her room, closed the door and walked over to her bed. Plopping down, she stared out the window to majestic blue skies glazed with marshmallow tufted clouds.

She liked California. Everything was beautiful here. The people were easy, friendly and carefree. The near-tropical summer consisted of windswept days and warm, balmy nights.

But suddenly, and for the first time since coming here, she missed home. She missed her small apartment and tiny balcony where she grew cactus in a vertical garden and the jasmine flourished over the rail grating. She missed her little kitchen, her bedroom of lavender blooms and country white lace.

She missed her mama.

And her friends.

She didn't see a future with Zane. As much as it broke her heart to think it, Zane wasn't available to her emotionally. He was hung up on her sister and losing her and their baby had scarred him for life.

"You can't get blood from a stone," she muttered. It was

one of her mama's ageless comments on life. It was right up there with another Holcomb favorite: You can take a horse to water, but you can't make him drink.

Ain't that the truth?

Jessica rose and eased out of her sundress. She opened the vast walk-in closet that doubled for a black hole and selected a pair of running shoes, shorts and a top. She redressed quickly and lifted her long locks into a ponytail. Giving herself a glimpse in the mirror, she saw someone she didn't recognize. She'd become a California girl like the ones the Beach Boys sang about: the blonde, tanned, skimpy shorts-wearing chicks who adorned the shores of the Pacific coastline.

Jess wasn't sure how she felt about that. She wasn't sure about anything right now.

She headed down the staircase and heard male voices. There was no way to avoid Dylan and Zane since she had to walk past the office to get out the back door. She stuck her head inside the room. "Hey, guys. I'm going for a run."

Zane glanced up, but she couldn't look him in the eye, and it dawned on her in that very second, that the sick feeling invading her belly was betrayal…the lyrics of a song hurting her more than perhaps being left at the altar by the wrong man. "We're almost through here. If you wait a sec…"

"I'll join you, too," Dylan was saying.

"Uh, no thanks. I think I'll go this one alone. You guys finish up your work. I'll see you later."

She turned, but not before she saw Zane's eyes narrow to a squint, trying to figure her out.

She cringed as she walked away. She'd been borderline rude, but she couldn't help it. She needed some time alone, away from the house and the influences that could very well blindside her again. She hurried out the door and raced down the steps. She headed to where the tide teased the sand under the glorious Moonlight Beach sunshine and began to jog.

She ran at a pace that would keep her feet moving for the longest amount of time. She dodged and weaved around Frisbee-tossing teenagers, small swimsuit-clad kids digging tunnels in the wet sand and boogie boarders crashing against the shore. Sea breezes kept her cool as she dug in, jogging farther and farther away. She headed to a cove, a thin parcel of land surrounded by odd-shaped rock clusters called Moon Point that extended into the sea, forming a crescent.

The rocks looked climbable, and she was in the mood for a challenge.

Up she went, gripping the sharp edge of one rock and then finding her footing on another. Winds blew stronger here, but she held on and worked her way up. She'd heard the view from Moon Point was the best. On a clear day you could see the Santa Monica Pier. Once she got the hang of it, she was pretty good at climbing, and best of all, she was alone. She had no competition for viewing rights. She reached the top in fewer than five minutes and planted her butt on a flat part of a rock.

A hand salute kept the sun from her eyes, and she looked out at the vast ocean view. It was amazing and peaceful up here. Quiet, as if she had the entire ocean to herself.

She could stay up here all day.

Waves rocked the Point, and the sea spray sprinkled her body. The drops felt cool and refreshing, but also woke her to the time. She'd been up on the Point for three hours. She'd hardly noticed the others who'd decided to join her. They'd come and gone, but she'd stayed.

She climbed down from the rock, a deceivingly much harder proposition than going up, and she walked along the shore that was slowly and surely becoming deserted by summer school buses and mothers eager to get on the road before traffic hit. She reached the strip of beach in front of Zane's house half an hour later, and her heart somersaulted when she spotted him on the deck.

He stood with feet spread wide as if he'd been there a long time. His beige linen shirt flapped in the breeze, and his eyes, those beautiful, deep, dark eyes, locked directly on her. There was no need to wave. They'd made their connection. She stifled a whimper and headed toward him.

He started to move toward her, climbing down the steps to the sand, a loving smile absent on his lips. This was not going to be an easy conversation. For either of them.

"Where in hell did you go?" he asked.

She blinked. He'd never spoken to her in that tone. "I took a run."

"You were gone for almost four freaking hours, Jess."

"Well, I'm back now."

His bronzed face reddened to deep brick. "I can see that. Why you'd go off in such a damn hurry?"

"I needed to be alone."

"On the beach? Must've been a thousand people out today."

That was an exaggeration. "Okay, fine. I needed to get away from you for a little while."

He jerked back. "Me? What did I do? And don't change the subject. I was worried."

"Why were you worried, Zane?"

"Because, damn it. I had no idea where you were. You could've gotten swept up by a wave, or some lunatic could've grabbed you, or you might have fallen and gotten hurt. You didn't have your cell phone with you. How was I supposed to know if you were all right? Who goes jogging for four hours?"

"I needed to think."

"So, did you?"

"Yes, up on Moon Point."

Zane rolled his eyes. "You climbed the Point?"

"It wasn't hard."

The sound of teeth grinding reached her ears, but he didn't say another word.

A sigh wobbled in her throat before she released it. She laced her fingers with his and he gazed down at their hands entwined.

"Zane," she said, softening her voice. "You were worried because you care some about me, but also because you feel responsible for me. You promised my mom that you'd watch out for me. Don't deny it. I know it's true. You didn't want to fail her. I get that. I actually appreciate that. But you don't have to worry about me. I'm not the same weak, heartbroken Jess that showed up on your door more than a month ago. I've changed."

A genuine spark of sincerity flickered in his eyes. "You're amazing, Jess. Strong and smart and funny and beautiful."

She hesitated a beat. His compliments nearly destroyed her. "Don't say nice things to me."

"They're true."

"There you go again, Zane."

"Can't help it."

"I'm leaving tomorrow." She had to be strong now. She couldn't show him how her heart was cracking at this very second.

"No, you're not."

She nodded. She wouldn't be persuaded.

"What can I say to make you stay?"

She could think of a dozen things, but she remained silent.

"Why, Jess? What's happened? You owe me an explanation."

In a way, she did. "You asked what you could say to make me stay? Well, I've got something to tell you to make you rethink that."

He squeezed her hand. "Never going to happen, Jess."

"I took a pregnancy test yesterday." The words were hard to get out, and tears burned behind her eyes unexpectedly. She was through with crying. Yet one lonely drop made its way down her cheek.

Breath rushed out of his mouth. The gasp was loud enough to wake the dead. He blinked several times, staring at her as if trying to make sense of what she'd just said. His hands dropped to his sides. He probably didn't even know they had. Just like that, she had her answer.

All remnants of anger left his eyes. They filled with… fear. And he began shaking his head as if he'd heard wrong. "You took a pregnancy test?"

"Yes. I've been feeling tired and nauseated and, well, I had some other symptoms."

The fear spread to his face, which seemed to turn a putrid shade of avocado green. At any minute, he might be the one upchucking. His body, on the other hand, became one rigid piece of granite.

"I'm not pregnant."

A sigh from the depths of his chest rushed out uncontrollably fast, his breath tumbling nosily. The relief on his face drifted down to the rest of his body, and his form sagged heavily. He looked like a man who'd been given a reprieve from the worst fate in the world.

Sadly, his reaction didn't really surprise her. She'd known all along. He didn't want her child. He couldn't handle the commitment of loving another human being more than anything else in the world. He'd been there, done that once in his life. He was still plenty scarred up on the inside, but his scars also showed in his lack of commitment to his career, his floundering around, trying to reinvent himself as an actor, maybe? Or a restaurant entrepreneur. He had clipped wings, and breaking his foot had served as a means for Zane to put a temporary halt to his life.

"Maybe I shouldn't have told you," she whispered. "Kept my trap shut."

"No, no. I'm glad you did." He straightened, the gentleman and dutiful decent man that he was taking hold. But nothing could've hurt her more than seeing, *living* his response. Witnessing the somber truth in his frightened eyes for those brief moments had dissected her heart.

Yet a ridiculously hopeful part of her wished he might have been glad or even receptive to the idea of her having his child. Even if it wasn't planned. Even if it hadn't been conceived in wedlock.

When Janie had told Zane about her pregnancy, he'd been over-the-moon happy. He sent her flowers every day for a week. He hired a decorator and told her to fix up a nursery any way she wanted. He'd written a song for the baby, a soothing lullaby meant only for their new family. He'd told his friends, his fans and the press. The town of Beckon had rejoiced. Their golden boy was going to be a father.

Now Zane reclaimed her hands. His were cold and clammy, and another pang singed her heart. "I wouldn't want you to go through something like that without telling me. I, uh, want you to know that if things had turned out differently, we would've worked it out, Jess."

She didn't want to know what he meant by *working it out*. How did one work out having a baby? It didn't sound like flowers and sweet lullabies. "I know. And now you understand why I have to leave tomorrow."

She couldn't find fault with him. She knew if he could've made her feel better, he would have. But the man didn't have it in him. He didn't love her. He was through with commitment. He'd already had the one great love in his life. The stony expression on his face said it all.

A cold blast coated her insides. The frost would linger even through the Texas heat of home. She loved Zane and wanted to have his child. But he would never know her feelings. He would come to think of her as his wife's sister again.

Sweet Jess.

She wasn't destined for love.

"I'll pack my bags tonight, Zane. Don't bother to see me off. I'm leaving before dawn."

Eleven

Jessica was all about change now, moving the desks around her classroom in a new way. She wanted to see each of her students' faces when she taught in front of the blackboard. Making a connection to them was of the utmost importance. She didn't want to see their profiles but look directly into their eyes to gauge their level of attention and encourage their participation. She had her lesson plans all laid out, her mind spinning about the mark she would make on her students' lives. Who didn't remember their first-grade teacher? And she hoped they would one day think upon her fondly and know she cared.

School started in Beckon just after Labor Day, one week from today. She was eager for the semester to begin, eager to put the past behind her. Scraping sounds echoed in the classroom as she moved chairs across the linoleum floor. She was actually working up a sweat. The summer heat hadn't relented yet. September was just as hot as June in Texas.

Just minutes ago, Steven had knocked on her door. She'd been surprised to see him, but one look at his sheepish face and she knew she'd never really loved him in that forever kind of way. He'd offered her excuse after excuse and finally apologized to her. She'd listened patiently and let him have his say, all the while thinking he'd actually done her a favor by not marrying her, brutal as it had been. When he was through, it was her turn to speak. She didn't swear, didn't get angry, but calmly and very systematically gave him a piece of her mind and then dismissed him.

The new Jess had finally been heard, and it had been liberating.

She kept her hands busy maneuvering desks, not wasting another minute on Steven. But in the silence of her classroom, her mind drifted back to Zane, as it always seemed to do, and her last day in California.

Zane wouldn't let her leave on her own that morning. He'd gotten up before dawn, insisting on driving her to the airport. He had no clue how terribly hard it was for her to say goodbye. He had no way of knowing that her rebound guy had become her Mr. Right and that he'd taught her what love was truly about.

Thanks to airport regulations, Zane couldn't walk her to her boarding gate, but he'd handled her luggage and helped her get as far as he could without garnering a reprimand from security. Luckily, it was the butt crack of dawn, as her friend Sally would put it, and the Zane Williams fan club members obviously weren't early risers. Zane had told her in the car that he didn't care if he was recognized or if the paparazzi were following them—which they weren't. He wanted to see her off.

"Well," he said, dropping her luggage at his feet and taking both of her hands. His dark lashes lowered to her, framing beautiful brown eyes that seemed to give her a view into his soul. "I'll miss the hell out of you, sweetheart."

He had a way with words. The corner of her mouth lifted. How could she not love this man who'd braved Homeland Security, a possible rash of Super Fans and the ungodly early hour to wish her farewell?

"Thank you, Zane." She looked away, into the street that was starting to swarm with taxicabs and buses. She couldn't tell him she'd miss him. That would be the understatement of the century. "I appreciate you letting me stay with you. I'll miss…California."

She'd become a California girl, by Beach Boy standards.

He moved his hands up her arms, caressing her skin, and she began to prickle everywhere he touched.

"Won't you miss me a little?"

"I can't answer that, Zane." *Don't make me.*

He nodded, and his magic hands continued up her arms. "I won't ever forget the time we've spent together. It's meant a lot to me."

Her eyes squeezed shut to hold back tears. She filled her lungs, steadied herself and stared right back at him. "I won't forget, either. I'd better go. They'll be boarding soon."

"Just a sec," he said and then planted a kiss on her lips that would've brought her to her knees if he hadn't been holding her arms. He kissed her for all he was worth. And then he moved his hands to her face and cradled her cheeks, lifting her chin to position his mouth once again and stake a claim in a whopper of a kiss that brought her up onto her toes.

When the kiss ended, he pressed his forehead to hers, and they stood that way for a long time with eyes closed, their breaths mingling.

Over the loudspeaker, her flight was announced. It was time to board.

"Damn," Zane muttered and stepped back.

She lifted her luggage and began the trek that took her away from the man she loved.

He didn't ask her to stay this time.

They both knew it was over.

She had walked away from him and never did look back.

Jess shook off that memory and after accomplishing what she set out to do in the classroom, she climbed into her car and turned on the radio. Zane's melodic voice came across the airwaves. "Great, just great." She didn't need any reminders of how much she missed him. She punched off the radio and cruised along the streets of Beckon, aiming her car for home.

She needed a good soak in the tub.

Or better yet, she'd go soak her head and be done with it.

"Happy birthday, Jessica. How's my girl today?"

"Hi, Mama." Jessica left the curb in front of her apartment and bounded around the front end of her mother's car. Climbing into the passenger seat, she leaned in for a kiss. Mama planted one right smack on her cheek. The none-too-subtle scent of Elizabeth Taylor's White Diamonds perfume matched the heavy humidity in the air, but it was comforting in a way, since the classic scent defined her mama to a T. And today of all days, Jess and her mother needed the comfort.

Mama wasn't the best driver, but she insisted on picking her up and driving today. Thankfully the roads in Beckon weren't complicated or crowded, because the way her mother drove scared the daylights out of her. She clutched the steering wheel like a lifeline and rocked the darn thing from side to side with nervous jerks. Amazingly the car continued down the road in a straight line.

She looked over her shoulder at an arrangement of bubblegum-pink daylilies and snow-white roses. "Pretty flowers, Mama."

"Janie's favorites. I've got a bunch for you back at the house, sweet darlin'." It had become a ritual to visit Janie's grave on their mutual birthday. Neither of them would have it any other way.

The cemetery was on the edge of town, and it didn't take long to get there. They both stepped out of the car and walked fifty feet to the beautiful monumental headstone that Zane had had constructed. "Looks like someone's already been here today," Mama said.

More than a dozen velvety red and white roses shot up from the in-ground vase. "Zane probably had them sent." He wouldn't forget Janie's birthday. He'd always made a big deal of it when she was alive, hunting for the perfect gift for her, making her day special in any way he could.

"I don't think he had them sent," Mama said, pointing to one rose in particular. "Look at that."

"His guitar pick," Jessica said softly. Black with white lettering, the pick placed between opened petals read, "Love, Zane."

"He's in town, Jess."

"Don't be silly, Mama. Zane doesn't come here. If he was in Beckon, it'd be all over the news by now. You know how the town loves him."

"And so do you, Jessica."

"Mama," she breathed quietly. "No."

"Yes, you do. You love that man. There's no need denying it. He's a fine man, decent, and oh, boy, he loved your sister like there was no tomorrow, but Janie's gone. And Lord knows I wish she wasn't, but if you two have something—"

"Mama, I wish Janie wasn't gone. I really do, with all my heart. But you've got it wrong." She wished her sister had lived. Her baby would've been almost two by now, and she'd be the favorite aunt. Aunt Jess. Janie and Zane were meant for each other.

She was a poor substitute for the real thing.

"We'll see."

Jess ignored her mama's ominous reply and hoped that Zane wasn't within one hundred miles of Beckon. Make that one thousand.

Mama laid the flowers down, and both said a silent prayer. They stayed like usual, half an hour, talking to Janie, catching her up on news. Then, with tears welling in their eyes, said goodbye. It was always the hardest day of the year, sharing a birthday with her sister and being able to live out her birthdays while Janie's were cut short.

Mama pulled through the cemetery gates and onto the road. "How about some barbecue for your birthday dinner? I invited Sally and Louisa and Marty to join us."

Her mother, bless her soul, didn't get to grieve for Janie fully on a day that would maybe bring about some healing. Because it was Jessica's birthday as well, she had to put on a cheery front, plaster a smile on her face and pretend her heart wasn't breaking.

"Sure, Mama, that sounds good."

Sally, her best friend, and Louisa, her mama's dear friend, would be there. Marty was Louisa's daughter and also a schoolteacher. Jessica sort of got Marty's friendship by default, which was okay by her. Marty was a wonderful person.

The parking lot at BBQ Heaven was full by the time they got there. Odd for a weeknight, and though the place had new owners who'd changed the name of the restaurant from Beckon Your Bliss BBQ, it still served the best barbecue beef sliders and tri-tip in three counties. There were times back in California when she'd craved those smoky, hickory-laced meals. Now her mouth watered.

They met their friends outside and entered the place together. Seating for five wasn't a problem, it seemed. Her mama must've made reservations. They were seated at the best crescent-shaped Red Hots candy-colored booth in the restaurant. Mama and Louisa sat in the middle so they could gab, and Jessica and her friends shared the end seats.

"Thank you all for coming," Jessica said. She was getting her life back in order. Seeing Marty and Sally helped. Of course, Sally knew all. She'd picked her up from the airport when she'd returned from Moonlight Beach, and Jessica had spilled the beans. She'd sworn Sally to secrecy that day, as if they were in high school, Jess finding a way to trust a friend again. It was all good.

"Sure thing, friend. Happy birthday. Wish I was twenty-six again," Marty said with a lingering sigh.

Louisa rolled her eyes. "You're only twenty-eight, sugar."

"I know, Mom, but twenty-six was a good year for me."

Sally gave Marty a look, and all three of them laughed.

"Happy birthday, Jessica," Louisa said, her voice somber. "I hope you can find some joy today."

"I'm sure she will," Mama said with enough certainty to make Jess turn her way. Her mother's light emerald eyes were dewy soft and smiling. It was great to see her so relaxed.

The waitress came by their table. Everyone ordered a different dish for sharing, with five different sides as well, garlic mashed potatoes, white cheddar mac and cheese, bacon baked beans, almond string beans and corn soufflé. No one would go home hungry.

Bluegrass music played in the background, but no one could hear a word. The place was hopping, conversations from crowded tables going a mile a minute.

She was halfway through her salad when someone tapped on a microphone, the screeching sound check enough to bust an eardrum. Finally, the sound leveled out, the background bluegrass was history, and George, the restaurant manager, spoke into the mike. "We have a little surprise in store for you tonight," he said from the front of the room. She had to crane her neck to see him above the heads bobbing to catch a look. "Our own Zane Williams is back in town, and he's got a new song he wants to sing for all of you. Sort of a trial run, so to speak. I know not a single one of you will mind being serenaded tonight. So let's give Zane a big Beckon welcome."

Applause broke out, and just like that, Zane stepped up with a guitar strap slung over his shoulder. His six-foot-two frame, black hat and studded white shirt made him stand out from the crowd like no one else could, especially since a spotlight miraculously shone on him like a sainted cowboy who traveled with his own glow.

Lord, help her. He was amazing. She'd almost forgotten how much. And her heart did a little flip. She faced her mother who refused to look at her. And suddenly it clicked.

The innuendo at the cemetery, her mother's suspicious behavior today, the *we'll see*s and the *I'm sure she will*s.

Oh, Mama, what did you do?

Sally was beaming and mouthing, *Did you know?*

She shook her head.

And then Zane commanded his audience with simple words. "Thank y'all for letting me interrupt your meal and try out my new song on you. George, I owe you one, buddy," he said, smiling at the man standing to his side. "This one here, it's intended to wish someone I love a happy birthday. So here goes. Oh, it's called 'Janie's Song.'"

*Oh*s and *ah*s swept through the crowd. Everyone knew about Zane's undying love for Janie. A cold rash of dread kicked Jessica in the gut. Her belly ached. Bile rushed up to her mouth. How could she sit here and listen to the lyrics of the song she'd secretly read, a tribute to the love Zane still had for Janie? His voice was a beautifully rich torture instrument that would crumble her heart to powdery dust.

Her gaze darted to the door. Could she make an escape without being noticed?

Zane began to sing. Too late for an escape. He had the floor and a captivated audience. The words she'd remembered, words she'd repeated inside her head a hundred times, poured out of his mouth in a ballad pure and honest, just Zane and his guitar.

"I will always love you, Janie girl. Without you here, my road was bleak, my path unclear. My heart was yours without a doubt…"

Her mama took her hand from underneath the table and squeezed. Jessica glanced at her and found warmth brimming in her eyes. Her mother nodded toward Zane with her chin, her gaze fondly returning to him. Jessica looked down. She couldn't bear to see him sing a love song to another woman, not even to Janie. Not now, not after what they'd shared together. Was that terrible of her?

He crooned, mesmerizing everyone in the place with his

deeply wrought emotions. The pain in his voice was unmistakable, but the lyrics that filled the now quiet room were new, different, changed.

"I loved you once, and it was fine. The finest love I'd ever known. But I'm movin' on, my Janie Girl, with a love so true, I know you'd approve. You see, my girl, you love her, too. You love her, too. You love her, too. You love her, too."

Jessica snapped her head up. Zane's eyes were closed, his head tilted, his hand strumming the chords on the guitar gently as the song eased out of him. He seemed free, liberated, somehow unburdened, even as he put his heart and soul into that song.

She stared at him, unable to shift her eyes away, her mind in an uproar. When he lifted his lids, he focused on her. Only her. He removed his hat in a gallant gesture, and the dark soulful depths of his eyes reeled her in further. All heads in the restaurant turned around. Some people were gaping, others smiling. She recognized quite a few who'd attended her almost-wedding. Her face flamed. What was he doing to her?

He removed the guitar strap from his shoulder and held his instrument with one hand now. He didn't seem to care that he was making a spectacle of himself. And her.

She rose from her seat. The spotlight swiveled to her and flashed in her eyes, making her squint.

Zane took a step toward her.

Her heart was beating so fast, she thought she'd faint.

There was only one thing she could manage right now.

She bolted.

Out of the restaurant.

Into the street.

And kept on running.

"Ah, hell," Zane muttered, ignoring the applause from the crowd and granting Mae Holcomb an apologetic shrug before he took off after Jess. It hadn't gone as he'd planned, that was for doggone sure. His chin held high, he walked out of the restaurant matter-of-factly as if women ran from him every day of the week. As soon as he made it to the street, he darted his head back and forth. Once he spotted Jess nearly a half a football field away, he took off at a sprint. If Doobie Purdy, his track coach, had seen her, he would've signed her up.

But he wasn't anything if not determined, his long legs no match for her. He caught up to her in no time but slowed to a few paces behind, rethinking what he wanted to say to her. He couldn't blow it. Not again. Jess meant the world to him.

"Go away," she tossed over her shoulder.

"That's not nice." What was nice was seeing her tanned, coltish legs making strides. Lifting his gaze higher to her beautiful backside reminded him of how soft and supple she was, how amazingly gifted she was in the female department.

She didn't slow her pace, not for a second.

"Ouch, damn it. I hurt my foot," Zane yelped.

She stopped then and turned, her eyes focused on his fake injury. He saw the depth of her compassion, the love she had for him glowing in her eyes—Dylan hadn't been wrong—and loved her so damn much right now, he could hardly breathe.

"You're not hurt, are you?"

"My heart is bleeding."

She gasped. A good sign.

"But your foot is fine, right?" She stared at his feet.

"Well, my foot could be hurt, Jess. Running like a bat outta hell to catch you in these boots isn't the kind of therapy I need."

She shook her head, and the gorgeous mass of blonde hair curled around her face. The run had put a rosy blush on her face, and the material of her coral dress lifted her ample chest with every breath she took, nearly killing him.

He inhaled now and was grateful she wasn't moving again. "You *really* don't play fair, Zane."

"I needed to see you today. On your birthday."

"Zane, what were you thinking? You made a spectacle of me in that restaurant. You of all people know I don't need another scandal in my life. I've had enough of being the laughingstock in this town. I… Why are you really here?"

"I came for you."

Hope popped into her eyes. Another good sign.

"You changed the words of the song."

"Dylan said he thought you'd seen those lyrics. He was right, wasn't he? Is that why you wouldn't stay with me?"

"Dylan? Are you taking advice from the Casanova now?"

"Don't knock Dylan. He's the one who made me see how much I missed you. How stupid I've been. And yes, after you left, I reworked the song, the lyrics coming easy and straight outta my heart. I sang it tonight just for you."

She folded her arms, and a warm glint entered her eyes. "But why there, in front of half the town?"

"I let you go. I was running scared. When you told me you might've been carrying my child, I couldn't deal with it, Jess. I've been blaming myself for Janie's death all this time, feeling guilty about losing her and our child. Deep down, I hated myself. I didn't think I'd ever want again, or love again. It was easier to live in the moment and not look to the future. But then you left, and I was hollowed out, gutted to my sorry bones. I missed you something fierce. I didn't think me saying it would be enough. I didn't know if you'd believe me unless I shouted it from the rooftops.

"I'm not doing the movie, and the restaurant is the last one I'm building. I'm going to finish up my tour, Jess. I'm through hiding my head in the sand. I'm through not being me."

The corners of her mouth lifted. He wanted to see her pretty smile again, but it wasn't there, not yet. "That's good, Zane. I'm happy for you."

Cars swerved around them. Someone honked a horn. Zane took her hand and guided her out of the middle of the street, to the sidewalk in front of the Cinema Palace. Ironically, it was nearly the same spot where he'd fallen in love with Janie. And now, here he was coming full circle, praying that her sister would agree to spend her life with him.

"Do you love me, Jess?"

She stared at him as if he were a three-headed monster. "Do you?"

She pulled her hands free of him. "Yes, you idiot."

His face split wide open, and he didn't care if he looked like a grinning fool. Joy rushed out so fast he couldn't stop himself from telling her his plans. "I'm selling off my place, Jess. Finally. The land where I lived with your sister will belong to someone else one day soon. I'll never forget Janie, but it's time to move on. There's this beautiful parcel of land I've got my eye on. But I want you to see it, too. I want you to love it as much as I do. I'm digging in and putting down roots again, here in Beckon."

"But you said you're going back on tour."

"I have to finish it up. I'm bound by the contract, but after that, Jess, I'll stay here in Beckon and tour only during the summer months, when you're not teaching."

The smile he was praying for was almost there. "Zane, what are you saying?"

"Oh, yeah, got ahead of myself, didn't I?" He inhaled deeply and took hold of her hands. "I've already spoken to your mama, Jess. She and I worked things out, and she's given me her blessing. Sweet Jess, my Jess, you've helped me heal my body and my heart. And I can't imagine my life without you. Jessica Holcomb, I'm getting down on one knee," he said, his knee hitting the pavement. He tilted his head up and gazed into her eyes. "You taught me to look toward the future again. Knowing you, loving you the way I do, has given me the courage I needed to find my true self. I'm not afraid anymore. And I'm asking you for a second chance. I'm asking you to share your life with me. I'm asking you to be my wife, Jess. And Lord knows, have my baby one day. I want that. I really do. I love you with all my heart. Will you marry me, sweet Jess?"

Her beautiful, soft, grass-green eyes teared up, but her smile was real and genuine and the most beautiful thing about her. She hesitated so long he thought he'd blown it, but then she pulled him up and he stood facing her, his heart in her hands. "No girl marries her rebound guy," she said, her smile widening. "But me. I love you, Zane. I want to be your wife and spend the rest of my life with you."

"I'm so happy you said yes. 'Cause I wasn't gonna take no for an answer. It's all sorta weird and wonderful and unexpected, sweetheart, but my love is true. You have to know that."

"I do. And I think just like you said in your song, Janie would approve. She's looking down on us now and giving her blessing, too."

Holcomb women sure had a hold on him. "I'd love to believe so."

"I believe it, Zane. Let's go back to the restaurant and share our good news. Mama looked worried when I walked out."

"She wasn't the only one." Zane took her into his arms and pressed a kiss onto her soft, sweet lips. Planting his stake, claiming his woman. He was gonna hold on tight and never let her go.

Ever again.

* * * * *

THE BILLIONAIRE'S DADDY TEST

CHARLENE SANDS

To the two new babies in my life!
You are welcomed and loved so much.
With four "princesses" now, you and your sisters have
made my "baby" research so much fun!
I am truly blessed.

One

Adam Chase had a right to know his baby daughter.

Mia couldn't deny that, but her heart still bled as if a dozen knives were piercing her. Darn her conscience for leading her to Moonlight Beach this morning. Her toes sifted through sand as she walked along the shoreline, flip-flops in hand. It was cooler than she'd expected; the fog flowing in from the sea coated the bright beach with a layer of gloom. Was it an omen? Had she made the wrong choice in coming here today? The image of Rose's innocent little face popped into her mind. Sweet Cheeks, she called her, because she had the rosiest cheeks of any baby Mia had ever seen. Her lips were perfectly pink, and when she'd smiled her first little baby smile, Mia had melted.

Rose was all Mia had left of her sister, Anna.

Mia shifted her gaze to the ocean. Just as she'd hoped, she spotted a male figure swimming way beyond the breaking waves hitting the shore. He was doing laps as if there were roped-off columns keeping him on point. If the scant research she'd found was anything to go by, it was surely him. Adam Chase, world-class architect, lived at the beach, was a recluse by nature and an avid swimmer. It only made sense he'd do his daily laps early, before the beach was populated.

A breeze lifted her hair, and goose bumps erupted on her arms. She shivered, partly from the cold, but also because what she came here to do was monumental. She'd have to be made of stone not to be frightened right now.

She didn't know what she'd say to him. She'd rehearsed a thousand and one lines, but never once had she practiced the truth.

With another glance at the water, she spotted him swimming in. Her throat tightened. It was time for the show, whatever that was. Mia was good at thinking on her feet. She calculated her steps carefully, so she'd intersect with him on the sand. Her hair lifted in the breeze, and another shiver racked her body. He stopped swimming and rose up from the shallow water, his shoulders broad as a Viking's. Her heart thumped a little faster. He came forward in long smooth strides. She scanned his iron chest, rippled with muscle—all that grace and power. The few pictures she'd found in her research hadn't done him justice. He was out-and-out beautiful in a godly way and so very tall.

He shook his head, and the sun-streaked tendrils of his hair rained droplets down along his shoulders.

"Ow!" Something pricked her foot from underneath. Pain slashed the soft pad and a sharp sting burned. She grabbed her foot and plunked down in the sand. Blood spurted out instantly. Gently, she brushed the sticky sand away and gasped when she saw the damage. Her foot was cut, slashed by a broken beer bottle she spied sticking out of the earth like a mini-skyscraper. If she hadn't been gawking…

"Are you hurt?" The deep voice reverberated in her ears, and she lifted her eyes to Adam Chase's concerned face.

"Oh, uh." She nodded. "Yes. I'm cut."

"Damn kids," he said, glancing at the broken bottle. He took her hand and placed it on the bridge of her foot. "Put pressure here and hang on a sec. I'll be right back."

"Th-thanks."

She applied pressure, squeezing her foot tight. It began to feel a little better, and the stinging dissipated. She glimpsed Adam as he jogged away. Her rescuer was just as appealing from the backside. Tanned legs, perfect butt and a strong back. She sighed. It was hardly the way she'd hoped to meet the very private Adam Chase, but it would have to do.

He returned a few seconds later holding a navy-blue-and-white beach towel. He knelt by her side. "Okay, I'm going to wrap it. That should stop the bleeding."

A huge wave crashed onto the shore, and water washed over her thighs. Adam noticed, his gaze darting through amazingly long lashes and roving over her legs. A warm rush of heat entered her belly. She wore white cotton shorts and a turquoise tank top. She'd wanted to appear like any other beachgoer taking a leisurely morning stroll along the water's edge, when in fact she'd deliberated over what to wear this morning for thirty minutes.

Now Adam Chase was touching her cautiously. His head down and a few strands of hair falling on his forehead, he performed the task as if it were an everyday occurrence. She had to admire him. "You seem to know what you're doing."

"Three years lifeguarding will do that to you." He glanced up and smiled, flashing a beautiful set of white teeth.

That smile buoyed her spirit a little.

"I'm Adam," he said.

"Mia."

"Nice to meet you, Mia."

"Uh, same here."

He finished his work, and her foot was tied tightly but with an excess of material hanging down. She'd never be able to walk away with any dignity. The makeshift tourniquet was ugly and cumbersome, but it seemed to do the trick. The bleeding was contained.

"Do you live close by?" he asked.

"Not really. I thought I'd go for a stroll along the beach this morning."

"Do you have any beach gear?"

She nodded. "It's about a mile up the beach." She pointed north. "That way."

Adam sat up on his knees and peered down at her, rubbing the back of his neck. "You really should have that cleaned and bandaged right away. It's a sizable gash."

She shivered. "Okay."

The water crept up to their legs again.

Adam frowned and glanced at her encumbered foot.

Pushing off from the sand, she tried to rise. "Oh!" Putting her weight on her foot burned like crazy. She bit her lip to keep from crying out any more and lowered herself back down onto the sand.

Adams's eyes softened. "Listen, I know we've just met, but I live right over there." He gestured to the biggest modern mansion on the beach. "I promise you, I'm not a serial killer or anything, but I have antiseptic and bandages in my house, and I can have you patched up pretty quickly."

Mia glanced around. No one else was on the beach. Wasn't this what she'd wanted? A chance to get to know Adam Chase? She knew darn well he wasn't a serial killer. All she knew was that he liked his privacy, he didn't go out much and—most important of all—he was Rose's father.

She could write volumes about what she didn't know about Adam Chase. And that's exactly why she'd come here—to find out what kind of man he truly was.

Rose's future was riding on it.

"I guess that would be okay."

Come to think of it, no one knew where she was today. Rose was with her great-grandmother. If Adam did have evil on his mind, it would be a long time before anyone came looking…

The mountain of a man scooped her up, and she gasped. *Pay attention, Mia.* Her pulse sped as he nestled her into his chest. His arms secure about her body, he began to carry her away from the water's edge. On instinct, she roped her arms around his neck. Water drops remained on his shoulders, cooling his skin where her hands entwined.

"Comfy?" A wry smile pulled at his lips.

Speechless, she nodded and gazed into his eyes. There were steely flecks layered over gray irises, soulful shadows and as mysterious as a deep water well. Oddly, she didn't feel *un*comfy in his arms, even though they were complete strangers.

"Good. Couldn't think of a faster way to get you to the house."

"Thank you?" she squeaked.

He didn't respond, keeping his eyes straight ahead. She relaxed a little until her foot throbbed. Little jabs of pain wound all around the bottom of her foot. She stifled a shriek when a few bright red drops of blood seeped from the towel onto the sand.

"Does it hurt?" he asked.

"Yes, this is…*awful*." She barely got the word out. Adam Chase or not, she wanted to crawl into a hole. What a way to meet a man. Any minute now, she'd probably bleed all over his gorgeous house.

"Awful?" He seemed to take exception with that. She wasn't complaining about his sudden caveman move, how he'd plucked her into his arms so easily. No, that part had been, well, amazing. But she felt like a helpless wounded animal. She couldn't even stand on her own two feet.

"Embarrassing," she muttered.

"No need to be embarrassed."

His stride was long and smooth as he moved over the sand toward his mansion. Up close, the detail of his craft showed in the trim of wide expansive windows, the texture of the stucco, the unique decorative double glass doors and the liberating feel of an outdoor living space facing the ocean—a billionaire's version of a veranda. Fireplaces, sitting areas with circular couches, overhead beams and stone floors all made up the outskirts of his house. The veranda was twice the size of her little Santa Monica apartment, and that was only a fraction of what she could see. Inside must be magnificent.

"Here we are," he said, steps away from the dream house.

"Uh, do you think we could stay out here?" She pointed to the enormous outside patio.

He blinked, those dark gray eyes twinkling. "Sure. If you feel safer outside."

"Oh no, it's not that."

His perfectly formed eyebrows arched upward. "No?"

"I don't want to ruin your carpeting or anything." Lord knew, she made a decent living at First Clips, but if she destroyed something in the mansion, it could take years to pay off a replacement.

"My carpet?" His smile could melt Mount Shasta. "There's not a shred of carpet in the house. I promise to keep you away from any rugs lying about."

"Oh, uh. Fine then."

He moved through the front doors easily and entered a massive foyer, where inlaid marble and intricate stone patterns led to a winding staircase. She gulped at the tasteful opulence. She clamped her mouth shut and held back a sigh from her lips. Was it the unexpected nuances she found in his stunning home, or was it the man himself who caused such a flurry in the pit of her stomach? His size commanded attention, the breadth of his shoulders, the bronze tone of his skin and, yes, the fact that he was shirtless and wet, his moisture clinging to her own clothes, his hands gripping the backs of her thighs.

A thrill ran through her, overriding her embarrassment.

He began to climb the stairs.

"Where are we going?" Up to his lair?

"The first aid supplies are in my bathroom. Mary is out shopping, or I'd have her go get them for us."

"Mary? Your girlfriend?"

His gaze slipped over to her. "My housekeeper."

"Oh." *Of course.*

"Have you lived here long?" She needed lessons in small talk.

"Long enough."

"The house is beautiful. Did you decorate it yourself?"

"I had some help."

Evasive but not rude. "I'm sorry about this. You probably have better things to do than play nursemaid to me."

"Like I said, I have mad lifeguarding skills."

Yes. Yes, he did.

Adam set the woman down on the bathroom counter. Long black lashes lifted and almond-shaped eyes, green as a spring meadow, followed his every movement. From what he could tell, she didn't have an ounce of makeup on her face. She didn't need it. Her beauty seemed natural, her face delicately sculpted, glowing in warm tones. Her mouth was shaped like a heart in the most subtle way, and her skin was soft as butter. His palms still tingled from holding the underside of her thighs as he'd lifted her off the hot sand. "Here we go. Just let me get a shirt and my glasses."

He grabbed the first shirt he found in his bedroom drawer and then came up with a pair of wire-rimmed glasses. Next he selected the medical supplies he'd need out of a closet in his bathroom. He found what he needed easily: gauze, peroxide, antibacterial cream. When it came to keeping things organized, he was meticulous. It was the way he rolled, and he'd taken more than a fair share of heat about it from everyone who knew him. That aside, he'd bet he'd shock his college pals if they saw the worn, tattered and faded to ghost-blue UCLA Bruin T-shirt he'd just thrown on. Adam almost cracked a smile. It was so unlike him; yet once a Bruin, always a Bruin. He wouldn't part with his shirt. He set his glasses onto the bridge of his nose. "Okay. Here goes. Ready?"

She nodded. "Go ahead."

Gently, he unwound the towel from her foot. "I want to take a better look at that gash."

"You're really nice for doing this," she said softly.

"Hmm."

"What kind of work do you do?" she asked.

He didn't take his eyes off her foot. It was small and delicate, and he was careful with her, surveying the damage and elevating the heel. "Uh, I'm self-employed."

"It's just that, well, this house is magnificent."

"Thank you."

"Is it just you and Mary living here?"

"Sometimes. Mia, do you think you could swivel the rest of your body up on the counter, near the sink, so I can see the foot a little better?"

"I think so." Holding the heel of her foot, he helped guide her legs onto the counter. She had to scoot back and pivot a bit until she filled half the length of the long cocoa marble commode. She couldn't be more than five foot five. Her foot hovered over the sink.

A tank top and white shorts showed off her sun-kissed body. Her legs were long and lean like a dancer's. Seeing her sprawled out before him, the entire Mia package was first-class gorgeous. He caught himself staring at her reflection. *Focus, Adam. Be a Good Samaritan.*

"So you went to UCLA?" she asked.

"Yeah. Undergrad." He stroked his chin and hesitated, staring at her foot. It had been years since his lifeguarding days. He'd never had qualms about giving first aid before. He'd done it a hundred times, including giving CPR to a man in his sixties. That hadn't been fun, but the man had survived and, years later, gratefully commissioned Adam to design a resort home on the French Riviera. It had been one of his first big architectural projects. But this was different somehow, with Mia, the beauty who had landed at his feet on the beach.

"Adam?"

He looked at her. A fleeting thought entered his head. For a woman in distress, she sure asked a lot of questions. It wouldn't be the first time someone tried an unorthodox way to interview him. But surely not Mia. Her foot was slashed pretty badly. Some women liked to talk when they were nervous. Did he make her nervous?

"Is it okay if I wash your foot?"

Her lovely olive complexion colored, and a flash of hesitation entered her eyes. "Do you have a foot fetish or anything?"

He grinned. Maybe he did make her nervous. "Nope. No fetishes at all."

She made a little noise when she inhaled. "Good to know. Okay."

He filled the sink with warm water. "Let me know if it hurts."

She nodded, squeezed her eyes shut and clenched her legs.

"Try to relax, Mia."

Her expression softened, and she opened her eyes. He rotated her slim ankle over the sink with one hand and splashed warm water onto her foot. Using a dollop of antibacterial liquid soap, he cleansed the area thoroughly with a soft washcloth. Heat rose up his neck. It was about as intimate as he'd been with a woman in months, and Mia, with her cotton-candy-pink toenails, endless legs and beautiful face was 100 percent woman. "The good news is, the bleeding has stopped."

"Wonderful. Now I can stop worrying about destroying your furniture."

"Is that what you're worried about?" He furrowed his brow.

"After the foot fetish thing, yes."

He shook his head and fought the smile trying to break his concentration. Not too many people made him smile, and Mia had already done that several times. "You can stop worrying. I don't think you'll need stitches either. Luckily, the gash isn't as deep as it looked. It's long, though, and it might be painful for you to walk on for a day or two. You can have a doctor take a look, just to make sure."

She said nothing.

He dabbed the cut with peroxide, and bubbles clustered up. Next he lathered her wound with antibiotic cream.

"How're you doing?" He lifted his head, and her face was there, so close, obviously watching his ministrations. Their eyes met, and he swallowed hard. He could swim a mile in her pretty green eyes.

She took a second to answer. "I'm, uh, doing well."

It was quiet in the house, just the two of them, Adam's hand clamping her ankle gently. "That's…good. I'll be done in a second." He cleared his throat and picked up the bandages. "I'm going to wrap this kind of tight."

He caught Mia glancing at his left hand, focusing on his ring finger, as in no white tan lines, and then her lips curled up. "I'm ready."

Suddenly, he'd never been happier that he was romantically unattached than right at that moment.

After Adam had patched her up, Mia's stomach had shamefully grumbled as he'd helped her down from the bathroom counter. She'd probably turned ten shades of red when the unladylike sound echoed against the walls. Luckily, he'd only smiled and had graciously invited her to breakfast. She had to keep her foot elevated for a little while, he'd said, and Mia had been more than willing to continue to spend time with him.

To get the scoop on him. It would take some doing; he was tight-lipped. Making conversation was not in his wheelhouse. But so many other things were. Like the way he'd immediately come to her aid on the beach, how thoughtful he'd been afterward, carrying her into his house, and how deadly handsome he looked behind those wire-rimmed glasses. *Oh, Mama!*

She sat in a comfortable chaise chair in the open-air terrace off a kitchen a chef would dream about. Part of the terrace was shaded by an overhead balcony. Adam was seated to her right at the table. Her foot was propped on another chair. Both faced the Pacific.

The morning gloom was beginning to lift, the sun breaking through and the sound of waves hitting the shore penetrating her ears. White curtains billowed behind her as she sipped coffee from a gold-rimmed china cup. Adam knew how to live. It was all so decadent, except that Adam, for all his good looks and obvious wealth, seemed down-to-earth even if he didn't talk about himself much. And she had to admit, her Viking warrior looked more like a beach bum in khaki shorts and a beaten-down Bruins T-shirt. But she still hadn't found out much about him.

"So you work as a hairdresser?" he said.

"Actually, I own the shop but I don't cut hair. I have two employees who do." She gauged his reaction and didn't elaborate that First Clips, her shop, catered to children. The hairdressers wore costumes and the little girls sat on princess thrones, while the boys sat in rocket ships to have their hair cut. Afterward, the newly groomed kids were rewarded with tiaras or rocket goggles. Mia was proud of their business. Anna had developed the idea and had been the main hairstylist while Mia ran the financial end of things. She had to be careful about what she revealed about First Clips. If Anna had confided in him about their business, he might connect the dots and realize Mia wasn't exactly an innocent bystander out for a beach stroll this morning.

Mary, his sixtysomething housekeeper, approached the table and served platters of poached eggs, maple bacon, fresh biscuits and an assortment of pastries.

"Thank you," she said. "The coffee is delicious." Adam had brought it out from the kitchen earlier.

"Mary, this is Mia," he said. "She had an accident on the beach this morning."

"Oh, dear." Mary's kind pale blue eyes darted to her bandaged foot. "Are you all right?"

"I think I will be, thanks to Adam. I stepped on a broken bottle."

Mary shook her head. "Those stupid kids…always hanging around after dark." Her hand went to her mouth immediately. "Sorry. It's just that they're in high school and shouldn't be drinking beer and doing who knows what else on the beach. Adam has talked about having them arrested."

"Maybe I should," he muttered, and she got the idea he wasn't fully committed to the idea. "Or maybe I'll teach them a lesson."

"How?" Mary asked.

"I've got a few things bouncing around in my head."

"Well, I wish you would," she said, and Mia got the impression Mary had some clout in Adam's household. "It's very nice to meet you, Mia."

"Nice meeting you, too."

"Thanks, Mary. The food looks delicious," he said. Mary retreated to the kitchen, and Adam pointed to the dishes of food. "Dig in. I know you're hungry." His lips twitched. When he smiled, something pinged inside her.

She fixed herself a plate of eggs and buttered a biscuit, leaving the bacon and pastries aside, while Adam filled his plate with a little of everything. "So you said you're self-employed. What kind of work do you do?"

He slathered butter onto his biscuit. "I design things," he said, then filled his mouth and chewed.

"What kind of things?" she pressed. The man really didn't like talking about himself.

He shrugged. "Homes, resorts, villas."

She bit into her eggs and leaned back, contemplating. "I bet you do a lot of traveling."

"Not really."

"So you're a homebody?"

He shrugged again. "It's not a bad thing, is it?"

"No, I'm sort of a homebody myself, actually." Now that she was raising Rose, she didn't have time for anything other than work and baby. It was fine by her. Her heart ached every time she thought about giving Rose up. She didn't know if she could do it. Meeting Adam was the first step, and she almost didn't want to take any more. Why couldn't he have been a loser? Why couldn't he have been a jerk? And why on earth was she so hopelessly attracted to him?

Had he been married? Did he have a harem of girl-friends? Or any nasty habits, like drugs or gambling or a sex addiction? Mia's mind whirled with possibilities, but nothing seemed to suit him. But wasn't that what people said about their neighbors when it was discovered they were violent terrorists or killers? "He seemed like such a nice man, quiet, kept to himself."

Okay, so her imagination was running wild. She still didn't know enough about Adam. She'd have to find a way to spend more time with him.

Rose was worth the trouble.

Rose was worth…everything.

"You're not going to be able to walk back," Adam said.

She glanced at her foot still elevated on the chair. Breakfast was over, and her heart started thumping against her chest the way it did just before panic set in. She needed more time. She hadn't found out anything personal about Adam yet, other than he was filthy rich and truly had mad first aid skills. Her foot was feeling much better, wrapped tightly, but she hadn't tried to get up yet. Adam had carried her to her seat on the shaded veranda.

She knew her flip-flops would flop. She couldn't walk in them in the sand, not with the bandage on her foot.

"I don't have a choice."

Adam cocked his head to the side, and his lips twisted. "I have a car, you know."

She began shaking her head. "I can't impose on your day any more. I'll get back on my own."

She pulled her legs down and scooted her chair back as she rose. "You've already done en—" Searing jabs pricked at the ball of her foot. She clenched her teeth and keeled to the right, taking pressure off the wound. She grabbed for the table, and Adam was beside her instantly, his big hands bracing her shoulders.

"Whoa. See, I didn't think you could walk."

"I, uh." Her shoulders fell. "Maybe you're right."

And for the third time today, she was lifted up in Adam's strong arms. He'd excused himself while Mary was cooking breakfast and taken a quick shower and now his scent wafted to her nose—a strong, clean, entirely too sexy smell that floated all around her.

"This is getting to be a habit," she said softly.

He made a quick adjustment, tucking her gently in again, and gave her a glance. "It's necessary."

"And you always do what's necessary?"

"I try to."

He began walking, then stopped and bent his body so she could grab her turquoise flip-flops off the kitchen counter. "Got them?"

"I got them."

"Hang on."

She was. Clinging to him and enjoying the ride.

Two

Adam carried Mia down a long corridor heading to the garage. After traveling about twenty steps, the hallway opened to a giant circular room and a streamlined convertible Rolls-Royce popped into her line of vision. The car, a work of art in itself, was parked showroom-style in the center of the round room. She'd never seen such luxury before and was suddenly stunningly aware of the vast differences between Adam Chase and Mia D'Angelo.

She took her eyes off the car and scanned the room. A gallery of framed artwork hung on the surrounding walls and her gaze stopped on a brilliant mosaic mural that encompassed about one-third of the gallery. Her mouth hung open in awe. She pressed her lips together tightly and hoped her gawking wasn't noticed.

"Adam, you have your own bat cave?"

His lips twitched. He surveyed the room thoughtfully. "No one's ever described it quite like that before," he said.

"How many people have seen this?"

"Not many."

"Ah, so it *is* your bat cave. You keep it a secret."

"I had this idea when I was designing the house and it wouldn't leave me alone. I had to see it through."

Score one for his perseverance.

"I don't know much about great works of art, but this gallery is amazing. Are you an art junkie?" she asked.

"More like I appreciate beauty. In all forms." His eyes

touched over her face, admiring, measuring and thoughtful. Heat prickled at the back of her neck. If he was paying her a compliment, she wouldn't acknowledge it verbally. She couldn't help it if having a gorgeous man hold her in her arms and whisper sweet words in her ear made her bead up with sweat. But she wasn't here to flirt, fawn or fantasize. She needed to finesse answers out of him. Period.

He stepped onto the platform that housed the car and opened the passenger door of the Rolls-Royce. "What are you doing?"

"Taking you home."

"In this? How? I mean, the car's a part of your gallery. And in case you haven't noticed, there's no garage door anywhere." She double-checked her surroundings. No, she wasn't mistaken. But just in case the bat cave had secret walls, she asked, "Is there?"

"No, no garage door, but an elevator."

Again her gaze circled the room. "Where?"

"We're standing on it. Now let me get you into the car."

Buttery leather seats cushioned her bottom as he lowered her into the Rolls, his beautiful Nordic face inches from her. The scent of him surrounded her in a halo of arousing aroma. Her breath hitched, she hoped silently. Mia, stop drooling.

"Can you manage the seat belt?" he asked.

Her foot was all bandaged up, not her hands, but still a fleeting thought touched her mind of Adam gently tucking her into the seat belt. "Of course."

He backed away and came around to the other end of the car and climbed in. "Ready?"

"For?"

"Don't be alarmed. We're going to start moving down."

He pressed a few buttons, and noises that sounded like a plane's landing gear opening up, filled the room. Mia had a faint notion that they were going to take off somehow. But then the platform began a slow and easy descent as the main floor of Adam's house began to disappear. Grandma Tess would call it an "E" ticket ride.

She looked up and the ceiling was closing again, kind of like the Superdome. Adam's gallery had a replacement floor. If he designed this, he was certainly an architectural and mechanical genius.

Score one more for Adam Chase.

Smooth as glass, they landed in a garage on the street level. More noises erupted, she imagined to secure the car elevator onto the ground floor. Inside the spacious garage, three other cars were parked. "Were these cars out of gas?" she asked.

A chuckle rumbled from his throat. "I thought this would be fastest and easier for you. And to be honest, it's been a while since I've taken the Rolls out."

She liked honesty, but surely he wasn't trying to impress her? He'd already done that the second he'd strode out of the ocean and come to her aid.

A Jag, an all-terrain Jeep and a little sports car were outdone by the Rolls, yet she wouldn't turn any one of them down if offered. "So, are you a car fanatic?"

He revved the engine and pressed the remote control. The garage door opened, and sunshine poured in. "So many questions, Mia. Just sit back, stretch out your leg and enjoy the ride."

What choice did she have? Adam clearly didn't like talking about himself. Anna's dying words rang in her head and seized her heart. Clutching her sister's hand, her plea had been weak but so determined. "Adam Chase, the baby's real father. Architect. One night…that's all I know. Find him."

Anna had been more adventurous than Mia, but now she understood why she'd known little about the man who'd fathered her child. Anna had probably done most of the talking. It had been during the lowest part of her sister's life, when she thought she'd lost Edward forever. Maybe neither one of them had done much talking.

She glanced at Adam's profile as he put the car in gear, his wrist resting on the steering wheel. Chiseled cheekbones, thoughtful gray eyes, strong jaw. His hair, kissed by the sun, was cropped short and straight. No rings on his fingers. Again, she wondered if he had a girlfriend or three. Everything about him, his house, his cars, his good looks, screamed babe magnet, yet oddly, her gut was telling her something different, something she couldn't put her finger on. And that's why she had to find a way to delay her departure. She didn't have enough to go on. She certainly couldn't turn her sweet-cheeked baby Rose over to him. Not yet.

He might not even want her.

Perish the thought. Who wouldn't want that beautiful baby?

"Are you sure you don't want me to drive you home?" he asked. "You can have someone pick up your car later if you can't drive comfortably."

"Oh no. Please. Just drive me to my car. It's not that far, and I'm sure I can drive."

Adam took his eyes off the road and turned to her. "Okay, if you're sure." He didn't seem convinced.

"My foot's feeling better already. I'm sure."

He nodded and sighed, turning his attention back to the road.

"How far?"

"I'm parked at lifeguard station number three."

"Got it."

It was less than a mile, and she kept her focus on the glossy waters of Moonlight Beach as he drove the rest of the way in silence. Too soon, they entered the parking lot. "There's my car." She pointed to her white Toyota Camry. He pulled up next to it. The Rolls looked out of place in a parking lot full of soccer-mom vans and family sedans. A mustard-yellow school bus was unloading a gaggle of giggling children.

"Hang on," he said. "I'll get your gear. Just show me where it is on the beach."

Whoops. She'd lied about that. She didn't have so much as a beach towel on the sand. Blinking, she stalled for time. "Oh, I guess I forgot. I must have put everything in my trunk before I took my walk."

Adam didn't seem fazed, and she sighed, relieved. He climbed out of the car, jaunted around the front end of the Rolls and stopped on the passenger side. She opened the car door, and he was there, ready to help her out.

His hands were on her again, lifting her, and a warm jolt catapulted down to her belly. She'd never felt anything quite like it before, this fuzzy don't-stop-touching-me kind of sensation that rattled her brain and melted her insides.

He set her down, and she put weight on her foot. "I'm okay," she said, gazing into eyes softened by concern.

"You're sure?"

"If you can just help me to my car, I'll be fine."

He wrapped his arm around her waist, and there it was again—warm, gooey sensations swimming through her body. She half hopped, half walked as he carefully guided her to the driver's side of the car.

"Your keys?" he asked.

She dug her hand into the front pocket of her shorts and came up with her car key. "Right here."

He stared at her. "Well, then. You're set."

"Yes."

Neither one of them moved. Not a muscle. Not a twitch.

Around them noises of an awakening beach pitched into the air, children's laughter, babies crying, the roar of the waves hitting the shore, seagulls squawking, and still, it was as if they were alone. The beating of her heart pounded in her skull. Adam wasn't going to say anything more, although some part of her believed he wanted to.

She rose up on tiptoes, lifted her eyes fully to his and

planted a kiss on his cheek. "Thank you, Adam. You've been very sweet."

His mouth wrenched up. "Welcome."

"I'd love to repay you for your kindness by cooking you one of my grandmother's favorite Tuscan dishes, but—"

"But?" His brows arched. He seemed interested, thank goodness.

"My stove is on the blink." Not exactly a lie. Two burners were out and the oven *was* temperamental.

He shook his head. "There's no need to repay me for anything."

Her hopes plummeted, yet she kept a smile on her face.

"But I love Italian food, so how about cooking that meal at my place when you're up to it?"

At his place? In that gorgeous state-of-the-art kitchen? Thank goodness for small miracles. "I'd love to. Saturday night around seven?" That would give her three days to heal.

"Sounds good."

It was a date. Well, not a date.

She was on a mission and she couldn't forget that.

Even if her mouth still tingled from the taste of his skin on her lips.

Adam removed his glasses and set them down on the drafting table. He leaned back in his seat and sighed. His tired eyes needed a rest. He closed them and pinched the bridge of his nose as seconds ticked by. How long had he been at it? He turned his wrist and glanced at his watch. Seven hours straight. The villa off the southern coast of Spain he was designing was coming along nicely. But his eyes were crossing, and not even the breezes blowing into his office window were enough to keep him focused. He needed a break.

And it was all because of a beautiful woman named Mia. He'd thought of her often these past two days. It wasn't often a woman captured his imagination anymore. But somehow this beautiful woman intrigued him. Spending those few hours with her had made him realize how isolated he'd become lately.

He craved privacy. But he hadn't minded her interrupting his morning, or her nosy questions. Actually, coming to her aid was the highlight of his entire week. He was looking forward to their evening together tomorrow night.

"Adam, you have a phone call," Mary said, bringing him his cell phone. Few people had his private number, and he deliberately let Mary answer most of the calls when he was working. "It's your mother."

He always took his mother's calls. "Thanks," he said, and Mary handed him the phone. "Hi, Mom."

"Adam, how's my firstborn doing today?"

Adam's teeth clenched. The way she referred to him was a constant reminder that there had once been three of them and that Lily was gone.

"I'm doing okay. Just finished the day's work."

"The villa?"

"Yeah. I'm happy with the progress."

"Sometimes I can't get over that you design the most fascinating places."

"I have a whole team, Mom. It's not just me."

"It's your company, Adam. You've done remarkable things with your life."

He pinched the bridge of his nose again. His mother never came right out and told him she was proud of him. Maybe she was, but he'd never heard the words and he probably never would. He couldn't blame her. He'd failed in doing the one thing that would've made her proud of him, the one thing that would've cemented her happy life. Instead, he'd caused his family immense grief.

"Have you spoken with your brother yet?"

He knew this was coming. He braced himself.

"Not yet, but I plan to speak with Brandon this week."

"It's just that I'm hoping you two reconcile your differences. My age is creeping up on me, you know. And it's something I've been praying for, Adam…for you and Brandon to act like brothers again."

"I know, Mom." The only justice was that he knew his mother was giving Brandon the very same plea. She wanted what was left of her family to be whole again. "I've put in a few calls to him. I'm just waiting to hear back."

"I understand he's in San Francisco, but he'll be home tonight." Home was Newport Beach for his brother. He was a pilot and now ran a charter airline company based out of Orange County. He and Brandon never saw eye to eye on anything. They were as different as night and day. Maybe that's why Jacqueline, his ex-girlfriend, had gotten involved with his brother. She craved excitement. She loved adventure. Adam would never be convinced that she hadn't left him for Brandon. Brandon was easygoing and free-spirited, while Adam remained guarded, even though he'd loved Jacqueline with all of his heart.

"Don't worry, Mom, I'll work it out with Brandon. He wouldn't want to miss your birthday party. We both know how important it is to you."

"I want my boys to be close again."

Adam couldn't see that happening. But he'd make sure Brandon would come to celebrate their mother's seventieth birthday and the two of them would be civil to one another. "I understand."

It was the best he could do. He couldn't make promises to his mother about his relationship with Brandon. There was too much pain and injury involved.

"Well, I'd better say goodbye. I've got a big day tomorrow. A field trip to the Getty Museum. It's been a few years since I've been there."

"Okay, Mom. Is Ginny going?"

"Of course. She's my Sunny Hills partner. We do everything together."

"And you haven't gotten on each other's nerves yet?"

A warmhearted chuckle reached his ears. It was a good sound. One he didn't hear enough from his mother. "Oh, we have our moments. Ginny can be overbearing at times. But she's my best friend and next-door neighbor, and we do so love the same things."

"Okay, Mom. Well, have fun tomorrow."

"Thanks, dear."

"I'll be in touch."

Adam hung up the phone, picturing his mom at Sunny Hills Resort. It was a community for active seniors, inland and just ten miles away from Moonlight Beach. Thankfully his mother hadn't balked about leaving Oklahoma and the life she'd always known after his father died. Adam had bought her a home in the gated community, and she seemed to have settled in quite nicely, her middle America manners and charm garnering her many friendships. The activities there kept her busy. He tried to see her at least once or twice a month.

Mary walked into his office. "It's dinnertime. Are you hungry, Adam?"

"I could eat. Sure."

"Would you like me to set you up on the veranda? Or inside the kitchen?"

"Kitchen's fine."

Mary nodded.

Mary asked him every night, and he always had the same answer for her, but he never wanted her to stop asking. Maybe one night he'd change his mind. Maybe one night he'd want to sit outside and see the sun set, hear distant laughter coming from the shoreline and let faint music reach his ears. Maybe one night he wouldn't want to eat in solitude, then watch a ball game and read himself to sleep.

"Oh, and Mary?"

She was almost out of the doorway when she turned. "Yes?"

"Take the day off tomorrow. Enjoy a long weekend."

Sundays and Mondays were her days off. Adam could fare for two days without housekeeping help, unless something important came up. He made sure it didn't. He had an office in the city where he met with his clients and had meetings with his staff. He often worked on his designs from home. His office was fully equipped with everything he needed.

"Thank you, Adam. Does this have anything to do with that lovely girl you met the other day?"

Mary had been with him since before he'd moved into his house. Some said she had no filter, but Adam liked her. She spoke her mind, and he trusted her, maybe more than some trusted their own relatives. She was younger than his mother but old enough to know the score. "If I told you yes, would you leave it at that?"

A hopeful gleam shined in her blue eyes. "A date?"

Of course she wouldn't leave it alone. "Not really. She's coming over to cook for me. As a thank-you for helping her."

Mary grinned, her face lighting up. "A date. I'll make sure the kitchen is well stocked."

"It's always well stocked, thanks to you, Mary. Don't worry about it. I imagine she's bringing over what she needs. So enjoy your Saturday off."

"And you enjoy your date," she said. "I'll go now and set the table for dinner."

She walked out of the room and Adam smiled. Mia was coming over to make him a meal. For all he knew, she felt obligated to reciprocate a favor. Not that what he'd done had been a favor; anyone with half a heart—that would be him—would've helped her out. Who wouldn't stop for a woman bleeding and injured on the beach?

A beautiful woman, with a knockout body and skin tones that made you want to touch and keep on touching.

He had to admit, the thought of her coming over tomorrow got his juices flowing.

And that hadn't happened in a very long time.

"Gram, this is so hard," Mia said, shifting her body to and fro, rocking baby Rose. The baby's weight drained her strength and stung her arms, but she didn't want to stop rocking her. She didn't want to give up one second of her time with Rose. Her sweet face was docile now, so very peaceful. She was a joy, a living, breathing replica of her mama. How could she lose Anna a second time? "I can't imagine not seeing her every day. I can't imagine giving her up."

"She's ours, too, you know." Grandma Tess sat in her favorite cornflower-blue sofa chair. As she smiled her encouragement the wrinkles around her eyes deepened. "We won't really be giving her up," she said softly. "I'm sure... this Adam, he'll do the right thing. He'll allow you contact with the baby."

"Allow." A frown dragged at her lips. She'd raised Rose from birth. They'd bonded. Now someone would have the power to *allow* her to see Rose?

"He may not be the father, after all. Have you thought about that?"

"I have," she said, her hips swinging gently. "But my gut's telling me he's the one. Rose has his eyes. And his hair coloring. She's not dark like us."

"Well, then, maybe you should get going. Lay the baby down in the playpen. She'll probably sleep most of the night. We'll be fine—don't you worry."

"I know. She loves you, Gram." Tears formed in her eyes. Her heart was so heavy right now. She didn't want to leave. She didn't want to see Adam Chase tonight. She wanted to stay right here with Rose and Gram. She caught the moisture dripping from her eyes with a finger and sighed. "I won't be late. And if you need me for anything, call my cell. I'll keep it handy."

She laid the baby down in the playpen that served as the crib in Gram's house. Wearing a bubblegum-pink sleep sack, Rose looked so cozy, so content. Mia curled a finger around the baby's hair and, careful not to wake her, whispered, "Good night, Sweet Cheeks."

She left the baby's side to lean down to kiss Gram's cheek. Her skin was always warm and supple and soft like a feather down pillow. "Don't bother getting up. I'll lock you in."

"Okay, sweetheart. Don't forget the groceries."

"I won't," she said.

As she passed the hallway mirror, she gave herself a glance. She wore a coral sundress with an angled shoulder and a modest hemline. Her injured foot had healed enough for her to wear strappy teal-blue flat sandals that matched her teardrop necklace and earrings. Her hair was down and slight waves touched the center of her back.

"You look beautiful, Mia."

"Thanks, Gram." She lifted the bag of foodstuffs she'd need to make the meal, glanced at Rose one more time and then exited her grandmother's house, making sure to lock the door.

The drive to Adam Chase's estate was far too short. She reached his home in less than twenty minutes. Her nerves prickled as she entered the long driveway and pressed the gate button. After a few seconds, Adam's strong voice came over the speaker. "Mia?"

"Yes, hello… I'm here."

Nothing further was said as the wrought-iron gates slid away, concealing themselves behind a row of tall ivy scrubs. She drove on, her hands tight on the steering wheel, her heart pumping. She had half a mind to turn the car around and forget she'd ever met Adam Chase. If only she had the gumption to do that. He would never know he had produced a child. But how fair would that be to him or to Rose? Would she wonder why she didn't know her father and try to find him once she grew up? Would she pepper her aunt Mia with questions and live her life wondering about her true parents?

In her heart, Mia knew she was doing the right thing. But why did it have to hurt so much?

She parked her car near the front of the house on the circular drive. Adam waited for her on the steps of the elaborate front door, his hands in the pockets of dark slacks. Her breath hitched. A charcoal silk shirt hugged arms rippling with muscle and his silver-gray eyes met hers through the car window. Before she knew it, he was approaching and opening the car door for her. His scent wafted up, clean and subtly citrus.

"Hello, Mia." His deep voice penetrated her ears.

She took a breath to calm her nerves. "Hi."

"How are you?" he asked.

"I'm all healed up thanks to you."

"Good to hear. I've been looking forward to the meal you promised." He stretched his hand out to her and she took it. Enveloped in his warmth, she stepped out of the car.

"I hope I didn't overstate my talents."

His gaze flowed over her dress first and then sought the depth of her eyes. "I don't think you did." A second floated by. "You look very nice."

"Thank you."

He spied the grocery bag on the passenger seat and without pause lifted it out. "Ready?"

She gulped. "Yes."

He walked alongside her, slowing his gait to match hers. As they climbed wide marble steps, he reached for the door and pushed it open for her. Manners he had. Another plus for Adam Chase. "After you," he said, and once again she stepped inside his mansion.

"I still can't get over this home, Adam. The bat cave is

one thing, but the rest of this house is equally mind-blowing. I bet it was a dream of yours from early on, just like your gallery garage."

"Maybe it was."

He was definitely the king of ambiguity. Adam, guarded and private, never gave much away about himself. Already he was fighting her inquiries.

"I've got wine ready on the veranda, if you'd like a drink before you start cooking."

"We."

"Pardon me?"

"You're going to help me, Adam." Maybe she could get him to open up while chopping vegetables and mincing meat.

He rubbed the back of his neck. "I thought I'd just watch."

"That's no fun." She smiled. "You'll enjoy the meal more knowing you've participated."

"Okay," he said, nodding his head. "I'll try. But I'm warning you, I've never been too good in the kitchen."

"If you can design a house like this, you can sauté veggies. I'm sure of it."

He chuckled and his entire face brightened. Good to see. She followed him into the kitchen, where he set her bag down on an island counter nearly bigger than the entire kitchen in her apartment. Oh, it would be a thrill cooking in here.

"So what's the dish called?"

"Tagliatelle Bolognese."

"Impressive."

"It's delicious. Unless you're a vegetarian. Then you might have issues."

"You know I'm not."

She did know that much. They'd shared a meal together. "Well, since the sauce needs simmering for an hour or two, maybe we'll have our wine after we get the sauce going."

"Sounds like a plan. What should I do?"

She scanned his pristine clothing. "For one, take your shirt off."

A smile twitched at his lips. "Okay."

He reached for the top button on his shirt. After unfastening it, he unbuttoned the next and the next. Mia's throat went dry as his shirt gaped open, exposing a finely bronzed column of skin. She hadn't forgotten what he looked like without a shirt. Just three days ago he'd strode out of the sea, soaking wet, taking confident strides to come to her aid.

"Why am I doing this?" he asked finally. He was down to the fourth button.

Her gaze dipped again and she stared at his chest. "Because, uh, the sauce splatters sometimes. I wouldn't want you to ruin your nice shirt."

"And why aren't you doing the same? Taking off that beautiful dress?"

Her breath hitched. He was flirting, in a dangerous way. "Because," she said, digging into her bag and grabbing her protection. "I brought an apron."

She snapped her wrist and the apron unfolded. It was an over-the-head, tie-at-the-waist apron with tiny flowers that didn't clash with her coral dress. She put it on and tied the straps behind her back. "There. Why don't you change into a T-shirt or something?"

He nodded. "I'll be right back."

By the time Adam returned, she had all the ingredients in place. He wore a dark T-shirt now, with white lettering that spelled out Catalina Island. "Better?"

The muscles in his arms nearly popped out of the shirt. "Uh-huh."

"What now?" he asked.

"Would you mind cutting up the onions, celery and garlic?"

"Sure."

He grabbed a knife from a drawer and began with the

onions. While he was chopping away, she slivered pieces of pork and pancetta. "I'll need a frying pan," she said. Her gaze flew to the dozens of drawers and cabinets lining the walls. She'd gotten lucky; the chopping blocks and knives were on the countertop.

"Here, let me." Adam reached for a wide cabinet in front of her and grazed the tops of her thighs with his forearm as he opened the lower door. She froze for a second as a hot flurry swept through her lower parts. It was an accidental touch, but oh how her body had reacted. His fingertips simply touched the drawer loaded with shiny pots and pans and it slid open automatically. "There you go."

She stood, astonished. "I've never seen anything like that. You have a bat cave kitchen, too."

"It's automated, that's all. No pulling or yanking required."

"I think I'm in heaven." How wistful she sounded, her voice breathy.

Adam stood close, gazing at her in that way he had, as if trying to figure her out. His eyes were pure silver gray and a smidgen of blue surrounded the rims. They reminded her of a calm sea after a storm. "I think I am, too."

She blinked. His words fell from his lips sincerely, not so much heady flirtation but as if he'd been surprised, pleasantly. Her focus was sidetracked by compelling eyes, ego-lifting words and a hard swimmer's body. *Stop it, Mia. Concentrate. Think about Rose. And why you are here.*

She turned from him and both resumed their work. After a minute, she tossed the veggies into the fry pan, adding olive oil to the mix. The pan sizzled. "So, did you help your mother cook when you were a boy?" she asked.

Grandma Tess always said you could judge a man by the way he treated his mother.

"Nah, my mom would toss us boys out of the kitchen. Only Lily was— Never mind."

She turned away from the clarifying onions and steaming veggies to glance at his profile. A tic worked at his jaw, his face pinched. "Lily?"

"My sister. She's gone now. But to answer your question, no, I didn't help with meals much."

He'd had a sister, and now she was gone? Oh, she could relate to that. Her poor sweet Anna was also gone. He didn't want to talk about his sister. No great surprise. She'd already learned that Adam didn't like to talk about himself. "Do you have brothers?"

"One."

He didn't say more. It was like the proverbial pulling teeth to get answers from him.

She added the pork to the mix and stirred. "Did you grow up around here?" she asked matter-of-factly.

"No, did you?"

"I grew up not far from here. In the OC." She didn't like thinking about those times and how her family had been run out of town, thanks to her father. She, her mama and sister had had to leave their friends, their home and the only life they'd ever known because of James Burkel. Mia had cried for days. It wasn't fair, she kept screaming at her mother. But it hadn't been her mother's fault. Her mother had been a victim, too, and the scandal of her father's creation had besmirched the family name. The worst of it was that an innocent young girl had lost her life. "Here, stir this for me," she said to Adam, "if you wouldn't mind. We're caramelizing the meat and veggies now and don't want them to burn. I'll get the sauce."

"Sure." He grabbed the wooden spoon from her hands and stood like stone, his face tightly wound as he concentrated on stirring. She was sorry she'd made him uncomfortable with her questions. But they had to be asked.

"Okay, in goes the sauce. Stand back a little."

He turned her way. "What's that?"

She gripped a tube of tomato paste in her hand and squeezed. Red paste swirled out. "Tuscan toothpaste."

He laughed, surprised. "What?"

"That's what we call it. It's concentrated sauce. Very flavorful. Take a taste."

She sunk her spoon into the sauce and then brought it to his mouth. His lips parted, his head bent and his eyes stayed on hers as she gave him a taste. "Might be a little hot."

He swallowed, nodding his head. "It's so good."

"I know. Yummy."

His eyes twinkled. There was a moment of mischief, of teasing, and his smile quickened her heart. "Yummy," he repeated.

The staunch set of his jaw relaxed and she stared at his carefree expression. She liked the unguarded Adam best.

After tossing in the herbs and the rest of the ingredients, she set the pan to simmer and they left the kitchen for the open-air veranda. "I don't usually come out here," Adam said, pulling out a chair for her. "But I thought you might like it."

The sun was dipping, casting a shimmering glow on the water. Hues of grape and sherbet tangled through the sky. It was glorious. There was nothing better than a beachside view of the horizon at this time of day. "Why not, Adam? If I lived here, I'd spend every night watching the sunset."

"It's…" His face pinched tight again, and she couldn't figure out if it was pain or regret that kept him from saying more. Maybe it was both? "Never mind."

Lonely. Was that what he was going to say? Was this intelligent, wealthy, physically perfect specimen of man actually lonely?

"Would you like a glass of wine?"

"Yes," she answered.

"Cabernet goes well with Italian."

"It does."

He poured her a glass, and she waited for him before taking her first sip.

"Mmm. This is delicious."

The veranda spread out over the sand in a decking made entirely of white stone. A circular area designated the fire pit and off to the side, a large in-ground spa swirled with invigorating waters. She'd been here before, sat close to this very spot, but she'd been too immersed in her mission to really take note of the glorious surroundings. Sheer draperies billowed behind them.

"I'm glad you like it."

What was not to like? If only she could forget who Adam Chase really was.

They sipped wine and enjoyed the calm of the evening settling in. A few scattered beachgoers would appear, walking the sands in the distance, but other than that, they were completely alone.

"Why did you leave Orange County? For college?" he asked.

"No, it was before that." The wine was fruity and smooth and loosened her tongue, but she couldn't tell Adam the reason her mother had picked up and left their family home. She'd been careful not to share the closest things about herself to Adam, in case Anna had divulged some of their history to him. While Anna had kept the last name Burkel, Mia had legally changed her name to her mother's maiden name, D'Angelo, as an adult. Mia was dark haired with green eyes, while her sister had been lighter in complexion and bottle blonde. She wondered if Adam would even remember much about Anna. It had been a one-night fling, and a big mistake, according to Anna. "After my mother and father got divorced, we came to live with my grandmother."

It was close to the truth.

"I see. Where did you go to school?"

"I graduated from Santa Monica High and put myself through community college. I bet you have multiple degrees."

"A few," he admitted and then sipped his drink. His gaze turned to the sea.

"You're very talented. I'm curious. Why did you decide to become an architect?"

He shrugged, deep in thought. Oh no, not another evasive answer coming on. Was he trying to figure out a way out of her question? "I guess I wanted to build something tangible, something that wouldn't blow over in the wind."

"Like the three little pigs. You're the smart pig, building the house made of bricks."

His lips twitched again and he lifted his glass to his mouth. "You do have a way of putting things. I've never been compared to a pig before." He sipped his drink.

"A *smart* pig, don't forget that. You build structures that are sturdy as well as beautiful."

He nodded. "Foundation comes first. Then I layer in the beauty."

She smiled. "I like that."

He reached for her hand. "And I like you, Mia." The hand covering hers was strong and gentle.

His eyes were warm, darkening to slate gray and as liquid as the sensations sprinting through her body right now. This wasn't supposed to happen. This intense, hard-to-ignore feeling she got in the pit of her belly. She couldn't be attracted to him. It was impossible and would ruin everything.

She slipped her hand from his and rose from her seat. "I think I'd better check on the meal."

His chair scraped back as he stood. Always the gentleman. "Of course."

She scurried off, mentally kicking herself. An image of Adam's disappointed face followed her into the kitchen.

Three

"Damn it." Adam squeezed his eyes shut. He'd almost blown it with Mia. She was skittish, and he couldn't blame her. She didn't know him. It had been his MO not to let people in, and he'd done a good job of avoiding her questions tonight. He'd lost the fine art of conversation years ago, if he'd ever had it. If only he wasn't so darn smitten with her. *Smitten?* Now that was a corny word. Hell, he was attracted to her, big-time. She was a breath of fresh air in his stale life.

He entered the kitchen holding two wineglasses he'd refilled and found her by the oven, wearing her little blue apron again. His throat tightened at the domestic scene. How long had it been since a woman cooked him a meal? Well, aside from Mary. A long, he couldn't remember how long, time. "Me again." He set down her wineglass. "What can I do?"

"How are you at making a salad?"

"I can manage that."

She stirred the sauce as he opened the refrigerator and grabbed a big wooden bowl covered with plastic wrap. He set it in front of her.

"How's this?"

"Looks beautiful." She smirked. "You work fast."

"Thank Mary. She anticipates everything." He opened a drawer and revealed a loaf of fresh crusty Italian bread. "Yep, even bread."

Mia smiled. "Thank you, Mary. The sauce is almost ready. I brought homemade tagliatelle. But I can't take credit for making it. There's no way I could duplicate my gram's recipe. She's the expert. She made it."

Several sheets of thin pasta were laid out on a chopping block. Mia rolled a sheet all the way up until it was one rather long log and then she cut inch wide strips and then narrower strips all the way down the line. "Tagliatelle doesn't have to be perfect. That's the beauty in the recipe. Once you've made the pasta, cutting it is a breeze." She unrolled two at different lengths and widths and showed it to him. "See?"

She added a sprinkling of salt to a boiling pot. "Here you go. Want to put these in as I cut?"

"I think you can double as a chef, Mia D'Angelo." They worked together, her cutting, him adding the pasta to the bubbling water.

"That's nice of you to say. But judge me in two minutes, when it's done."

"If it tastes anything like it smells…" The scent of garlic and herbs and the meaty sauce spiked his appetite. The homey aroma brought good memories of sitting down to a meal with his mom and dad, brother and sister. "It'll be delicious."

"I hope so."

He helped Mia serve up the dish, and they sat down outside again. It was dark now; the moonlight over the ocean illuminated the sky. Mary had placed domed votive candles on the table, and he lit them. He couldn't remember having a more relaxed evening. Mia didn't seem to want anything from him. She was the real deal, a woman he wouldn't have even met, if she hadn't injured herself practically on his doorstep. She was curious, but she wasn't overbearing. He liked that she made him laugh.

Steam billowed from the pasta on his plate and he hunkered down and forked it into his mouth before his stomach started grumbling. The Bolognese sauce was the best he'd ever tasted, and the pasta was so tender, it slid down his throat. The dish was sweet and savory at the same time, just the right amount of…everything. "Wow," he said. "It's pretty damn good."

She grinned. "Good? Your plate is almost empty."

"All right. It's fantastic. I'm going in for second helpings. If that's okay with you?"

"If you didn't, I'd be insulted." She ladled another portion of pasta onto his plate and grated parmesan cheese in a snowy mound over it. "There—that should keep you happy for a while."

"I'll have to double my swim time tomorrow."

"How long are you out there usually?"

"I go about three miles."

"Every day?"

He nodded. "Every day that I'm home."

She swirled pasta around her fork. "Do you travel much?"

"Only when I have to. I'm doing a big job right now on the coast of Spain. It might require some traveling soon."

"I'd love to travel more. I rarely get out of California. Well, there was this one trip to Cabo San Lucas when I graduated high school. And my father's family was from West Virginia. I spent a few weeks there one summer. But oh, your life sounds so exciting."

It wasn't. He didn't enjoy traveling. He liked the work, though, and it was necessary to travel at times. Adam pictured Mia on the southern coast of Spain with him, keeping him company, lounging in a villa and waiting for him to return home from work. He saw it all so clearly in his mind that he missed her last comment. He blinked when he realized he'd been rude. "I'm sorry—what did you say?"

"Oh, just that I've always wanted to see Italy. It's a dream of mine, to see where my mother's family was from. That's all."

He nodded. Many people would love to trace their roots, but if Adam never entered the state of Oklahoma again, he wouldn't miss it. Not in the least. After Lily died, their family had never been the same. Some nights he woke up in a sweat, dreaming about the natural disaster that had claimed his sister's life. "I can understand that. Italy is a beautiful country."

"Have you been there?"

"Once, yes."

She took a long sip of wine. His gaze was riveted to her delicate throat and the way she took soft swallows. He didn't want the evening to end. If he had his choice, she'd be staying the night, but that would have to wait. Mia couldn't be rushed, and he wasn't one to push a woman into something she wasn't ready for. "After dessert, would you like to take a walk on the beach? I promise I'll bring a flashlight, and we'll be careful."

Mia turned her wrist and glanced at the sparkly silver bracelet watch on her arm. "I would love to, but it's getting late. Maybe just dessert this time. But I'll take a rain check on that walk."

Late? It was a little after ten. "You got it. Another time then."

They brought the dishes inside and Adam pulled out a strawberry pie from the refrigerator. "Mary brought this over this morning. That woman is a saint. I gave her the day off, yet she still came over with this pie."

Fresh whipped cream and split strawberries circled the top of the pie.

Mia took a look. "Wow, it's beautiful. Mary reminds me of my gram. Eating is a priority. And she makes enough food for an army. You'll never go hungry if my gram is around."

"I think I like her already." Adam grabbed a cake knife from the block.

"You would. She's the best."

Adam made the first cut, slicing up a large wedge of pie. "Whoa," Mia said, moving close to him. "I hope that piece is for you."

Her hand slid over his as she helped guide the knife down to cut another thinner wedge. Instant jolts hit him in the gut. Mia touching him, the softness of her flesh on his. She'd gotten under his skin so fast, so easily. Her scent, something light, flowery and erotic, swam in his head, and he couldn't let her go.

"Mia," he said. Turning to her, the back side of his hand brushed a few strands of hair off her face. Her eyes lifted, jade pools glowing up at him. They both dropped the knife, and he entwined their fingers, tugging her closer until her breasts crushed against his chest. "Mia," he said again, brushing his mouth to her hair, her forehead and then down to her mouth. His lips trembled there, waiting for invitation.

"Kiss me, Adam," she whispered.

His mouth claimed hers then, tenderly, a testing and tasting of lips. Oh God, she was soft and supple and so damn tempting. He was holding back, not to frighten her, holding back to give her time to get used to him. Every nerve in his body tingled.

She touched his face, her fingertips tracing the line of his jaw. A sound emerged from his throat, raw and guttural, and as her willing lips opened, he drove his tongue into her mouth. Her breath was coming fast—he could feel it, the rapid rise and fall of her breasts against his chest. His groin tightened, and he fought for control. He had to end the kiss. Had to step away. She turned his nerves into a crazed batch of male hormones. He swept his tongue into her soft hollows one more time, then mastered half a step back, breaking off the connection.

It was too much, too soon and crazy. She brought out his primal instincts. The jackhammering in his chest heated his blood. He held her in his arms, his forehead pressed to hers; then he brushed a kiss there. "Go out with me tomorrow night, Mia," he whispered. There was raw urgency in his request. Did he sound desperate?

Her expression shifted from glazed-over passion to concentration. Her silence worried the hell out of him. "Okay," she finally whispered back, her voice breathy and as tortured as his. "I'd better go now, Adam."

He didn't want her to leave. He couldn't get enough of her, but he wasn't going to press his luck. She wasn't a one-night-stand type of woman, and he was glad about that. "I'll see you out." He took her hand, the strawberry pie forgotten, and walked her to the front door. Rubbing the back of his neck, he gazed into her eyes. "Thanks for the meal."

"My pleasure."

"It was delicious." So was she. "I'll need your address."

"Six four, six four Atlantic. It's easy. Apartment ten, first floor."

He repeated her address, cementing it into his brain, and then opened the door for her. "I'll walk you to your car."

It was only a few steps, but he took her hand again, fitting it to his and she turned her leaf-green eyes his way. He melted a little inside. It would be a long twenty hours. "I'll pick you up at seven?"

"That's perfect."

Breath released from his lungs. "See you then."

He bent his head and placed a chaste kiss on her lips. Her sweet taste and softness seared him like a sizzling-hot branding iron.

He shut her car door. As she started the engine he gave her a smile, lifting his hand in a wave. Mia wiggled her fingers back and drove down his driveway, turning onto Pacific Coast Highway.

He stood rooted to the spot, breathless.
Mia D'Angelo had literally stumbled into his life.
What kind of fantastic dumb luck was that?

Four

"It's gonna cost you, Mia." She glanced in the ladies' room mirror of the nightclub, frowning at the reflection staring back at her. She was going to tell Adam the truth, sometime tonight during their date. She couldn't put it off any longer. Deep down in her heart, she knew Adam Chase was a decent man. She could feel it in her bones. She'd had a few boyfriends who'd been bad mistakes. Boyfriends who had cheated on her or given her a sob story every time they ran out of cash. How many times had she dipped into her own pocket to lend them a hand only to be taken advantage of again?

She wasn't that naive woman any longer. She'd learned from her mistakes, especially after she'd been burned by a master, her dear old dad, who was a terrible father and an even worse husband. He'd cheated on her mom and done much worse. A drunk and a womanizer, he'd brought shame and heartbreak to the family. He'd taken a life, running down an innocent young girl while under the influence. Gin was his poison of choice, and he'd reeked of it when he'd been hauled off to jail.

But Adam Chase, swimmer, rescuer, talented architect, wasn't a mistake. It was a feeling she got every time she was with him. Even though trying to delve into his past to learn more about him proved fruitless—the guy didn't like talking about himself—Mia owed it to Rose and to Adam to reveal her secret.

It had been on the tip of her tongue to reveal the truth a couple of times tonight. Once, just as she was about to say something, the waiter had come by with their meal and she'd lost her nerve. And later, as she was about to speak up again, the band had kicked up, drowning out her thoughts. Adam had asked her to dance then, and she couldn't refuse those expectant eyes gleaming at her. She'd taken his hand and danced close to him, losing herself in the music. Losing herself in him.

Now she had no excuse. She was going to march right out here, sit down next to him and ask for his patience and understanding. This was it. The time for stalling was over. This was going to be the hardest thing she'd ever had to do in her life. Tears stung her eyes and threatened to ruin her mascara. She dabbed at them with a tissue, took a breath and bucked up.

Her high heels clicked against the wood floors like a death march as she made her way back. The room was dark, the blues music in tune with her edgy mood. Keeping her eyes averted, unable to look Adam in the eye, she reached their table. Her mouth dropped open and she quickly clamped it shut. Sitting next to her date was none other than Dylan McKay.

Movie star. Sexiest man of the year. Box office gold. So much for her well-rehearsed confession. Her mind fuzzed over. She was looking at Hollywood royalty.

Both men instantly rose to their feet. "Mia D'Angelo," Adam said. "I'd like you to meet my neighbor Dylan."

"Hi, Mia." He extended his hand.

"Hello." She placed her hand in his and smiled casually as if she met megastars every day of the week. "Nice to meet you."

"Same here. I have to say I'm impressed. Not too many people can get Adam out of the house. Lord knows, I've tried a hundred times."

Adam shot him a glare. "Give it a rest, McKay."

Dylan flashed a brilliant ultrawhite smile, mischief playing in his eyes. "Adam and I have been neighbors for a few years now. He keeps to himself, but he's a good guy." Dylan winked, and Adam seemed to suffer through it. It was hard not to smile, Dylan was a charmer. Gosh, she'd seen every one of his films. Dylan pulled out the seat for her before Adam could get to it. She caught him frowning.

"Thank you," she said. She lowered herself down, and he scooted the chair in.

"Don't you have to be going?" Adam remarked, giving Dylan McKay some sort of male signal with his eyes. Mia stifled a chuckle.

"Yes, actually. I have a hot date with an older woman. She loves jazz."

Adam's brows shot up. And then he seemed to catch on. "Your mom's visiting?"

Dylan nodded. "She loves jazz. She brought my little sis with her this time. I'd bring them over, but I don't want to bust in on your date."

"The way you did?" Adam said drily, taking his seat.

Dylan didn't take offense. "Hey, I didn't want to be rude and not say hello." Dylan bent over to Mia, and she peered directly into his clear blue eyes. "Are you Italian?"

She nodded. "My family's from Tuscany."

"It's a beautiful country. I want to do another film there, just to absorb the culture and the food. Have you ever been?"

"No, it's a dream of mine to go one day. My gram tells some great stories of the old country."

"You'll get there. Nice meeting you, Mia. Adam. Have a nice evening, you two."

"Thanks." Adam rose to shake his hand. They seemed to have an easy friendship.

As he took his seat, Adam said, "Well, now that Dylan gave me his seal of approval as a nice guy, will you dance with me again?"

He was already rising, taking her hand and piercing her with those sharp metallic eyes. A soft, sultry, bluesy tune whispered over the conversational hum of the night-club. He tugged her to the middle of the dance floor and brought her in close, folding her hand in his and placing it on his chest. "Thank you for not going all fan-crush crazy for Dylan. His ego's big enough."

"He came across very down-to-earth."

"He's easy with people. That's probably why he's loved by the masses."

Adam was the exact opposite of Dylan, quiet and closed off. For all she knew, the only thing they had in common was that they both lived on Moonlight Beach, and were probably billionaires or close to it. "You like him."

Adam gave a short nod. "He's a good friend." He tightened his grip on her and whispered, "Are you enjoying yourself tonight?"

"Very much."

Adam brushed a soft kiss to her hair, and she melted into him. "So am I," he whispered into her ear.

As they danced silently, his heartbeat echoed into her chest. Feeling the music, moving to the rhythms, the sax-ophone delivering gloriously soulful notes, she was float-ing on air. When the music stopped, Adam didn't move. He pushed a strand of hair from her face, gazing at her as if she was made of something precious and fine. Then he touched his mouth to hers, a tender claiming of her lips that stole her breath. His hands roamed over her partially backless dress possessively; her skin tingled where his fin-gers touched her skin.

His breath hitched, a small guttural sound emanating from his throat, as he continued to kiss her. Luckily, they were still ensconced on the crowded dance floor with cou-ples waiting for the next song to begin. When the music started up again, he tugged her off the floor and they re-turned to their table, but he didn't sit down. Instead he took her face in his palms, gave her another wonderful kiss and gazed deeply into her eyes. "Mia, I have to get you home."

Why? Would he turn into a pumpkin at the stroke of midnight? But then he inched closer. Restraint pulled his face tight, his eyes pleading, and she instantly understood why he needed to get out of the nightclub.

She nodded, a beam of hot tingling heat spreading through her body. "I'm ready."

The courtyard near her apartment was dimly lit. Rays of moonlight reflected off a pond and flowed over the hibiscus bushes by her front door. "Thank you for a lovely evening," she said, turning to Adam. He let go of the hand he held and mumbled something she didn't quite hear. Her brain had scrambled during the limo ride home between bouts of sensual caresses and kisses that sent her soaring into the stratosphere.

She'd lost her nerve, once again. And she vowed, tomorrow, after all this heat and energy died down, she'd meet with him on neutral turf and tell him the truth.

"I'm sorry—what did you say?" she asked.

He braced his arms against the front door and trapped her into his body's embrace. His scent, a hint of lime and musk emanating from his pores, did wild things to her. Her thoughts, her body, were keyed into him. Below her belly, she ached and tingled, the pressure building. Her breasts pressed the boundaries of decency and the pebbly tips jutted out, stretching the material of her dress.

"Invite me in, Mia."

And then his lips were on hers again, taking her in another mind-numbing kiss. Her soul was seared, branded by a man she hardly knew. Yet it felt right. So very right. How could she be so attracted to the same man her sister had slept with? Conceived a baby with? This wasn't going to happen. It couldn't.

Her little plan was backfiring.

Because as much as the battle raged inside her head with all those thoughts, she couldn't stop kissing Adam. She couldn't stop wanting him. She hadn't yet said yes or no, and his kisses kept coming, delving and probing her mouth, his lips teasing and tempting hers. She tingled and ached for him, and when he placed the flat of his palm across her chest, rubbing at the sensitive tip through her clothes, a flood of warmth pooled down below, and a strangled sound rose from her throat. "Adam."

She was breathless, out of oxygen and falling fast.

He was an amazing kisser.

He was probably an amazing lover.

How long had it been since she'd been flipped inside out like this?

Maybe never.

She slipped a hand into her beaded purse, grabbed for her key and pressed it into his hand. "You're invited in," she said, her voice a raspy whisper.

"Thank God." Adam blew out a relieved breath.

She moved slightly away from the wall, her body ragged and limp already, just from his kisses.

A thought scurried into her mind of the baby's gear. *Oh no!* Was it all tucked away? Mentally picturing each room, she summed up that the coast was clear. For now, and that was all that mattered.

She didn't want to think further than this moment. She couldn't refuse Adam anything. In seconds, she was inside her apartment, deep in his embrace.

If she expected him to rip at her clothes, he didn't. He took her hand in his and brushed a soft caress to her mouth. More deliberately now, he spoke over her lips. "This is crazy. I don't want to rush you, Mia."

Adam, always rational. She was beginning to understand that about him. Even in the heat of passion, he thought of her feelings. His eyes were hot embers, his body on fire, yet he slowed down enough to make sure he wasn't taking advantage of her or the situation. "I don't feel rushed, Adam." Her voice softened as she confessed the truth.

He drew breath into his lungs as if he'd prayed for that answer and nodded.

She pushed his dinner jacket off his shoulders and he wiggled out of it. He wore no tie, but he unfastened the top buttons on his shirt. She took his hand and led him to the sofa. He sat first and tugged her down onto his lap. "You're beautiful." The heat in his eyes bored straight into her, and then his lips were on her again, his tongue mating with hers.

She gripped his shoulders, touched his hot sizzling skin from beneath his shirt. His strength rippled through her body and heightened her thrill. A low guttural growl rose up from his throat and touched something deep and tender in her heart. Nothing else existed in the world. It was all Adam. Adam. Adam.

He lowered her down slightly, holding her by one strong arm as the heat of his palm covered her breast. It swelled even more, aching for his touch. It was easy for him to slip down the one shoulder strap of her dress. The material and her strapless bra edged down; cool air hit her exposed chest. She arched for him, and he bent his head, taking her into his mouth.

She moaned as he suckled gently, his tongue moistening her extended nipples. Mia wiggled, and he held her arms firm, stroking her over and over, torturing her with swipes that left her breathless. The apex of her legs began to throb, a deep building of pressure that would soon need release.

His mouth left her breast then to reclaim her lips. The hem of her dress was pushed up and the rough planes of his hand cupped her leg, skimming the underside of her thigh, back and forth.

Her mind swam with delicious thoughts as pressure climbed. His fingertips came close to her sweet spot, and she ached for his touch.

"You want this, right?" he rasped, his fingers teasing closer.

"Yes," she breathed, her pulse racing. "I want it."

It wouldn't take much to send her over the edge. She was almost there already. She'd never been so in tune with a man before. She'd never had this kind of immediate response. And she wasn't ashamed that she was practically begging him to take her.

His fingers slipped beneath her bikini panties, and his touch brought a sudden sharp breath from her lips. "Easy, sweetheart. I won't hurt you."

She nodded, unable to utter a word.

As he moved over her, moisture coated his fingers, and, ever so slightly, her body began to rock and sway as he stroked her. Sensations swirled, and she gave herself up to the wondrous feeling. Adam's mouth on hers, his tongue inside her and his fingers working magic—she was too far gone to hold back. She let go and moved with him now. He pressed her harder, faster and she climbed as high as she could go.

"Mia." His voice tight, he seemed just as consumed as she was.

Her body gave way, releasing the strain, the heavy weight loosening up and shattering. Her eyes closed, she merely allowed herself to feel. And it felt mind-blowingly wonderful.

She opened her eyes to Adam's stare. The hunger on his face told her he was ready for more.

He brought down the hem of her dress and replaced the strap over her shoulder. She was being lifted again, tucked into his arms. Kissing her throat, he whispered, "Where's your bedroom, sweetheart?"

She pointed toward the darkened hallway. "The last door on the left."

He began to move slowly, cradling her. "Are you okay?"

She gave a slow nod. "I'm perfect." There was no shame.

She couldn't wait to be with him again, to have him inside her. She was just getting started. How many years had she gone without? Now, having Adam as a partner, her bones jumped to life.

"I agree. You are."

The compliment seeped into her soul.

He walked past Rose's bedroom. The door was shut, hiding her nursery, but a jolt of guilt-ridden pain singed her. She didn't want to think about that right now. Things were getting complicated.

They neared her bedroom door.

And then she was nearly falling out of his arms.

He tripped, and she went down with him. The stumble brought him to his knees. He never let go of her, though—good lifeguarding skills—and he laughed in her ear. "I've still got you. Sorry for the stumble. I must've stepped on something."

He set her down gently and searched the floor, picking up the mystery item that caused the fall.

Her eyes squeezed shut.

"What the hell is this?"

He groped at the stuffed snowman with the giant carrot nose. Olaf, the character from *Frozen*. She remembered Rose dropping it as she was getting ready to go to her grandmother's house. She'd meant to grab it but had totally forgotten.

"It's a toy I forgot to pick up."

"Do you moonlight as a babysitter or something? Or do you have a thing for weird-looking snowmen?"

She sighed. Then stood up and flipped the light switch on.

Adam squinted and gazed at her through narrowed eyes. "Mia? I was just kidding. Why are you frowning?"

Her heart sank, and tears burned behind her eyes. The night would bring on so many changes. Rose's innocent face flashed. For a split second, she thought about bail-ing. About lying to Adam and sending him packing. In her dreams, Rose was hers, Gram would live forever and they'd be a family.

"Mia?" Adam rose from the floor. She couldn't put this off any longer. It was time. She had the perfect opportunity to tell Adam about Rose. To lie now would only prolong the inevitable and make things harder than they already were.

"Adam, that's Olaf. It's, uh…it's your daughter's favorite toy."

It took all of her effort to get Adam to sit down at the kitchen table so she could explain. As she filled the coffeemaker, she sensed his gaze boring into her like a pinpointed laser beam and her neck prickled. He kept looking at her as if she were from outer space.

"This is some kind of joke, isn't it, Mia?"

"No joke. You have a daughter."

He shook his head. "I'm still waiting for your explanation. You can't just blurt out I've got a daughter and then decide we need to discuss this over coffee, as if we were talking about the weather. Christ, Mia. I've had people try to infiltrate my territory and invade my privacy. I admit you're good. You found a way to get my attention. Even it if did cost you pain and a little bleeding. Hell, you had me fooled. Whatever you want, just spill it out, so we can get this over with."

Her head whipped around, her eyes burning hot. "I'm not trying to fool you or invade your precious privacy, Adam. And you wouldn't say that if you knew Rose. That baby is the sweetest thing on this earth." She simmered down. She so didn't want to have a confrontation. "We need to discuss this calmly, rationally."

"How do you know I have a daughter? Who is she to you?"

"She's…my niece."

"Your niece?" His voice rose, piercing her ears. He hadn't expected that, but the truth deserved to be told now.

"Yes, my niece. About a year ago, you spent some time with my sister. Her name was Anna Burkel."

Adam frowned and darted his eyes away, as if trying to recall.

"She was dark blonde and pretty and, well, you spent one night with her."

Adam turned back to her and blinked. "She's your sister?"

Trembling, she poured coffee into mugs and brought them to the table in her small kitchen. Steam rose up and she stared at it a second. All of her mistakes came bounding back at her, and her hand shook as she set the mug down in front of him. "Yes, she was my sister."

"Was?"

"She died after giving birth to Rose. It was a complicated delivery."

Adam didn't offer condolences. He was in shock, staring at her face, but seeing straight through her. "Keep going, Mia. I'm not connecting the dots."

Her heart pounded. This wasn't going well. And it was probably going to get a lot worse. "I'll try to explain. When you met Anna, she was at a low point in her life. She was in love with Edward, her fiancé of two years. They had planned to get married that summer, but then Edward broke it off with her. I doubt she told you any of this, on... on that night."

He shook his head. "No, she didn't. I only remember that she looked lonely. I was at an art museum in the early hours, just when it opened," he said, gazing out the window to the dark sky. "I only make rare visits. But she was there, too, wandering around, and we were enthralled with the same piece. She said something that intrigued me about the artist. She seemed to know a lot about art. We had that in common. We struck up a conversation and ended up spending the day together. Are you saying she got pregnant that night?"

"Apparently."

"Apparently," he repeated. "Well, what is it Mia? Yes or no?" He rose from his seat and began pacing. "Are you trying to hustle me?"

"No! Damn it, Adam. I'm not doing that. And, yes, she got pregnant that night."

"So why didn't she try to find me and tell me about the baby?"

"Because she didn't tell anyone she was carrying your baby. She kept the secret from everyone, including her fiancé. She got back together with Edward just one month later and, and…" Oh, man, this was harder to admit than she'd thought. Saying the words out loud made her sister's deed seem conniving and sinister. What she'd done was wrong, and Mia had been shocked to learn the truth on Anna's deathbed. But how could she blame her sister now? She'd paid the worst price, dying before she got to know her sweet child.

"And she pretended that the kid was his?" Adam's lips twisted into a snarl. She didn't think his handsome face could ever appear ugly, but right now it did.

She nodded.

He stopped pacing and closed his eyes as if absorbing it all. "I'm not convinced the child is mine. How can you be so sure?"

"Because my sister was dying when she confided the truth to me, Adam."

"And?"

She bristled. "If that's not enough, Rose has your eyes."

"What does that mean?"

"How many children do you know have silver-gray eyes?"

"I don't know many children, Mia."

Now he was being obtuse. Yes, it was a lot to lay on him and she hadn't planned on his finding out this way… accidentally. It would've been much better if she could have confessed the truth to him during a long soulful talk, the way she'd hoped.

"How old is the baby?" he asked.

"Rose is four months."

His hands went to his hips. He might've been a gunslinger, eyeing his opponent. He stood ramrod stiff and ready to do battle. "Four months? The child is four months old?" He paced again, moving briskly, and she imagined his head was ready to spout steam any second. "So what was all this about?" He gestured to her apartment, the couch where she'd come undone in his arms and all the rest, by making a circle with his hand. "Were you trying to soften the blow? Because, Mia, you're good. I'd say you're a pro."

The "pro" comment had her walking up to him, her nerves absolutely raw. "Don't insult me, Adam. Bullying doesn't work on me."

She'd been called many names in high school after her father had sullied the Burkel name. It had hurt her beyond belief. She'd felt dirty and shamed. Mean-spirited folks aimed their disgust and revulsion at her entire family, instead of the one person who'd actually been guilty of hideous crimes. James Burkel deserved their distrust, but not the rest of her family. They'd been innocent victims, as well.

From that day on, Mia had vowed not to allow anyone to bully her again.

"You sure had me fooled." And then Adam's eyes widened and he pointed a finger at her. "Did you plant that broken bottle on the beach, just to meet me?"

"Don't flatter yourself, Adam. I was trying to meet you, yes, that's true, but I wouldn't bloody myself. That was an accident."

"But it did the trick, didn't it?"

Oh man. She couldn't deny it. "Yes, it served my purpose."

"And that was to what? Screw me, as many ways as you could. And I'm not talking about sex, but honey, after tonight, if the shoe fits."

Fury blistered up and her hand lifted toward his face. He stared her down, and she dropped her hand, not because she was afraid of Adam, but because she didn't approve of physical violence of any kind. There had been one too many slaps to her mother's face by dear old dad for her to ever want to repeat that behavior.

He sensed her displeasure and backtracked a little. "I apologize for that. But just tell me why you waited for four months and why, when we first met, you didn't immediately tell me about Rose?"

"For one, my sister died before I could get much information out of her. She told me your name and that you were an architect. Do you know how many Adam Chases there are in the United States? Logic had me narrowing it down to a handful of men, but then I found a recent picture of you…which, by the way, wasn't easy to find. You're not exactly press happy, are you?" She didn't expect him to answer. It was common knowledge that he was a recluse, or whatever kind of label fit a man who didn't like people or being out in public. "When I saw a picture of you, and homed in on your eyes, well, then I knew it had to be you."

"What else?"

"Nothing else. Isn't that enough? I was right. You were with my sister."

"What about this Edward guy? Does he still believe the baby is his?"

An exhausted sigh blew through her lips. This had been a trying day, and her emotions were tied up into knots. "No, Anna left it up to me to tell him. He didn't believe me at first and I understood that. He didn't *want* to believe it. He had already bonded with Rose. When the DNA test came back, he was devastated. He'd lost Anna, and then to find out Rose wasn't his… I've been raising Rose ever since."

"Where is the baby now?"

"With my gram." Taking her eyes off Adam, she glanced at the wall clock. "I have to get her soon. She'll be fast asleep."

"I want to see her, Mia. Tomorrow morning. First thing." It was the first time Adam Chase barked an order at her.

"I'll have to make arrangements. I'm expected at work, but I'll be there."

"See that you are. Who watches the baby when you're working?"

"I do. She's too much for my gram all day. I take her to the shop, and she's pretty good. She takes naps. And some days I work part-time or work from home. She's my little mascot."

"You never explained why it took you so long to reveal this little secret. Why didn't you just come out and tell me about her?"

His eyes locked in on her, and it was clear he wouldn't let her off the hook. She could tell him she was charmed and mesmerized by him. But that would only compound the problem. Her palms began to sweat. "You're not going to like it."

"I've liked nothing about his evening, so why stop now?"

Ouch, another sharp blow. She felt something for Adam Chase, and it hadn't been one-sided. But that was beside the point. "Rose is precious to me. She's all I have left of my sister and she's an amazing, beautiful, smart baby. I'd die for her, Adam. I couldn't just turn her over to a stranger. I had to get to know you as a person."

"Those nosy questions you kept asking me."

She nodded. "But you gave nothing away about yourself. I mean, other than you're a brilliant architect and you're pretty handy with a first aid kit."

A low guttural laugh crept out of his mouth. The sound

made her skin crawl. "You've got to be kidding? You were judging me? If Rose is my baby, where do you come off not telling me immediately?"

She had to make him see her logic. Certainly, he wouldn't condemn her for her actions. He had to see she had the baby's welfare at heart. "It's only because I was trying to protect Rose. Think about it, Adam. All I knew about you is that you had a one-night stand with my sister. That doesn't make you father material. I had to make sure you weren't—"

"What? An ax murderer? A criminal?" Blood rose to his tanned cheeks.

She nodded slowly. "Well…maybe," she squeaked. "I had to know you weren't a jerk or a loser or something."

His eyes widened.

Stop talking now, Mia.

"So you made yourself my judge and jury? Did I pass your test? I must have…since you practically let me—" His eyes roamed over her disheveled dress. "Never mind." He pushed his fingers through his hair. "I can't believe this."

"I was going to tell you tonight. I had it all planned, but then we kept getting interrupted."

"If I hadn't stepped on that toy, I might never have learned the truth."

"That you have a daughter?"

"Whether this child is actually mine remains to be seen. I meant I would've never found out what a liar you are."

He grabbed his jacket from the sofa and strode toward the front door. Handling the knob, he stopped and stared at the door, refusing to look at her another second. "Bring her over in the morning. If you don't show, I'll come for her myself."

"We'll be there, Adam."

He walked out, and the sound of the door slamming made her embattled body jump.

So far her "daddy test" plan was an epic fail.

Five

Adam gazed out his bedroom window to view overcast morning skies. His eyes burned like the devil. He shut them and flopped back against his mattress. "Ow."

Hammers pounded away in his skull, but he'd have to ignore the rumble. He had more pressing things to think about than his hungover state. He'd had too much mind-numbing vodka last night. In just a few hours, he'd come face-to-face with Mia again. The conniver. The liar. The woman who'd deceived him for days. He'd let down his guard, just like he had with Jacqueline, and look how that had ended. He'd given her his heart and trust and shortly after, she'd broken it off with him, falling madly in love with his brother instead. Nice.

He pinched the bridge of his nose and filled his lungs with air.

And now Mia claimed he'd fathered her sister's child. He didn't trust Mia D'Angelo as far as he could toss her. But the baby was another matter. If she was his, he'd make things right. Last night, before he'd taken to drink, he'd put the wheels in motion to find out his legal rights in all this. And to find out who Mia really was.

He remembered more and more about the night he'd shared with Anna. It had been on the anniversary of his sister's death, some twenty years ago. He'd gone out, because staying in always made him think too hard about Lily and then the guilt would come. So he'd escaped to the museum and had met an equally lonely woman and they'd had a nice time. Nothing too earth-shattering, and, afterward, they'd both agreed it was best not to see each other again. No phone numbers were exchanged. They'd barely known each other's names. It had been an impetuous fling.

A knock at the door sounded loudly. "It's Mary. I brought you something to make you feel better."

"Come in." He sat up. His head was splitting like an ax to logs. The tomato drink flagged with a celery stem popped into his line of vision. "I thought you might need this."

How did she always know what he needed?

"I saw an empty Grey Goose bottle on the counter and figured this might be a welcome sight this morning."

"Thanks. It's exactly what I need."

She handed him the glass. "Bad night? Or an extremely good one?"

He took a sip. "Might be a little bit of both. Take a seat." He gestured to the chair by the window. "I have something to tell you. We're going to have two visitors today…"

Two hours later, Adam walked out of his bedroom showered and dressed in a pair of jeans and an aqua-blue polo shirt. He was too keyed up to eat breakfast and his head-shredding hangover didn't allow his usual morning swim. Instead, he grabbed a mug of coffee and wandered outside. He walked to the outer edge of his stone patio and gazed at the steady waves pounding the shore. He sipped coffee, staring out.

The last time he'd thought about fatherhood, he was getting ready to ask Jacqueline to marry him. He'd fallen hard for her and thought they were in tune with one another. So much so, he'd wanted to spend the rest of his life with her. But life never turned out as expected. He'd been shell-shocked when Jacqueline broke it off with him. Shortly after, he'd accidentally found out she'd fallen in love with Brandon.

There'd be no marriage. No family with Jacqueline for him.

As it turned out, Brandon hadn't lasted long with Jacqueline. She'd left him three years later, after a tumultuous relationship, and finally married a college professor. She was living a quiet life on the East Coast now. His mother had given him the scoop, though he kept telling her it wasn't any of his business anymore.

Now his every thought revolved around being a father. A chill ran down his spine thinking of all the ways his life would change after meeting Rose. But first and foremost, he had to find out if she was his daughter.

Mary's voice from behind startled him. "Adam, they're here."

He pivoted around to see Mia holding the baby in her arms. Behind them, long sheer drapes flapped gently in the breeze, fanning around them as if framing the Madonna and her child. He held his breath; his limbs locked in place. They both wore pink, Mia in a long flowery summer skirt and a pale blouse. The baby, wrapped in a lightweight blanket with only her face peeking out, had sandy-blond hair. That was all he could see of her as he stood a good distance away. Mia gazed at the child she held, her eyes filled with love and adoration, and the sight of her again packed a wallop to his gut. She didn't look like the conniving liar he'd pegged her for last night. But he wouldn't be fooled again. Too much was at stake.

This could be a scam. Mia could be a gold digger. Maybe she'd conjured up all of this after learning about the fling he'd had with her sister. The baby might be an innocent pawn in the sick game she was playing. *Remember that, Adam.*

His gaze went to Mary, standing near them, her hand on her heart, her light eyes tender on the baby. "I'll take it from here, Mary. Thanks."

"Yes, thank you, Mary." The women exchanged a glance. "She's precious."

"Yes, she is," Mia responded.

"I'll leave you two to talk it out."

Adam waited for Mary to leave. Then he set the coffee mug down and strode the long steps toward them. Mia cradled the baby possessively, holding her haughty chin up, suddenly defiant. What did she think he'd do, wrestle the baby out of her arms and banish her from his house forever?

He faced Mia and swiveled his head to see the baby's face. Soft gray eyes, circled with a hint of sky blue, looked up at him. Adam's heart lurched. Oh, God, she did have his eyes.

"This is Rose."

He nodded, his throat tight.

"She was born on May first."

Mia unfolded the blanket, showing him her chubby little body outfitted in a frilly cotton-candy-colored dress. Ruffles seemed to swallow her up. Her little shoes and socks matched her dress. "She weighed seven pounds, seven ounces. She's almost doubled her birth weight now."

"She's a beauty," he found himself saying. His child or not, he couldn't deny the truth. "Let's get her inside the house."

"Good idea. She's probably going to need a diaper change soon. She feels a little wet."

Adam gestured for her to go first. She stepped inside the kitchen. He pressed a button on the wall and the sliding doors glided shut. "Where do you want to change her?"

"Mary said she put her diaper bag in the living room."

"In here," he said and moved ahead of her.

She followed him down the hallway and into a room he barely used, filled with sofas, tables and artwork. A bank of French doors opened out in a semicircle to a view of the shoreline.

"Mary says I don't use this room enough," he muttered,

lifting the diaper bag overflowing with blankets, bottles, rattles and diapers. "All this stuff is hers?"

"That's only part of it."

Mia's lips twitched, not quite making it to a smile. Her eyes were swollen and her usual healthy-looking skin tone had turned to paler shades.

"Where do you want to change her?" asked Adam.

"On the floor always works. She's starting to roll and move a lot. It's safer for her than putting her on the sofa where she might topple. Hand me a diaper and a wipe out of there, please?"

Adam dug into the bag, pulling the items out, while she kneeled onto the floor, laid the baby's blanket down and then placed Rose on top of it. "That's right my little Sweet Cheeks—we're going to clean you right up."

The baby gave her a toothless grin and Adam had to smile. She was a charmer. Mia pressed a kiss to the top of her forehead. "Bloomers off first," she said, pushing them down beautifully chunky legs. "Now your diaper."

The baby kicked and cooed, turning her inquisitive little body to and fro. Something caught his eye on the back of her leg as the ruffles of her dress pulled up. A set of light brown markings, triangular in shape, stained her skin on her upper back thigh. Mia laid a hand on her stomach to hold her still while she cleaned the area with a diaper wipe. Adam kneeled down beside her to get a better look at that mark. He pointed to her thigh. "What's that on the back of her leg?"

Mia rolled the baby over ever so gently to show him. "This? It's nothing. The pediatrician said it's a birthmark. She said it'll fade in time and would be hardly noticeable."

Adam drew a deep breath. "I see."

The birthmark caught him by surprise. Up until now he hadn't been convinced about Rose's bloodlines. Gray-blue eyes were rare but not proof enough. But a family birthmark? Now that wasn't something he could ignore.

He'd been born with the exact marking in the same location, upper back thigh. Adam's father had had it, but as far as he knew, Lily and Brandon had escaped that particular branding. "I have the same birthmark, Mia."

Her eyes flickered.

"I still want a DNA test." His attorney had told him it was a must. For legal reasons, he needed medical proof. "But now I know for sure. Rose is my child."

The moment had finally come. Adam understood he was Rose's father. The birthmark she hadn't given a thought to had convinced Adam. Mia wanted this, but where did they go from here? How should they proceed? Adam hadn't said much of anything as to his plans. He'd asked countless questions about Rose, though. What was she like? Did she sleep through the night right away? Had she ever been ill? What foods did she like to eat?

Calmly and patiently she answered his questions as they sat on the sofa that faced the Pacific Ocean. Adam gawked as Mia fed the baby a bottle of formula.

He reached out to touch her hair, wrapping a finger around a blond curl. "She's been good, hasn't she?"

"She's usually very good. Not too many things upset her. She only makes a peep when she's tired. I rock her to sleep and that calms her."

"Do you sing to her?"

"I try. Thank goodness she's not a critic."

Adam laughed, a rich wholesome sound that would've had her smiling, if the situation was something to smile about.

"When she's done with her bottle, I'd like to hold her."

Mia drew breath into her lungs. The thought of handing her over to Adam, if only for a little while, turned her stomach. Soon she'd lose Rose to him forever. She had a right to see her from time to time, but it wouldn't be the same as raising her, day in and day out. Nothing would be the same.

Oh, how her heart ached. "Sure."

The baby slurped the last drops of formula, and Mia sat her on her lap and burped her, explaining to Adam how to do it in an upright position. The baby belched a good one, and she smiled. "That's my little trouper."

She hugged Rose to her chest, kissed her forehead and turned to Adam. "Are you ready?"

"Yes, but keep in mind, I haven't held a baby since my sister was born. And then I was only a kid."

"Just put your arms out, and let me give her to you."

He did just that, and she placed Rose into his arms. "She holds her head up now all by herself, but just make sure she doesn't wobble."

Mia positioned Adam's hand under the baby's neck and extended his fingers. Adam darted a glance at her. Their eyes connected for a second, and then he was focused back on the baby.

Rose squirmed in his arms, her face flushed tomato red. And then her mouth opened, and she let out an ear-piercing wail.

Adam snapped his head to her for help. "What do I do?"

"Try rocking her."

He did. It didn't help.

"What am I doing wrong?" he asked.

She didn't know. Usually Rose wasn't fussy. "Nothing. She doesn't know you."

Her wails grew louder and louder, and Mia's belly ached hearing her so unhappy.

"Maybe that's enough for right now," she said, reaching for the baby.

Adam was more than willing to give her back. "Hell, I don't know what I did to upset her."

"Please don't swear around the baby. And you did nothing wrong."

Mia put her onto her shoulder and rocked her. She stopped crying.

Adam shook his head. "Okay. What now?"

"Well, I'm due at First Clips in a little while. Rose and I should get going."

Adam's gaze touched upon the baby, a soft gleam shining in his eyes. He opened his mouth to say something, and then he clamped it shut. Was he going to refuse to let Rose leave? That could never happen. He wasn't properly equipped to have a baby here. And clearly he didn't know what to do with her. "I want to see her tomorrow. I want her to know me."

"I'll stop by again. Same time?"

He nodded and then helped her pack up the baby's stuff. He looked on fascinated as she strapped Rose into the car seat. "You'll have to teach me how to do that."

"It's not that hard." A man who designed state-of-the-art houses shouldn't find it a challenge to buckle a baby up. "Tomorrow, you'll fasten her in."

"All right."

She slung the shoulder bag over her shoulder and Adam lifted the bucket, walking her outside to her car. On the way out, little Rose peered up, watching him holding the handles of her car seat, and squawked out several complaints. Once at the car, they made an exchange. He took the diaper bag off her arms and she lifted the bucket onto its base and snapped it in, giving it a tug to make sure it was in tight. "There you go, little one."

"The baby rides backwards?" Adam asked.

"Until she's much older, yes."

He shrugged. "I guess there's a lot to learn."

"Tell me about it. I was petrified when I first took Rose home from Edward's house. It was a hard day for everyone."

Adam glanced at Rose again. Maybe he didn't have much sympathy for what she'd gone through, losing her sister, telling Edward the truth and then raising Rose these past months, but she'd done what she thought was right.

"I'll call you tonight," Adam said.

"Why?"

"She's my daughter, Mia. I've already missed enough time with her." There was no mistaking his condemning tone. He held her guilty as charged. "I want to know everything about her."

Yes, she was right. No sympathy.

She drove off his property as he stood in the driveway, hands in his pockets, watching her drive away and looking like he'd lost his best friend.

"Morning, Mia. Bad news. The rocket ship's on the fritz again." Sherry greeted her at the back entrance of First Clips and opened the screen door for her. Situated in the heart of the Third Street Promenade, the shop catered to an elite clientele of children from ages one to twelve years. "How about I watch the baby while you do your magic on that crazy machine."

Mia sighed. "I wish you and Rena would learn how to fix the darn thing. It's just a matter of replacing shorted fuses."

"I can calm a kid and cut hair on the wildest child, Mia, but you know I'm not good with mechanics. Luckily, our next client isn't due for another fifteen minutes. And she'll be sitting on the princess throne."

Baby Rose loved to watch the lights flicker on and off on the First Starship seat but she also loved the shiny tiaras and lighted wands the girls played with while seated on the Princess Throne.

Mia handed Sherry the handle to the baby's car seat. "Here you go. Auntie Sherry will watch you while I make all the pretty lights work again."

"Hello there, Rosey Posey. How's my little angel today?"

Rose cooed at her aunt Sherry. Today Sherry wore a

carnation-pink chambermaid costume with white ruffle sleeves. Her thick blond hair was up in a fancy do and she looked fit to coif the hair of the finest royalty. Sherry was a stylist extraordinaire.

Mia set about fixing the dashboard on the rocket ship. It took her all of five minutes to replace the fuses, and when the mission was accomplished she found Sherry rocking Rose to sleep in her office, which doubled as the baby's nursery. "Shh…she's out," Sherry whispered. "Sweet little thing." Sherry lowered her into the playpen as Mia looked on.

Sherry and Mia strolled into a small lounge that consisted of a cushy leather sofa and a counter with a coffee machine on top and a small refrigerator underneath.

"She's such a doll," Sherry said.

Mia smiled, grabbing two mugs and setting them out. "For everyone but her father." Steam rose up as she poured the coffee. She handed Sherry a cup, took her own and they both sat down. They held their mugs in their laps.

"Still? It's been how many days?"

"Today makes four. She's not warming to him, and I think he's really frustrated. He thinks if she sees him for more than an hour or two, she'll get used to him. And he has to get used to her, too. He's very unsure when he's holding her."

"It doesn't seem like a wealthy guy like that would be unsure of anything."

Mia sipped her coffee. "Babies are in a category all their own. They throw most men off-kilter. Doesn't matter how powerful or rich they are, there's something about babies that frighten them. They think of them as fragile little creatures."

"My brother has a six-month rule," Sherry said. "He won't hold a baby until they're sturdy little beings."

"What about little Beau? Did he back off from holding his own son?"

"He made an exception for Beau, but he still waited a good couple of weeks before he held him."

"Wow."

"I know. Me? I couldn't wait to get my hands on Beau. And you know how I feel about Rose. I love her like she's my own niece."

"I know, Sherry. She loves you, too. You're her auntie Sherry."

"I love that. So what about Adam?"

"What do you mean?"

"Well, you said he doesn't venture out much, he's sort of a recluse and he's got his head stuck in a computer all day. So, is he a geek?"

A sound rumbled up from her chest. "Not at all."

An image of Adam striding out of the ocean, toned and tanned, shoulders broad, arms powerful, beads of water sliding down his body as he made his way to her, wouldn't leave her head alone.

Rena stepped into the room wearing a metallic silver jumpsuit with triangular collar flaps. She was the First Starship captain. "Oh I came just in time." She poured herself a cup of coffee. "Tell us more about Adam."

"You know all there is to tell," Mia said. "As soon as he found out who I really was, he turned off completely. Shut me down. He's only interested in Rose. And right now she's not cooperating with him. It's sort of sad, seeing the disappointment in his eyes every time we leave."

"Turned off, completely? Does that mean he was turned *on* at one point?" Sherry asked.

Mia rubbed at the corner of her eyes, stretching the skin to her temples. She hadn't told her friends about her dates with Adam or the kisses they'd shared. Or the way he'd made her come undone on her living room sofa that night. It seemed like eons and not days ago since that happened. She couldn't tell Gram the details of what had transpired with Adam that night. Goodness no. "Well, maybe. As I told you before, we spent some time together. I was trying to get to know what kind of person he was and, yes, judging him to see if he was worthy of Rose."

"You had every right," Sherry said.

"You couldn't just drop her off and hope for the best," Rena said.

"Thanks for the support. It means the world to me, but, unfortunately, Adam doesn't see it that way. And well, I thought we might have had something pretty special."

Two sets of eyes pierced her, waiting for juicy news.

She went on. "Let's just say on a scale of one to ten, our date was an eleven. I know enough to believe it wasn't one-sided. He is very charming when he lets down his guard."

"You didn't tell us you went on a date!" Rena said.

"Was it flowers and chocolates?" Sherry asked.

"More like an amazing dinner and lots of dancing," she explained.

"Holding tight. Whispers in the ear?" Rena asked.

Mia nodded.

"And good-night kisses?"

"Oh yes, delicious good-night kisses."

"Mia, did you do it with him?" Sherry asked, darting a bright-eyed glance at Rena.

"Of course not." But almost, she wanted to add. Something made her hold that part back. She wasn't ready to tell them she'd come close to giving Adam her heart and her body that night. She'd lost her head and been fully consumed with passion. Had it been desperation that drove her or something else?

Their shoulders slumped; the fire in their eyes snuffed out. Her love life disappointed her friends. Oh well, what could she say? It disappointed her, too.

"He's filthy rich," Rena said.

"And rock-star handsome," Sherry added. "We wouldn't blame you."

"Or judge you," Rena said. "You've had it rough lately."

"You guys are the best. But he's Rose's father. And I have to watch my step from now on. Her future is on the line. That's all that matters to me right now."

"You're late." Adam grumbled, opening her car door for her.

His *pleasant* greeting grated on her already shot nerves. "Only by fifteen minutes. It's Friday night. There was a ton of traffic on the PCH." She climbed out of the driver's seat, taking the diaper bag with her.

Adam scratched his head. "If you'd let me have a car pick you up, we wouldn't run into this problem."

"Adam, we've been over this. Does your car drive *over* traffic? Because if you had one that did, I'm sure it would replace the Rolls in your gallery."

Adam's mouth clamped shut. A tic worked at his jaw. He didn't like her attitude? Well, she wasn't crazy about his. This was her third stop today. She'd worked long hours, then rushed out of the salon just so she could get here on time. She'd hit bad traffic, which was no joy. And when she'd pulled up to his house, he was waiting for her outside like an irate parent, his displeasure written on the tight planes of his face. Where was that beautiful man she'd met on the beach?

"Come inside," he said.

He reached for the handle of the baby seat but thought better of it. Rose was awake, her gaze glued to his. One false move could start her on a crying jag. Once again, disappointment touched his eyes as he took the diaper bag off her shoulder and grabbed her purse. She followed him inside to the living area. It was after six, a beautiful time of day at the beach. The sun was fading and a glow of low burning light flowed in through the bank of opened French doors. A slight breeze blew into the room, ruffling the leaves on the indoor plants.

"If it's cold for the baby, I can shut the doors."

"No, this is fine. She's been inside all day. She could use a little air." And so could she. Her nerves were frazzled and the temperature was just right to cool off her rising impatience with Adam.

Once they were situated, Mia unfastened Rose from her restraints and picked her up. "There we go, Sweet Cheeks." Mia kissed both of the baby's cheeks, and Rose opened her mouth to form a wide toothless smile. Then she propped the baby on her lap and cradled her in the crook of her elbow.

Adam looked on. Longing was etched on his perfect features, and a twinge of guilt and sorrow touched her heart. He wanted to bond with Rose so badly, and she was having none of it.

"I'd like to hold her," Adam said.

"Okay. Come sit down next to me first."

He did. The scent of him—sand and surf and musk—packed a wallop. He was a towering presence beside her. If only she wasn't so darn attracted to him. "Let's give her a few minutes."

"Okay."

"Talk to me. Let her get used to the sound of your voice again." They'd done this before, and it hadn't worked. Maybe tonight it would make a difference.

"What would you like to know?"

"Everything. But you can start by telling me how your day went."

Adam hesitated. His face was pinched tight. She pictured the debate going on in his head before he finally agreed to open up. "Well, I took my usual swim this morning, after you left."

"Don't you swim just after dawn?"

"I'm a stickler about that, yes. But I woke up later than usual today and I didn't want to miss seeing Rose."

"How far did you swim this morning?"

He glanced at the baby. Rose's eyes were intent on him. It was uncanny how she measured him.

"Four miles."

"Four? I thought you usually did about three?"

"I, uh, had a little more energy to work off this morning."

"Why?"

He glanced at Rose.

"Oh." Rose had been unusually clingy and wouldn't let Adam get anywhere near her.

He didn't say more. "So then, what did you do after your swim?"

He lifted his head and stroked his chin thoughtfully. "My mother called."

"How nice. Do you speak with her often?"

"About once a week. It was a short conversation."

How she missed her own mother and the conversations they used to have. With Anna and her mother gone, she had only Gram. Her grandmother was wonderful, and Rose's arrival had given Mia's life more purpose.

"After that it was business as usual. I did some drafting, took a few calls. Went into the office for a few hours and got home in time to meet you."

"You didn't hesitate to scold me about being late."

Adam shot her a glance, bounded up from the sofa and walked over to the French doors, running his hands through his hair. Turning to her, his eyes were two tormented storm clouds. "Look, I'm sorry about that. I was worried about her. Do you have any idea how much I want to be a part of her life? I've already missed her first four months. I don't want to miss any more time with her."

She nodded. "Okay. I can understand that."

"Well, that makes me feel a whole lot better that you understand I want to know my daughter. I want to love and protect her."

"Adam."

"Let me hold her, Mia."

"Let's play a game with her first. She loves peekaboo. It might make her warm up to you."

"All right, fine." He softened his tone. "How do we do that?"

"I'll show you." She laid the baby down on a blanket on the floor. "Want to play peekaboo, Sweet Cheeks?" Rose's eyes followed her movement as if anticipating something more fun than a diaper change. "Come down here with me, Adam."

Adam scooted next to her, his thigh brushing hers as he positioned himself. Her body zinged immediately, which annoyed her. He didn't think much of her these days, and she should get the hint already. "Reach over to the bag and hand me a receiving blanket," she ordered.

Adam rummaged through her bag and came up with one. "This good?"

"Yes, thank you," she said and softened her tone. "Now watch."

Mia brought the blanket very close to Rose's face and left it there for three seconds so that she couldn't see them, and then quickly removed it. "Peekaboo!"

Rose broke out in cackles. It was the sweetest sound.

"See, she loves this game. Now you do it, Adam." She handed him the blanket.

"Okay, I'll give it a try. Here we go."

Adam repeated the same moves. "Peekaboo!"

Rose stared at him, her mouth curving up slightly, but no real smile emerged. Her legs were kick, kick, kicking. It was something she did when she was excited.

"Try it again. At least she's not crying."

"Okay."

He went through the peekaboo ritual again. The baby studied him. Her inquisitive eyes roamed over his face as if she couldn't quite figure him out. Mia felt like she had the same problem.

"I'm going to pick her up now," Adam said. He bent

and gently lifted her, cradling the back of her head and her buttocks. "That's it, little Rose," he said, carefully rising with her in his arms.

As if Rose finally realized what was happening, she turned abruptly in his arms, her body stretching out, stiffening up. Adam caught her before she wiggled free of his hold. She reached for Mia, her arms extended and pleading. Then she let out a scream.

Mia jumped up. "Rose!"

Adam held her back, firming up his grip. "Let me hold her, Mia. I'll walk her around and talk to her. She can't cry forever."

Mia bit her lip. Her stomach ached. It was torture hearing Rose cry and seeing her desperately reaching for her. "It might be longer than you think."

"Be positive, Mia. Isn't that what you tell me?"

"But she's crying for me."

"Maybe she wouldn't if she didn't see you. I'll take her in to see Mary."

He headed toward the kitchen, gently bouncing the baby in his arms. "Sing to her," she called to him. "She loves music."

Adam nodded and walked out of the room. She closed her eyes. But that only concentrated the baby's screeching cries over Adam's rendition of "Old McDonald Had a Farm." Her heart lurched, and she bit down on her lower lip to keep from calling to her.

She couldn't stand it.

She walked over to the French doors and stepped outside.

Mia sat across from a stony-faced Adam at the dinner table. Mary had left for the day, and Rose slept on her blankets on the floor of the living room. Mia pushed chicken Florentine around on her plate. Mary had outdone herself today with the meal, but Adam's quelling silence soured her stomach of any appetite she might've had.

He sipped wine, a fine Shiraz that went well with the meal. But Adam hadn't touched his food, either. He stared off, his gaze on the shoreline and the high tide rising. A gentle breeze blew by, coming in through the expanse of the open kitchen area, and she shuddered.

Adam glanced at her. She shook her head—she wasn't cold.

Not from the winds anyway.

"She wouldn't go to Mary, either," Adam said, mystified. "And Mary is good with children."

"I know. I heard Mary trying to calm her."

"She cried for twenty minutes in my arms. I tried everything."

He had. He'd sung out of tune to her. He'd bounced her. He'd taken her outside to see the beach. Then he'd sat down on a glider and swayed back and forth, trying to keep her from squirming out of his arms. Mia had hidden herself from the baby's sight and stolen quick glances. She couldn't help worrying over Rose. She'd taken care of her every need for four solid months. It had been a very hard twenty minutes, seeing the baby's anguish and knowing she needed her aunt Mia.

"She's too attached to you, Mia."

She jumped at his comment. "What does that mean?"

"It means that I want my daughter to know me. And that's not happening right now."

"Give it time, Adam."

"You keep saying that. How much time? The longer she's with you and you alone, the more attached she'll become. Isn't that obvious?"

"No, it's not obvious. She'll warm up to you. These are new surroundings, and she's only known you for a few days. She's fine with Rena and Sherry at the salon. She goes to them—so I know it's not just me she wants."

"Is it supposed to make me feel better knowing my daughter will go to perfect strangers, but she won't let her own father hold her, not even for a minute, without exercising her very healthy lungs?"

"Rena and Sherry are not perfect strangers. They are her family."

Adam's face reddened. "I'm her family, Mia."

Oh man. This evening wasn't going well. Her stomach lurched. Dread crept along her spine and knotted her nerves.

He bounded up and pushed his hands through his hair. He always did that when he was agitated. Several sandy-blond strands stood straight up, but Adam could get away with that look. It was appealing on him, a little muss to disrupt his perfectly groomed appearance.

"There's only one solution, Mia."

Her throat constricted. She buttoned her lips.

"Rose has to live here with me."

Oh God. Oh God. Oh God.

Her worst fears were coming true. She knew this day would eventually come, but hearing him say it ripped her apart. "No."

"No? Mia, she belongs with me. I've already missed so much time with her. Four months to be exact. I may not be a perfect father to her right now, but I've got to keep trying. I know if she's here, she'll come to accept me quicker. You can visit her any time you'd like. It's a promise."

Her eyes burned; the tears threatening to flow were white-hot flames. Her body shook, her lips quivering. "No, Adam. I can't leave her."

Adam watched her carefully. This was so hard. She tried to be brave, to put up a good front, but she was ready to fall apart. Any second now, she'd shatter into a mass of tears.

"I'll hire you on as a babysitter," he said, softer.

"A babysitter?" What was he saying? She sobered a little. Grabbing the table for support, she rose on wobbly legs. She couldn't sit still another second. "You want to pay me to take care of my beautiful niece? My own flesh and blood?"

"Hell Mia, do you have a better idea?"

"I already have a job, thank you very much. I own First Clips. I'm needed there."

His lips tightened to a thin line. His eyes became two stormy gray clouds. A battle seemed to rage inside his head. Seconds ticked by. Finally, he sighed as if he'd lost something treasured. "Fine, then. Just move in with me."

"M-move in with you? You couldn't possibly want that."

A wry laugh rumbled from his chest. "I don't see that I have a choice. If I want Rose here..."

"Then you're stuck with me, is that what you were going to say?"

"Don't put words in my mouth, Mia." He gave his head a shake. "You don't have any idea how important this is to me, or I wouldn't even consider inviting you into my home."

"But we'd be living together."

She caught his shudder. No, he didn't want this any more than she did.

"It's a big house," he countered, "and a solution to our problem. You both move in. You can come and go as you please, and I'll be able to see Rose whenever I want. She'll be here every day and night. And she'll come to accept me."

"I don't know," Mia said, stalling. The idea was sprung on her so quickly, she needed time to think it through.

"Mia, it's the only way to ease Rose into this transition more comfortably. It's best for her."

She didn't know if that was true. Adam wasn't thrilled with having her live with him. How could he be? It wasn't for romantic reasons. For all she knew, he hated her or at best resented her for the lies she'd told.

"I don't know if I can do it, Adam."

"And I don't see that we have any other choice. You want to be with Rose as much as I do."

"I know she's your daughter and you want to get to know her, but I don't understand why you are so insistent about this since you're clearly not comfortable around babies."

He stared at her, or rather, stared straight through her as if thinking hard about her question.

Finally, he sighed. "I have my reasons."

She shrugged, palms out gesturing to him for an answer.

"It's personal."

Of course. How could she believe he'd give her an upfront honest reason. That would mean he'd have to divulge something about himself.

She didn't see that she had any choice in the matter. "When and for how long?"

"Move in by the end of the week." He blinked, and then added, "We'll have to take it one day at a time from there."

She gulped.

"Just say yes, Mia."

It probably *was* the best solution for Rose. And Mia couldn't give her up cold turkey. She'd be getting what she ultimately wanted, a chance to keep Rose with her most of the time. Nothing would change other than her location. They'd just hang their hats at this gorgeous beach house instead of at her small apartment.

Her mouth opened and she heard a squeak come out. "Yes?"

Adam nodded, satisfied.

But just as he turned away, a shadow of fear entered his eyes.

The recluse's life was about to change dramatically.

And so was hers.

Six

The guest room on the second story of Adam's home was amazing. It wasn't cozy like her own bedroom, but she could certainly make do with the king-size bed, bulky light wood furniture and much more square footage than she'd need for her yoga workouts. There was a one-drawer desk by the window, a view of the ocean she couldn't complain about, a lovely white brick fireplace and a sixty-inch flat-screen television hanging on the wall. All her clothes would fit into two dresser drawers and one-tenth of the walk-in closet. Adam had let her choose her room and she'd chosen the one that suited her tastes the most. Namely, it was right next door to Rose's nursery.

"Oh listen, Rose. Hear the big trucks? They are coming with your brand-new furniture." Propped on pillows on the bed, Rose kicked her legs and watched her put her clothes away in the closet. The baby was learning how to roll, though she hadn't quite gotten the hang of it yet. Even so, Mia kept an eye on her every second. It was a long way down to the floor for a four-month-old.

Last night, Adam had enlisted her help in picking out nursery items the baby would need from a catalog, including a crib and dresser. Less than twenty-four hours later, they had arrived. Through the magic of…Chase money.

She sighed, although she was glad Adam insisted on buying Rose all new furniture. The baby deserved as much and it meant that Mia could keep Rose's nursery intact at her apartment for those times, if ever, she would take Rose there.

With a fold and a tuck, the last of her sweaters were stacked neatly into the dresser drawer. As she closed the drawer slowly with the flat of her hands, a shiver coursed through her body. Her future was uncertain. She'd been driven out of one home already. How long before Adam added to her pain? How long before she felt like that same unwanted, sullied guest that had overstayed her welcome and been asked to leave? And how could she leave Rose?

Grandma Tess hadn't taken the news lightly of Mia moving into Adam Chase's mansion. Mia had put a happy face on it, trying not to worry Gram with her own doubts. Gram didn't want her getting hurt. There'd been enough heartache in their family recently. Mia couldn't disagree. But she did point out the obvious. Adam was Rose's legal father—the DNA test results had come back positive—and he could provide Rose with a great future.

Sherry and Rena had a different opinion. They saw her move as an opportunity for Mia to spruce up her nonexistent love life. Mia had been dating the vice president of a financial firm six months ago, and her two pals had been sorely disappointed to learn that she'd broken it off with him weeks later. He'd been a player, fooling with women's hearts. Mia recognized the signs and the lies immediately. And she wanted none of those games. She'd seen what her mother had gone through, putting up with her father. Mia didn't want to make the same mistake. Rena and Sherry saw moving in with the mysterious, deadly handsome Adam Chase as a romantic adventure. Mia only saw it as a necessity. He'd given her no other option.

A sudden quiet knocking broke into her thoughts. She turned to the door she'd left partially open, and Adam popped his head inside. "How's it going?"

"We're doing fine. I'm just about unpacked."

Adam glanced at the baby on the bed. "May I come in?"

She nodded.

He took a few steps inside and gave the room a once-over, his gaze stopping on the items she'd put on the dresser—a framed photo of her mother and Gram in the early days and another of her holding the baby along with her gal pals at First Clips—then walked over to the bed, making eye contact with Rose.

She'd thought better of putting out Anna's picture right now, but she would eventually give it to Rose. The child had a right to know all about her mother.

"The movers are downstairs, ready to come up," he said, turning to her. "Would you mind showing them where you'd like everything to go?" He shrugged. "I haven't got a clue."

The irony hit her hard. The master designer needed help arranging baby furniture. "I can do that."

"Great."

Mia bent and gathered Rose into her arms. "Come on, Sweet Cheeks. We're gonna see your new digs."

Adam's lips twitched and a beam of love glistened in his eyes. He reached his hand out as if to stroke the baby's head, then retracted it quickly.

Mia pretended not to notice.

Thirty minutes later the movers were gone and the nursery was almost all set up. She sat on a glider, entertaining Rose with a game of patty-cake while Adam sat cross-legged on the floor staring at screws and nuts and wooden slats of the crib he'd laid out. "So you're telling me you put Rose's crib together all by yourself?" He spared her a glance over his shoulder.

"I sure did."

He scoured over the small-print instructions for all of ten seconds, his brows gathering. "I see."

"What?" she asked. "If a mere woman can do it, you should be able to knock it out without a problem?"

"I didn't say that," he said, his tone light.

She chuckled. "It was implied. I'm curious—why didn't you have the movers set it up?"

He swiveled around to face them, those gray eyes soft now on the baby. "It's the least I can do for Rose. A father usually sets up his baby's crib, doesn't he?"

A lump formed in her throat. Her heart grew suddenly heavy. The man who had everything wanted to do something meaningful for his child. "Y-yes. I suppose he does."

He nodded and turned back to his task.

"I'll put her sheets and towels into the wash," she said, rising. "They'll be ready for her tonight."

"Mary's got that covered."

"But does she have the right—"

"She raised three children," Adam said. "She knows all about laundering baby clothes."

"Oh, right. Okay."

"If you don't mind, I'd like you to stay in here until I get this thing put together."

"Don't mind at all. I can lend a hand if you get confused."

Adam turned to her. She grinned ear to ear and the frown on his face disappeared. Gosh, the man almost cracked a smile. "Smart aleck."

The house was finally quiet of noises that would fill his life from now on. Rose playing with her toys, Rose taking a bath, Rose crying for her bottle. Adam breathed a sigh of relief. This was his daughter's first official night in her home. He'd built the crib she was sleeping in now, his heart bursting as he looked at her small chest rising and falling with steady breaths.

Assembling the crib hadn't been too much of a challenge after all. His only struggle had been afterward, when he'd discovered eight leftover screws and bolts. He'd checked over the crib twice, pulling and tugging at it, testing the sturdy factor and only after Mia told him that the same thing had happened to her he relaxed about it. The leftovers, she said, are either spares or a result of incompetence on the manufacturer's part. Either way, she'd given him her seal of approval on the crib.

And somehow, that had mattered to him.

Adam touched a small curl on Rose's head. If only he could bend over and kiss her sweet cheeks, wish her a good-night the way a father should. But he couldn't chance waking her and, worse yet, having her scream mercilessly at him.

She'd warm up to him. She had to. How long could he go without holding his own child?

He'd been given a second chance with Rose. He'd do better than he had with Lily. His sister had counted on him and when he'd let her down, it had cost her her life. That pain was always with him and drove him to the outskirts of life. He vowed solemnly not to ever let Rose down. Raising her, he'd try to make up for his failures with Lily and then maybe, he'd find a way to forgive himself.

Having Mia move into the house seemed like the only solution to keep Rose happy and content while living under his roof. For Rose's sake, he'd do anything to make up for lost time. Neither he nor Mia wanted it this way, but for all his business smarts and college degrees, he couldn't figure a way around it.

The architect couldn't draft a better design than the plan he'd come up with, so now he had two new females living under his roof.

Adam left his sleeping daughter and walked downstairs to the kitchen. Mary was long gone. She'd been smitten by Rose and had stayed longer than usual to make sure all was right with the nursery. Rose hadn't warmed to her either yet. Seemed she was all about Mia right now.

He dropped two ice cubes into a tumbler and poured himself a shot of vodka. Stepping outside, the cool salty air aroused his senses and he inhaled deeply. It was cleansing and peaceful out here.

To his left, movement caught his eye. He found Mia standing at the outer rim of the veranda where a low white stone wall bordered the sand. She watched the waves bound upon the shore. And Adam watched her. Breezes lifted the hem of her loose-fitting blouse, her long dark hair whipping at her back, her feet bare. She looked beautiful in the moonlight, and Adam debated going to her. He couldn't trust her. The lies she'd told him, the deceit she'd employed that had gotten them all to this point, painted an indelible mark on his soul. He'd be a fool to let her get under his skin again.

And Adam Chase was no fool.

Yet, he was drawn to her... Something was pulling at him, urging him to walk toward her and not stop. He had to see her. To talk to her. It was unlike anything he'd ever felt before. He took the steps necessary to reach her.

His footfalls on the stone alerted her to his presence. She turned to him. "Adam."

"Can't sleep?"

She shook her head. "I'm kind of keyed up. All these changes." Her shoulder lifted. "You know what I mean?"

"I think I do."

He shook his glass and the ice clinked. "Would you like a drink?"

Her eyes dipped to his glass. "No thanks. It's late. I should go check on Rose."

"I just did. I was in there before I came outside. She's sleeping."

Mia held a remote video receiver in her hand. She glanced at it and nodded. "I can see that."

"A pretty cool invention," he said.

"The best. I don't know how I'd ever get more than five feet away from her room without it. Even so, I get up during the night to check on her. It's a habit. Like I said, I really should go in."

"Am I disturbing you, Mia?"

Her gaze drifted to his mouth, then those amazing eyes connected to his. "It's your house, Adam," she said softly. "I might ask you the same thing. For all I know, you might have a nightly ritual of having a drink outside by yourself."

"Just me and my thoughts, huh?" If she only knew the pains he went through not to think. Not to let the demons inside. He sipped vodka and sighed. "You don't have to walk around on eggshells while you're here. For now, this is your home. Do whatever you please." Under a beam of moonlight her smooth olive complexion appeared a few shades lighter. He remembered touching her face, the softness under his fingertips when he'd kissed her. "We're going to be seeing each other a lot. I mean, my main focus is Rose. I want her to get used to me."

She turned away from him. "I get it. You're stuck with me. If you want to see Rose, I come along with the deal. Is that what you're trying to say?"

"It's just fact, Mia. And I can think of a lot of worse things than being stuck with a gorgeous woman living under my roof."

Mia snapped her head around, her eyes sharp and searching, her lips trembling.

Just days after meeting her, she'd gotten to him. She'd warped his defenses and he'd let her in a little. She'd made him think long range…he hadn't been that happy in a long time. But the path she'd led him down was broken and dangerous. He was too careful a man to venture in that direction again.

Boisterous voices carried on the breeze and reached his ears. Adam peered down the shoreline and made out half a dozen teens tripping over themselves, slinging loud drunken words, many of them profane.

He grabbed Mia's hand. "Shh. Come with me," he said leading her into the shadows behind a five-seat sofa. "Duck down."

He slouched, tugging her with him. They landed on their butts on the cold stone.

"What are you doing?"

"Shh," he repeated. "Lower your voice. It's the kids who've been vandalizing the beach," he whispered. "I still owe them for leaving that broken bottle in the sand and hurting you."

"How can you be sure they're the same kids?"

"Doesn't matter. News travels fast. They'll put the word out not to come here anymore."

"So, what's the plan?"

"Come with me and I'll show you."

Moving through the shadows, they entered the house. Adam left Mia at the foot of the stairs. "I'll check on the baby on my way back," he said.

Three minutes later, dressed in shorts and running shoes, he nodded at Mia as he reached the bottom step. "Not a peep out of her. She's still sleeping. Come—follow me outside."

They stayed out of the light as they returned to the spot near the sofa. "Okay, here's what I want you to do. Give me five minutes and be sure to watch. You'll get a kick out of it."

Adam explained the plan. Then he slunk through the darkness to the house next door that he'd once leased to his friend, country superstar Zane Williams. Zane was gone now, living back in Texas with his fiancée, and the house was empty. Well out of view, he trekked down to the shoreline and began jogging along the bank, heading toward the kids. He came upon them appearing as a midnight runner working up a sweat and breathing hard. Just as he reached them, he dug his heels in the sand and hunched over, hands on knees, and pretended to be out of breath. "Hey…guys." A dozen eyes watched him. "Anybody…have…some water?"

"Water?" one of the kids said. "Does it look like we have water?"

The kid tipped his bottle and slurped down beer. Then the big shot slung the bottle and it whizzed right by Adam's head. A crash competed with the roar of the waves as the bottle shattered against a metal ice bucket. Shards of glass scattered onto the sand. Adam ground his teeth. Maybe he should call the police.

Then one curly-haired boy stepped up and a plastic bottle of water was pushed into his hand. "Here you go, man. Drink up. You look like you could really use this."

The kid had compassion in his eyes. Okay. No cops. They were just stupid kids. They couldn't be more than sixteen years old. "Hey, thanks a lot. You know," he said, rising to his height and uncapping the bottle. "Just a heads-up, but you should be more careful. I mean, coming here and boozing it up right under the nose of a retired police captain."

"What?" the big shot said. "No way."

"Yeah, he moved into that house a few weeks ago." He pointed to the empty house. "I see his wife outside most nights watching the waves as I run by."

The boy craned his head in that direction. "That's far away. I can't see anything. Which means they can't see us."

"Okay, suit yourself. But I hear the captain's a hard-ass about underage drinking. Just a warning to you. Thanks for the water." Adam began jogging away. A siren bellowed, the sound screaming and urgent, disrupting the quiet of the night. Adam turned and looked into the big shot's eyes, wide now and panicked, his innocent years showing on his frightened face. The boys jumped to attention, all six of them darting fearful glances at each other.

One of them shouted, "Run!"

And they flew out of there, leaving their booze behind, kicking up sand and bumping into each other as they dashed down the beach. They'd run a good mile before they'd stop. The run and fright alone should sober them up.

Adam jogged over to Mia, who came out of hiding, holding the siren in her hand. She turned it off. "Did you see them run?" he asked.

"I sure did. Wow. This thing sounds like the real deal. Where did you get it?"

"It's a long story, but it's from my lifeguarding days. Sounds authentic because basically it is." Adam glanced down the beach, his mouth beginning to twitch. He hadn't had that much fun in a while. "I doubt they'll ever come back. Some might've learned a lesson. I can only hope."

He turned to find Mia smiling at him, her eyes warm and gentle. His heart began to thump, and blood pumped hard and fast through his veins.

One smile. One gentle look.

It shouldn't be that easy for Mia to affect him.

"You did this because they hurt me?"

"Yeah," he admitted. "They shouldn't be drinking at their age. Disturbing the peace and—"

Her lips touched his cheek in a kiss that was chaste and thankful. Her hair smelled of sweet berries.

"Mia," he said, folding her into his embrace.

"Adam, what are you doing?"

He whispered, "If you're going to thank me, do it right."

Mia came up for air a minute later. Her lips were gently bruised from Adam's kisses. The taste of him still lingered on her mouth. As he held her in his arms under the moonlight, she trembled.

It was crazy. This couldn't happen. They had a tentative relationship at best, and throwing romance into the mix would complicate everything. Adam clearly wasn't her biggest fan, and yet how could she forget how wonderful those first few days had been between them, when he didn't know who she was or what she'd done?

She hadn't forgotten about how his touch once made her giddy. How, before the truth was revealed, she had been lost in the moment and had almost given herself to him. Good thing that hadn't happened,

"Now, that was a proper thank-you." His hot breath hovered over her lips and she thought he would kiss her again. And once again, she might not stop him.

The baby's cries interrupted him. "Rose," she said, reaching for the baby monitor on the sofa and glancing at it. "She's awake, Adam. Fussing around."

Adam took the monitor from her hand and also looked.

"I've got to go to her," she said, walking quickly toward the doors.

"I'm coming."

Adam caught up to her and entwined their fingers. They headed upstairs together and when they reached the threshold to the nursery, Mia stopped and turned to him. "Maybe you should stay out here," she said.

Adam's head shook. "No, I'm coming in. She has to see me here. It's better that I'm with you."

"Okay." Rose's cries stopped the minute she saw Mia. She picked her up and cupped her head, kissing her rosy soft cheeks. "I know, my baby girl. This is all so new for you. But I'm here now. And so is your daddy."

Mia turned Rose toward Adam. She took one look at him and immediately swung her head in the opposite direction.

"Hi, Rose," he said anyway. "Sorry you can't sleep. Daddy can't, either."

Something lurched in Mia's heart as Adam spoke so tenderly and patiently to Rose. And hearing him call himself "Daddy" brought tears to her eyes. Her stomach ached. It seemed to do that a lot lately. Losing Rose would destroy her, she was sure, but how could she possibly not encourage the baby to know and love her father?

Mia turned so that Rose faced Adam. "Will you let Daddy hold you while I get you a bottle?"

Adam put out his arms to his daughter. Rose tightened her grip around Mia's neck, squirming up her body. Mia tried to pry her off, but Rose was determined not to go to her daddy. Mia didn't fight her. She stepped away from Adam and strode to the other side of the room. "It's okay, baby girl. It's okay. Adam, maybe you could warm up her bottle? I'll rock her."

Adam nodded and walked out of the room.

While he was gone, Mia changed the baby's diaper and then plunked down on the glider and began rocking the baby. By the time Adam returned, Rose was calmer and relaxed. Quietly, he handed Mia the bottle and sat cross-legged on the floor, facing them. Rose sucked on the bottle, keeping a vigilant eye on Adam. He said nothing, merely watched as Rose's eyes eventually closed. There were a few halfhearted attempts to suck the last inch of the formula down before Rose fell back to sleep.

"She's out," Mia whispered.

Adam nodded, the yearning in his expression touching something deep inside.

"Do you want to put her into the crib?" she asked.

"She'll wake if I do that." His voice was quietly bereft. Adam believed Rose had a sixth sense about him.

"No, I can almost guarantee you she won't wake up. She's out."

A childlike eagerness lit in his eyes and he stood. "Yes, then. Hand her to me."

Mia rose from the glider and transferred the baby carefully into Adam's arms. The baby didn't move a muscle. Mia sighed, grateful Rose didn't make a liar out of her.

Holding the infant in his arms, Adam's expression changed. The hard planes of his face softened. His gunmetal-gray eyes melted into longing, pride and love. It was beautiful to see.

But heartbreaking, too.

Mia stood back, away from Adam, overseeing him putting Rose down to sleep.

Not a whimper from Rose as her body touched down on the baby mattress.

Standing over the crib, Adam watched the baby sleep. Mia turned away, leaving the two of them alone. The bonding was happening right before her eyes. She was facilitating it to some degree. It was the right thing to do, but that didn't stop fearful jabs from poking her inside reminding her, her days with Rose at Moonlight Beach were numbered.

Saturday afternoon, Mia was just walking into the house with Rose after working a half a day at First Clips when she spotted Adam at the edge of the patio in very much the same place they'd kissed the other night. "Come on, Rose," she cooed. "Your daddy didn't see you this morning." Adam had made it clear he expected to see Rose at every opportunity. Mia couldn't balk at that. Or that Rose needed the fresh air. Most of her days were spent inside the salon.

She plopped a sunbonnet on Rose's head to shield her eyes from the sun. The hat matched a purple-and-white Swiss polka-dotted dress and bloomers that Adam had given her. She pictured him venturing out to shop for baby clothes and, well, she just couldn't grasp that notion. Yet Mary had insisted Adam had done the shopping with no help from her. She had to admit Rose looked especially adorable today.

With Rose in her arms, kicking her bootie-socked feet happily, Mia ventured outside. That beautiful kiss he'd planted on her hadn't been discussed or repeated. She'd thought that after she'd helped Adam chase off those teens, they'd broken new ground. Not the case apparently. Adam had retreated, probably kicking himself for letting down his guard and showing some emotion.

"Adam, we're home."

He turned around, but it wasn't Adam at all. The man had similar sharp features, a chiseled profile, strong jaw and shoulders just as broad. Stepping closer, she noted he wasn't nearly as tall and his eyes were a deep and mesmerizing blue. There was kindness on his face and a grin that touched something delicate in her heart as he gazed at the baby. "Sorry to disappoint. I'm Brandon. Adam's younger brother."

He put out his hand. "And you are?"

"Mia." She blinked. Adam hadn't told his brother about her and the baby?

They shook hands. "And who's this pretty little thing?"

She couldn't help responding kindly to him. He had a beautiful baritone voice that elevated as he asked about the baby. "This is Rose."

"Rose? Named after a flower," he said, his voice lowering, a veil dimming over his eyes. "Well nice to meet you two stunning ladies," he said. His eyes shined again. "I'm waiting for Adam. Mary said he's due back soon."

"He must be at the office. I think he had a meeting."

Brandon eyed her curiously, the smile never leaving his face. She didn't know what to say to him. Should she spill the beans? Adam was such a private person he might never forgive her if she did. It might be grounds for him tossing her out of the place.

"Is there something I should know? Am I an uncle?"

Mia shuddered.

Brandon's affable expression changed. "Sorry. She's got my brother's eyes."

There was no way around it. Brandon had guessed the truth. "Yes, Rose is Adam's child. I'm her aunt Mia."

"Aunt?"

She nodded. "It's a long story—better to be told by Adam, I think."

Brandon stared at her and then focused on his niece. "I'm an uncle."

Footsteps on stone had her turning to find Mary heading their way. *Thank goodness for the interruption.*

"Lunch is waiting, if you're hungry. I've got coffee, tea and lemonade ready in the kitchen."

Mia was famished. She'd eaten very little that morning. Rose had been in a mood and she'd missed breakfast. She should refuse, but how rude would it be to make Adam's brother eat alone? "Thanks, Mary."

"Shall I warm up a bottle for the little one?" Mary asked.

"I gave her a bottle a little while ago, but I appreciate the offer."

They entered the kitchen and ate lunch together, while the baby played quietly in the playpen. Brandon respected her wishes and didn't ask too many questions about the situation with Rose, other than how much she weighed at birth, how old she was and how Adam was taking to fatherhood. She skirted around the last question and turned the conversation to him. She found out he was a charter pilot working out of an Orange County airport and loved flying. He spent the remainder of their lunch speaking about his escapades in foreign countries, dealing with Homeland Security, and he told a few outrageous stories about the celebrities he'd flown around the world.

Rose began to cry and Mia rose immediately. As she lifted her out of the playpen, the baby whimpered still and Mia knew she had no time to lose. Rose could bellow with the best of them. "Sorry, she's hungry now. I've got to warm a bottle."

Brandon stood and walked over to her, holding out his arms. "No problem. Can I help?"

Mia tried not to let her eyeballs go wide. He didn't know

what he was asking. "Oh…uh. She's squeamish around strangers. I don't think she'll go to you."

"Can we try?" He had persuasive eyes, clear and so startling crystal blue a person could definitely lose their way in them.

"Sure." One second and he'd be handing her back.

"This is your uncle Brandon, Sweet Cheeks. He wants to hold you while I make your bottle."

Mia made the transition carefully, and Rose, the little sprite, didn't make a peep as Brandon settled her into his arms. He began moving, walking, pacing and rocking her as Mia looked on. Astonished, she'd almost forgotten about warming her bottle. "She's a sweet one," he said.

Mia gulped before giving him a smile. The baby was putty in his arms. Was that a good thing? Maybe Rose was finally coming around.

She made quick work of heating the formula in a bottle warmer. Once done, she placed the bottle above her arm and let a few drops drip onto her wrist. Brandon watched. "A test in case it's too hot."

"Gotcha." The baby was fascinated by him. She kept looking into his eyes, responding to his voice.

"I usually feed her in the living room. Mary likes that we're using that room."

Brandon followed her and sat down fairly close on the sofa. "Mind if I feed her?"

"Uh…no, I don't mind." The baby might even let him.

Mia handed him the bottle and the baby latched on to the nipple right away. She slurped and made sucking noises. "She's quite a guzzler." He chuckled and seemed comfortable holding an infant.

"She is growing like a weed."

Brandon took his eyes off the baby to give Mia a look. "I knew a Mia once, an older Italian woman who herded sheep. I can tell you stories…"

"Please do," she said. She enjoyed his company. He

was a charming, funny man who wasn't afraid to talk about himself, and she didn't mind the distraction from his brother, who would rather have a root canal than smile.

They were quietly laughing, Brandon just finishing a story about his crazy stay in Siena, the baby peacefully asleep in his arms, when Adam walked into the room. He stopped midway and gave Mia a cold glance before sending a grim look to his brother. His eyes were filled with indignation.

"Brandon." He kept his voice low, menacing. "What are you doing here? I didn't expect you until Monday."

"There was a change in plans."

Adam's mouth twisted in an unbecoming snarl. "There always is."

"Sorry, bro. I didn't think it would be a problem."

"It is a problem."

Adam frowned at Mia. There'd be no more smiles today for anyone.

"The baby is a stunner, Adam. Congratulations."

Adam blinked, his gaze shifting from her to the baby. "It's none of your concern, Brandon."

"Hey, you're a father, Adam. And that makes me this one's uncle. That's something to celebrate. Isn't she the reason you summoned me here?"

Adam's teeth clenched. He kept his focus on Rose now, in his brother's arms. Mia could only imagine what thoughts plagued his head. The baby wouldn't go to him, yet she took to Brandon, Adam's obviously estranged brother, like peanut butter to jelly.

"Does Mom know she's a grandmother?" Brandon asked.

Adam shook his head. "Not yet."

Mia rose from her seat. "Maybe I'd better let you two talk this out. Brandon, I'll take the baby—"

"Leave her be, Mia." Adam's voice was rough, his gaze

chillier than a deep freeze. "I don't want to break up your little party."

"It's not a party, for heaven's sake, Ad—"

He faced her, betrayal shining in his eyes. "Did you tell him everything?"

"She told me nothing," Brandon interjected in her defense, which only seemed to irritate Adam further.

"I'm asking Mia," he said, enunciating each word.

Defusing the situation was tricky. "No, I only told him that Rose was yours and that I'm her aunt. I thought it best for you to explain the details," she said.

He pinned her down. "That's all?"

She nodded and glanced at Brandon. "He was kind enough not to pressure me with questions."

"My brother's a regular Mr. Nice Guy."

Brandon rose now, careful with the baby in his arms. "Adam, don't take your sour mood out on Mia. Okay, so I showed up a few days early. My bad. Obviously, you've got issues going on here that you need to work out. I'll leave and come back another time."

Adam gave his head a shake. If he hoped to clear away his foul mood, it didn't work. "No. I need to talk to you. Tonight. We'll talk after dinner."

Brandon approached Adam with the baby, ready to hand her to him. Mia immediately stood and intervened. "I'll take her."

Wouldn't that just put a perfect ending on this afternoon for Rose to leave Brandon's arms only to start sobbing uncontrollably when Adam took hold of her. The scene played out in her head with HD clarity. She couldn't allow that to happen.

Brandon swiveled around, and opened his arms enough for Mia to gently take Rose from him. Little sleepyhead kept on sleeping, thankfully.

"Like I said, don't let me break up your little party. I have work to do."

Adam stalked out of the room leaving Brandon and Mia standing there, dumbfounded.

Seven

Adam pushed his hands through his hair half a dozen times as he paced the floor in his home office. He'd deliberately set his office in the front of the house, so he wouldn't be distracted by the roar of the ocean, beachgoers' voices carrying inside the room or a brilliant sun setting over the California shoreline. His windows open, sea breezes blew inside and ruffled the papers lying on his drafting table. He walked over and put a pewter paperweight over them. He wasn't going to get any work done today.

Brandon was here. It had been two years last Christmas since he'd seen him. His mother had insisted her boys share the holiday with her. They'd gone to her home at Sunny Hills and spent nine hours of rigid politeness being around each other. His mother's attempt at reconciliation hadn't worked and it had been awkward as hell. Adam wasn't ready to forgive Brandon for stealing Jacqueline away. Brandon, in one way or another, had been the source of pain for him all of his life. Yet, Brandon was the son whom his mother loved most. Deep down, Adam thought his mother had never forgiven him for what happened to Lily, though she'd never admitted that to him. Adam gnashed his teeth. Hell, he'd never forgiven himself. And he'd never divulged to his mother Brandon's part in Lily's death. Only Adam knew the absolute truth about what had happened that day.

Earlier today, when he'd seen Brandon holding Rose,

acid had spilled into his gut. He'd held back a barrage of curses. Brandon, the charmer, had already won Rose over, while Adam stood on the sidelines waiting and hoping his little baby would come to accept him.

Later that night over dinner, all was quiet. Mia didn't say a word that wasn't directed to the baby. Brandon was treading carefully, too. Several times, he'd caught Brandon shooting Mia conspiratorial sideway glances. Somehow Adam had become the villain.

Fine by him.

He was too wound up to give a damn.

Mia rose from the table after her meal and lifted the baby from her playpen. Rose clung to her neck so sweetly Adam ached inside. "I think we'll turn in early tonight," she said. "Good night, Brandon. Adam."

The sun had just set and it was especially early for her to hit the sack. Even little Rose didn't go to bed until nine. Mia wasn't fooling him. He'd behaved badly earlier this afternoon and she was annoyed with him. He probably deserved her scorn. And it was better that he speak with Brandon in private anyway. He was ready with a condensed version of the story to tell his brother about Rose. He didn't need Mia interjecting facts.

"Good night, Mia," Brandon said, rising to his feet. "Nice meeting you. And give that little one a good-night kiss from Uncle Brandon."

Mia smiled warmly at him. "I'll be sure to."

She was halfway out the door, when Adam spoke up. "I'll be up in a little while. Keep her awake until I get there."

Mia whirled on him instantly, shooting him twin green daggers with her eyes.

Great.

"Rose will sleep when she's tired, Adam, which I think was about five minutes ago. We're not waiting up."

He rolled his eyes. "Fine. Good night, then."

As soon as she left the room, Brandon grinned like a schoolboy. "You sure know how to charm them."

He bounded up, striding out of the kitchen to the bar outside on the patio. Fresh briny air smacked him in the face, and it was far gentler than Mia's reprimand. Technically, he could demand that she obey his wishes. He was Rose's father. He had all rights when it came to his daughter, but he'd never pull that card on Mia. Not unless she gave him good reason to.

He grabbed two highball glasses from underneath the white-and-black granite-topped bar and poured them both a drink. Brandon preferred bourbon, but Adam wasn't feeling especially generous tonight. He poured vodka into both glasses and handed him one as he walked up. "I'm going to make this quick. Want to take a seat?"

"Okay." The iron legs of the chaise scraped across the stone decking as Brandon pulled the chair out and sat down. He lifted his glass. "Thanks," he said and took a sip. His facial muscles tightened as he swallowed the strong liquor and leaned back.

Adam didn't want to start out on a bad note with his brother. He was ready to put the past behind him for his mother's sake, but having Brandon show up unannounced today and finding him holding his baby, his perfect little child who couldn't stand the sight of her own father, had snapped his patience.

He didn't like seeing Mia's eyes go warm and gooey over Brandon, either.

He dismissed that notion. Mia wasn't his concern. His mother and his child were his priorities now.

"So, tell me about the kid, Adam. She's yours—that much I know. And her mother is gone?"

He nodded. "Mia's sister died shortly after the birth."

"That's rough. Were you two close?"

"No, it wasn't like that. We barely knew each other."

"But you're certain the baby is yours?" Brandon asked.

"She is. DNA tests confirmed it. She's got the Chase birthmark, if DNA wasn't enough proof." A wry laugh erupted from his chest.

"No kidding. And what about Mia?"

"She spent months raising her and now she's moved in here, helping to make Rose's transition easier."

"Man, you sound like you're talking about some business merger or something. It's clear Mia loves that child. What about you?"

"Of course I love Rose. She's my daughter." It was love at first sight. On his part, anyway.

"You didn't pick her up when I tried to hand her to you. I haven't seen you hold her. And what's with you ordering Mia around like she's your indentured servant?"

Adam drew oxygen into his lungs. The chilly air helped keep his hot temper at bay. "None of that is important right now." He wasn't going to reveal how Mia had duped him when they first met. How she'd been doing her own form of investigation to make sure he was father material. Or that his daughter screamed blue murder when he tried to hold her. Wouldn't Mr. Charming have a good laugh over that one? "Look, I had an affair with Mia's sister. It wasn't serious and it ended mutually. I only learned weeks ago from Mia that Rose was conceived when we were together.

"So now I've got the baby here and we're trying to figure it out. Rose will always live with me."

"So you and Mia aren't..."

Adam shook his head a little too vehemently. "No. She's gone as soon as we feel Rose has acclimated to...the surroundings."

"Gone? Isn't that cold, Adam? She loves that child. It's clear Rose has formed a strong attachment to her. Who wouldn't? Mia's sweet and gorgeous and—"

"Brandon, lay off, okay? I said we're trying to figure it all out. And what makes you an expert on Mia D'Angelo anyway? You've known her for less than six hours."

"We talked. I have good instincts about people. She's a keeper."

Adam clenched his jaw. Was his brother really trying to give him romantic advice? "Do you want to know why I asked you to come here?"

"Has something to do with Mom. Her birthday's coming up." Brandon sipped his drink.

"That's right. It's her seventieth, and she wants only one thing from us."

"I can only guess."

"You got it. She wants us to patch up our differences. She wants to see her family whole again." It would never be, without Dad and Lily, but that was beside the point.

Brandon shoved the tumbler aside and leaned in from his nonchalant position on the chair. His elbows came to rest on the patio table. "I've tried, Adam. But you weren't ready to hear me."

Adam stared toward the ocean. The swells were high now, breaking on the shore in white foam that cleansed the sand. If only he could cleanse away the bitter pain that seeped into his soul that easily. Maybe that's what he was hoping for with those daily dawn swims, to wash away all the bad things in his life.

Brandon had always been at the very core of his pain. He'd been selfish and self-serving as a young boy, but Adam had never told his mother the true story. Because ultimately, he'd been the older one. He'd been responsible for Lily. "I'm listening now, Brandon."

"You're doing this for Mom."

He shrugged. "Does it matter why?"

Brandon drew a deep breath. "I guess not. I never meant to hurt you, Adam. As much as you may not want to hear this, I swear to you—Jacqueline and I never went behind your back."

Adam looked into his tumbler, sighed and then polished off the rest of it. He let the burn of alcohol settle in his gut before turning to face his brother. "No. You did it right in front of me."

"Not true. I admit, I fell for her from almost the moment I met her. Right here in this house. But she was your girlfriend, Adam. And I saw how much you cared for her. I never acted on my feelings. I never flirted. I never—"

"You were just your usual charming self."

"I am who I am."

Adam scoffed. "You're saying you couldn't help yourself?"

"No, that's not what I'm saying. You have to believe me. I fell hard for her, but never once thought about trying to come between you. I pretty much kept out of your hair. If you remember, I hardly showed up around here while you were dating. And when you two broke up, I struggled with that, but I didn't call her. I wanted to. I was in love with her, Adam. I'm sorry, but that's the truth. And I tried not to think about her. I figured out of sight, out of mind. Then one day, out of the blue, she called me. She had a friend who wanted to charter a flight for a special anniversary party. It began just by talking on the phone. A few dinners later, we were both in love. That's exactly how it happened, Adam. She didn't break up with you because of me."

Adam's mouth tightened. He gazed out to sea again, nodding his head. What was done was done. He'd have to live with Brandon's explanation for now. It had been six years. Jacqueline was out of the picture and his sister Lily wasn't ever coming back. If mending fences with Brandon would make his mother happy, he'd do it. "Okay. I understand."

Brandon slumped back against the chaise, his eyes incredulous. "You do? Just like that? For years, you've kept your distance. Now, you believe me?"

He'd recently discovered that he no longer cared about the situation with Brandon and Jacqueline. As far as he was concerned, it was ancient history. "I believe you didn't know how much it would affect me."

"We didn't sneak behind your back."

"Got it."

Though in Adam's rule book, he'd never go after his brother's girl, broken up or not. "Now, can we talk about Mom's birthday?"

"Sure…" Brandon smiled with a gleam in his eyes, reminding him of the young boy who'd always gotten away with stealing the last cupcake in the batch.

Adam tiptoed up the stairs after he and Brandon hashed out the details of their mother's birthday party. An hour had passed since Mia had taken the baby up to bed and he was certain the baby had already fallen asleep. Just watching Rose sleep was a relaxing balm, a way to calm his nerves and smooth out the kinks going on in his brain. She did that for him. He loved her with all of his heart, and it unnerved him how much she already meant to him.

He walked into the nursery lit by a Cinderella night-light and peered inside the crib, only to find it empty.

Slowly, he turned and crept out of the room. The door to Mia's room was ajar. He peeked inside and found the two of them asleep on the bed. Mia wore the same dress she'd had on during dinner, the hem of soft periwinkle cotton hiked up to her thighs. Her tanned legs were exposed and bent at the knees, protecting the baby with her body. She lay on her side facing him, two perfect breasts partially spilling out of her neckline and long raven strands of hair tickling her flesh as she took easy breaths. As sexy as she was in sleep, Adam only saw beauty now as she lay beside his child swathed with pink-and-brown teddy bears on her nightdress. Her breaths were strong and steady.

Tears stung his eyes, and the allure of their peaceful sleep brought him into the room. He stood over both of them for several seconds and recognized the yearning eating at him. He hadn't spent any time with Rose today. He'd missed his nightly ritual of holding her as she slept and laying her into the crib. It was such a small thing. One he never wanted to miss.

Nimbly, Adam kicked off his shoes and lay down on the bed. The mattress groaned and he winced, freezing in place. When no one stirred, he took great precautions stretching out his body, inching his way, trying not to wake either of them. Then he positioned his body exactly like Mia, a matching opposite bookend to complete the fortress around Rose's little sleeping self.

She was so small, so precious. Moving only the muscles necessary, he wound a curl of her blond hair around his finger. It was soft and as fine as silk. His eyes closed. He wanted to plant a loving kiss on her sweet cheeks. He wanted to speak to her, without her going ballistic on him, and tell her eye to eye how much he loved her.

When he opened his eyes, Mia was staring at him, those jade shards of ice from before melting to a bright warm glow. "Hi," she whispered over the baby. He could barely hear her.

"Hi."

"We tried to wait up."

So that's why they are on her bed tonight. After all her blistering, she thought enough to try to wait for him.

"Thanks. It took longer than I thought."

"You were grumpy tonight." She moved hair off her face, pushing the strands from her eyes. God, she was beautiful.

"My brother brings that out in me. He's gone. For now."

"Do you want to put her down in her crib?"

"Will that wake her?"

Mia glanced at the slumbering baby. "I doubt it. She's pretty tired."

He nodded. "Okay, then."

"You go on and do it. I'll stay here."

He stared at her for the beat of a second. "You're sure?" She wasn't going to oversee him putting the baby to sleep? He'd never done it without her watchful eye before.

"Yes."

Mia was a mystery to him. She'd lied to him, pretending to be an innocent bystander on the beach when they'd first met, and had kept up the deceit for days. Normally, Mia was extremely possessive about Rose. He didn't know what to make of her sudden generous attitude toward him. He certainly didn't trust her. Days earlier, he'd put the wheels in motion to find out what he could about her. More than she was willing to tell him. And he'd be interested in learning who Mia D'Angelo really was. Did she have any skeletons in her closet? He felt justified in his investigation because she had great influence over his daughter. A father had to protect his child, even from possible unknown threats.

Never taking his eyes off Rose, he slipped gently from the bed and bent to scoop her up. Fitting her little body across his arms, he braced her head with his right hand. She smelled of fresh diapers and baby shampoo, innocence and sweetness. He cradled her closer, absorbing all that goodness. She stirred from his movements, her hands fisting and her body arching in a stretch. He rocked her back and forth the way Mia had taught him, and she settled back into a peaceful sleep. Then he headed to the nursery and stood over the crib, hating to give her up. These were the only minutes in the day he could be this close to her. He could hold her all night and not tire of it, but he couldn't chance waking her. He laid her down, and she immediately turned her face toward the wall. She slept the same way he did. He smiled and after a few minutes inched away, his eyes on her as he backed out of the room.

Mission accomplished. He'd put his baby down all by himself. He felt over the moon.

Mia was waiting for him in the hallway. "Is she down?"

"Yeah, she stirred for a second but didn't wake up."

She smiled. "She does that."

Adam gazed into the warm glow of Mia's eyes again, the love shining through clearly despite the dim lighting. She looked mussed, a little tumbled and sexier than any woman he'd ever known.

"I'm glad you were able to put her down tonight."

"You waited up for me. Why?"

She shrugged. "You ordered it."

He took a step closer to her. Dangerous but he couldn't help himself. "If it came out that way, I apologize."

"I'm teasing, Adam. Do I look like a woman who'd cave to bullying tactics?"

"Definitely not." She looked like a woman who needed to be kissed and then some. "Why then?"

Her delicate shoulder lifted. "You were so tense around your brother, I figured you'd need Rose to soothe you."

"Oh, so *she* soothes *me*? Not the other way around. Is that what you're saying?"

"Uh-huh. Are you denying it?"

After a moment of thought, he replied, "No, I can't deny that."

"I didn't think so. Adam, what's up with you and your brother?"

He sighed and gave her a long look. He didn't want to have this conversation with her. He didn't want to have *any* conversation with her. "I don't want to talk about Brandon right now," he whispered, taking a step closer. "There are better things to do."

She gulped, and her gaze dipped to his mouth and lingered.

"Thank you for waiting up for me."

"It wasn't anything—"

"It was plenty," he whispered. His lips hovered over hers. Her breath smelled sweet and minty and when she sighed over his mouth, he could almost taste her.

"Adam," she whispered. A warning?

He thought she'd deny him a kiss, but instead she reached for his shirt collar and then slowly glided her fingers to the back of his neck. She locked her hands in place behind his head. The woman was unpredictable, and it only made her more appealing. Roping her around the waist, he pulled her closer.

She gazed at him, her eyes filled with the same warm glimmer she reserved for Rose. Resisting her now was impossible. He'd seen her laughing with Brandon, and that was all it had taken. If he had anything to say about it, Brandon wouldn't get within a mile of her.

He pressed his mouth to hers, and she fell into his kiss with a whimper of longing. A shudder ran through him. She affected him. And he couldn't help himself.

Her lips parted, and he didn't hesitate to plunge deeper and sink into the sweetness of her mouth.

He hadn't forgotten about that night in her apartment. He'd been lost in her and the heady way she'd responded to him. He'd touched the most intimate parts of her body, and she'd loved every second of it. During these past few nights, he'd lain awake in his bed thinking about her sleeping down the hall. Thinking about where that night would've led, if she hadn't dropped that bombshell on him.

There would be no bombshells tonight and he was ready to finish what he'd started.

Eight

"Adam, we can't." The words fell from her lips limply. They *were*, and she was helpless how to stop it.

His palm flattened against the center of her chest as he forced her back up against the wall. She was trapped by his body, cocooned in his heat. It was so unexpected, so thrilling a move her heartbeat began to pound up in her skull. His aggression excited her and his kisses wiped out any idea of a real protest. "Mia, tell me you don't want this and I'll back off."

He pulled away from her lips to trail hot moist kisses on her throat, gently nipping at her skin with his teeth. A path of fiery heat sprinted down her belly. She was dying with want, her traitorous body giving in to his passion, while a banner across her mind shouted no.

He whispered in her ear, "I'll take your silence as a yes."

A shiver ran through her, yet her mouth refused to open.

Adam kissed her then until she was breathless. His fingers fumbled with the spaghetti straps of her dress, sliding them down. Then with a few hastened tugs, the garment fell to a puddle on the floor around her feet.

She stood before him in her black bra and French-cut panties. He scanned over her body with a sharp intake of breath. "Mia," he said almost painfully. "What am I going to do with you?"

She had a pretty good idea and it didn't scare her. Well, just a little bit, considering who Adam was. He'd been her sister's lover once. She'd resigned herself to that already and didn't relate the mystery man she'd searched for with this living, breathing, sexy man who'd just picked her up into his arms.

He kissed her again and she held on to him as he carried her to his room.

She was lowered down on the bed, and he stood in front of her, flipping the buttons of his shirt. His chest appeared before her eyes, toned, rippled and solid. She sat there shaking, in awe of his upper body. If the lower half matched his brawn...

His eyes bored into her. "Come here, Mia."

The tone of his voice insisted on full obedience. Not that she would've disobeyed his command. She knew what she wanted and rose from the bed.

And then her world tipped upside down. Adam claimed her lips again and again and then he found other places to tease and torture with his mouth. His touch was magical, his hands knowing how to please, his fingers strumming her like a finely tuned instrument. Those firm demanding lips took her to heaven and back. He wreaked havoc on her body, one hand holding her in place while the other elicited moans of agonized pleasure.

"That's it, Mia. Fall apart in my arms."

His urgent command did the trick. The magician made her come apart at the seams, and she crumbled into a thousand wonderful satisfying pieces. She had the feeling Adam was just getting started.

He held her against him, cradling her so close she heard his rapid-fire heartbeat. Her hair was gently pushed off her face, tucked behind her ear and he placed easy quick kisses there to soothe her. She was loose like a rag doll and beautifully sated.

"Do what you want with me," he whispered.

Another thrill traveled south to regions of her body just satisfied. To have him at her mercy made liquid of her bones. Trembling, wicked thoughts entered her head. She was needy and throbbing again, and as she reached out to touch his slick moist skin, her hands shook. He was perfect, trim and muscled and as firm as granite. He shuddered under her hands, and she gazed into his eyes. They were soft, wistful, almost pleading. She had power over him. It was a heady notion and the biggest turn-on.

She lifted up to kiss him as she continued to probe his body. When her splayed hand reached beyond his belt buckle to tease the tip of his manhood, his breath came out as a sharp potent gasp. He was firm and large below the waist, another big-time turn-on.

"Touch me, sweetheart."

It was as much a dare as a request.

Mia wasn't one to back down from a dare. She covered the length of him with one hand and stroked over his trousers again and again. *Oh my.*

A deep barrel of a groan rose from his throat. And then she was being lifted again, Adam's soft curses ringing in her ears about enough foreplay or something. She hid a grin and was lowered rather unceremoniously onto a massive bed. "You said do what I want with you."

"And you're going to pay for that one."

"I'm waiting," she shot back. Where did she get her nerve?

He unbuckled his belt and removed his pants in a rush and joined her on the bed. *Oh my, again.* He had impressive architecture.

He rolled away from her and fiddled with a drawer in the end table. While he was doing that, she calmed herself by looking over the amazing bedroom. The corner room was angled and two entire walls were windows that looked out to sea. The rooms were tastefully decorated and—

He dumped five condom packets on the bed.

Her brows lifted. She had no idea Adam had such lofty plans for her. "Still waiting."

He groaned and grabbed her waist, lifting her above him. She settled, facing him in a straddle position over his thighs. "I want to see your face when I make love to you." Reaching up, he unhooked her bra and signaled for her to remove her panties.

No more fooling around. This was serious. *He* was serious, and the intensity in his eyes scared her a little. Her arms were braced by his hands and he began to massage them, up and down, caressing her limbs as if she were a precious jewel. It was pure heaven, and her anticipation grew. With a simultaneous tug of her arms, she fell forward, and he captured her mouth and kissed her soundly on the lips. The tips of her breasts touched his chest. The coarseness of his skin abraded her nipples, making them pebble up. He flicked his thumb over each one, and a shot of liquid heat poured down her body. She was beginning to ache in pleasant, searching ways. Adam kept it up, kissing her, touching her, making her come alive again.

She couldn't ignore his need, pressing firm against her belly. She touched him there and more soft curses rang from his lips. Hot silk in her hand, she pleasured him as he'd pleasured her, his moans and grunts encouraging her to go on.

Adam's eyes were wild now, smoky and dangerous. He hissed through his teeth, a warning for her to stop. Then his palms were on her waist, guiding her up onto him. They were both ready. She sank down into his heat and two instant moans of relief fell from their lips.

"So good," Adam muttered.

It was. She was filled with him, and it was only more beautiful when he began moving, his hands still on her waist, leading her, helping her find a rhythm that suited them both. He moved with her, slowly building up to a speed neither could maintain for too long. His hands went to her hips, and he rose up partway, encouraging her to wrap her legs around him. And it was like that for a while, each coming together, moving, looking into each other's eyes as he drove farther and farther.

He kissed her breasts, her throat, her chin, and when he reached her lips, he fell back against the pillows, taking her with him.

He arched his hips and pumped, keeping his eyes trained on her. Her hair spilled over the sides of his face and once again, he pushed the strands back, maintaining eye contact.

"Are you there?" he asked.

She nodded.

And then he unleashed the power of his body, sinking farther into her. She whimpered, her cries oddly quiet. It was so damn good, she was stunned almost silent.

Adam climbed with her, his body taxed but relentless. She let go a powerful release, and this time her mouth opened to a scream of pleasure.

Adam, too, made manly noises that seemed to promote his inner caveman. He huffed and grunted, and then she fell on top of him in a heap of boneless rapture.

By far, Adam Chase had given her the best night of loving in her life.

Mia rose from Adam's bed and tiptoed past the nightstand, where two remaining condom packets were left untouched. She was sore in places she hadn't been sore in years, but that wasn't the worst of it. She'd managed to have sex with Rose's father three times during the night. After the first time, the baby had woken and Mia went to her. Adam hadn't been far behind; he'd apparently become a light sleeper, since Rose had arrived here. Adam had warmed her bottle while Mia diapered her. Together, in the night-lighted room, they'd taken care of the baby. Once Rose had fallen back to sleep, Mia handed her off to Adam to put her down.

She'd been halfway to her own room when Adam took her hand and led her back to his big master bed. She hadn't gone kicking and screaming, and that was part of the problem. It had been so good between them she hadn't wanted the night to end. Adam hadn't let up on her and she'd met him touch for touch, kiss for kiss. After bout three, Adam held her tenderly in his arms, whispered soft words of her beauty, but he hadn't asked her to stay the night with him.

And once he'd fallen asleep, she'd returned to her own bed.

Now footsteps approached her room, and she listened carefully. Her door creaked open and Adam poked his head inside. They made eye contact and the door opened wider. Adam stood in the threshold, gazing at her in the predawn light. Disapproval marred his handsome features. "I'm going for a swim," he said. "Mary's not due for three more hours."

"Okay," she said. "I'll listen for Rose." If that's what he was getting at. She always listened for Rose, and this morning was no different.

He nodded, his gaze sharp on the covers she held up to her throat. After what they'd done to each other last night, it was a silly thing to do. But she felt vulnerable now and didn't know what he was thinking. Or feeling. Adam wasn't one to show emotion. Even now, after the passionate night they'd shared, his face was blank, his eyes unreadable, except for that note of disapproval she couldn't miss.

"Fine," he said. "You feeling all right?"

She'd had a hot night of sex with the handsomest man on the beach and all she could do was nod and answer, "Yes."

He blinked, stood there a few seconds and then closed the door.

Mia knocked her head against the pillows. What was that all about? Damn him. Why was he so closed off?

Was he not a morning person? How would she know— he never talked about himself. He didn't let anyone in. And what made her think he would ever let *her* in? Just because they'd satisfied their base needs last night didn't mean he would actually confide in her about anything.

She refused to think of last night as a mistake, but a little voice inside her head told her that very thing, over and over.

Where they went from here was anyone's guess.

Grabbing the baby monitor, she rose from bed and walked to the bathroom. She used a dimmer switch to adjust the lighting just so, and set the controls on the whirlpool tub. The jets turned on with a blast and bubbles rioted around the oval bathtub. She lit a few scented candles and soon vanilla and raspberry flavored the air, the flickering flames reflecting off the water. She was never one to pamper herself, but today luxury was called for. With luck, the baby would sleep another hour or two.

It would give her time to come to grips about her strong feelings for Adam Chase.

The genius recluse.

Adam stood at the edge of the veranda, his foot atop the stone border, gazing at Mia and the baby playing a game at the water's edge. The baby was smiling and every so often a breeze would carry Mia's animated voice to his ears as she played toe-tag with the incoming waves. He sipped coffee from a steaming mug. How had his life gotten so complicated?

He'd woken up early this morning to find Mia gone from his bed. He'd wanted her there last night. And this morning, he'd wanted to wake to the sweet scent of her luxurious body, to see her hair splayed across the pillow. He'd wanted to trail kisses across her soft shoulders and whisper good morning to her.

He'd worried that he'd been too rough with her, too forceful, too demanding of her body. When he found her gone from his bed, he'd worried that he'd hurt her. Thoughts of last night flashed before his eyes. There wasn't a doubt in his mind that he'd given her pleasure, but how much was too much? And had it been a stupid, mindless mistake, to take his daughter's aunt to bed? Carnal desire aside, he didn't want to ruin things between them. Mia would be in Rose's life forever.

"Here Adam—take this to Mia." Something was shoved into his free hand. He hadn't heard Mary come up behind him, and he looked down at the wicker basket he now held.

"What is it?"

"Mia's breakfast. Yogurt and granola, toast and juice. She has the day off, but she didn't eat anything this morning. There's some other things in there, too, if you'd like."

He gazed at Mia again. She'd taken a seat on a blanket under one of his multicolored umbrellas, the baby propped in her arms. "No, I'm good right now."

Mary relieved him of his coffee mug. "Go on now. Take her the basket. I know you want to."

Mary's eyes twinkled. He nodded. "Fine, if you want to shirk your duties."

"That's me—always finding my way out of doing work around here."

Mary was the best housekeeper he'd ever had. She'd been with him since before he'd come to Moonlight Beach. He wouldn't want anyone else taking care of his home.

"Fine. Shirker."

"I'll be eating bonbons on the sofa in you need me," Mary said as she walked away.

"Smart aleck," he muttered and stepped onto the beach barefoot.

It was a short walk to where Mia had planted herself. He supposed she'd want to have *the talk*. Adam hated those "what happens now" questions that he couldn't answer. Since Jacqueline, the women he'd been with had been few and far between, but almost all of them wanted to know where they'd stood with him after a night of sex.

Once he reached the blanket, he crouched down, setting the basket next to Mia. "Here you go. Compliments of Mary. Breakfast."

Mia turned to him, her sunglasses shielding her eyes. She removed them and glanced at the basket. "That's very nice of her," she said and finally looked at him. Her eyes were a gorgeous shade of rich green, reminding him of morning grass on the pastures in Oklahoma. He was struck silent for a second. "I'll thank her when I go in," she said.

The baby stared at him, her lower lip jutting out and trembling. Her pout broke his heart all over again. What would it take for Rose to accept him?

"Mind if I join you?" he asked.

She hesitated for longer than he would've liked. "No, be my guest."

He scooted onto the blanket on the other side of the baby. He hated that he had to keep his distance from her to keep her happy. Maybe he should keep his distance from Mia, too.

Too late for that.

"You weren't hungry this morning?" He looked into the basket and found a dish of vanilla yogurt topped with granola and raisins, pastries, a bottle of orange juice and fruit.

"Not really. I had coffee."

"Yeah, me, too."

He watched the waves bound in and out. Her silence unnerved him. Had he done something wrong? Other than the obvious, making love to a woman he had no right making love to.

Her hair was pulled into a ponytail that extended to the middle of her back. She wore black shorts and a pretty white scoop-neck tank with a glittery pink tiara painted over her chest. Mia looked delicious in anything she wore.

"You didn't stay the night with me," he said finally. It had been on his mind all morning. "Why?"

He braced himself for her answer. While he knew darn well they shouldn't be entering into an affair, hearing her put a halt to it wouldn't be welcome news. He couldn't imagine not touching her again. She was under his roof and so darn beautiful; it would be the greatest test to his willpower to keep away from her.

"You didn't ask me to."

His mouth nearly dropped open. "I figured you'd know that I'd want to wake up with you."

"Adam," she said, sighing. "Are we really going to have this talk?"

This talk? *The talk?* "Well, hell yeah, we should talk. Don't you think so?"

"I don't see the point."

He clenched his teeth. "You don't see the point?"

"It's weird, Adam. That's all. You and me, after what happened between you and my sister. Are you making comparisons? Did I measure up?"

He blinked, obviously surprised. "Mia, what's going on between you and me has nothing to do with that. Well, indirectly it does, since if Rose wasn't born, I wouldn't have gotten to know you. What's done is done, Mia. I can't change the past. Is that why you're upset?"

"No, Adam. That's not it."

"Then what is it?"

Their voices were raised, and Rose's lips began to quiver. Her face flushed red, a precursor to crying that he'd come to recognize. Mia scrambled to her feet, taking the baby with her. "It's nothing," she said, her voice lower and steady for the baby's sake. "Nothing whatsoever. I'm going inside. The sun's getting too hot for the baby."

A few scattered rays of sunlight beamed through the clouds, hardly enough heat to warrant taking the baby inside. He rose to his feet. "Wait a minute, Mia. Don't leave. We need to figure this out."

"Is that an order?"

He sighed. He hated that she played the martyr. If she was confused, well, so was he. But what they shared last night, all night, was pretty damn amazing. "It's a request. What's gotten into you today?"

"You, Adam. You've gotten into me. How does it feel not having your questions answered? Not knowing where you stand? Not good? Well, welcome to my world."

Crap. He stood there mystified, watching her walk away.

What on earth did she want from him?

And when he figured it out, would he be able to give it to her?

"I can't believe my son didn't tell me about this little one, the minute he learned he was a father," Alena Chase said to Mia.

Mia sat next to Adam's mother on the sofa, with Rose seated comfortably on her lap. Alena's birthday celebration was set for six o'clock that night, and Adam had picked up his mother early to give her the news. He was off somewhere now, speaking to Mary and the catering staff.

Alena had a pleasant voice that hinted at her southern beginnings. Her eyes were a brilliant blue-gray very similar to Adam's, and she wore her thick white hair curled just under her chin in a youthful style. Her face was smooth for a woman her age and only crinkled when she smiled. There were plenty of smiles. She absolutely glowed around Rose. Mia could relate. She'd thought she might feel threatened by yet another Chase laying claim to Rose, but she didn't feel that way about Alena.

"I think it's taken Adam a while to come to grips with it himself," Mia said. She didn't come to his defense for any reason other than to keep Alena's feelings from being hurt. Leave it to Adam to let two weeks go by before he told his mother the truth. "I think he wanted to surprise you for your birthday."

Alena took Rose's small hand in hers and gave it a little shake and then stroked the baby's soft skin over and over.

"Such a sweet surprise. I can't even fault Adam—I'm too happy about becoming an instant grandmother today. It's the best gift in the world. Now I have my entire family here for my birthday."

Brandon sat down and scooted close to Mia, his arm resting behind her on the back of the sofa cushions. "That's just what you wanted, right, Mom?"

She nodded, her gaze never leaving Rose. "Yes. Just what I wanted."

Alena hadn't judged her. She hadn't asked a lot of questions, either. She wondered how much of the true story she'd gotten from Adam when he'd picked her up this morning. Adam, the great communicator.

Mia had made a special point to keep her distance from him all week. She couldn't out and out ignore him, because he expected to see the baby, but she'd found excuses to work later than usual at First Clips every day. There were a dozen good reasons why she needed to avoid him, but the main one popped into her head day and night and wouldn't leave her alone.

She was falling for him.

And that was a disaster in the making.

Adam walked into the room and all eyes turned to him. He took in their cozy scene on the sofa, his gaze lifting to Brandon's arm nearly around her shoulders. His nostrils flared a bit, and a tic worked his jaw. Surely, he didn't think that she and Brandon…

He took a seat opposite them, his back to the ocean, and spoke to his mother. "All is set for the party tonight."

"That's fine, son. I can't wait to introduce this little one to my friends."

Adam nodded. "She'll steal everyone's heart."

"She looks so much like Lily did at this age," his mother said, her eyes misting up.

Adam stared straight ahead, not saying a word. His throat moved in a giant swallow. On a Richter scale of curiosity, Mia registered the highest magnitude. Adam's life was one big mystery to her.

"Sorry Adam, I know you don't like to talk about Lily, but it's just that I feel she's—"

"Mom, she looks more like Adam, I think." Brandon intervened, giving each of them a glance.

"Actually, the baby has her mother's nose and mouth," Mia said softly, gazing at the baby in her arms. Her heart lurched. "She looks a lot like Anna."

Alena blinked, and then lowered her head. "Oh, dear. I'm sorry if I'm being callous." She seemed genuinely contrite. "I'm sure Rose has many of your sister's features. That poor girl, losing her life that way. You must miss her terribly."

"I do. Every day. We were close."

"I'm so smitten with the baby, I can hardly think straight. Can you forgive me?"

Mia nodded. "Yes. Of course. I understand."

Mary walked into the room to announce that lunch was being served on the veranda outside. It was her cue to escape the tension surrounding Adam's family. There seemed to be many unspoken words between them. "Rose needs a diaper change and a nap before the party. I'll take her upstairs now."

"I'll bring up your lunch if you'd like," Mary said.

"Oh, that's not necessary. I'm not very hungry. I'll come down later and eat something."

Mary tilted her head, a note of disapproval in her expression.

"I promise," Mia said. "I'll eat something in a little while."

Mary let it go with a nod. It was sweet the way Mary mothered her.

She made her escape to their rooms upstairs. It would be a big day for Rose, and she really did need a nap. She took one look at the baby making clicking noises and searching with her mouth for the bottle Mia had forgotten to bring up. "Oh, baby. What a dummy your auntie is."

"Is this what you're looking for?" Mia jumped and turned to Adam. He gestured, holding Rose's bottle. "It's ready to go. And, no, you're not a dummy. Maybe you're a little too anxious to get away from my family, though."

Mia's shoulders slumped. "Was I that obvious?" Adam looked a little worn around the edges. His face sported stubble, his eyes appeared sleep weary and not every hair on his head was in place. He looked approachable, normal, but still hot enough to heat her blood.

"Only to me."

"It's not your family, Adam. It's me. I feel...out of place. I know nothing about them, and I have no idea what you've told them about me."

"They know only what they need to know about you. All good things."

"You didn't tell them the entire truth?"

He cracked a rare smile. "Mia, really? You think I'd want them to know how I really came to meet you? What purpose would it serve?"

He was right and it eased her mind that he'd protected her from his family's mistrust and scrutiny.

"So they know nothing about how I—"

"No. They know you had trouble finding out who I was and that once you found me, you immediately told me I had a daughter. That's all they need to know."

"Okay, but I did what I did only because—"

"I know your reasons, Mia. No need to rehash them."

Adam set the bottle down beside the diaper changer and glanced at Rose. Mia had her diaper off and was cleansing her bottom. Adam reached for a diaper and opened it, his eyes, as tired as they appeared before, now beamed with love for his daughter. It transformed his whole face, and Mia would never tire of seeing that adoring expression on Adam. She lifted the baby's legs up a few inches, and Adam slid the diaper underneath her soft-cheeked bottom.

"We're becoming a well-oiled team," Adam said. "I'd like to think so anyway."

Mia finished diapering her and sat down on the glider. The baby latched on to the bottle instantly, guzzling the nipple and taking long pulls of formula.

Adam sat down on the floor beside the glider, watching her feed the baby. It was becoming a ritual, Adam waiting for the time when the baby slept, so he could hold her for precious moments and put her down into her crib.

Only minutes later, the bottle was sucked dry and the baby's eyes had drifted closed. When Mia nodded to Adam, he helped her up and the hand he'd placed on her shoulder sparked a riot of emotion. He hadn't touched her for days and she'd hoped to be immune, but that night of shared passion was never far from her mind. She'd done a good job of keeping her distance from him since, yet her body responded to him like no other man she'd ever met before. Drawing in her lips, she nibbled on them and sighed.

"Here you go." Carefully, she handed Rose off to him and walked out of the room. It was his special time with his daughter and Mia could grant him that. At any other part of the day, Rose didn't want to have anything to do with her father.

Mia was standing at the window in her room watching the tide roll in, when she heard a knock on her door. She turned to find Adam there. "Do you have a minute?"

"Is Rose down?" she asked.

"Sleeping like an angel."

"Shouldn't you be having lunch with your family?"

"I'll go down in a few minutes. My mother never tires of being with Brandon."

There it was again, spoken with no sarcasm, yet Adam's choice of words was very revealing.

"Come in."

He approached her and for a few seconds was quiet, standing by her side watching the surf curl into waves that beat upon the shore.

"What is it, Adam?"

He sighed and his gaze flowed over her. "It's you, Mia. You're doing your best to avoid me."

"I won't deny that."

His brows lifted as if he didn't expect her to be so blunt. "Why?"

Did he really want to have this conversation now, on the day of his mother's party? "Let's just say I don't find you…" She stopped. Was she really going to say she didn't find him appealing, attractive—she wasn't into him? Yeah, right. And the sun didn't rise in the east every day. "You and I aren't compatible." She shrugged. That would have to do.

"Liar."

"What?"

"We're very compatible. In case you're forgetting that pretty fantastic night together. I'm having a hard time forgetting it. And I heard no complaints from you that night."

She blushed. "I mean outside of the bedroom."

"How so?"

"Adam, you're a recluse. Not only do you hide inside your house—you don't engage with people. You're closed off. You give nothing of yourself away, and I already have trust issues with men. So, you see, it's impossible. Besides, there's Rose to think about."

"Leave Rose out of this. What do you mean, you have trust issues?"

"Something's clearly eating at you, and you won't tell me what it is."

"I don't know what you're talking about," he said, eyes wide as a schoolboy's.

"Okay, fine, Adam. If that's how you want to play this. There's really nothing much more to talk about. Now, if you don't mind, I have some work to do before the party tonight."

"Mia, don't dismiss me."

She lifted her face to his, shaking her head and wishing for things to be different. "Then tell me the truth, Adam." The plea in her voice was softly spoken. "Talk to me."

"I'll tell you one truth." He cupped her face in his hands and, before she knew what was happening, placed a solid, smoldering kiss on her lips. A guttural moan rose from her throat as he drew her closer, his body pressed to hers, hips colliding, chests crushing.

He ended the kiss abruptly and spoke over her bruised lips. "Compatible."

He was almost to her door, when he turned to her and tossed out, "For your own sake, stay away from my brother, Mia. He's trouble."

Nine

Trouble was charming. *Trouble* offered her a drink and bantered with her during the party, while Adam stayed back overseeing the celebration with his foot braced against the wall on the veranda. *Trouble* wasn't trouble at all. He seemed like a man eager to get to know his niece. Brandon would leave Mia and Rose's side and venture to the opposite end of the patio to entertain one of his mother's guests and then come back to say something clever to Rose. Mia had no interest in Brandon, other than he was Rose's uncle and so far, proved to be a pretty nice guy, yet Adam hadn't balked at the chance to warn her about him. Why?

"I can't believe she's my granddaughter," Alena said, rocking the baby gently, with the expertise only a mother would know. Rose seemed to enjoy it. So far, not a peep out of her as Alena held her. Adam had given Rose the outfit she wore today. It was a lavender satin little thing, with frills and lace, made by a designer. Her shoes and socks and bonnet all matched. Several of Alena's friends surrounded her, their gazes focused lovingly on grandmother and baby. Alena was in birthday heaven.

"She's lucky to have you," Mia said. She couldn't begrudge the baby the love of her grandmother. Rose deserved to be loved by everyone in her family.

Alena's eyes welled with tears. "Thank you. It's nice of you to say. I hope to be seeing a lot of her. She's the blessing I've been praying for."

"I think Rose would enjoy spending time with you, Alena."

Rose, as if on cue, began to fuss.

"There, there," Alena said, changing her position and rocking her a little more forcefully. Rose was having none of it. Her mouth opened to tiny cries that grew increasing louder. "Whoops, I think she needs her auntie Mia."

Alena transferred the baby into Mia's arms, just as a hush came over the twenty-five other partygoers. Mia turned to see what the big deal was all about. In walked Dylan McKay, only the most celebrated movie star of this decade, with a young woman on his arm. He smiled amiably at everyone and strode directly over to Alena. He took her hands in his. "Alena, happy birthday," he said, giving her a big smooch on the cheek.

Women had swooned over far less attention from Dylan McKay.

"Dylan, I'm very glad you came."

"I wouldn't miss it." Alena's face was in full bloom.

"This is Brooke, my little sis."

"Hi," Brooke said. She was very attractive and up until that moment, Mia suspected she knew what had been on everyone's mind when Dylan had walked in with her. Dylan McKay was fodder for the tabloids and the entire world supposedly knew who he was dating, made-up scandals or not. "Nice to meet you."

"The very same here, my dear. Thank you both for coming."

"I hear there's someone else for me to meet." Dylan turned her way. "Hi again, Mia," he said. "We've met once before." His daunting blue eyes bored into her, and she almost swooned herself.

"Yes, we have. Hello, Dylan. It's nice to meet you, Brooke."

Alena sent an adoring look at Rose. "And this gorgeous little babe is my granddaughter, Rose."

Mia wasn't new to celebrities. First Clips catered to a

high-end clientele, but she'd never spent time with anyone in the same caliber as Dylan McKay. Adam never mentioned to her he'd invited them, but of course, why would he break the mold? After that kiss today, her relationship with him was even more complex than ever.

Adam finally left his wall space and approached the group. "Dylan, Brooke," he said amiably. "Welcome."

Dylan nodded, his focus solely on Rose. "She's beautiful, Adam. Congratulations."

He extended his hand, and the two men shook. "Thanks. Can I get you and Brooke a drink?"

"Sure, I'll go with you. Brooke, are you okay here?" Dylan asked.

"Of course. You know I love babies. Do you mind if I hang out with you?" she asked Mia.

"Not at all," Mia said. "I'd like that."

"Great," Dylan said. "I'll be back in a little while."

Dylan walked off with Adam and Brooke turned her attention to Rose. "May I hold her?"

Mia smiled warmly. "You can try."

"So you're a daddy now?" Dylan said, taking a sip of Grey Goose. They stood a few feet from the bar, out of the way of the bartender, who was making cocktails for the guests.

Dylan's appearance impressed his mother's friends, but that was not why he'd been invited. Dylan truly cared for Alena Chase. She reminded him of his own mother, who was living a quiet life in Ohio as a retired school principal. And in his own way, Dylan McKay was old-fashioned about family. He was a good son and brother from what Adam could tell.

"It appears that way. It came as a shock, but I'm getting used to the idea."

Dylan glanced into the crowd surrounding Mia and the baby. "The baby also came with a pretty hot-looking nanny.

Or haven't you noticed?" He grinned that winning mega-watt grin that earned him millions.

"I've noticed. But don't let your imagination run wild. Mia isn't her nanny. She's Rose's aunt and she's off-limits." To every man here under the age of sixty, he wanted to add, which meant Dylan and Brandon.

"Possessive," Dylan said.

Adam shrugged. It did no good explaining the situation to Dylan. The guy formed his own impressions and usually they were dead-on. "Not really. Just looking out for my daughter's welfare."

"Hmm. Yeah, I can see that. She's living with you, isn't she?"

"Rose? Yes, she's my daughter."

"I meant Aunt Mia."

Of course that's what he meant. "It's a temporary arrangement. Now change the subject, Dylan."

"Okay, but first let me say I'm very happy for you. It may not be a perfect situation, but that baby will bring you a world of joy."

Dylan wanted to find a woman he could settle down and raise a family with. He'd dated a bunch of women already and hadn't found *the one*. The man loved kids and wanted a few of his own. Sometimes, fame came with a huge price, and he was never sure who he could trust, who was the real deal.

Adam could relate. He didn't trust easily anymore. He thought he knew what love was, but apparently he'd been wrong. Having his heart carved up and laid out on a silver platter could do that to a man.

"Your mom looks happy, Adam."

"She's getting exactly what she wants. Brandon and I have patched up our differences. The baby is the icing on the cake for my mother. A baby bonus."

"Yeah, well, babies have a way of softening people. So, you've forgiven Brandon?"

One night over a bottle of fifty-year-old Chivas Regal whiskey, Adam had divulged his heartache about Jacqueline and his brother to Dylan. He was the only person who remotely knew the story. Apparently, Dylan had been dumped once, too, before he'd become famous, and the scars had left an indelible mark on him.

"For the most part, yeah."

He glanced over to the fire pit. Brandon was standing beside Mia, and their laughter drifted to his ears. What did the two of them always seem to find so funny? Adam fisted his free hand as he sipped his drink.

Dylan followed the direction of his gaze "You sure? Because you're looking a lot like the jealous husband right out of my last movie about now."

Adam glared at Dylan.

"Hey, don't kill the messenger. Listen, if you're interested in her, you should do something about it. She's the whole package."

"How on earth do you know that?"

"Hell, Adam. I read people. And if she wasn't, you wouldn't trust your baby with her or look like you want to strangle your brother right about now."

Adam drew a sharp breath. "Shut up."

"You know I'm right."

"What happened to changing the subject?"

"Okay, fine. Are you going to Zane's wedding next week?"

Country superstar Zane Williams had been his other next-door neighbor on Moonlight Beach until he'd fallen in love with Jessica Holcomb, his late wife's sister, and moved back to Texas. "I am. How about you?"

"I'm bummed that I can't. I'm set to film up north next week."

"Are you taking Brooke with you?"

Dylan's gaze reverted to his foster sister, who was playing with little Rose. "No, Brooke's too busy with her new business. She's moving into her own apartment this week," he said. "Things are going well for her."

The chef interrupted his next thought. "Dinner is ready, Mr. Chase. Would you like to announce it, or shall I?"

"You do it, Pierre, and thank you."

Adam and Dylan walked over to the fire pit where Rose was staring at the stone gems casting off light and heat. She seemed fascinated by the crystallized display, and Adam got a kick out of seeing life through her untarnished eyes.

"Mom, we're ready for dinner. Chef made all of your favorites."

His mother looked up. "Mia and Rose will sit with us at our table?"

"Yes."

"And Brandon, too?" she asked.

"Of course, Mom. Today is all about family."

Mia's head lifted. Her eyes softened as they met his, and Adam winked at her.

She tilted her head to one side.

Then she smiled, a beautiful, heart-pulling smile that settled around his heart.

"The party was really nice," Mia said to Sherry on Monday morning as they prepared to open the doors at First Clips. The first appointments were due at nine. Sherry arranged her hairbrushes, combs and scissors, while Mia looked over the appointment book. Rose was perfectly happy swatting at the toys hanging over the handle of her infant seat. "Adam's mother is smitten with Rose. She said it was the best birthday of her life."

"I would imagine. Learning that she had an adorable granddaughter could only put a smile on her face. But, Mia, was it hard seeing her with the baby?"

Mia thought about it a second. "Not really. I thought it would be. Gram is the only grandmother Rose has known, so I worried that it might seem strange and, I don't know, kind of disloyal. But it wasn't that way at all. Alena is a warm person and she's careful not to be heavy-handed when it comes to Rose. She stayed over the weekend, and we got to know each other a little. For her birthday, I had a picture of Rose taken shortly after her birth blown up and framed. Alena cried when I gave it to her and told me how much she appreciated it. She left this morning and you should've seen her when she kissed Rose goodbye. It was really touching. "

"So, now it's just you and the hunky architect living in that big old mansion again?"

"Technically yes. But it isn't like that, Sherry."

"Okay, if you say so. Did I tell you how jealous I am that you partied with Dylan McKay? Mia, you're mingling with Hollywood royalty."

"About ten times this morning."

"Oh man, Mia. If I didn't love you so much, I'd hate you."

"Thanks… I think."

Rena walked in wearing a cerulean satin princess gown à la Cinderella. Her hair was piled up on her head; a tiara dotted with gemstones caught the overhead lighting. "Morning ladies. How's everyone today?"

"Dylan McKay was at the party over the weekend," Sherry announced.

"No way he was," Rena said. Contrary to her words, her face lit up. "He wasn't there, was he?"

"If I promise to tell you, you have to promise not to hate me."

Rena gave Sherry a glance. She was feigning a frown and nodding her head. Rena's eyes widened. "I promise," she said. "Now tell me all about it."

She recounted the brief conversations she'd had with Dylan to her friends, and as they worked through the morning, they managed to keep all their appointments on schedule. Five boys and seven girls were clipped and groomed and had walked out with smiles on their faces. By eleven-thirty, Mia's stomach growled. She hadn't eaten much that morning. As she headed to the back lounge, taking the diaper bag with her, she spotted Rena and Sherry ogling a man through the shop window.

"He's heading this way," Rena said. "Would you look at him? He's a ten, if I ever saw one."

"Ten and a half," Sherry added. "Bone structure counts extra, you know."

"I take it you're not talking about shoe sizes," Mia said, preoccupied with getting Rose's bottle out of the diaper bag.

"No, but oh man, Mia. This guy is hot. I bet he'd put your Adam to shame."

"He's not *my* Adam." She was curious enough to move over to the window beside her friends. She followed their line of vision and oh! Thump. The overfilled diaper bag slipped from her hand. She gulped. "That *is* Adam."

The girls shrieked. "That's Adam," Sherry said. "Oh, Mia. Now I really do hate you."

"Me, too," Rena said.

"Oh, be quiet, you two." What was he doing here? Adam was too busy perusing the storefront sign to notice the three of them all lined up, gawking at him.

The next thing she knew, he was reaching for the doorknob. The overhead chime rang out a rendition of the *Star Wars* theme and he walked in. The girls bumped shoulders, waiting in attendance. They probably looked like the Three Stooges on a bad day.

"Hello," he said, eyeing the girls first. Mia had to admit, their starship captain and princess getups were a bit distracting.

"Hi," the two chorused in unison.

Mia stepped up. "Adam, what are you doing here?"

He shrugged. After he lifted his shoulders, the beige

zillion-dollar suit he wore slipped right back into place. "I came to see your shop."

Rena made an obvious throat-clearing sound, and Mia got the hint.

"Oh, right. Adam, let me introduce you my friends. They staff the shop along with me. This is Rena and Sherry. Adam Chase."

He took both of their hands and gave a gentle one-pump handshake. "Nice to meet you ladies. I've heard good things from Mia about you."

"Same here," Sherry said. "I mean, Mia talks about you all the time."

Mia nibbled her lip.

Adam glanced at her, and she looked away.

"Where's Rose?"

"She's in the lounge, napping," Rena volunteered. "We take turns with that precious bundle. Sherry and I are her honorary aunties."

Adam nodded. "I know she's in good hands." He turned to Mia. "If you have a minute, I'd like to speak with you."

"Now? Here?" She was curious. Why couldn't it wait until she got home?

"Yes, if you have the time."

"Oh, um. Sure. Follow me and I'll give you the nickel tour. We can talk in the back room, and you can see Rose."

"Sounds like a plan."

It really did only take two minutes to show Adam the entire shop. They wound up in the lounge area where Rose was sleeping. "She's still asleep," she whispered. "Sometimes she sleeps in the infant seat and sometimes I put her down in the playpen. I keep this place spotless and she's in good hands with Rena and Sherry, so you don't—"

Two of his fingertips brushed over her mouth, stopping her from saying more. The pads were rough over her lips, but a sweet tingle washed through her anyway. "Mia, you don't have to explain. I'm not here to inspect the place."

"Then why are you here?"

"I came by to see where my daughter spends a lot of her time. And I came to ask you to lunch."

"Lunch? You want to have lunch with me?"

"You look surprised. Don't you take a lunch break?"

"Yes, but…why?"

He released a big sigh. "I'm trying, Mia."

"Trying to do what?"

"Not be so closed off."

They sat across from each other in a hole-in-the-wall restaurant in Santa Monica, three blocks away from her shop. Seaboard Café boasted the best seafood in town. The baby enjoyed the short walk in the stroller and was now sitting in her infant seat next to Mia, taking in the surroundings with inquisitive eyes. Mia's heart seemed to be in a perpetual state of melt mode lately. She'd gone gooey soft inside when Adam confessed he was trying not to be so closed off. For her? If only she could be sure. But oh wow, that seemed to come out of the blue. And it made her giddy.

Adam stood for a moment and removed his jacket. "You mind?"

She shook her head. He could undress in front of her anytime he wanted.

He unfastened his tie and folded it into his jacket pocket and then unbuttoned the first two buttons on a crisp cocoa-brown shirt. He'd come into the shop looking sharp and handsome, but he was no less gorgeous now. The girls would never let up on her now that they'd laid eyes on him.

He sat down, shot his daughter an adoring look and said, "I like your shop. It was hard to picture in my mind. Now, I can visualize children sitting in those chairs getting their hair cut."

"We still have our challenges. Sometimes we get a child who is frightened or stubborn. All the bells and whistles in the world won't get them to sit in the chair. Sherry has actually cut a child's hair, sitting in the rocket ship, while the child stood up. The kid absolutely refused to do it any other way. We have learned to be flexible."

"It's a great idea, though. A very unique approach for a hair salon. Was it your idea?"

"No, I'm not that imaginative. It was Anna's. She was the mastermind of First Clips."

Adam nodded. And then hesitated. His lips pursed, tightening up. He seemed to have something to say, but he kept silent.

"What is it?" she asked.

"Your sister. I'm sorry she died, Mia."

Mia's heart pounded hard, the way it did whenever Anna's death was brought up. "Thank you."

"What you said about me comparing you to her, that isn't true. It never crossed my mind."

Mia's eyes narrowed on him. "Not even a little?"

"No. Not even a little."

"I wasn't too happy with you when I said those things."

"I know."

The waitress came by to take their order. Mia ordered a bay shrimp salad to Adam's grilled salmon. A loaf of pumpernickel bread and cheesy biscuits were placed on the table along with garlic-infused butter. Mia's mouth watered. When Adam offered her the bread, she grabbed a cheesy biscuit.

"Hungry?"

"Starving."

"Dig in. So when does the baby eat?"

"She'll be fussing the minute my food arrives, I'm sure. She has an inner time clock that keeps Aunt Mia in shape. My hips are grateful."

"So am I." A wicked smile graced his face.

"Is that so?" She chuckled and didn't know what to make of Adam today. "Tell me that when it happens to you."

"I'm waiting for the day when Rose lets me feed her."

"The pediatrician said he might give me the okay to start feeding her solid foods. She might be eating with a spoon soon."

"So soon? I'll never get to feed her with a bottle."

"Yes, you will, Adam. She'll come around. And she'll be drinking from a bottle for a long time."

"I'd like to go to her next pediatrician's appointment with you. When is it?"

"Next week. I was going to ask you to join us, if you weren't too busy."

"I'm never going to be too busy for Rose," he said emphatically.

After their meals arrived, Mia got two bites of her salad in before the baby squawked and squirmed uncomfortably in her seat. "See, I told you. She has a sixth sense." She smiled at Rose. "You don't want your auntie Mia getting chubby, do you?"

"I'm recognizing her different cries now. That's definitely a hunger cry." He dug into the diaper bag and grabbed the bottle. He gave it a few shakes and handed it to her. "I wish she'd let me help you more."

Mia lifted the baby out of the infant seat. "You're welcome to try anytime you want, Adam." She gestured with the bottle.

"Not now. I wouldn't want to get kicked out of this place. The food is good. I'd like to come back."

"Chicken," Mia said, grinning. Rose was getting good at holding the smaller four-ounce bottles on her own. Mia fed the baby with one hand and picked up her fork and took bites of her salad with the other.

"You make it all work, Mia." Adam's note of admiration wasn't lost on her. "You multitask like a pro."

"Thanks. Are you buttering me up for something?"

He cut into his meal and chewed thoughtfully. "Why, because I'm paying you a compliment?"

"Well, yes. There is that."

"You caught me. But I'd give you the compliment even if I didn't have something to ask you."

"So, I was right?"

"Yes." He braced his arms on the table's edge and leaned forward, capturing her attention. "I want to take you and the baby away for the weekend."

"What?" She couldn't possibly have heard him correctly.

"I'm going to a wedding, and I want to take you with me."

She absorbed that for a moment. "You want me or the baby?"

"Both of you, of course."

Meaning, he wanted Rose with him, and the only way that could happen was if she went, too. They were a package deal.

"My friend is getting married, and you're both invited. It's in a small town in Texas. We'll leave Friday morning and be home by Sunday afternoon. It's short notice, but I'm hoping you'll say yes."

"I don't know, Adam." She began shaking her head. "Taking Mia on a plane can get complicated. I'd have to check it out with her doctor. Wouldn't it be easier for you to go without us?"

"I'm chartering one of my brother's planes. So we'd have a ton of room and all the conveniences we'd need. The trip is less than four hours, Mia. And well, I don't want to stall the small amount of progress I've made with Rose. The truth is, I don't want to miss a minute of time with her."

It was a tough situation. Mia was pretty much at his mercy. If he wanted to take his daughter somewhere, Mia would always be the tagalong. "Texas?"

"It'll be fun. A change of scenery. The wedding is being held in a barn on his property."

"Whose property?"

"Zane Williams."

Mia shrieked. "*The* Zane Williams. The country superstar?"

He nodded, blinking at her outburst.

"For heaven's sake, Adam. Don't you know any normal people?"

He chuckled. "Zane is as down-to-earth as they come. He's a great guy, and he wants to meet my daughter. Mia, I really want you there with me. It's not just about the baby."

Could she believe that? Should she trust him enough to believe he genuinely wanted her with him? "Give me some time to think about it."

"Okay. I can do that."

The meal was over, and Mia fastened Rose into her infant carrier again. Adam paid the check and picked up the carrier, inserting it into the stroller base. With a click, the baby was latched in. He was getting good with the baby's gadgets.

Adam assumed the position, taking hold of the stroller handle. "Ready, my pretty little Rose? Daddy's going to take you for a walk." She lagged behind as he strolled the baby out of the restaurant and onto the sidewalk, heading back to the shop.

There would be nothing left of her heart if Adam continued being so sweet and loving. He wanted to be a father in every sense of the word. How could she stand in his way?

She already knew what her answer to the weekend trip had to be.

She couldn't seem to deny Adam Chase anything anymore.

Ten

The plane trip was as comfortable as Adam said it would be. Rose slept most of the time in her car seat, and Mia and Adam played games with her during the rest of the trip. Mia had half hoped the pediatrician wouldn't give Rose permission to fly, but that hadn't been the case at all. Rose had gotten the all clear. And now Adam sat facing Mia in a stretch limo loaded down with baby equipment, heading toward Beckon, Texas.

"Tell me about Zane and his fiancée," Mia asked Adam, keeping her voice low. The baby's eyes were drifting closed again. Mia wished she could join her in a nap. "You told me that he'd leased the house next door to you and that you'd become friends during that time. But that's all I know, really."

Adam poured her a glass of lemonade from the bar and extended his arm to hand it her. "Thanks."

"You haven't read about it? It's big entertainment news. I guess the story got leaked out about Zane falling for his late wife's sister. They fell in love when Jessica came to Moonlight Beach to heal her wounds from being dumped at the altar."

"I don't have much time to read that stuff, Adam."

Adam poured himself a glass of lemonade, too, and took a sip. "Jessica is a nice woman. You're going to like her. She's a schoolteacher. I got to know her a bit when she lived here."

"And so will this wedding be a three-ring circus?"

"It shouldn't be. They were keeping their wedding plans a secret. Zane had rumors spread that they were hoping to get married next summer on the beach where they met. So, hopefully, this small farm wedding won't attract attention."

"I hope not, for their sake. They deserve to have a private ceremony."

His eyes flickered as he flashed a smile. That killer rare smile did things to her insides. Then he slid across from his seat to sit beside her and brought his hand up to her face. The gentle touch had her lifting her chin, and their eyes met as his arm wrapped around her shoulder. "I'm glad you're with me, Mia."

"Me, too," she said, taking a swallow of air.

His head bent toward her, and her mouth was captured in a long delicious kiss that was sweet, soothing and different from the way he'd kissed her before. "It's a long ride," he said. "Why don't you close your eyes and get some rest?"

It was just what she needed. The plane trip and all the preparations beforehand had worn her out. "Sounds perfect."

He cradled her in his arms and coaxed her head onto his chest. He smelled of musk and man, so strong and so good. The sound of his heart beating, the rapid thump, thump, thumping, calmed and comforted her as she drifted off.

A kiss to her forehead snapped her eyes wide-open. "Wake up, sweetheart."

Mia pushed up and away from Adam's grasp to get her bearings. The limo was parked in front of a hotel. All those miles of flatlands were behind them. "Did I sleep the whole way?"

"You and Rose were sleepyheads."

She gazed at Rose in the car seat. Her eyes were just now opening. "Wow, I didn't mean to sleep so long." She fiddled with her mussed hair. She must look a wreck.

"You needed the rest. You do a lot, holding down a job and taking care of Rose."

"I love it."

"I know, but that doesn't mean it doesn't wear you down at times."

She couldn't disagree. She'd been getting up with Rose twice a night the last few days. The baby was cutting teeth and wasn't sleeping through the night.

The chauffeur opened the door, and Adam unsnapped the baby out of the infant seat. He handed her off to Mia before she fussed and then extended his hand to help them out of the car. After Adam gave the driver instructions regarding the baby equipment, he guided her to the front desk and checked them into the only two-room suite on the premises.

Beckon wasn't a destination stop, but Zane Williams had put their little town on the map. He was their pride and joy. That much she knew about the country star.

As they entered the elevator, Adam whispered in her ear. "I can't promise you a five-star hotel. But I was assured it's a decent place."

"All I need are clean sheets and a nice bathtub and I'm happy."

"Is that all it takes to make you happy?"

"Uh-huh." She glanced at him. There was a lightness to Adam lately that kept her on her toes. "And what makes you happy?"

"Whatever makes you happy, Mia."

If he wanted her to jump his bones, he was halfway there. She liked this new Adam. He was charming and sweet. It sort of unsettled her, though. His abrupt turn-around seemed too good to be true.

"Right answer," she said as she stepped out of the elevator to face their suite.

Adam opened the door and they stepped inside. "Wow, this is nice," she said immediately. It was spacious with a flat-screen television on the wall and two lovely sofas facing a fireplace. A double door opened to one large bedroom and a master bath.

A large bouquet of pink lilies filled a glass-blown lavender vase that sat on the fireplace hearth. Adam walked over to it and read the card. "It's from Zane and Jessica, welcoming us to Beckon."

"Nice of them," she said. Rose was getting heavy in her arms. "Adam, can you lay a blanket down, please?"

He jumped to help her, retrieving the blanket from the diaper bag. Kneeling down, he placed it in the center of the room, and Mia met him there as she laid the baby down on her stomach. "Tummy time," she said. Then she gazed at Adam. "There's only one bedroom," she blurted. It was one of the first things she'd noticed about the suite.

"You and the baby take the bedroom. I'll sleep in here," he said. "I'm sure the sofas fold out into beds."

Their eyes locked, and warmth heated her cheeks. It was one thing living under Adam's roof in a huge mansion of sixteen rooms. A person could go all day without bumping into anyone else, but here? *Awkward.*

"You're pretty when you blush," Adam said.

Her shoulders slumped. No sense skirting the issue. "It's not as if we haven't slept together, Adam. But we have to be careful for Rose's sake that we don't make a mistake."

"I agree. We're on the same page, Mia."

"We are? Okay, good." As long as she made herself clear. Adam had no clue how hard it would be to go to bed tonight knowing he was only steps away. She wasn't as immune to him as she pretended, especially lately. He'd been a dream these past few days. "So what's on the agenda today?" she asked.

"Well, first we take a little rest and get settled. And later tonight there's a welcome barbecue at the farm. Zane's in the process of building Jessica a house, so it'll be on his property, but prepare to rough it a bit."

"You didn't design the house by any chance?"

"It's their wedding present. Zane had specifics and I helped him along."

"It's probably going to be fantastic, a dream home."

"I hope so."

"If you designed it, it will be."

Adam's expression softened and warmth filled his eyes. "Thank you."

She stared at him. "You're welcome."

Their luggage arrived at the door, breaking the moment, and they spent the next twenty minutes unpacking and setting up the baby's equipment.

By six o'clock they were standing on Zane Williams's property, a vast amount of land accented by cottonwoods and lush meadows. Off in the distance, she saw the house under construction and could only imagine how beautiful it would be when it was done. Adam told her there were balconies and terraces to the rear of the home facing a lake.

The party invitation had said ultracasual. Mia wore a soft cotton paisley dress and tall tan leather boots. Adam told her she looked very much like a country girl. Adam did the cowboy thing justice, too. He wore jeans, a belt buckle, boots and a black Western shirt with white snaps. He could easily play the sexy villain in a Western movie in that getup.

"Ready?" he asked.

She nodded and Adam placed a hand to her back as they headed on foot toward the festivities held under tall thick oaks shading the area. Mia pushed the stroller, and when the terrain got a little too rough, Adam took over. As they approached a set of picnic benches with candles burning and vases filled with willowy wildflowers dotting the length of the dressed tables, intense hickory scents flavored the air and worked at her appetite. Beyond the benches, smoke billowed from three giant smoker barbecue grills.

"Howdy," said a voice she recognized. She owned at

least three of Zane Williams's albums. And sure enough, he was approaching them, holding the hand of a pretty blonde woman. "Adam, I'm glad you could make it. Congratulations on being a daddy."

The men shook hands and the woman placed a kiss on Adam's cheek. "Yes and congrats from me, too, neighbor. So glad you all made it for our wedding."

"I am, too, Jess. You're looking beautiful and very happy," Adam said.

She winked. "Never could pull the wool over your eyes, Adam. And who are these gorgeous ladies?"

Adam made the introductions. Mia couldn't believe Zane Williams actually gave her a warm hug and thanked her for coming. "Nice meeting you and congratulations. Little Rose, is she?"

"Yes, she was named after my mother," she told the couple.

"Pretty name," Zane said, crouching down to get a better look at Rose. "She's got your eyes, Adam. Such a pretty little thing."

"And you're the baby's aunt?" Jessica asked softly, eyeing the baby.

"Yes, I'm Aunt Mia." There was no need to go into further detail. She didn't know how much Adam had told them, but she was certain it wasn't all that much.

"Well, I hope you have a nice time this evening," Zane said. "We've invited our closest friends and family. Before we eat, we'll go around and introduce you to everyone."

"Sounds good," Adam said.

Mia raised her brows. There must be fifty people in attendance. Small for wedding standards, but would Adam make the rounds to meet everyone or stay in the shadows like he always did?

"Would you like to sit down?" Adam asked after Jessica and Zane left. "Looks like we can take our pick of seats."

"Actually, I'd like to walk around a bit. If you don't mind trudging around with the stroller."

"Not at all." They headed away from the festivities, staying to flat grounds, Rose cooing and gurgling as they bumped along a grassy path. "I didn't know Rose was named after your mother."

"She was. Rose was her middle name."

"Makes me wonder what else I don't know about you. And don't say, welcome to my world."

Mia's breath caught. At some point, she'd wanted to tell Adam about her life and share her innermost secrets. But did she know him well enough? So far the men in her life had only disappointed her. If Adam hurt her, she'd be devastated. She'd wait for the time when Adam met her halfway. Right now, he already knew much more about her than she knew about him. "How about, welcome to my universe?"

"Very funny, Mia." But Adam was smiling, and he didn't press her.

They walked along in silence and returned in time to meet Zane and Jessica's family and friends. All the while, Adam stayed by her side and was cordial to everyone, shaking hands, making small talk.

They sat down to the best barbecue Mia had ever eaten. She tasted a little of everything. The spareribs were to die for. The corn on the cob smoked in their husks and flavored with honey butter, insane. The chicken, shrimp and brisket were all tender and tasty. Mia had never eaten so much in her life.

Zane and Jess sat down with them after the meal. Mia was enamored by the love they shared. Zane's eyes gleamed when he looked at his fiancée and spoke about the house they'd live in and the children they hoped to have one day. Mia's heart did a little tumble. How lovely to see two people so blessed by love. Her mother had never had that. And Mia's track record with the opposite sex wasn't all that good, either. She'd met too many men like her father. Flakes, liars or losers. She'd weeded out quite a few, and what was left in the dating pool hadn't been all that inspiring.

From under the table, Adam's hand sought hers and he entwined their fingers. It seemed like such a natural move and yet it meant something monumental. She glanced at his strong profile as he bantered with Zane and clung on to her hand, his thumb absently stroking over her skin.

Sweet, amazing sensations whipped through her. Somehow, after their arguments, their intense lovemaking and their time spent with Rose, after pranking those teens on the beach, kissing under the moonlight and holding hands under the table, Mia had fallen fully and deeply in love with Adam Chase.

She loved him. There wasn't anything she could do about it.

She'd put up a good battle. She'd tried to talk herself out of it. She'd tried to keep her distance, falling short of her goal a time or two, but it was no use. Adam wasn't a flake, a liar or a loser. He was pretty wonderful. And she was about to give him the one thing she hadn't given another man. Her full trust.

"Well, it's time for me to punish y'all with a song or two," Zane was saying. The sun had set and glass lights slung from tree to tree lit the night. "We've got a fire going. Come on around to the fire pit and bring the baby, too. I'll sing her a lullaby."

"I'll round up our guests," Jess said "Mia, I'll come sit with you in a while."

"I'd like that."

Adam helped her up and gave her a kiss on the cheek. "What was that for?"

"Just because," he said and squeezed her hand before he let her go.

Could he be feeling the same sentiment and mood as

her? Was being outdoors under the stars with all the talk of love and marriage getting to him?

With darkness came cooler breezes, and Mia shivered a bit. "Rose is going to need a sweater," she said.

"I'm right on it." Adam reached into the basket under the stroller and gave her a choice of a blue knit sweater or a black-and-pink sequined Hello Kitty jacket.

"Such a good daddy."

"Unless you think it's too cold for the baby," he added. "If you want to head back to the hotel, I'm fine with it."

"And miss a private performance by Zane Williams? Not on your life." She nabbed the jacket out of his hands.

Adam laughed.

It was such a beautiful sound.

Adam laid the sleeping baby into the play yard, her own personal bed brought from home. Mia loved the way he handled Rose now, confident but also so tenderly it made her heart sing. Standing together in the hotel bedroom, they watched her take peaceful breaths. Adam reached for Mia's hand again, and their fingers naturally entwined. She could stay this way forever, in the quiet of the night, with the man she loved and their little bundle of sweetness.

"The party knocked her out," Adam said.

"It's been a long day."

"Are you tired? Should I leave you, so you can get some sleep?"

"No, stay." The night had been perfect and she didn't want it to end.

"Let's have a drink." He lingered one more second over Rose and then led her into the living room. "Have a seat," he said, leaving her by the sofa. "I'll get us something from the bar."

Instead Mia walked over to him and laid her hand on his arm. "Adam, I don't need a drink."

He turned to her, his brows lifting. "You don't?"

She shook her head. "I don't," she said softly, staring into his eyes.

His lids lowered, and his arms wrapped around her waist. "What do you want, sweetheart?" he rasped.

Mia rose up on tiptoes and pressed her lips to his. She'd taken him momentarily by surprise, but Adam was fast on his feet, and she loved that about him. He drew her up, cradling her body to his, deepening the kiss and letting her know with deep-throated groans that he wanted her as much as she wanted him.

Their kisses led to the shedding of their clothes and the two of them falling onto the sofa cushions. Adam's hands roved her body, his touches eliciting white-hot sensations that brought her to the brink of ecstasy. She cried out quietly, muting her sighs with closed lips. Adam was an expert at drawing her out. And when he coaxed her to do the same to him, she didn't disappoint. Her caresses led to bolder moves as she explored his body and made love to him in every way she knew how.

She gave him her whole self, holding nothing back. Making love on a sofa brought out Adam's inventive side. He positioned her in ways that heated her blood and made her ache for more. Mia was happy, so happy she didn't want to think about where this would lead. She shut her mind off to anything but good thoughts and as she climbed higher and higher, Adam wringing out every last ounce of her energy, each powerful thrust brought her closer to completion. And then it happened. His name tumbled from her lips over and over and her body splintered.

Adam wasn't far behind, and as he held her, his face inches from hers, his eyes locked on hers, he bucked his body one last time and shed a release that brought them both earth-shattering pleasure.

He collapsed on top of her, and she bore his weight. Her hands played in his sweat-moistened hair as his mouth found hers. His kiss was gentler now, easy and loving. "Are you okay, sweetheart?" he murmured.

"Mmm." She was humming inside, feeling wonderful, filled with love.

Adam rolled off her, taking her with him so she wouldn't fall off the sofa. It was a tight fit, but there wasn't anywhere she'd rather be. "Mia, we're good together." He kissed her forehead.

It was hardly a declaration of love, but if it was the best he had to offer, she'd take it. "We are."

A cool blast of air made her shiver. It was hard to believe since Adam's body was a hot furnace. But the air conditioner was running and the room was growing chilly.

"You're cold?"

"A little."

"Let me get the sofa bed ready, Mia. I want you with me tonight. Will you stay?"

"I'll stay."

"Good." She was lifted off him and kissed soundly on the lips. "You go check on Rose. I'll only be a minute."

She grabbed Adam's shirt, fitting her arms through the sleeves and scooted out of the room. The baby was still peaceful and sleeping on her back, her cheeks as rosy as ever, such a pretty sight. She was plenty warm in her sleep sack.

When she returned to the room, the bed was made up and Adam was waiting. He patted the spot beside him and she climbed in next to him. The back of the sofa as their headboard, they used pillows to prop up. Adam put his arm around her shoulders and she snuggled in, bringing a sheet over them. "Better?" he asked.

"Much. The baby is still asleep."

He kissed her forehead. "I haven't been this happy in a long time."

She let those words sink in. "Since when, Adam?"

He was silent for a while. Had he been thinking out

loud? Did he regret revealing that much to her and had she overstepped again, trying to get information out of him? He let go a deep sigh, and her breath caught. Then he spoke. "I was almost engaged once. I thought we were perfect together. Her name was Jacqueline."

"What happened with her?" she asked in a whisper.

"She broke it off. Pretty much broke my heart. I thought we were crazy in love, but it turned out I'd been wrong about our relationship. I'd never been poleaxed like that before. You know, it was like a sucker punch to my gut."

"I'm so sorry, Adam."

"That's not all. About a month later, I called her. It was late at night and I couldn't sleep. I'd been rehashing everything and it all seemed so wrong. I thought surely she was having doubts about the breakup. It was all a big mistake. I can still remember the shock I felt when I heard my brother's voice on the other end of the phone. For a few seconds, it didn't quite click. I thought I'd dialed the wrong number. And when it hit me, my head nearly exploded. I'm surprised I didn't grind my teeth to the bone. Of course, Brandon made all sorts of excuses, but he didn't deny the fact that he and Jacqueline were together."

"Oh, Adam. Really? Brandon and Jacqueline? That was the ultimate betrayal."

"I thought so. Believe me—I wasn't happy with either one of them. I didn't speak to Brandon until they broke up three years later. He cheated on her, and she finally wised up and dumped him."

"Wow. So that's what you have against him. I get it now. You must've loved her a lot."

"It was years ago, Mia. I'm over her, and Brandon is who he is. My mother has been after me for years to mend fences. Somehow it's my fault all of this happened. She believes Brandon didn't go after Jacqueline until after she broke up with me. I can't blame Mom. She wants us to be close like we once were."

"What happened is clearly not your fault," Mia said. "But you have forgiven your brother, haven't you?"

"There's a difference between forgiving and forgetting. I'm not holding a grudge. But I can't forget who Brandon is."

"Is that why you warned me about him?"

She set her hand on his chest and stroked him tenderly, sliding over his skin, hoping to soothe him, calm him, make the pain go away. He reached for her hand and lifted it to his lips, placing a kiss on her palm. They were finally connecting, finally making headway.

"If he goes anywhere near you, there's no telling what I'd do to him."

Warmth spiraled through her body, a slow flow of heat that surrounded her entirely. "You don't have to worry—there's only one Chase I'm interested in." She kissed his shoulder, and he gazed into her eyes. There was no mistaking the gratitude and relief she found in them.

"I'm glad." He sighed heavily as if relieved of his burden. "I feel like I've been given a second chance with my life. I don't want to blow it again."

"Adam, what do you mean, second chance? Are you talking about your sister? Is it about Lily?"

His eyes closed then, as if the pain was too much. He shook his head. "Yes, but I can't talk about Lily now, Mia. I can't talk about my sister."

"Okay." There was enough force in his voice to make her a believer. "You don't have to tell me."

"Thank you, sweetheart."

Adam was trying. It was all she could ask of him.

The old barn was decorated with wildflowers, lilies and white roses. Sprays of color splashed over haystacks, and snowy sheer curtains were draped from rafter to rafter overhead. Hundreds of flameless candles cast romantic lighting over the entire interior of the barn and lanterns on pickets defined each row of white satin chairs tied with big bows.

"It's beautiful," Mia said. She sat beside him in the last row. A precaution, she'd said, in case the baby fussed, she could duck out and make a quick escape.

"*You're* beautiful," he whispered. "The place is okay."

The jade in her eyes brightened, and he winked playfully. Mia wore a stunning pastel-pink dress that met her waist in delicate folds, accented her sexy hips and flowed to her knees. Her hair was down and curled, and her olive skin absolutely glowed. Rose looked cute as a button. She wore pink, too, her dress a mass of fancy ruffles. A big matching bow wrapped around her forehead. She was smiling now, her eyes gleaming as she took in the candles and colorful flowers surrounding her.

Adam knew a sense of peace. This moment in time couldn't be more perfect. He reached for Mia's hand—he'd been doing that lately, sometimes without realizing it—and held it on his knee.

Violins began to play, and people milling about promptly took their seats.

Zane appeared, walking in from the side entrance, wearing tuxedo tails and his signature cowboy hat, looking happier than he'd ever seen him. Zane took his place next to the minister at the back of the barn. A ray of sunshine poured over him from the loft window—he had his own personal spotlight—as he searched the aisle for signs of his bride.

And then the orchestra kicked up, playing a classic version of "Here Comes the Bride."

A hush fell over the barn.

Jessica stepped up and all eyes turned toward her. Chairs creaked and shuffling sounds echoed against the walls as everyone rose to their feet.

"I love her dress," Mia whispered.

Ivory and satin, with lace everywhere, Jessica made a lovely bride.

She'd been jilted at the altar once before, but if Adam knew Zane, he was more than going to make up for that.

Jessica made her trip down the aisle, smiling, her face beaming, the bouquet of star lilies and gardenias trembling in her hands.

She reached Zane, and everyone settled back into their seats.

The minister gave a lovely speech about second chances, and something hit home for Adam as he reached for Mia's hand again. He'd liked waking up with her this morning. Almost as much as he'd enjoyed taking her to bed last night. And afterward, he'd managed to give her a glimpse into his life. He'd told her things about Brandon and Jacqueline he'd never shared before with another human being. He'd shared his heartache with her, the betrayal that ruined him for love.

He'd been over Jacqueline for a long time. But he'd never get over Lily. Mia hadn't pressed him last night about her, and he'd been relieved. He kept those memories buried.

Rose began to kick in her infant seat. She had a shelf life of about twenty minutes, before things got out of hand. Her complaints started quietly and Mia took out a long-necked giraffe teething toy. She handed it to Rose, and that seemed to settle her.

Zane and Jessica exchanged vows, making mention of the woman they'd both loved and lost, Janie Holcomb Williams, and promised to do her memory honor by living a good and happy life. Adam had never met Zane's first wife, but he knew the heartache her death had caused to both Jessica and Zane. It was a touching moment, and even Mia shed a tear or two.

Now the minister was asking if anyone knew a reason why the couple shouldn't be joined in holy matrimony, and Rose's mouth opened as if on cue. A belch blasted from her lips, so loud it was hard to believe the uncouth sound had come from such a tiny person.

The entire assembly laughed. Zane and Jessica glanced over their shoulders and chuckled, too.

Mia gasped and looked at Adam in wide-eyed shock, but then a slow grin spread across her face and they both burst out laughing, like everyone else.

The minister made a joke about that not counting, garnering a few more chuckles and he proceeded with the ceremony.

After the wedding, the barn was transformed into a reception hall. The orchestra was replaced by Zane's country band, and a dance floor was laid down. Appetizers were passed around and a bar was set up. It all flowed smoothly.

Mia had the baby out of the infant carrier now and was swaying to the music. Rose was cackling, making those little sounds of happiness that ripped into his heart. He wound his arms around both of them, Rose sandwiched in between, and swayed with them, rocking back and forth to the music. It seemed as long as Mia was present, his finicky little daughter would tolerate him.

"Now that's a sight to behold."

Adam turned to the smiling groom. "Hey, buddy. Congratulations." He shook his hand and gave him a light slap on the back. "Great ceremony."

"Thanks. Thanks. We did it. Jess is a beautiful bride, isn't she?"

"She is." Mia stepped up to give him a hug. "Congratulations. I feel honored to have been invited."

"Hey, well, you and this little one are part of Adam's family now." Zane smiled and playfully wiggled Rose's toes. "She even participated in the ceremony."

Mia's gaze shot up. "Oh, gosh. I'm sorry about the disruption. You never know what these little ones are going to do. Leave it to Rose to make her presence known," she said.

"She's a glutton for attention. She doesn't get that from me," Adam said.

"Oh, so you're saying it comes from my side of the family," Mia teased.

"Hey, we didn't mind. Honestly," Zane said.

"Not at all," Jessica said as she joined Zane, slipping her hand in his. "It was just what the ceremony needed, a little levity."

Jessica's appearance brought another round of hugs and congratulations. And shortly after, the announcement was made that dinner was ready.

Halfway through the meal, Adam's phone vibrated. He pulled it out of his pocket and frowned when he saw the name lit up on the screen. He wanted to ignore the call and finish his meal with Mia, but something told him he needed to answer his brother's call. He kissed Mia's cheek, breathing in her intoxicating scent and rose. "Excuse me. I've got to take this call. Are you going to be all right?"

"We'll be fine. Rose needs a diaper change. I was just about to take her."

"Okay, I'll meet you back here and we'll finish our meal."

He walked out of the barn and strode toward the construction site, away from the music and conversations and picked up on the fifth ring. "Brandon, it's Adam. I'm at a wedding in Texas. What's up?"

"Adam. You need to come home right away. Mom's had a heart attack."

Eleven

Adam held his mother's pasty hand, gazing into her soft blue eyes. A pallor had taken over her skin as she lay in the hospital bed. She was hooked up to IV tubes and oxygen, yet she managed to smile. "Hi, Mom."

"Adam, you came." Her voice was weak.

"Of course I came." He squeezed her hand. He'd flown half the night to get back to Los Angeles, hoping he wouldn't be too late. He'd had a limo waiting at the airport and had come first thing. Mia and the baby were driven to Grandma Tess's home so she could spend time with Rose.

"I'm so glad you both are here," Mom said, glancing at Brandon, too.

Brandon stepped up. "Of course we're here."

"I'm sorry to worry you. I don't know what happened. One minute I was fine, shopping with Ginny, and the next thing I know, my legs went out from under me. I felt terribly weak, and a few kind people at the mall brought me over to a bench and sat me down. Someone called nine-one-one."

"I'm glad they did. You need to be here," Brandon said. He'd been in constant contact with Adam, letting him know the status of the tests they were doing. "Mom, you've had a bad attack of angina. It's not life-threatening, but you do have to take it easier now. Eat better, watch your diet. You'll probably be put on medication, too."

"They're keeping me here for a few days."

"Just for observation," Brandon said. "They've got a few more tests to run, and they want to monitor you. I think it's a good idea."

"I do, too," Adam said, greatly relieved the emergency wasn't more serious. He wasn't ready to say goodbye to his mother.

Tears filled her eyes. "I was shopping for Rose. Oh dear… I want to see her grow up, Adam. I want to be around for all of it."

"You will, Mom." She didn't get to see her own daughter grow up. She didn't have the chance to raise Lily. "You'll see Rose as much as you want. I'll make sure of it, Mom. I'll be sure to keep my baby safe." His voice cracked. Fatigue, worry and regret had him spilling out words he'd always wanted to say. Words that he'd harbored for years. "I won't let you down the way I did with Lily."

"Oh no…you didn't… Please don't feel that way. I don't blame you. I never did, son. And that was before Brandon told me the truth earlier today." Her face tightened, the wrinkles around her eyes creasing.

Adam whipped his head around. "Brandon, what did you tell her?"

"The truth, Adam," his brother said. His jaw tight, the hard rims of his eyes softened. "I told Mom about how you covered for me during that storm. How you wanted to leave the storm cellar and check for Lily and how I lied to you. I told you Lily was with Mom, when I knew it wasn't true. I was too scared to let you go looking for her up at the house. I didn't want you to leave me alone. You were my big brother and I needed you to protect me." Brandon put his head down.

Adam let that sink in. Seconds ticked by, his mind scrambling for answers. "Why now?" he asked Brandon.

"Because he thought I was dying, Adam."

He stared at his mother. Then blinked. She'd shocked him, but her expression now was solid and more alive than when he'd first walked into her room. "It's been bothering him for years—isn't that what you said, Brandon? And today you thought I might die before you could confess the truth to me."

"Mom, you're not dying." His brother's voice was deep and compassionate.

"From your lips to God's ears." Her pained sigh resounded in the quiet room. Her head against her bed pillows, she closed her eyes. "The truth is, I've been blaming myself all these years. I shouldn't have left Lily alone with you boys." Her voice was soft, reverent and full of regret. She peered at both of them. "She was only six. You were twelve, Adam, and Brandon was eight. I knew we lived in tornado country. It was to be a quick trip to the grocery store, but I should've taken Lily with me. She wasn't your responsibility—she was mine. I'm more to blame than anyone. I'm only grateful, when that tornado ripped through our land, you boys didn't die along with her. Adam, you took your brother to safety and kept him there. Or maybe all three of you would've died."

Brandon had tears in his eyes. "I told Adam I saw Lily go in the car with you, so he wouldn't leave me alone. I lied, and Lily died."

"You were so young, Brandon," Mom said. "I understand how scared you must've been. But have you ever once considered that you might have saved both of your lives that day?"

"No, Mom, I never did. And I've hated myself ever since." Brandon spoke quietly, his voice nearly breaking.

Adam winced and breathed deep, keeping his emotions at bay. He couldn't break down now. He couldn't show the world, or his family, his vulnerability, yet the scars within him were on fire. He was burning and didn't know how to stop it.

He'd never known Brandon felt guilty about Lily's death. They'd never spoken of it. Adam had always blamed himself for not seeing through Brandon's lies, for not knowing his little brother had been too frightened to let him go after Lily. He was older, the responsible one when his mother wasn't around. He should've checked on his sister regardless of what Brandon told him. But often he questioned whether he would've actually taken those steps up from the storm cellar even if Brandon hadn't stopped him. He'd been afraid, too; the noises outside had been horrifying. Adam had always wished he would've done something different. Been stronger. Acted braver.

His head pounded. All these years, he'd resented Brandon and had been more than willing to hate his brother when he'd discovered his involvement with Jacqueline, but now... He wasn't sure about anything.

"I'm sorry, Adam," Brandon said, his face flushed. He was trying valiantly to hold back tears.

It was a genuine, heartfelt apology. He never thought he'd hear those words from Brandon, and in the course of a few weeks, he'd heard them twice.

"I've let you carry this burden all these years. The truth is, I think I intentionally sabotaged my relationship with Jacqueline because I knew I didn't deserve her and because I'd hurt you. I've been a coward. About everything."

Adam swallowed.

"I know you've despised me. I can't blame you, Adam. But I'm apologizing for all I've done that has hurt you."

"I don't despise you, Brandon."

"You boys were always fighting," his mother said. "But I knew back then, just as I know now, you love each other. So shake hands once and for all. Heaven knows there's enough guilt in this room to feed the devil. The past has hurt all of us. It's time to move on."

They looked at each other now, and the hope and apology in Brandon's eyes had Adam extending his hand. Brandon clasped it. "You're a good man, Adam. Always have been."

He nodded, too choked up to speak.

The nurse walked in. "Excuse me, but you have another visitor," she said to his mom. "But I'm afraid we can allow only two visitors at a time. One of you will have to leave."

Mia stood at the door, holding a vase of spring flowers. "Is it okay?"

Adam gazed at Mia. She was a bright and wonderful light shining through all of his past darkness.

"I'll leave, so you three can spend time together." Brandon offered. He walked to the door and gave Mia a kiss on the cheek. "Thanks for coming," he said and walked out of sight.

"I don't want to interrupt," she said to Adam, still not moving.

And it hit him, just like that. He *wanted* her there. He needed her support. Especially after the conversation he'd just had with Brandon. She'd come, and that meant a lot to him. "Please, come in."

"Yes," his mother said quietly. "It's good to see you, dear."

"I was worried about you, Alena," Mia said, walking into the room. Adam took the flowers and placed them on a small table under the television where his mother could see them easily.

"The flowers are lovely," his mother said. "Thank you."

"I was hoping you'd enjoy them," Mia said.

"Mia, I'm sorry to interrupt your plans with my son this weekend. I feel awful about that."

"Don't think of it. Your health is important to us. You've just got to concentrate on getting better." Mia reached for her hand. "How are you feeling now?"

"Better. It was frightening, I will admit. I had an angina attack that knocked me for a loop. I have to stay a day or two for monitoring, but then I'll be going home."

"That's great news," Mia said, her eyes so beautifully hopeful.

"Where is Rose today?"

"My grandma Tess is watching her for a few hours."

"That's nice. I hope you'll let me babysit one day, too."

"I'm sure you will."

"Come sit and tell me all about the trip. How did Rose do at the wedding?"

Mia lowered down on the edge of the bed. "Well, uh…" Her eyes met his, and they shared a conspiratorial moment. Little Rose was the maker of many stories, and this one would surely bring a smile to his mother's face. She could use a little levity. The last few minutes had been laden with grief, guilt and regret.

Adam breathed a sigh of relief, taking a step back, allowing Mia to comfort his mother.

"She did fine, except for this one moment during the ceremony…"

The next day, Mia walked through the door lugging Mia in her infant seat in one arm and a file folder she'd brought from First Clips tucked under the other arm. Since the wedding and Alena's health scare she wanted to work from home more these days, to be closer to Adam. Rose had a way of cheering him up, even if she still wasn't too keen on him. Adam adored being with her. And one day soon, his daughter would come to accept him. Every day together brought them closer and closer. Mia sensed that Rose was warming to him.

She was heading upstairs to her room, when she spotted a young woman sitting on the living room sofa speaking with Mary. She set down her files on the entry table and unfastened the straps of the carrier, lifting Rose into her arms. "Let's see what's going on," she said, kissing the baby's forehead. The baby gurgled, and Mia's heart warmed. Casually, her curiosity getting the better of her, she strolled into the living room.

"Hi, Mary. We're home," she said.

The woman popped up from her seat immediately and

turned to her. The spunky blonde was all smiles as her gaze locked on to the baby. "This must be the little darlin', Rose."

One glance at Mary's sheepish expression sent dread to her belly. "Hello, Mia."

Mia waited, staring at the woman who couldn't be more than twenty-two.

"Mia D'Angelo, this is Lucille Bridges," Mary said. "She's from Nanny Incorporated."

"I have an appointment with Adam Chase this afternoon," the woman added.

Nanny Incorporated? Adam had called a nanny agency? The blood in her veins boiled. The girl wouldn't take her eyes off Rose. Mia hugged her tighter and stepped back.

"I was just explaining to Miss Bridges that Adam isn't home. He must've forgotten about his appointment with all the commotion this past week. I've called him, but he hasn't answered his phone."

"He's at the hospital visiting his mother." She eyed the girl cautiously. "I'm sure he won't be home for quite a while."

"That's okay. I understand. I've left my references with Mary. I've been with the agency for three years and I have impeccable referrals," she said.

Wow, three whole years.

"Do you think I can say hello to the baby while I'm here?"

Mia's nerves jumped. She shot a glance at Mary.

"Uh, I think Aunt Mia was just about to put Rose down for a nap. It's past her naptime, isn't it, Mia?"

"Right," she gritted out. How could Adam do this to her? "Rose is quite a handful when she's tired."

"I know how babies can be. I helped raise four siblings."

Mia couldn't take it another second. Adam's betrayal and deceit didn't sit well in her gut. "I'm sure Mary can show you out. I've got to take the baby upstairs now."

"Oh, uh, sure. Bye-bye, Rose. Nice meeting you, Mia."

She headed for the stairs without responding.

She couldn't. Her throat had closed up.

She was in shock.

Trembling, she stood in the kitchen doorway, watching Adam forage through the refrigerator. It was after seven, and he'd just come home.

"I asked Mary to go home early," she said.

Adam backed up and peeked at her. "Good idea. I see she left us dinner." He pulled out covered dishes and set them on the counter. Lifting a lid, he said, "Looks like we're having rosemary chicken and—" he lifted the next lid "—glazed carrots."

"I won't be having dinner…w-with you." Her darn throat constricted again. Her anger had never subsided; neither did the hurt. She'd cried and cried all afternoon. Like a fool.

Adam stopped what he was doing to really look at her. "Why, sweetheart?" He approached her. "You're pale as a ghost. Are you feeling sick?"

He wrapped his arms around her, and for one instant, she relished it, squeezed her eyes closed and sought the pleasure of him, before she set both hands on his chest and shoved with all her might. Surprise more than force made him stumble back, his eyes wide and confused. "Yes, I'm sick, Adam. Of you. And all your secrets, lies and deceit. When were you going to tell me you were hiring a nanny for Rose? Were you going to hire someone, then toss me out onto the street? Was that your plan all along?"

Adam's tanned face flushed with color instantly. "Mia, for goodness' sake, calm the hell down."

"No, Adam. I will not calm down," she shouted. "How do you think I felt coming home to find a blonde bimbo nanny sitting on the couch, waiting for you?"

"Mia," he said, exasperated. "I meant to speak to you

about it. But then Mom had her attack and it slipped my mind."

"It slipped your mind!" Mia was one step away from losing it entirely. "It should've never *been* on your mind. Do you think I can't care for Rose? Am I lacking in some way? Or has the recluse in you decided that I'm getting too close, invading your precious privacy?" She gestured an air check with her index finger. "Checked me right off, didn't you?"

"No, of course not!"

She folded her arms. "I don't believe you."

"Shh, Mia, keep your voice down. Where's Rose?" he asked.

"Sleeping upstairs." She grabbed the monitor attached to her belt and showed him. "Regardless of what you might think of me, I'd never put Rose in danger. See, I'm watching her. She's my baby, too, Adam. You had no right. No right, going behind my back like that."

"Mia." His voice was an impatient rasp. "I know you'd never put Rose in danger. And if you'll let me explain what I was thinking."

"Apparently, you weren't thinking. Adam, that girl was a kid. I don't care that she claimed to have impeccable references—she doesn't know Rose, not the way I do."

Adam walked to the bar at the end of the huge granite counter and slapped a shot glass down. He filled it with vodka and downed it in one gulp. He didn't hesitate to pour a second shot.

"Alcohol never solved any problems, Adam."

He gulped the second shot and poured a third. "Don't lecture me, Mia. I won't get behind the wheel of my car and slaughter some poor innocent girl."

Mia froze. The swirling tirade in her head ready to lash out of her mouth vanished. She hadn't heard right, had she? "What?"

He slugged back the third shot and hunkered down, bracing his elbows on the counter. "Nothing."

"It was something, Adam." She walked over to him and spoke to his profile. "How do you know about that?"

"Know what?" He refused to look at her. It wasn't a coincidental statement. Adam Chase didn't leave things up to chance.

"About my father."

Silence.

"Adam, if you care one iota about me, you'll tell me how you know that right this minute."

Silence again.

Adam didn't care. Maybe he never had. She was through with Adam Chase. He would never let her in, never trust her. She turned her back on him and walked away. She was almost out of the kitchen when his voice broke the silence.

"I had you investigated."

A gasp exploded from her mouth. She whirled around. "You did what?"

He turned to face her. His expression was coarse, his eyes raw, not filled with the apology she'd expected. "I didn't know a thing about you, Mia. And when you came to me with that story about your sister and Rose, I didn't know if I could believe a word out of your mouth. After all the lies you'd told me when we first met, I had to find out more about you. I had to know who was coming to live in my house and help raise my daughter."

"You didn't trust me to tell you the truth."

"No, I didn't."

"I would have one day, Adam. I was waiting for you to open up to me. But I can see that will never happen." She sighed, the conversation sapping her strength. "So, you know everything?"

He nodded.

Shame washed over her. She was the young Burkel girl again, whose father had mowed down a young teenager, a girl who'd had a full life yet to live. He'd been drunk, coming home from a scandalous affair with a married woman. The town scorned the Burkels. She couldn't go anywhere without being harassed or whispered about. It was equally painful going to school. Young Scarlett Brady, the victim, had been a classmate and the daughter of a revered police captain. Everyone knew and loved Scarlett. When her mother decided to move them to Grandma Tess's home, their neighbors put up balloons in celebration on the day they'd moved out. The memory brought fresh shivers.

"You didn't even tell me your real name, Mia. What was I to think?"

He'd had her investigated like a common criminal. She cringed at the thought. How so like Adam, though. Sweeping heartache invaded her from top to bottom. "That maybe I didn't lead a charmed life. That maybe my family suffered and we'd paid a big price for my father's deeds. That maybe I make mistakes, unlike you."

"I make mistakes, Mia."

"Yes, you're right. *This* was a big mistake. But that doesn't make what you've done any easier to take."

Adam wadded up the note Mia had left for him on the kitchen table that morning. She needed time to think, away from him. She had taken Rose with her, but she'd call often and let him know how Rose was doing. She'd be at her grandma Tess's home for the next few days. He was welcome to come visit her anytime. And please, don't call the police—she hadn't kidnapped his daughter.

What the hell. He'd never accuse her of kidnapping. That last part really gutted him through and through. Mia would never allow any harm to come to his daughter. He trusted Mia with Rose and knew he wasn't equipped to take care of the baby on his own. Not yet. Not like Mia could. He missed the both of them, like crazy.

Adam tossed the note, missing the trash can in his

office, and rubbed his temples. He had a headache that wouldn't let up. How had he thought he'd get any work done today? It was a foolish notion. Mia had called him twice already today with an update about Rose. She'd eaten a good breakfast. She'd pooped her diaper. She'd taken her for a walk around the neighborhood with her grandmother this morning.

"When are you coming home?" Adam had asked.

"I don't know, Adam," she'd replied coolly. The aloof tone of her voice worried him.

He knew when she did come home, nothing would be the same.

"Adam, Brandon's here," Mary announced at his doorway. "He's waiting for you downstairs."

"It's about damn time," he said, bounding up from his desk. "Thanks, Mary."

He strode down the stairs to find Brandon in the living room with a drink in his hand, a whiskey. He'd also had a tumbler of vodka ready for him. "So, Mia's gone?" Brandon held out the glass to him.

He should refuse the drink. Last night, he'd nearly polished off half a bottle and his head still throbbed. "Just one." He took it from his brother and nodded. "Yeah, she's gone."

"Let's sit outside, Adam. It's a cool afternoon. It'll help clear your head."

"Is that what I need?"

"Oh, I think so, brother." He led the way outside, where breezes took away the heat of the day. The sun, lowering on the horizon, cast a brilliant gleam on the water. "I have to say, I was surprised to get your call."

Adam shrugged. He was surprised he'd called his brother, too. Just went to show how crazy confused he was right now. "We might as well start behaving like brothers."

"You had no one else to call," Brandon stated and then sat down on a lounge chair.

Adam chuckled, taking a seat, as well. "Okay, guilty." He really didn't confide in anyone about personal matters. Trusting his brother didn't come easy, but Mia and Rose were important to him and oddly, he believed Brandon could help him sort this out. "You know women, Brandon. And you know me."

"I'm glad to help, bro. Go on. Tell me what happened with Mia."

"All of it?"

"Everything. I'm no relationship expert, but I've made enough mistakes now that I've gotten pretty good at rectifying them. And, yes, I do know women."

Adam spelled it out for Brandon. Telling him exactly how he'd met Mia on the beach. Explaining Rose's negative reaction to him and how Mia coming to live with him had been necessary, at least in the beginning. He recounted the past few weeks, up to a point.

"Have you slept with her?" Brandon asked.

"Why does that matter?" Adam shot back.

"Just the fact that you're asking, means you need more help than I originally thought."

"Okay, yes. Damn it. We've been together, more than once. That's all you need to know. And I think she had feelings for me."

"Had?"

"I blew it with her."

"Yeah, well, going behind her back to search for a nanny might do that."

"I explained the reason I did that."

"To me, but you never told Mia your reasons."

"I never had the chance. I wanted her to calm down so I could explain it rationally to her, but then I made that slip about her family and I was forced to tell her I'd had her investigated."

"The final nail in the coffin."

Adam nodded and admitted quietly, "I did it for Rose."

"I believe you, but you're going to have a hard time convincing Mia about your intentions, because you won't open yourself up. She's been telling you all along that's what she wants. Why are you holding back? It's obvious you're crazy about her."

"It is?"

"Aren't you?"

Adam gave it some thought. "With Rose came Mia. I think of them as one. I guess I never realized it before. They were a package deal almost from the beginning."

"You adore Rose. *And Mia.* They are a gift. All tied up into a bow for you. So what are you afraid of, Adam?"

Adam rubbed his temples again. The pain in his head pounded with the truth. He'd been plagued by guilt and uncertainty for years, safeguarding his heart so securely, that he'd kept himself away from serious relationships and love. He'd hidden behind his work and his need for privacy. "Mia was right. I've been closed off a long time. I don't know how to let anyone in."

"You let me in, Adam. Of course it took Mom's health episode to accomplish that, but I think you're ready to let Mia in. If she wasn't important to you, you wouldn't have called me. And don't give me that business that you were worried about how to get Rose home without hurting Mia in the process. If you want Rose back, all you have to do is go get her. You have legal rights to her, Adam. But you want more than that. And I'm telling you, don't wait until it's too late. The clock is ticking. Go after what you want right now. Tell Mia how you feel. And hurry the hell up."

"I hate it that you're right," Adam said, finishing his drink.

"And I hate it that you've got a gorgeous woman and child waiting for you." Brandon smiled. "I've had to live knowing you'd saved my life and there was no damn way for me to reciprocate. At least now I feel I may have helped save yours."

Adam smiled back. "That makes us even."

"Get your child and woman back first. Then we'll be even."

The front porch swing moaned as Mia rocked Rose in her arms. The quiet sound lulled the baby to sleep. This house had been her home once, when Grandma Tess had taken all of them in, and now she was back, feeling that same sense of loss, the hurt blistering her up inside. Her grandmother was a rock, a solid, rational, wise woman and Mia needed to be here with her now. She needed the comfort Grandma Tess provided. She always knew the right thing to say. Mia was wounded. She'd begun to trust again. She'd believed in Adam Chase. She'd let go her fears and put her faith in the power of her intense feelings for Adam. He'd sure had her fooled.

Initially she and Adam had spoken about her nanny duties and taking it day by day with no real end in sight. Now that the time had come, Mia couldn't face leaving Rose in the hands of another…a stranger. No matter what had happened between her and Adam, Mia was prepared to forgive and forget in order to live under Adam's roof and care for her niece, if he allowed it.

If that meant swallowing her pride, she would do it. She'd return to Moonlight Beach and keep out of Adam's life the best she could. If she didn't do that, what kind of life would Rose have? She'd have every material thing she might want—Adam's wealth could provide that—but what about love? What if Adam couldn't open himself up to loving his own daughter? What if he held back with her, the same way he'd held back with Mia?

She peered at the slumbering angel in her arms. "Sweet Cheeks, your auntie Mia will not abandon you," she whispered. "Don't worry."

Mia was almost lulled to sleep, too. Gentle breezes reaching this far inland soothed her tired bones until the humming roar of an engine coming down the street reached her ears. She opened her eyes and leaned forward in the swing, watching a Rolls-Royce park in front of the house. The gorgeous car stuck out on this middle-class street, like a diamond among mere stones.

Adam climbed out of the car, and their eyes met. She wasn't surprised to see him. She knew he wouldn't let Rose out of his sight for long, but they'd agreed that he'd call before coming over. Of course, Adam hadn't abided by that rule.

As he wound around the car and approached, a bouquet of lavender roses in his hand caught her attention. Did he think flowers would solve anything? He reached the porch and set one foot on the first step. "Hello, Mia."

She gasped inside, her heart racing like crazy.

"Adam."

He glanced at Rose, love beaming in his eyes. "How long has she been sleeping?"

"Only a few minutes."

"Is your grandma Tess home?"

"Yes."

"I would like to meet her."

"Now?"

"Yes, right now. It's about time I met her. Don't get up. Let the baby sleep. I'll knock and see if she comes to the door."

He walked past her and gave three light raps to the door.

Adam was full of surprises today. Of course Grandma Tess came to the door, and she graciously greeted Adam, bleeder of her heart, and let him inside.

"What on earth?" Mia muttered.

Rose stirred restlessly, stretching out her arms, and Mia pushed off with her bare feet to start the swing swaying again while she strained to listen to the quiet conversation going on in the house.

She sighed. She couldn't hear a thing.

A short time later, Adam walked out the door, minus the flowers. "Mind if I sit with you?"

She shrugged and he sat down. "I like your grandmother, Mia. She's a nice lady."

They spoke softly to keep from waking the baby.

"You were supposed to call to let me know you were coming."

"I didn't want to chance you telling me no."

Adam pushed a hand through his hair. He breathed deeply and turned to face her. "I've missed you, Mia."

"You miss Rose."

"I miss both of you." His eyes narrowed as if he was choosing his words carefully. "You know what I saw when I pulled up to the house just now? I saw my family. You and Rose and me, we're a family. And it doesn't scare me anymore to think it, to say it or to feel it."

"Don't, Adam. You don't have to pretend. I've already decided for Rose's sake I'll come back to Moonlight Beach."

Adam's eyes gleamed and he smiled. "Oh, so you've decided that you can tolerate me. You're making the ultimate sacrifice for the baby by being in my presence."

Had he gone crazy since she'd left him? "Why are you smiling?"

"Because you are so full of it, Mia." What *did* Grandma Tess say to him?

"I beg your pardon?"

"You are. And if you just listen to me for one minute, I'll explain about the nanny."

"Don't forget about the investigation. I'd love to hear your excuse for that one."

"Fine. I'll tell you everything. I hope that'll make up for hurting you. Because, sweetheart, the very last thing in the world I want to do is hurt you again."

He was getting to her. His body nestled next to hers, the tone of his voice and the sincere way he spoke only added to her slow melt. "Start from the beginning, Adam. Leave nothing out."

As Adam spoke about Lily, his little sister who'd looked up to him, who'd followed him around like a lost puppy, who'd trusted him like no other, Mia bit her lip to keep tears from spilling down her cheeks. His voice broke a few times, recounting that horrible day when the tornado ripped through his town and took Lily with it. He spoke of grief and guilt and heartache. About his relationship with his mother and his brother, about how he'd shouldered the blame and let that come between him and his family. He spoke about Brandon, too, and how they'd finally patched up their differences and about how he'd asked Brandon for advice today, needing his brother now more than he ever had before.

Mia was seeing a side of Adam that he'd never revealed. She could relate to the pain they'd endured as a family, the loss, the heartache. "I'm glad you told me."

"I want there to be no secrets between us, Mia." He put his arm on the back of the porch swing and even though he wasn't touching her, his presence surrounded her and she felt safe and protected.

"About the nanny," he said. "It was just a thought to make your life easier. I've seen how hard you work. You come home looking tired and drained at times. I know how much Rose means to you, and you do it without complaint. But you hold down a full-time position, take care of Rose and your grandmother and have to put up with me. It's a lot of responsibility. The nanny idea came to me, only as a means to provide you with some backup. Believe me, I was going to run it by you, but then we started getting closer and I didn't want to ruin what we had going. Being with you two in Texas was wonderful. I've never been happier, and I did tell you that."

"You did," Mia admitted.

"And then Mom got sick and we had to rush home. The

whole thing slipped my mind. Mia," he said, his arm wrapping around her shoulder. "No one could replace you." The depth of his voice had her believing him.

A tear trickled down her cheek. "Thanks."

He went on, "Do you remember how we met?"

"Of course, I cut my foot and bled all over you."

Adam chuckled. "Not quite. But you came to Moonlight Beach to find out what you could about me, right? Why did you do that?"

"I've already told you. I couldn't just turn Rose over to a stranger. I needed to find out what kind of person you were."

"Exactly. I regret having you investigated now, but weeks ago when all I knew about you were the lies you'd told me, I needed to know the same thing. You were going to live under my roof and help me raise my daughter. What I did wasn't too different than what you did. We just had different ways of going about it. We were both trying to protect this little girl." He pointed to Rose, love shining in his eyes. "Because she's precious to both of us."

"Adam, the difference is I would've answered all of your questions truthfully. You, on the other hand, went out of your way to evade mine."

"True. That was the old Adam. I don't like to talk about myself."

"You really mean you don't like letting people know you."

"You know me now, Mia. You know everything about me. And I'm happy about it. Loving you has changed me."

Hot tingles rose up from her belly. "What did you just say?"

Adam grinned. "I love you, Mia. At first I thought my feelings were just for Rose, but Brandon, of all people, helped me see what was right in front of me. I'm in love with you, Mia. You and Rose own my heart."

"We do?"

"Yes, you do."

Adam leaned over and brushed his lips over hers. She'd never known a sweeter kiss. "Oh, Adam." Tears spilled down her cheeks freely now. She could hardly believe this was happening. She moved closer to him on the porch swing, and his next kiss wasn't sweet at all, but soul-searching and magical.

"I love you, Adam Chase. I tried really hard not to."

"I'll take that as a compliment, sweetheart, and thank God you love me. Must've been my mad first aid skills."

A chuckle burst from her lips. "That was it. That's why I love you so much I can hardly stand it." The baby fussed, a little sound of displeasure. "Adam, I think the baby wants her daddy."

"I'll take her," Adam said, and she transferred Rose into his arms. Adam cuddled her close and turned to face Mia. "Before she wakes up and howls, I have a question for you." A hopeful glint entered his eyes.

"What is it?"

"I've asked for your grandmother's blessing and she's given it to me."

Mia took a big swallow at the reverent tone in his voice.

"I've never asked this of another woman. Will you come home to Moonlight Beach and be my wife? You, me and our little Rose, we're already a family, but I want to make it official because I love both of you with all my heart. I'm asking you to marry me, Mia."

Mia touched his arm and gazed into his beautiful eyes. She no longer had to hold back her love for him; she let it flow naturally, and it was liberating and wonderful. "Yes, Adam. I'll marry you."

"We'll have a good life, Mia. I promise. I want to take you to Italy. We'll honeymoon there, the three of us."

"It's always been a dream of mine."

"I know, sweetheart. I want to make your dreams come true."

Their gazes locked, and warmth seeped into her heart. She loved this man like crazy. He would be a wonderful father and an attentive, loving husband. She had no doubt.

"Uh-oh," Adam said. "Looks like little sleepyhead is waking up. Do you want her back?"

"No, you hold her, sweetheart."

"Okay, but she's not going to like this."

Rose's eyes opened, she fidgeted and took a glance around. Her lips parted and they waited for her complaint.

"Coo, coo." Precious sounds reached their ears.

She gurgled a few times, and then her chubby hand reached up to touch Adam's face.

His brows lifted, creasing his forehead. "Would you look at that."

"I'm looking," she said, awed. Her little Rose had perfect timing.

The baby peered at her daddy's handsome face. Her mouth opened and spread wide, revealing a gummy toothless beautiful smile.

Adam's eyes welled up. "I think I've won her over, Mia."

"Adam Chase, only you can win two female hearts in one day."

"Our sweet little matchmaker helped make that happen."

"She's brilliant, just like her daddy."

Adam kissed her then, and Mia's heart swelled. Their baby Rose did have a way about her. She was going to wrap them both around her finger.

And there was no place either of them would rather be.

* * * * *

ONE SECRET NIGHT, ONE SECRET BABY

CHARLENE SANDS

Special thanks to my wonderful son-in-law, Zac Prange, who helped me with the on-set moviemaking details of this story. Your support and expertise really meant a great deal, keeping the story honest and authentic. With love to you, Nikki my fabulous daughter, and of course your two sweet princesses who brighten our lives every day, Everley and Lila.

One

She wasn't a one-night stand sort of girl.

Emma Rae Bloom was predictable, hardworking, ambitious and least of all, adventurous. *Boring.* She never did anything out of the ordinary. She was measured and sure and patient. *Double boring.* The one time she'd crushed that mold, breaking it to bits, was at her neighbor Eddie's blowout bash at Havens on Sunset Boulevard in celebration of his thirtieth birthday last month. She'd partied hard, lost her inhibitions as well as her mind during the now infamous Los Angeles blackout and wound up in bed with her best friend's brother, Hollywood heartthrob in the flesh, Dylan McKay.

She'd had secret dibs on Brooke's brother since the age of twelve. He was the older boy with sea-blue eyes and stubble on his face who'd treated her kindly and given her a measuring stick to compare all men against.

There was no going back to reclaim their night together, although her memory of her time with Dylan was almost nonexistent. Just her luck, she had her first ever one-night stand with the hottest guy on earth and her mind had gone as foggy as a London winter day. Too many mango mojitos could do that, she'd been told.

She stood at the port-side railing of Dylan's yacht now. As he approached her, his head wrapped with gauze bandages, a haunted look on his face spoke of sadness and grief. It was a somber day, but beaming rays of sunshine and stunning marshmallow fluff clouds didn't seem to know that. She pushed her sunglasses farther up her nose, grateful to hide her true emotions.

Roy Benjamin was gone, killed in the freakish stunt accident on the set of Dylan's Navy SEAL movie. The tragedy had rocked Hollywood insiders and made a big splash on the news, even eclipsing the story of how the lights went out in the city just the day before. It wasn't just Roy's death that had rocked the entertainment world and hit the headlines with a bang, but Dylan's amnesia resulting from the same blast that had killed his friend.

"Here, have a soda." Brooke walked up beside her brother and offered Emma a glass. "You look like you could use one."

"Thanks." She accepted the benign drink. No more alcohol for her, thank you very much. "It's a hard day for everyone." She sipped her cola.

Standing between her and Brooke, Dylan wrapped his arms around them. "I'm glad you both are here with me today."

Emma's nerves squeezed tight. She hadn't seen Dylan since the night of the blackout. The supportive arm around her shoulders shouldn't elicit any of the sensations she was having. It shouldn't. She sighed. His hand caressed her upper arm lightly, sending shock waves through her system. As the yacht backed out of its slip, his body lurched, two hundred pounds of solid granite shoulder to shoulder with her. She stopped breathing for a second and gripped the railing.

"Of course we'd be here," Brooke said. "Roy was a friend of ours, too. Right, Emma?"

She gave Dylan a quick smile. It was such a tragedy that a man so vital and strong as Roy had died at such a young age. He was a Dylan look-alike, his stunt double and a close friend to the McKays. Emma only knew Roy through them and he'd always been nice to her.

Dylan's lips curled up a little, the subdued smile of a man in mourning. "I miss him already."

He tightened his hold, bringing their bodies close. He was the consummate movie star, sunglasses shading his face, blond hair blowing in the breeze and a body carved from hard gym workouts and daily runs. He was Hollywood royalty, a man who'd managed to steer clear of lasting relationships his entire adult life. Darkly tanned, as talented and smart as he was good-looking, he had it all.

Emma should be concentrating on Roy's death instead of her dilemma. Yet as she'd dressed this morning readying for Roy's memorial, she'd rehearsed what she would say if Dylan remembered anything that happened between them during the blackout.

I wasn't myself that night. The blackout freaked me out. I've been afraid of the dark since I was a kid and I begged you to stay with me. Can we just go on being friends?

Now it looked as if she could dodge that confession. Soul-melting blue eyes, dimmed now from grief, settled upon her as they always had. He saw her as his sister Brooke's friend, nothing more. He had no memory of their night together. The doctors termed it dissociative amnesia. He was blocked and might never remember the hours or days leading up to the blast that took his friend's life and sent a hunk of shrapnel tunneling into his head. He'd been knocked unconscious and had woken up hours later, in the hospital.

He let her go to sip his soda and she began breathing normally again. Cautiously she took a step away from him. Having his hand on her played too much havoc with her brain. She had escaped telling him the truth today, and the devil on her shoulder whispered in her ear, *Why rock the boat?* Clever little fiend. *This can be your little secret.*

Could she really get away with not having to tell him?

She battled with the notion as the yacht made its way out of Marina del Rey, traveling past the docks at a snail's pace. Pungent sea scents filled her nostrils, seagulls squawked overhead and one white-winged bird landed on a buoy and quietly watched the yacht head into open seas.

"I guess it's time," Dylan said, minutes later, once they were far enough out to sea. Dylan wanted to do this alone, with just his family. Later today, a memorial would be held at his Moonlight Beach home open to Roy's friends and fellow crew and cast members, the only family he'd ever known. That's when Emma and Brooke would go to work, hosting an informal buffet dinner in Roy's honor. It definitely wasn't a Parties-To-Go kind of event, but Dylan had turned to them for help. "Roy always joked, if he missed the net from a ten-story fall, to make sure I tossed his ashes from the *Classy Lady.* He loved this boat, but I never thought I'd ever have to do this."

Brooke's doe eyes softened on her brother and Emma hurt inside for both of them. Brooke and Dylan were miles apart in most things, but when push came to shove, they were always there for each other. Emma envied that. She had no siblings. She had no real family, except for foster parents, two people who'd taken her in and then neglected her as a child. She hadn't hit the jackpot in the parent department, that was for sure. Not like Brooke. Brooke was Dylan's younger foster sister whom his parents had eventually adopted. They were totally amazing. They'd been better parents to Emma than the two who'd collected monthly checks on her behalf.

Dylan made swift work of saying heartfelt words about his friend, his voice tightening up to get it all out, right before he opened the urn, lifted it up and let the wind carry Roy's ashes out to sea. When he turned around, tears filled his eyes and his mouth quivered in heartbreak. She'd never seen this vulnerable side of Dylan and she gripped the railing tight to keep from going to him. It wasn't her place.

Brooke went to him and cradled him in her arms the way a mother would a child, whispering soft words of sympathy in his ear. Dylan nodded his head as he listened to his baby sister. After a few minutes he wiped the tears from his eyes and the solemn expression from his face. He gave Brooke a sweet smile.

Dylan McKay was back.

It was the first time Emma had ever seen him let his guard down.

It touched her soul.

Secret dibs.

Dylan's kitchen could swallow up her little apartment in one large gulp. Every kind of new age appliance ever conceived was set on the shiny onyx granite counter and in the textured white cabinets. It was a culinary dream kitchen and his housekeeper, Maisey, made great use of it. She'd cooked up a storm for the fifty-plus people who'd come to pay their respects to Roy Benjamin. Aside from Maisey's home cooking, the caterers Emma had commissioned delivered trays of finger foods, specialty breads and appetizers. Everyone from grips to the president of Stage One Studios was here. Emma and Brooke, dressed in appropriate black dresses with little ornamentation, set out the food and offered drinks to the guests. They weren't acting as Parties-To-Go planners today as much as they were Dylan's hostesses for this sad event.

"Did you see what Callista is wearing?" Brooke muttered under her breath.

Emma set out a plate of sweet-cream-and-berry tarts on the dessert table, shooting a quick glance to the living room, where many of the guests were gathered. Callista Lee Allen, daughter to the Stage One Studio mogul, was on Dylan's arm, hanging on his every word. She wore Versace, and the only reason Emma knew that was because she'd overheard the blonde gloating about it. It was a silver glimmer dress with detailed layering and jewels dripping off her throat and arms. "I see."

"It's not as if the Fashion Police are trolling. Roy deserves better. This day isn't about her."

Emma grinned. "Tell me how you really feel, Brooke. At least she talks to you. I'm invisible to her." Being a friend of Dylan's sister didn't rank high enough on Callista's status scale to award Emma an iota of her attention.

"Be grateful. Be very grateful."

Emma stood back from the arrangement, giving the presentation scrutiny. They'd draped the dessert table with tablecloths in varying colors and edged each platter with flowering vines. This is what they did. And they did it well.

"It's none of my business, but Dylan's on-again, off-again relationship with her isn't good for him," Brooke said.

Emma shot them another glance. Callista's eyes flashed on Dylan's bandage, one hand possessively on his arm as she reached up with the other to touch the injury. Emma watched the scene play out. Dylan was deep in conversation with Callista's father and didn't seem to notice her unabashed attention.

Sucking oxygen in, Emma glanced away and tamped down pangs of jealousy swimming through her body. She'd be ten times a fool to think she'd ever have a chance with Dylan. He was her friend. Period. "He's a big boy, Brooke."

"I never thought I'd say this, but thank God my brother doesn't commit. She's all wrong in so many ways." Brooke lifted her hands in a stopping motion that was her signature move. "But like I said, none of my beeswax."

Emma smiled at her friend and put the finishing touches on the dessert table. Maisey had made coffee and there was hot water and a sampler box of teas available.

Dylan approached, gorgeous in a tailored dark suit and tie. He'd changed his clothes from the jeans and black silk shirt he'd worn this morning on the yacht. "Do you two have a minute?" he asked quietly. His brows were gathered in question. Brooke and Emma nodded and he guided them to the far side of the kitchen, out of earshot of anyone. It was all so curious.

"You girls have done wonderful today. Thank you," he began and then shook his head. "I'm figuring you'd give it to me straight. Callista and I...are we a thing again?"

Emma held her breath. She wouldn't comment on her thoughts about the bottle blonde. Dylan didn't exactly confide in her about his love life, but his earnest question made her stomach ripple in guilt. She had a truth to tell him, too, and maybe it would help spark his memory, but it could also make things weird between them, which was the last thing she wanted.

Brooke seemed eager to answer, but shook her head as if formulating her thoughts. "You don't remember?"

"No. But she's acting like we're ready for the altar. From what I remember, that wasn't the case. Am I wrong?"

"No, you're certainly not wrong," Brooke shot back. "Not even close. Before...before your accident, you told me you were going to break it off with her for good."

"I did? I don't remember." Poor Dylan was struggling. His gaze lifted to the wide windows that opened out onto the sea, as if he were searching for answers there. He seemed lost right now, not his usual self-confident, always-one-step-ahead-of-everyone, charming self.

"If she says it's more, Dylan, I'd be careful," Brooke offered. "She's banking on your amnesia to worm her way back into your…"

Dylan turned to his sister, his brows lifting and a crooked smile emerging. "My what?"

"Your good graces," Emma finished for her.

Dylan slid her a knowing look. "Always the diplomat, Em. But somehow, I don't think that's what Brooke was going to say." He began nodding. "Okay, I get the picture." He glanced at Callista, who was now surrounded by a few other actors in the film. She was deep in conversation yet constantly casting him furtive glances at every opportunity, sizing him up and staking her claim.

Brooke was right—Callista was all wrong for Dylan. How difficult it must be for him not to remember some things, not to have a grasp on his feelings. "You're the only ones I can trust," he said. He rubbed his brow, just under his bandage. "I can't tell you how bizarre this feels. I see some things clearly. Other things are fuzzy at best. And then there's a whole chunk that I don't remember."

Emma plunked three ice cubes into a glass and poured him a root beer, his favorite from childhood. "Here, drink up."

"Thanks," he said, "though I could use something stronger."

"The doctor says not yet. You're still on pain meds." Brooke's internal mother came out. It really was sweet seeing how close the two had become since the move from Ohio to Los Angeles years ago.

"One drink won't kill me."

"Let's not find out, okay? I was worried enough when you were sent to the hospital. And Mom just went home two days ago. If I have to call her again to tell her you're back in Saint Joseph's, she'll have a heart attack."

Dylan rolled his eyes. "You see how good she is, Emma? She knows exactly how to lay on the guilt."

A chuckle rumbled from Emma's throat. "I know all about Brooke's tactics. I work with her."

"Hey!" Brooke said. "You're supposed to be on my side."

"Like I said, Emma's a diplomat. Thanks for the drink." He lifted his glass in mock toast and then pivoted around and walked away.

"He'll be okay," Brooke said, watching him head back to his guests. "We just have to do whatever it takes to help him along."

Dread formed a tight knot in Emma's stomach. She hated keeping secrets from Brooke. They usually shared everything. But how exactly could she come out and say, *I begged your brother to sleep with me the night of the blackout and all I remember is his body on mine, heated breaths and sexy words whispered in my ear.* She didn't remember how she got in bed or when he left her that night. She couldn't recall how they'd ended things. Were there parting words recognizing the big mistake? Or had he promised to call her? He had no knowledge of what they'd done, but geesh, she didn't recall much of that night, either.

"Oh, brother," she mumbled.

"What?" Brooke asked.

"Nothing. Nothing at all."

"Brooke, you did a wonderful job today," Callista said, leaning her arms over the granite island, spilling her cleavage and smiling her billion-dollar smile. The sun was setting and all but one guest had left the memorial service. "You helped make the day easier for your brother."

"It wasn't just me, Callie," Brooke said. "Emma did her

fair share of the work and we'd both do anything to help Dylan get through this day."

Callista's gaze darted Emma's way as if she'd just noticed her standing there. *Hello, I'm not invisible.* "Of course, you, too, Emma." She spoke to her as if she were a child. What was it with rich powerful women that made them feel superior, just by right of wealth? Emma could probably run circles around her SAT scores. "You did a marvelous job."

"Dylan's a special guy and I'm happy to help."

Callista gave her a cursory nod, eyeing her for just a second as if measuring the competition, and then turned away, writing her off.

"Brooke, do you know where Dylan is? I want to say goodbye to him and tell him his eulogy was touching."

"Yeah, I do. He said to say goodbye to you for him. The day tired him out. He went to sleep."

"He's in bed already?" Callista straightened and her gaze moved toward the hallway staircase. She knew exactly where Dylan's bedroom was. "Maybe I should go up and wish him good-night."

"He, uh, needs uninterrupted rest. Doctor's orders." Brooke's accomplished smile brought Emma a stream of silent chuckles. Leave it to Brooke. She was in defense mode now.

"Yes, of course, you're right." She nibbled on her lip, shooting another longing glance at the staircase. Then her expression changed. "He does need to rest up so he can be back on set as soon as possible."

The SEAL movie had been shut down for a month already and it was costing the studio big bucks, so Dylan's return to the set was essential. Even Callista recognized that fact. "Tell him I'll call him."

"Will do, Callie. I'll walk you out."

"Oh, that's not necessary," Callista said.

"I don't mind."

After the two left, Emma couldn't contain her laughter. She knew for certain Callista Lee Allen hated to be called Callie, yet she let Brooke get away with it because she was Dylan's sister.

What a day it had been. Selfishly, Emma was glad it was over. She didn't like walking around with a cloud of guilt over her head. She hoped "out of sight, out of mind" would work on her. As soon as she left Dylan's house, maybe her head would clear and she'd be free of this grating bug gnawing at her to tell Dylan what happened between them.

Finished with her duties, the house clean and back to normal, thanks to Maisey and her efforts, Emma took a seat on one of the many white leather sofas in the living room. A pastel pop of color fading on the horizon grabbed her attention as she looked out the window. The sunset was beautiful on Moonlight Beach. She leaned back, closed her eyes and listened to the sound of the waves breaking on the shore.

"Mission accomplished," Brooke said, clapping her hands. "She's gone."

Emma snapped to attention as Brooke sat down beside her. "You're a regular Mama Bear. Who knew?"

"Normally, Dylan can take care of himself, but right now, he needs a little help. What else are meddling little sisters for anyway?"

"To keep conniving women away from him?"

"I try my best." Brooke propped her feet on a cocktail table and sighed. "I'm getting excited about the celebrity golf tournament coming up. This is one of the biggest events we've ever booked. And we got it all on our own. No intervention from Dylan. They don't even know he's my brother. Dylan doesn't play golf."

"I don't?" Dylan walked into the room looking adorably rumpled. It was the five-o'clock shadow, the mussed-to-perfection hair and those deep blue bedroom eyes that did Emma in. He wore a pair of black sweats and a white T-shirt.

"No, you don't," Brooke said, eyeing him carefully.

He grinned. "Just joking. I know I don't play golf. At least I have memories of tanking every shot. Never did get the hang of it."

"Brat. What are you doing up?"

On a long sigh, he ran a hand down his face. "I can't sleep. I'm going for a walk. I'll see you guys later. Thanks again for everything."

Brooke's mouth opened, but he was out the back door before she could stop him. "Darn it. He's still having dizzy spells. Will you go with him, Emma? Tell him you're in the mood for a walk, too. He already thinks I baby him enough."

Emma balked. She was three minutes away from escaping to go home. "I, uh…"

"Please?" Brooke begged. "If you're with him, he won't get it into his head to start jogging. I know he misses it. He's been complaining about not doing his daily runs. It's almost dark on the beach. He could collapse and no one would know."

It was true. The doctor said he shouldn't overdo any physical activity. How could she deny Brooke the peace of mind? She'd been worried sick about her brother lately. "Okay, I'll go."

"That's why I love you." Brooke sounded relieved.

Emma bent to remove her heels and rose from the sofa. "You better," she said. "I don't chase handsome A-list movie stars for just anyone." With that, she walked out the back entrance of Dylan's mansion, climbed down the stairs, searched for signs of him and took off at a jog when she'd seen how far he'd already traveled.

"Dylan," she called, her toes squishing into wet sand as she trudged rapidly after him. "Wait up."

He turned around and slowed his pace.

"Would you like company?" Her breathing ragged, she fibbed, "I feel like a walk, too."

"Let me guess. Brooke sent you."

She shrugged. "Maybe I just felt like taking a walk?"

His mouth lifted in a dubious smile. "And maybe the moon is green."

"Everyone knows the moon is made of cheese, therefore it's yellow."

He shook his head, seeming to relinquish his skepticism. "Okay, let's walk. Actually, I would like your company."

He took her hand, his fingers lacing with hers.

How…unexpected. Her breath froze in her chest.

"It was a nice memorial, wasn't it?" he asked as he resumed walking.

There was a slight tug on her hand that woke her from her stupor and she fell in step with him. "It was heartwarming. You honored Roy with a wonderful tribute to his life."

"I'm the only family he had, aside from his crew. He was a great guy and it's just a ridiculous shame. Roy was obsessed with his stunts. He spent his whole life perfecting them. He was the most cautious man I've ever known. It just doesn't make sense."

"They're saying it was a freakish accident."

Dylan took a sharp breath. "That's what they say when they don't know what happened. It's the standard answer."

They walked on in silence for a while, the heat from where he held her hand warming her entire body. It was actually a perfect evening for a stroll on the beach. Breezes blew at the twist of hair at the back of her head. She reached up and pulled it out of its band, freeing the long waves that touched the middle of her back.

"So tell me what's going on in your life, Emma."

Her brows gathered at the oddity of the request. Dylan knew just about everything about her. She was Brooke's friend and business partner. She lived in a tiny apartment twenty minutes away from Moonlight Beach. She loved her work and didn't go out much.

Oh, no! Did he remember something? Blood drained from her face as her mind worked overtime for signs that he'd remembered that blackout night. But as she dared to gaze at his profile, his eyes didn't probe her but stayed straight ahead, his neutral expression unchanged. She let out a relieved sigh. Maybe he needed to break the silence. Maybe he was just making conversation. And maybe her guilty conscience was wringing her dry.

"The same old, same old," she answered. "Work, work, work."

"Still hoping to make your first million before thirty?"

Her laugh came out a little too high-pitched. Brooke must've told him of her long-term goal. How embarrassing. Ever since she was a child, money had been scarce. Her foster parents didn't have much and were stingy in sharing. She didn't know that until she'd grown into a teen, of course, and witnessed how they'd splurge what they did have on each other. Never her. She grew up mostly wearing thrift store clothes. From the age of thirteen, Emma knew she'd have to find her own way in the world. She'd worked her ass off, achieving a full scholarship to college, and vowed she'd become financially independent one day. The promise she made herself was that by the age of thirty, she would make her first million. She had several years to go, but her hopes were high of expanding Parties-To-Go into a million-dollar franchise.

"Your sister, my best friend, needs to button her mouth."

"Don't blame Brooke," he said softly. "I think it's commendable to have goals."

"Lofty goals."

"Attainable goals and you work hard, Emma."

"Without your investment, we wouldn't even have a business."

"I just helped you get started, and in the two years since you've been working at it, you've come a long way."

"We owe you, Dylan. You've been amazing. We want to make you proud."

Dylan stopped, his Nikes digging into the sand, and when she turned to him, a genuine smile graced his handsome face. Gone was the sadness from before. A glint of appreciation twinkled in his eyes. "You don't owe me anything. And I am proud. You're a hard worker, and you're paying me back faster than I expected or wanted. But, Em, I have to tell you, as much as you believe Brooke has helped you through the growing-up years, you've helped her, too. She came to California hoping to become an actress. God, it's a tough business. I've been lucky…more fortunate than I could've hoped, but it's not the same for Brooke. She's much happier now, being in business with her best friend and earning a legitimate living doing what she loves. I owe that to you. So thank you for being…*you*."

Dylan leaned in, his face coming within inches of hers. Her heart rate escalated as she stared at his mouth. She understood now why his female fans swooned. He was breathtaking and yummy. There was no other way to describe it. "You're the amazing one, Emma," he whispered.

Her mind going fuzzy, she whispered back, "I am?"

As he inched closer, taking her into his arms, angling for her cheek, her entire body relaxed. Of course, he'd give her a sisterly kiss on the cheek. She closed her eyes.

His warm lips came down softly.

On her mouth.

Oh, she'd died and gone to heaven. His lips were warm and giving and soothing. She wrapped her arms around his neck and brazenly returned the kiss. Wow. It was all so new. And exciting. Dylan McKay was kissing her on Moonlight Beach at sunset and she was fully in the moment this time. There were no gaps of memory from a fuzzy brain. There wasn't anything but right now, this speck of time, and she relished the taste of him, the amazing texture of his firm lips caressing hers, the strength and power of his body close to hers.

But something still seemed slightly off with his kiss. She couldn't quite put her finger on it. Was it just that she was fully aware, fully attuned to him right now?

Dylan broke off the kiss first, and instead of backing away, he grasped Emma to his chest tightly like a little boy needing the comfort of his favorite stuffed toy. Elmo or Teddy or Winnie the Pooh.

She stood in his embrace for long moments. He sighed and continued to hold her. Then his mouth touched her right earlobe and he whispered, "Thank you. I needed your company tonight, Emma."

What could she say? Was she foolish enough to think he remembered their night of passion and wanted more? No, that wasn't it. Dylan needed comforting. Maybe what she considered to be a heart-melting kiss, only counted as a friendly measure of comfort for a man whose life was full of adoration. At least, she could give him that.

Her secret was safe.

"You're welcome, Dylan."

Glad to be of service.

Two

Dylan wasn't himself. That had to explain why he'd kissed Emma as though he meant it. Actually, he *had* meant it in that instant. She was familiar to him. He knew the score with her, his sister Brooke's best friend. Someone he could trust. Someone he could rely on. The meds he was taking lessened his headaches and he was recovering, feeling better every day. But having a chunk of his memory gone affected his decision making and confidence, made him vulnerable and uncertain.

But one thing he was certain about: kissing Emma had made him feel better. It was the best kiss he'd had in a long time. It packed a wallop. He knew that without question. Those big green eyes that sparkled like emeralds wouldn't steer him wrong. He'd needed the connection to feel whole again. To feel like himself.

Had he gotten all that from one mildly passionate kiss? Yeah. Because it was with Emma and he knew his limitations with her. She was untouchable and sweet with a side of sassy. So he'd kissed her and let the sugar in her fill him up and take away the pain in his heart.

"You're quiet," he said to her as they walked back toward his house. "Was the kiss out of line?"

"No. Not at all. You needed someone."

He covered her hand with his again and squeezed gently. "Not just anyone, Emma. I needed someone I could trust. You. Sorry if I came on too strong."

"You...didn't."

But she didn't sound so sure.

"It was just a kiss, Dylan. It's not as if you haven't kissed me before."

"Birthday kisses don't count."

She was quiet for a second. "I didn't have a lot of affection when I was younger. Those birthday kisses meant a lot to me."

He gave her another quick squeeze of the hand. "I know. Hey, remember the face-plant kiss?"

"Oh, God. Don't bring that up, Dylan. I'm still mortified. Your parents went to a lot of trouble to make that cake for me."

He chuckled at the image popping into his head. "Damn, that was funny."

"It was your fault!"

Dylan's smirk stayed plastered on his face. He couldn't wipe it clean. At least his long-term memory was intact. "How was it my fault?"

"Rusty was your dog, wasn't he? He tangled under my feet and in that moment I figured it was better to fall into the cake than snuff out your dog. I would've crushed that little Chihuahua if my full weight landed on him."

"What were you, twelve at the time?"

"Yes! It said so on the birthday cake I demolished."

Dylan snorted a laugh. "At least you got to taste it. It

was all over your face. The rest of us just got to watch. But it was worth it."

"You should've given me my birthday kiss before your mom kindly wiped my face clean. Then maybe you wouldn't have felt so deprived. The cake was good, you know. Chocolate marble."

"Oh, don't worry, Em. I wasn't deprived."

She stopped abruptly, taking a stand in the sand, pulling her hand free of his and folding her arms across her middle. "What's that supposed to mean? You enjoyed seeing me fall?"

The phony pout on her face brought him a lightness that he hadn't felt in more than a week, since before the accident.

"Oh, come on, Miss Drama Queen. It was many moons ago." And yes, he knew stuntmen, Roy included, who couldn't have done a better pratfall. It had been hilarious.

"Me? Drama queen? I don't think so. I'm standing here, looking at a true-life drama king. Mr. Winner of two Academy Awards and God only knows how many Golden Globes."

"Three." He grinned.

She rolled her eyes. "Three," she repeated.

He walked back to where she'd made her stand and grabbed up her hand again, tugging her along. He liked Emma Rae Bloom. She'd had a tough life, raised by neglectful foster parents. Just by the grace of all good things, she'd become his sister's best friend, and thus, a member of the McKay clan.

They were almost back to his house. It was sundown, a time when the beach was quiet but for the waves washing upon the shore. Moonlight illuminated the water and reflected off the sand where he stopped to face Emma. "Well, you've succeeded where many have failed this week, Em. You've put a smile on my face."

Her pert little chin lifted to him, and he balked at the urge to take her into his arms again. To kiss that mouth and feel the lushness of her long hair against his palms. She was petite in size and stature, especially without shoes on, and so different than the tall lean models and actresses he'd dated.

He wouldn't kiss her again. But it surprised him how badly he wanted to.

He pursed his lips and went with his gut. "Hey, you know, I've got this charity gig coming up. If the doctors say I'm good to go, I'd love for you to join me for the meet and greet at Children's West Hospital."

Emma turned away from him now, to gaze out to sea. "You want me to go with you?"

"Yep."

"Don't you have agents and personal assistants to do that sort of thing?"

"Em?"

"What?"

Tucking his hands in his pockets, he shrugged. "It's okay if you don't want to go."

She whipped her head around, her eyes a spark of brightness against the dim skies. "Why do you want *me* to go?"

"The truth? I'm a little mixed-up right now. Having a friend come along will make me feel a little safer. I haven't been out in public since the accident. Besides, I know the kids will love you. I was going to ask Brooke, too."

"Oh." She ducked her head, looking sheepish. "These kids, are they all ill?"

"Mostly, yes. But many are in recovery, thank goodness. I'm slated to do a promo spot in a few days with some of the kids to raise funds and awareness about the good the hospital does. I've donated a little to the new wing of the hospital and I guess that's why they've asked me."

"You donated 1.3 million dollars to the new wing, Dylan. I read that online. It's going to be amazing. The new wing will have a screening room with interactive games for the kids."

He smiled. "So what do you say?"

"Yes, of course I'll go."

"Thanks, Em. Now, let's get back inside before Brooke sends out a search party for us."

Emma's laughter filled his ears and made him smile again.

Late Wednesday afternoon, Emma hung up the phone with Mrs. Alma Montalvo, rested her arms on her office desk and hung her head. The client was delirious about details and had sapped Emma's energy for two long hours. Yes, they'd found a local band to play fifties tunes. Yes, they'd rented a '57 Chevy and it would be parked strategically at the top of their multitiered lawn for added effect. Yes, they'd have a photo booth decked out with leather jackets, poodle skirts and car club insignia for the guests to wear as they had their photos snapped. Yes, yes, yes.

Thank goodness the party was this Saturday night. After it was over, she and Brooke could take their big fat check from Mrs. Montalvo and say, *Hasta la vista, baby. Parties-To-Go has come and gone.*

The chime above the door rang out Leslie Gore's classic song "It's My Party" and Emma glanced up.

"Hey, I thought you were going home early today," Brooke said, entering their Santa Monica office.

"I thought I was, too, but Mrs. Montalvo had other ideas."

Brooke rolled her eyes. "We'll impress the hell out of her, Emma. The party is going to be top-notch."

"It better be. I've put in extra hours on this one."

Brooke grinned and set down shopping bags on the

desk adjacent to Emma's. The office furnishings were an eclectic mix, all colorful and light to convey a party atmosphere for clients. The desks were clear Plexiglas, the walls were painted bright pastels and the chairs were relics that had been upholstered in floral materials. Photos of their parties and events adorned the walls from hoedowns on local ranch properties to rich, elaborate weddings with a few celebrity endorsements mixed in, thanks to Dylan.

They had two part-time employees who came in after school and on weekends to answer phones, do online research and work the parties whenever needed.

"Take a look at this," Brooke said, pulling a mocha cocktail dress from a box in one of the bags. "Isn't it… perfect? I got it at the little shop on Broadway."

"Wow, it's gorgeous. And not black. I bet it's for the San Diego golf dinner, right?"

Brooke was shaking her head. "Nope, not at all. You'll never guess."

Emma's thoughts ran through a list of upcoming events and couldn't come up with anything. "Don't make me, then. Tell me!"

Brooke put the dress up to her chin, hugged it to her waist and twirled around, just like when they used to play dress-up and pretend to be princesses ready to meet their special prince.

"I have a date." Brooke sang out the words and stomped her feet.

It shouldn't be that monumental, but Brooke seldom dated. After graduating from college, they'd both been focused on the business. And Brooke was picky when it came to men. So this was a big deal, judging by the megawatt, light-up-Sunset-Boulevard smile on her face. "The best part is, he doesn't know who I am."

Or rather, who her brother was. Most people, men and women alike, showed interest in Brooke once they found out that Dylan was her big brother. It sucked big-time and made Brooke wary of any friendliness coming her way. She was never sure if there was an ulterior motive.

"I mean, of course he knows my name is Brooke. We met at Adele's Café. We were both waiting for our take-out lunch orders and it took forever. But once we got to talking, neither of us minded the long wait."

"When was this?"

"Yesterday."

"And you didn't tell me!" Wasn't that like breaking the BFF rule?

"I didn't know if he'd call." She hugged the dress one last time, before carefully stowing it back in the box. "But he did this morning and asked me out for the following weekend. And get this, he wanted to see me sooner but I told him about the event this weekend and he seemed really disappointed. We don't have anything next weekend. Tell me we don't. The golf tournament is in three weeks, right?"

Emma punched it up on her computer and glanced at their calendar. "Right, but you're so excited, even if we had an event, I'd relieve you of your duties. I've never seen you so gaga. What's his name?"

"Royce Brisbane. He's in financial planning."

Emma dug her teeth into her bottom lip to keep from chuckling. "You, with a suit?"

"Yes, but he looks dreamy in it."

"Wow, Brooke. You really like this guy. You shopped." Brooke was not a shopper. She had one color in her wardrobe arsenal, basic black, and she wore it like armor every day.

"I think I do like him. A lot. It was so easy talking to him. We have a lot in common."

"Tell me more."

After getting the full details on Royce Brisbane, Emma's thoughts went to Brooke's upcoming date on the drive home.

Emma had to admit, the guy sounded good on paper. If he made Brooke happy, then she was all for it. She hadn't seen Brooke smile so much in months. That could be a good thing, or a bad thing. A very bad thing. The more you care about someone, the more they could potentially hurt you. But Emma wouldn't poke a hole in Brooke's happy balloon; her friend deserved to have a good time.

Emma parked in her apartment structure and climbed out of her car. Her legs were two strands of thin spaghetti tonight. It was an effort to walk across the courtyard to her front door. She shoved the sticky door open with her body and glimpsed her comfy sofa with cushy pillows and a quilt she could curl up in. She dropped her purse unceremoniously onto the coffee table, sank down onto the sofa and let out a relieved sigh.

A hundred details ran through her head. The upcoming golf event was first and foremost in her mind. It wasn't for a few weeks yet, but it was a big opportunity for the business. She did yet another mental check, making sure all bases were covered, before she could really relax. Somewhat confident she hadn't forgotten anything, she lay her head down and stretched her legs out, allowing the cushions to envelop her weary body.

If only she could go mindless for a while. Sometimes she envied people who could close everything off and go blank. Just…be. She tended to overthink everything, which made her excellent at her job, but a sad prospect for a carefree lifestyle.

The night of the memorial for Roy Benjamin played in her head and she immediately zoomed in on Dylan McKay. The way he had held her on the beach, the way she had felt when his hand covered hers possessively, the way his mouth had moved over hers and claimed her in a kiss. It wasn't a birthday kiss. It wasn't a friend's kiss, either, though Dylan seemed to think so. It was much more for her. And the memory floated through her body and filled in all the lonely gaps.

Secret dibs.

She smiled. It was never going to happen, yet part of her fantasy had come true. Dylan had made glorious love to her. Okay, so she wasn't sure about the glorious part. She'd been too out of it to know if he was a good lover or not. But in her fantasy world, Dylan was the best. *Appeal* magazine had said so, too. He'd been voted Most Sexy Single this year. And there had been endorsements by his former girlfriends. So it had to be true.

Her eyes grew heavy. It was a battle to keep them open with the cushions supporting her fatigued body and the quilt covering her. All tucked in, she gave up the fight and surrendered to slumber.

Ruff, ruff...ruff, ruff.

Emma bolted upright, her eyes snapping to attention. She found herself on the sofa, half covered with her favorite quilt. How long had she been out? Squinting, she glanced at the wall clock. It was eight thirty. Wow, she'd been asleep for ninety minutes. She'd never taken a nighttime nap before.

Ruff, ruff...ruff, ruff.

Her phone rang again. She grappled for it inside her purse and put it to her ear. "Hello."

"Hello."

It was Dylan. There was no mistaking that deep baritone voice that had half the female movie-viewing population panting to hear more. "Oh, hi."

She hinged her body up, planted her feet on the ground and shook her head to clear away the grogginess.

"I didn't wake you, did I?"

Did she sound as if she'd been sleeping? She tried her best to pretend she was wide-awake. "Not at all. I'm up."

"Busy?"

"No. Just sitting here…going over a few details in my head." A yawn crept out and she cupped her hand over her mouth to hide the sound. "What are you doing?"

"Nothing much. I spoke with Darren on the phone and my manager stopped by to check on me tonight. To be honest, I'm going a little stir-crazy."

"You're used to being busy."

"I can't wait to get back to work. But then, I'm dreading it at the same time."

"I get it. It's because of Roy. It'll be strange for you to go about your daily routine knowing that he's gone and you're going on with your life."

"How come you're so smart, Em?"

"I got lucky in the brains department I guess." She chewed on her lip. She still wasn't comfortable speaking to Dylan with this big black cloud hanging over her head. It made her feel guilty and disingenuous. And why was he suddenly her best friend? Did that knock to his head change his perspective? They'd always been cordial, but since his rise to celebrity status, she hadn't exactly been on his radar. All of a sudden, he was behaving as if they were best buds.

He was disoriented. Fuzzy in the brain. And in need of someone he could trust. But as soon as he was comfortable in his own skin again, things would change. She had no doubt. Dylan was a busy, busy man, sought after by the masses and the media, with who knew how many opportunities for work.

She scrunched up her face. *Don't get used to his attention, Emma.*

"Well, I won't keep you," he said. "I'm calling to confirm our date."

Date? A bad choice of words. "You mean the hospital thing?"

"Yes, it's this Friday morning. How about I swing by your place around nine to pick you up?"

"That's fine. I'm still not sure of my part in all this, but I'm happy to help out."

"You are helping out. You're helping *me*."

The way he said it, with such deep sincerity, tugged her heart in ten different ways. And it dawned on her that it wasn't just returning to work he was partially dreading, but going out in public for the first time with everyone expecting to see Dylan McKay back in true form. That was clearly worrying him. He didn't know if he was ready for that. He needed the support of his sister and friend.

"And you're going to make a difference in a lot of children's lives."

"I hope to. See you around nine, Em. Sleep tight."

"You, too."

Emma ended the call and sat there for a few minutes taking it all in again. She had to stop dwelling on Dylan McKay. Food usually kept her mind occupied. But oddly, she wasn't hungry. In fact, the thought of eating right now turned her stomach, so she nixed that plan and picked up the TV remote. She hit the on button and her small flat-screen lit up the dark room. The channel, tuned to the local network, was airing a movie. She settled back, propping up her feet, and stared ahead.

Dylan McKay's handsome face popped up, filling most of the screen, his bone-melting blue eyes gazing into the pretty face of Hollywood's latest darling, Sophie Adams. The cowboy and his girl were about to ride into the sunset. The camera zoomed in for the movie-ending kiss, and just like that, something cold and painful snared Emma's heart as Dylan's mouth locked onto Sophie's.

Hitting the off button did little to calm her. Why couldn't she get away from Dylan?

Falling for the unattainable was romantic suicide. She wasn't that stupid.

She'd just have to get over her secret dibs.

End of story.

She was ready at precisely nine o'clock. When the doorbell rang, she took a quick glance in the mirror, checking her upswept hairstyle, snowy-white pants and the sherbet-pink blazer she wore over a dotted swiss top. A tiny locket nestled at the base of her throat; that, silver stud earrings and a fashionable chunky watch were all the jewelry she'd opted for. She was going for a professional look without appearing unapproachable to the children. A little thrill ran through her body. Seeing Dylan aside, she was looking forward to meeting the kids, knowing firsthand how hard it was for a youngster to be outside the mainstream. She'd been one of those kids. Lucky for her, she had been healthy, but she'd been different, unloved and unwanted, and she'd never really felt as if she belonged.

Today was all about the kids.

She opened the door and was immediately yanked out of her noble thoughts as she took one look at Dylan standing on her doorstep. She'd expected his driver. But there Dylan was, in the flesh, his bandage gone now, the scar on the side of his head that would eventually heal only making him appear more manly, more dangerous, more gorgeous. Dressed in new jeans and a tan jacket over a white shirt, he smiled at her. "Morning. You look great."

She didn't feel great. She had woken up pale as a ghost and feeling boneless from tossing and turning all night. But his compliments could get to her, if she put stock in them. He was smooth. He was the consummate lady-killer. He knew which buttons to push to make females fall at his feet. And with her, she was sure, he wasn't even trying.

"Thank you. Is Brooke with you?"

He shook his head. "Brooke cracked a tooth this morning. She called me in a panic and said she had to get it fixed right away. I guess it's because of your event tomorrow, but she bailed. She's got a hot date with the dentist in twenty minutes."

Or rather a hot date with Royce next week and she couldn't go toothless. "Oh. Poor Brooke."

"She didn't call you?"

Emma lifted her phone out of her purse and glanced at the screen. "Oh, yeah, she did," she said. "Looks like a voice mail this morning. I was probably in the shower."

Dylan's eyes flickered and roamed over her body. Gosh, he was Flirt Central without even knowing it.

"I'm ready. Or would you like to come in?" Oh, boy, had she really invited him in? The last time he'd been here, they'd…

He glanced behind her and scanned her apartment as if seeing it for the first time. It was clear he didn't remember coming here.

She put those thoughts out of her mind and wondered what he would think of her two-bedroom apartment tucked into an older residential area of Santa Monica. There were no views of the ocean, no trendy, glamorous furnishings or updated kitchen. But it was all hers. And she loved having…stuff of her own.

"Maybe some other time," he said politely. "We should probably hit the road."

After she locked up her apartment, Dylan took her arm and guided her through the courtyard to the limousine parked by the sidewalk. "Here you go," he said as the driver opened the door. She slid in and Dylan followed. "I haven't gotten clearance to drive yet," he explained as he settled into the seat across from her by the window.

But it wasn't as if being carted around in a limo was foreign to him.

"Thanks again for coming with me today."

Again, she was struck by his sincerity. "You're welcome. Actually, I'm looking forward to it."

He stared at her, waiting for more.

She shrugged. "It's just that my own childhood wasn't ideal. If I can do something for these kids, even just as a bystander, I'm all for it. But how are you doing? This is your first venture out in public since the…"

"Accident?" His lips tightened and he sighed. "Let's just say, I'm glad you're here."

"Even though you'll have your team waiting for you there?"

"My agent and PA are great, don't get me wrong. But they see me one way. I don't think they get how hard this has been for me. Losing those days of my life, and losing Roy, has put me at a disadvantage I'm not used to. There are missing pages in my life."

And she could fill in some of those blanks if she had the courage.

He reached for her hand and laid their entwined fingers on the middle seat between them. "Brooke had good reason to jump ship today. I'm just glad you didn't bail."

"I wouldn't."

"I know. That's why I asked you to join me. I can count on you."

They reached Children's West Hospital, a beautiful building with white marble walls and modern lines. The limo slowed to a stop right in the circular drive that led to the entrance.

"Ready for the show?"

Several news crews were waiting like vultures, snapping pictures even before the driver got out of the limo. Dylan made headlines everywhere he went, and his first time out in public since the accident was big news. She recognized Darren, his agent, and Rochelle, his prim assistant, also waiting along the lineup. "Ready." Emma gave off much more confidence than she was feeling.

Dylan waited two beats, sighed as if grasping for strength and then nodded to his driver, who had one hand on the door handle. The door opened and photos were snapped immediately. Dylan got out, waved to the crowd and then reached inside to take her hand. She exited the limo and was dragged into the fray by Dylan, who seemed to tighten his hold on her. A hospital official came forward to greet them and introductions were made as security guards ensured that none of the news media followed them into the hospital lobby. His agent and PA also followed behind, eyeing everyone. Still, Emma saw cameras pressed up against the windows, the paparazzi snapping photos of Dylan and his entourage as they moved along the corridors with Richard Jacoby, the hospital administrator, and a few other ranking hospital officials.

Mr. Jacoby stopped at a double-wide door and turned to their small group. "The children are excited to meet you, Dylan. We've gathered our recovering patients here, in the doctor's lounge. And later, we'll go up to see the other children who are still in treatment."

Emma assumed that he was talking about the kids who couldn't make it out of bed. Her heart lurched and she braced herself for what was to come.

"Afterward, we'll shoot your promo spot with Beth and Pauly."

"Sounds good to me," Dylan said.

"We had a little movie premiere of *His Rookie Year* last night for everyone to get acquainted with who you are. Most of them already knew of you. Eddie Renquist was quite a character."

The rated-G movie hadn't won Dylan any awards, but he'd garnered a whole new audience of youngsters with that role. It was on Emma's Top Ten Favorite list.

"After you," Mr. Jacoby said, and they entered a large room filled with kids of all ages, sitting on grown-up chairs, their eyes as big as the smiles on their faces. They began waving at Dylan. With Emma at his side, he made his way over and spoke to each child. The younger boys called him Eddie and asked him all about baseball, as if he really was a star athlete like his character in the film. Dylan was quite knowledgeable actually and always reminded them he was only acting out a role. Some of them got it, others weren't quite sure. The girls were all over the map, the teens telling him he was hot and they loved him, while the younger ones wanted to shake his hand or give him a hug.

Dylan wasn't stingy with his hugs. He gave them freely and laughed with the kids, shook hands and recited lines from his movies when asked. Some of the kids with shaved heads had peach fuzz growing. They were the lucky ones, the ones who would eventually go home to live normal lives. Some wore back braces or leg casts; others were in wheelchairs. But all in all, every one of them reacted positively to Dylan. He was good with them and managed to bring Emma into the conversation often.

"This is my friend Emma. She plans parties and knows a lot about everything," he said.

"Have you ever planned a Cinderella party?" one of the younger girls asked.

"Well, of course. Cinderella and Belle and Ariel are friends of mine," she said.

A cluster of little girls surrounded her and asked her dozens of questions.

Dylan caught her eye and nodded as he continued to make his way around the room. Once Dylan had greeted every single child, he came to stand at the front of the room and asked if they would like to sing a few songs. "Emma has a great voice and knows lots of songs."

It wasn't exactly out of her wheelhouse to entertain children, but this had come out of the blue. "Oh, of course. We can do that." She jumped right in.

She led them in Taylor Swift and Katy Perry songs as well as a song from *Frozen*, for the little ones, and then Mr. Jacoby signaled to her that their time was up. Dylan walked over to his personal assistant and she handed him a packet of cards.

"Thanks for giving me a chance to meet you all," he said to the kids. "I'm going to come around the room again one more time and hand out movie passes for you and your families."

And afterward, they were whisked away, riding up in the elevator to the third floor where the really ill children lay in beds. What really struck Emma was how happy all the children seemed to be, despite the bald heads, wires and tubes going through them, limbs in casts and machines humming. Experiencing their unqualified acceptance and genuine gladness to see them was as heartwarming as it was heartbreaking. Emma sent up silent prayers for all of them, wishing that affliction wouldn't strike ones so young. But their spirit was amazing and many adults, including her, could learn from their sense of joy and gratefulness.

Dylan treated these kids in the same way he had the others. No pity shone in his eyes; instead, there was a sense of camaraderie and friendship. He was one with them, talking movies and baseball and family with these wonderfully unaffected children.

"It's a lot to take in," Dylan said once they were alone in the hallway.

"They're sweet kids."

"They shouldn't have to deal with this crap. They should be allowed to be kids."

This wasn't just a photo op for Dylan. "You're a softy. Who knew?"

She knew. She'd seen it firsthand and she'd learned something about Dylan today. His compassion for the less fortunate was astounding.

"Shh. You don't want to wreck my image, do you?" He grinned.

"Heavens, not me."

His agent and PA called him away, and he excused himself. When he returned, he was frowning. "The little boy Pauly who was to do the shoot with us had a setback. He's not healthy enough to do the promo spot right now. They're giving me the option to do it with only Beth or to pick another child, or I can wait for Pauly. The camera crew is all here, everything's set up, but here's the thing. Pauly was really looking forward to this. They tell me it's all he's talked about all week." Dylan ran a hand down his face. "What do you think?"

He was asking her advice? She didn't know about the technical nature of this business or the cost involved, but she had only one answer for Dylan. "I'd wait for Pauly. It might make the difference in his recovery, if he has this to look forward to."

Dylan smiled wide, his eyes locking to hers in relief. "That's what I was thinking, too." He leaned over and kissed her cheek. "Thanks."

He turned away before he could take in her shocked expression. He'd kissed her again.

It had to be the surroundings, the children, the good that he'd done today to brighten lives here at Children's West Hospital, and that's all Emma would read into it.

When they walked out of the hospital a short time later, the press vultures were waiting, snapping pictures and shooting questions at him from behind a roped-off line. She stood in the background with Darren and Rochelle, noting how perfectly Dylan handled the situation, stopping them with a hand up. "I'll make a brief statement. As you can see, I'm doing well and recovering. I'll be back to work very soon, but today is not about me. It's about the wonderful work this hospital is doing for the children. The doctors and staff here are dedicated and so willing to give of themselves. We're hoping to shine a light on Children's West Hospital today. Visit their website to see how you can help these brave children. Thank you."

With that, Dylan ushered Emma into the limo and it sped off before she could get her seat belt on.

"Whoa," he said, and for the first time today, she glimpsed beads of sweat on his brow.

"Dylan, are you okay?"

He sank down, shrugged into his seat belt and tossed his head against the headrest. "I've been better."

"Dizzy spell?" She clamped her own seat belt on.

"Nope, it's just a little bit…crazy, isn't it? I'm not feeling myself just yet."

"That's understandable, Dylan. You've been through a lot. But you handled them like a pro."

He turned to her, shaking his head. "Maybe I should've kept you out of it. Your picture might just make the front page of some of those rags."

"I did hear several questions shouted about the red-head." A giggle sounding more like a hiccup escaped her mouth. She'd lived in Los Angeles long enough to know how desperate the paparazzi could be. "I noticed you ignored those."

"Think they'd believe me if I said you were a friend of the family? Not on your life. Let 'em guess."

"Yeah, let them guess." Bet they'd never guess she'd been the one-night stand Dylan McKay had no memory of. Now, that was a story for the tabloids.

"Thank you for coming with me today. It made a difference having you here."

She was his surrogate sister. She didn't mind. Not today.

"You know, I'm glad I came, too, and if I helped you in the process, that's a bonus."

"You did." Dylan leaned over, gave her a sweet kiss that seemed to linger on her lips, then retreated to his seat and closed his eyes. "Thanks."

She was pretty sure surrogate sisters didn't get kisses like that.

In fact, she didn't remember much about his kisses at all.

And that stumped her. A man like Dylan…well, a girl shouldn't forget something like that, drunk on mojitos and in a blackout or not.

The Montalvo party went off without a hitch, except for one boisterous guest who'd gotten smashed on martinis and fallen off the top tier of the multilevel grounds. Luckily for him, it was only a five-foot drop and he'd fallen on a shelf of border boxwoods that pinched like the dickens but broke his fall and prevented major damage. After causing a momentary ruckus, the man sobered up real fast, skulked off like a pup with his tail between his legs, and the party picked up again from there.

Emma was proud of the display they'd put on for the fifties party and their company was hired on the spot by a theatre producer in attendance to host a similar event. It had been a win-win night.

She'd worked her butt off these past few weeks. Brooke had her head in the clouds after her date with Royce and they'd seen each other three times since. Emma didn't mind picking up the slack, except that she'd been extremely tired and with her resistance down she managed to catch Brooke's cold. Now both of them weren't feeling well. But while Brooke had only sniffles and sneezes, Emma had an upset stomach, as well. She couldn't look at food for days and even now the thought of eating anything but a piece of fruit made her tummy grumble. And the big golf tournament event was in just four days.

"Emma, get your ducks in a row," she muttered. She lay on her bed praying for strength. A commercial for a big sloppy hamburger came on the television screen and she didn't turn her head away in time. "Oh, God." Her stomach soured instantly and her legs tangled in the sheets as she fumbled from bed and raced to the bathroom. She landed on her knees and made it to the toilet just as her stomach contracted.

Wonderful…just wonderful. After she flushed the toilet she sat back on her knees. The little energy she'd had this morning had seeped out of her. But the flu bug would not get her down. She wouldn't miss their big charity event coming up. She grasped the bathroom counter for support and lifted herself up. Her head spun for a second, until finally her eyes focused and she mustered every ounce of strength to stay upright.

"Okay, Emma," she whispered. "You can do this."

Carefully, she stepped away from the sink. The merry-go-round in her head was gone. *Thank you, Flu Gods.* But just a second later gripping pain attacked her stomach. "Oh." She held her belly and flew toward the toilet again. Sinking down onto the floor, she emptied everything into the porcelain bowl, until there was nothing left.

An hour later, after managing to climb her way back into bed, her body shaking, her bones weak, she clutched her cell and pushed Brooke's number. "Hi," she whispered.

"What's wrong?"

Brooke knew her so well.

"I'm down, Brooke. Can't make it out of bed right now. The flu."

"Oh, Em. I'm so sorry. I got you sick and now you're getting the brunt of it. You sound terrible."

"My stomach's finally eased off, but it wasn't pretty an

hour ago. I'm so…tired. I'm gonna try to make it into the office later today."

"No, you're not. You need to stay in bed all day and rest. I've got things handled here. You know we've been right on schedule with this charity event. I just have a few last-minute things to take care of. You rest up and get better so you can make it on Friday."

"Okay, I think you're right."

"Sleep. It's the best thing for you."

"Thanks, and, Brooke, no way am I missing this weekend."

"I'll come over later and bring you some soup."

"Ugh, no. Just the thought of food right now turns my stomach."

"All right. I'll call you later."

When the call ended, Emma turned her head into her pillow, closed her eyes and slept the entire day. She woke up bathed in a stream of dim light coming from the night-light on the opposite wall. She blinked herself awake. Outside, darkness had descended, but she was safe, protected. Since the night of the blackout, she kept night-lights on day and night in her apartment to keep from ever being alone in total darkness. She also now had an entire bedroom shelf devoted to pillar candles, scented and unscented. It didn't matter, as long as they did the trick. She took them with her when she traveled, too, just in case, and had also started carrying a mini flashlight in her purse. Not that she couldn't use her cell phone—someone had turned her onto a flashlight app, which came in handy—but cell phone batteries died on occasion and she couldn't chance it.

A look at her cell phone now revealed that it was seven twenty-five. Wow, she'd slept for nine hours. Funny, but she didn't feel rested at all. Or hungry. Just the thought of food made her queasy all over again.

Brooke called and they spoke for half an hour, going

over the final details of the golf event, the dinner, dancing, silent auction and raffle. At two thousand dollars a head and with an expected one hundred fifty guests in attendance, there were lots of fine points to check on.

"I'll see you tomorrow, Brooke," Emma said, feeling optimistic as she hung up the phone. Her stomach had eased back to normal and she figured she'd been through the worst of it.

By the morning of the next day, she knew that she'd figured wrong. She emptied her stomach twice before it settled down. She managed to go into the office, but once Brooke took a look at her pasty face, she ordered her back to bed. Emma didn't have the strength to argue.

By Thursday morning, nothing had changed. She spent the morning in the bathroom next to her new best friend. Suspicions were running rampant in her head. What if she didn't have the flu? What if there was something else wrong with her? Something permanent? Something rest and hot soup wouldn't cure?

Eyes wide-open now, she fought the invading rumblings in her belly, quickly dressed and dashed to the local drugstore. Once she got back home, she peed on a stick at three different intervals of the day, only to get the same result each time. Opening her laptop, she keyed it up and researched a subject she thought would be years down the road for her.

She was as sure now as she would ever be; she had all the symptoms.

She was pregnant.

And Dylan McKay was her blackout baby's father.

Three

"You're trying to hide a smile, Brooke. You don't fool me."

"I'm not trying to fool you, Emma. I think it's kinda cool that you and my brother…"

"No, it wasn't like that, really." Oh, boy.

Having Brooke stop everything at the office and come over right away might have been a mistake. But this was big and she couldn't hide her pregnancy from her best friend. Especially not when Brooke had a stake in this, too; she was Dylan's sister after all. Emma needed her right now. She had no one else to turn to and time was running out. She had morning sickness, big-time. Immediate decisions had to be made and she'd have to deal with Dylan at some point.

"We're not romantically involved," she said to Brooke.

Her friend sat on the sofa next to her, her mouth twitching, the smile she couldn't conceal spreading wider across her face. This was no laughing matter. Obviously, Brooke thought differently.

She'd given Brooke the bare facts about what had happened that night between her and Dylan, explaining how she'd panicked when all the lights had gone out in that nightclub. The entire city had gone dark from what she could tell and she hadn't been in any shape to drive home. At least she got that part right. No drunk driving for her.

But instead of Brooke coming to pick her up as she'd hoped, Dylan had come to her rescue, as any good guy would. Emma tried to make clear to Brooke that she'd been the one to initiate the lovemaking. Emma remembered that much; she'd begged him to stay with her. She had no recollection of exactly how it all went down, those hours fuzzy in her head, but it was all on her. She'd been scared out of her wits and inebriated. And Dylan was there. She'd lived out her fantasy with him that night, but she didn't tell Brooke that. Some things were better left unsaid.

"Brooke, I'll say it again, and this is hard to admit, but I probably climbed all over him that night. I swear, he didn't take advantage of me." The worst would be that Brooke would hold anything about that night against Dylan.

Brooke covered her ears. "Emma, pleeeze! No details. I can't think of Dylan that way." And then she lowered her hands. "But it's sweet that you're trying to protect him. You don't want me to think badly of my brother. I get that, Em. And I don't. No one's to blame."

"Okay, no details." Not that she could remember any. "Dylan doesn't know any of this happened."

"Are you sure of that?"

"I'm sure. I'd know it, if he remembered. I'd see something in his eyes. And he's never mentioned my phone call that night, or the fact that he came to pick me up from the nightclub. When he came to my apartment the day we went to the children's hospital, he didn't seem to recognize anything as familiar. I'm certain that night was erased from his memory."

"I think so, too. Just making sure there were no signs."

"Nope, not a one."

Brooke nodded and then gazed warmly into Emma's eyes for several ticks of a minute. "You're going to be the mother of my niece or nephew," she said as softly as Emma had ever heard her speak. The tone was rich and thick as honey. "And my brother is going to be a father."

The way Brooke put it was sort of beautiful. Emma could get lost in all the wonder of motherhood, of nurturing a new life and having a man like Dylan father her child. But the wonder didn't come close to erasing the plain facts. That she and Dylan didn't plan this child. That he didn't even have a clue what was happening, yet his life was about to change forever.

"Oh, Brooke. I'm just wrapping my head around it. The baby part has me feeling…I don't know, protective already and scared." Emma shivered. "Very scared."

"You'll be fine. You have me. And Dylan. He'd never turn his back on you."

"Gosh, it's all so new. Part of me feels guilty not telling him about that night. It might've triggered some of his memories."

"You'll have to tell him now, Em. He has a right to know."

It was inevitable that she tell Dylan. But she wasn't looking forward to that conversation. Gosh, he'd been like a big brother to her and now nothing between them would ever be the same.

"I know. I will."

"Good. You're in no shape to do the golf event, Em. You're exhausted and still having morning sickness."

Emma chewed on her bottom lip. She didn't want to miss this weekend. All those hours, all that planning. Brooke needed her, but how could she function when she was running to the bathroom all morning long? "Yes, but it's getting better. Maybe I could come along and help out in the afternoon and evening."

Brooke was shaking her head. When had she turned into a mama bear? "I've got it covered, Emma. You can't come. You'd be miserable. I've got Rocky and Wendy on standby."

The part-timers?

"I've been briefing them and they're up for the task. I don't want you to worry about a thing. You should concentrate on the baby and feeling better. We'll do fine."

"Are you saying you don't need me?"

"I'm saying, we'll make do without you, but of course, we'll miss you. Thanks to your unending efficiency, we've got all the bases covered. You should take this weekend to adjust to all of this. That's what I want for you. It's what you need."

Emma sighed and gave her friend a reluctant nod. Brooke was right. She couldn't very well carry out her duties in San Diego with her stomach on the blink every hour and her body feeling as though it had been hit by an eighteen-wheeler. "Okay, I'll be a good girl."

"It's too late for that," Brooke replied with a grin.

"Don't I know it."

Brooke's eyes melted in apology. "You're not letting anyone down, Emma. Just the opposite. I know the situation isn't ideal right now, but you're having a baby with Dylan. My best friend and my brother...how can I not think it's just a little bit wonderful?"

Brooke's arms came around her and the hug warmed all the frigid ice flowing through her veins. She was wrapped up in comfort and support and friendship. "How come you always know the right thing to say?"

"Since when?"

"Since...now."

"Oh, Emma. Do you want me to be there when you tell Dylan?"

"No!" Emma pulled away from her friend. The thought of having that conversation gave her hives, but having Dylan's baby sister there? There was no number on the Awkward Scale high enough to describe such a scene. "It'd be too weird. I can't even picture any of this in my head right now, but I suspect this is one time I need to be alone with Dylan."

The tight lines on Brooke's face crumbled and her expression resumed some semblance of normalcy. "Whew, thanks. I have to agree. I love my bro and I love you, but…"

"But I made my bed, now I have to toss off the tangled sheets and come clean."

"Yeah," Brooke said, giving her that same melting look. "Something like that, sweetie."

"Promise you won't worry about me this weekend?"

"If you promise me the same. Don't give a thought to the golf event."

They stared at each other, knowing unequivocally that would be impossible.

"Sure," Emma said.

"Gotcha," Brooke added, her smile falsely quick. Then Brooke kissed her goodbye on the cheek and brought her mouth near her ear to whisper, "The sooner you tell Dylan, the better."

"I know," she said, nodding. "I will."

Problem number one: she didn't have a clue *how* or *when* she could bring herself to do that.

"A little bit of fresh air will do wonders for you, Emma," Dylan said as he strolled into her apartment wearing jeans and a vintage T-shirt, the Stones logo stretching wide across his chest. The shirt hugged him tight and hinted at a ripped torso underneath. Before she got caught ogling, she shifted her attention to his face and was struck by the scruffy, tousled look that appealed to her on so many levels, it was ridiculous. "Brooke is worried sick about you."

Emma had had about half an hour advance warning from Dylan that he was coming to visit her, his text announcing he was on the way, leaving her no option. He was on a mission, commandeered by Brooke, no doubt, and Emma had raced around her apartment destroying evidence of just how sick she'd been. She'd picked up blankets tossed across the sofa and folded them, sprayed the room with cinnamon spice air freshener—the place now smelled like Christmas—slipped off her smelly sweats, taken a shower and put on a sleeveless denim dress and a pair of tan boots.

Evenings were her best time of day lately, so she was pretty sure that she could pull off seeing him without doing a sprint to the bathroom. "I'm feeling much better, Dylan. There's no need for you to be here. Gosh, you must have better things to do on a Friday night."

He smiled her way, that megawatt lady-killer smile that either slowed breathing or caused it to race. Right now, her breath caught in her throat and she reminded herself to breathe. He was just a man.

And the father of your baby.

"Nope, no plans. And since I'm already here, I was hoping not to eat alone tonight. Come back to the house with me. Maisey's made an amazing meal. We can eat on the patio. It's a gorgeous night."

God, getting some fresh Moonlight Beach air did sound appealing. She'd been stuck in her house for eons, it seemed.

Her hesitation wasn't lost on him. He eyed her carefully, taking a quick toll of her state of health. She didn't want to seem ungrateful for the gesture although she knew he was here solely at Brooke's bidding.

"Brooke says you haven't been eating. You need a good meal, Em."

She did, and her traitorous stomach growled quietly, but he didn't appear to notice, thank goodness. "I don't know."

"You want to. Come for an hour or two."

It was hard to refuse, with the look in those beautifully clear sky-blue eyes. When aimed at her, she usually succumbed. It had always been that way. What could she say? She, like a zillion other adoring fans, had it bad for Dylan McKay. And she knew darn well, he wouldn't be here if it weren't for Brooke's nagging. She wouldn't get off his case if he didn't succeed in making sure Emma was well cared for tonight.

Why had Brooke put her in this position? As sweet as it was, she wasn't anyone's charity case. She hadn't been for a long time, and she wasn't ever going back there. She'd learned to fend for herself since her foster care days and didn't want to be thought of as an obligation in order to ease anyone's conscience. She had a mind to refuse him flat, but those bone-melting eyes kept a vigil on her and a look of hope spread across his face.

"Well, maybe just for a little while, but only to get you off the hook with Brooke."

Gesturing in his own defense, he turned his palms up. "I don't know what you mean. This was my idea."

She snorted. "And the sun doesn't shine in LA."

Glancing out the window at the dimming skies, he grinned. "It isn't at the moment."

Okay, she could share a meal with him. She didn't have to tell him the truth. Not yet. She wasn't ready for that, and this way, he'd report back to Brooke that all was well and she'd have the rest of the weekend in peace. "I'll get my jacket, then."

He nodded, looking ridiculously satisfied.

A few minutes later, they were barreling down Pacific

Coast Highway in his licorice-black SUV, the windows down and warm spring breezes lifting her hair. Dylan, recently cleared to drive again, was concentrating on the road, and she took a second to gaze at his profile. He had classic good looks: a solid jawline, a strong chin, a nose that was just sharp enough to suit his face and eyes the color of Hawaiian waters, deep blue with a hint of turquoise. His hair was streaked by the sun, a little long right now so that it swept over his ears. Most times he wore it combed back away from his face, but there were these locks that always loosened from the pack to dip onto his forehead that drove her crazy.

Would their child have his hair? His eyes?

Or would the baby look more like her? Green-eyed with dark cranberry tresses?

Her stomach squeezed tight thinking of the secret life inside her, growing and thriving despite her frequent bouts of nausea. She really did need a nourishing meal and Maisey's cooking was too good to turn down.

"Here we are." Dylan pulled into the gated circular driveway of his beach home. There were times she couldn't believe this was all his. He'd grown up in a normal American household, the son of a high school principal and a civil engineer. Dylan's dad had died one year before he was due to retire, but Markus McKay had lived a full and happy life. The love he'd had for his wife and family, the life they'd led filled with generosity and kindness, had restored Emma's faith in mankind.

Once he parked in the multicar garage on the property, Dylan made an attempt to wind around the car to open the door for her, but she was too quick. She stepped out on her own, ignoring how his smile faded as she strode past him toward the service door that led into his house. "Hey, Sparky, wait up," he said, coming to stand beside her.

He unlocked the door and opened it for her. She took

a step to enter, just as his arm shot out, blocking her way in. Suddenly, surprisingly, she was trapped between his body and the door. Trapped by the compelling scent of him. Several beats ticked away and then she lifted her lids and locked onto his gaze.

"Do me a favor," he said softly, the fingers of his free hand coming to rest under her chin. His innocent touch kicked her senses into high gear. He didn't wait for her answer, but continued, "Don't pretend you're completely recovered just to prove a point. I see how tired you are. Your face is pale, and you've obviously lost weight."

He'd hit the nail on the head. The shudder that erupted inside probably wasn't visible on the outside, but boy, oh boy, how it rattled her all the way down to her toes. His noticing her body was shock enough, but noticing how bad she looked brought new meaning to her humiliation. What next? Would he point out her warts and moles, too?

"I've been around the theatre long enough to know an act when I see one. All I'm asking is for you to relax tonight, eat a delicious dinner and have a good time. You don't have to pretend with me. Just be yourself."

As he lowered his arm allowing her to pass, Emma blurted, "Yes, Dr. Dylan. Will do." All she needed now to accompany the nod she gave him was a military salute.

His eyebrows lifted at her sarcasm. "Your mouth... sometimes I want to—" And then he leaned in before she could grasp his intention and brushed a soft kiss to her lips.

She gasped, raking in air, but quickly recovered. "Shut me up?"

He shook his head, chuckling. "That's one way to put it. But I was thinking of it more as a way to sweeten the sass blistering your tongue."

Well, he'd shut her up *and* sweetened her mouth with one tiny kiss. Dylan could get away with things like that. He'd been gifted with an accommodating good nature that charmed any woman in his path. She'd seen it over and over again. His reputation with the ladies had been mulled over, talked about and dissected by the media. Magazine covers, television interviews and social media platforms had him figured out. He wasn't one to be tied down, but he'd gotten away with it with the press, because he never infringed. He'd been crowned a one-woman kind of man, and the woman he was currently dating received all of his attention. A smart move on his behalf, it kept him out of trouble.

And all it had taken was a power outage burdening most of the city one night to shake his very well-protected reputation. Only, he didn't know that yet.

Oh, boy, when Emma did things, she did them all the way.

The minute they entered his luxurious home, Dylan went about opening the massive beveled glass French doors in the living room. Balmy breezes immediately rushed in bringing scents of salty sea air and powdery sands. Emma followed him into the kitchen, where he opened the doors leading to the Italian-stone-and-marble patio deck. Succulents and vines grew vertically up one wall in a landscaping masterpiece Dylan had recently commissioned, adding just the right touch of greenery to the outdoor landing. Patio tables and a cozy set of lounge furniture were strategically placed around a stone fire pit to allow the best views of the Pacific.

"Want to have a seat out here?" he asked. "I'll heat up the food Maisey left for us and you can soak up some fresh air."

She'd rather do something with her hands than sit outside. Alone. In the dark. "No, thanks, I'll help you."

"Suit yourself. But I can handle it. I give Maisey the weekends off usually."

"You mean you cook for yourself?"

He smiled as he walked over to the double-door cabinet refrigerator and grabbed a covered dish. "Unless Maisey takes pity on me and leaves me something wonderful like this chicken piccata, I've been known to throw a meal together." He set the dish down and opened the oven door.

"Impressive," she said.

"I can also wash a dish and toss dirty clothes in the washing machine, too."

He gestured and she grabbed a casserole dish of rice pilaf from the fridge and handed it to him. Into the oven it went, right next to the chicken. A basket of bread, something garlicky with bits of sun-dried tomatoes, was nestled on the onyx counter next to a tray of homemade chocolate chip cookies. All the combined scents should make her queasy, but she found them actually whetting her appetite. She was hungrier than she'd been in a week. "Such skills. I'm impressed."

Once the meal was set to reheating, Dylan leaned against the granite island, folding his arms across his torso, and pinned her down with those baby blues. "You're forgetting how I grew up. Mom and Dad expected us to do everyday chores, just as they did. I washed cars, cooked meals, did laundry, made beds, and good God, I even scrubbed toilets."

"I bet you don't anymore."

He shrugged and slid her a crooked grin. "Not if I can help it."

Thinking about her recent toilet incidents, she didn't blame him. "Your mom and dad were wonderful people. They taught you well."

"Yeah, but at the time I didn't think so. I did more work than any of my friends. Before I could go out and play ball, I had a list of chores to get through. Weekends were especially gruesome."

"They were building character."

"Yeah, now I play characters on the screen."

"And you still wash dishes and make your own meals. The last conversation I had with your mom, she told me how proud she was of you."

"She is now, but when I left college in my sophomore year to pursue an acting career, my folks were both pretty bummed. Especially my dad. He had high hopes of me going to medical school. He lost his chance at being a doctor and tossed all of his hopes and guilt onto me. He wanted to be a pediatrician." He made a noisy sigh and scrubbed at the dark blond stubble on his chin. "I guess I really disappointed him when I ran away with Renee."

Renee had been no good for Dylan. Emma had heard that a zillion times from Brooke and Dylan's folks. Emma hadn't been too happy with her, either. At the tender age of fourteen, Emma's heart had been crushed when Dylan had fallen in love with a cheerleading beauty who'd convinced him he could make it big in the movies. She had connections. She could get him in to see all the right people.

"Maybe it wasn't in the cards for you to be a doctor. Your dad lived long enough to see your success. He had to know you made the right decision for yourself."

"Dad didn't think I knew what I was doing. And maybe I didn't. Renee was my first girlfriend and I was crazy about her." He pumped his shoulders a couple of times, hopelessly, and something faint and hidden entered his eyes. "But enough about ancient history. How about a soda?" He opened the fridge again. "Lemonade? Wine or beer? Anything else? Maisey keeps the fridge pretty stocked."

"Water sounds good." It was safe. She couldn't trust her stomach right now, and even before she'd found out about the baby, she'd given up alcohol.

He handed her one of those cobalt blue water bottles

that cost more than a glass of fine wine and then plucked out an Indian Brown Ale for himself. His throat moved as he tipped the bottle to his lips and took a swig. She looked away instantly. She was never one to hide her emotions and the last thing she needed was to have Dylan catch her eyeing him.

They'd had their one night. Unfortunately neither of them remembered it.

Dylan's cell phone rang out the theme song to his latest action flick. How many people actually had their very own ringtone? He grabbed it off the counter and frowned at the screen. "Sorry, Emma. I have to get this. I'll make it quick. It's the head of the studio."

"Go right ahead. I'm fine right here." She gestured for him to take the call.

He nodded, his eyes sparkling with gratitude as he walked out of the room, the cell to his ear. Emma grabbed the salad from the refrigerator, set it on the granite island and then scrounged through drawers to find tongs. Coming up with a pair, she leaned against the counter as Dylan's voice drifted to her ears.

"It's Callista's thirtieth birthday? Yeah, I think she'd love a party. Up at your house?"

And then after a long pause, "I'll do my best to be there, Maury. Yes, yes, I'm recovering nicely, thank you. I'm back at work on Monday. Thanks for the call. See you soon."

He walked back into the kitchen, frowning and running a hand down his face. "Sorry," he said. "Business crap."

"Sounds like Callista's having a party." She tilted her head. "Sorry, I overheard."

"Yeah, she's turning thirty. Maury likes to remind me he's not getting any younger. He expects me to be there." Dylan sighed.

Maury Allen had power and influence. That much, Emma knew. According to Brooke, he'd been pushing for

Dylan to make a commitment to his daughter, but so far, Dylan had resisted. Their relationship had been on and off for three years. "And you don't want to go?"

Dylan leaned back against the counter, picking up his beer. "Maury's been good to me. Gave me my first break. I sort of owe him my loyalty. If he wants me at his daughter's birthday celebration, I'll go."

Dylan McKay and Callista Lee Allen made a gorgeous couple. Whenever they were together, there were headlines. To all the world they probably seemed like a perfect match.

Which made Emma's predicament suddenly jump to the forefront of her thoughts and curdle her stomach. She was feeling a little weak-kneed anyway and needed to sit down.

Dylan's hand came to her elbow and his eyes locked onto hers. "Emma, are you okay? You're looking pale. I need to get food into you. Come, sit down."

Why was he always touching her? She had enough to deal with right now, without getting all fan crazy over Dylan's slightest brotherly touch. "Okay, maybe I should sit."

He guided her to the outside patio table closest to the kitchen. "Wait here. I'll get some plates and bring out the food."

She sat, dumbfounded by her fatigue, and stared straight out to sea. The waves gently rolled onto the shore, and stars above lit the sky as low-lying fixtures surrounding the deck gave off soothing light. Fresh scents from the vertical garden on her right drifted to her nose and the whole effect made her feel somewhat better.

Emma wasn't a wilting flower. Nothing much rattled her, well, except being alone in complete darkness. Overall, considering her lousy childhood, she'd fended well in the world, but this whole Dylan thing—secretly carrying his child, losing her cookies every morning and not holding up her end with Parties-To-Go—overwhelmed her. The walls were closing in from all directions and right now her body wasn't up for the fight.

Dylan came back loaded down with food and went about serving her as if she was the Queen of England. Then he offered her the tan suede jacket she'd brought from home. "It's getting a little cool out here," he said.

She nodded and he helped her put her arms through the sleeves. "There you go. Better?"

She nodded. The jacket fit her snugly. She wondered how much longer she could wear it and then, just like that, tears welled in her eyes. Her mouth began to quiver.

It had to be hormones.

Dylan didn't seem to notice. He was too busy making sure she had everything she needed at the table. "Eat up, Emma."

He finally sat and they both picked up their forks. The food was delicious and she managed to eat half of everything on her plate. An accomplishment, considering she hadn't eaten this much in days.

"You're not worried about your girlish figure, are you?" he asked, eyeing her plate. His grin and the twinkle in his eyes were right on par for Dylan.

"Should I be?"

His lids lowered as he slowly raked his gaze over her body. "Not from where I'm sitting."

She had no comeback. He'd once touched every inch of her and seemed to have no complaints that she could remember.

She managed a smile, though suddenly her energy waned. "The food was amazing. I feel full and satisfied," she fibbed. Actually, she wasn't feeling so great. "Please be sure to thank Maisey for me."

"I will."

"Dylan?"

"Hmm?"

"I'm really exhausted. Would you mind taking me home?"

He hesitated and something that resembled regret flickered in his eyes. "Sure…if that's what you want."

"It is." She rose and pushed back her chair. Before she could take a step, heat washed up and over her, spinning circles inside her head. Her legs buckled and soon she was falling, falling.

And then Dylan's arms were around her, easing her to the ground. "Emma!"

A sharp pat to the face snapped her eyes open. She'd been slapped.

"Emma, thank God. You fainted."

Her head felt light and she saw two Dylans leaning over her on bent knee. "I did?"

"Yeah, you were out for a few seconds. I'm going to get you inside and call 911."

"No, no!" His words were enough to rouse her and refocus her eyes. "I don't need the paramedics."

"You do, honey. You've been sick for days now. You should see a doctor." The resolve in his voice frightened her. This was going sideways fast.

"No, no. I'm not sick."

"Something's wrong with you, Emma. I have to get you help."

"Dylan, no." She gazed into his worried face. "I know what's wrong. I'm not sick."

"You're not?"

She shook her head. "No, I'm not. I'm…pregnant."

Four

"Pregnant?" Had he heard Emma right? He didn't know she'd been seeing anyone. He softened his voice, attempting to keep his surprise concealed. "You're pregnant, Em?"

She nodded, chewing on her lower lip, her eyes down.

Where was the guy? Did he bail on her? And why did he feel sharp pangs in his gut consisting of an emotion he refused to name? "Are you sure?"

"Yes," she whispered, still averting her eyes.

It seemed that she hadn't come to grips with it yet. Softly, he brushed fallen locks off her forehead, the tendrils flowing through his fingers like silk, which brought her pretty green eyes up to his. "Well, damn."

She swallowed.

"Is it okay for me to lift you up now?"

He was holding the top half of her body off the ground. Another few inches and she would've landed hard on stone.

"I think so. I'm not dizzy anymore."

He knew something about getting dizzy. Luckily, that

hadn't happened to him for days now. "Okay, slowly," he said.

He brought his face close to hers, breathing in a sweet scent that reminded him of lavender. God, he liked her. There was something sweet and real about Emma Bloom. She'd spent a lot of time in the McKay household while growing up and he'd always looked upon her as a second little sister. But now he wasn't altogether sure why he felt so close to her. Or why, whenever given a chance, he chose to kiss her. It was almost second nature with him lately, holding Emma and kissing her.

Gathering her in his arms, he guided her up, keeping her body pressed close to his. Her breasts crushed his chest and he tried not to think about how soft and supple they felt. Once they were upright, he kept his hold on her. "Do you think you can stand on your own?"

"Yes, I think so."

"I won't let go of you completely. I'll hold on to your waist, okay?"

She nodded. Color had come back to her face. It wasn't rosy, but she didn't look like a sheet, either, so that was a good thing.

She was unusually quiet and there was a stark look on her face. Stronger breezes had kicked up on the patio and it was getting chilly. "Let's go inside."

He stood beside her now, wrapping an arm around her slender waist. "I've got you." Shoulder to shoulder, they took small steps. They bypassed the kitchen and moved into the larger living room. Dylan stopped at his buttery leather couch, the most comfortable seat in the house, and helped her sit down. Her silence unnerved him. Was she embarrassed, scared, regretful? Hell, he didn't know what to say to her when she was like this.

"Thank you," she mumbled.

"You're sure you're okay?"

"I'm feeling better, Dylan.

"You really should see a doctor."

She looked down at the hands she'd folded in her lap. So unlike Emma. "I plan to."

"Does Brooke know?"

She nodded. "I told her just recently."

"I don't mean to pry, but what about the baby's father? Does he know?"

She shook her head. "Not yet."

Dylan didn't want to stick his nose into her business, but Emma hadn't led a charmed life. The kid didn't deserve to go through this alone. Dylan wasn't good with stuff like this, but she was here and had fainted in front of him. With Brooke gone for a few more days, Dylan had to step in. "I'm not taking you home until I'm sure you're feeling better."

"Dr. Dylan," she said, her lips quirking up. Signs of the real Emma Rae Bloom were emerging.

"Your friend Dylan."

She looked away.

"Let me get you some water. Hang on."

He left the room, and when he returned with a glass, Emma's eyes were closed, but there was no peace on her face. He sat down beside her quietly and put the glass in her hand.

She turned to him then and whispered, "Dylan...I need to talk to you."

"Sure. Okay. I'm listening."

Her chest heaved as she filled her lungs, as if readying for a marathon. And then she began. "You know how I was raised. My foster parents weren't very attentive, but they gave me a home. They fed me and I had clothes on my back."

They were reckless and selfish bastards. Heavy drinkers. But Dylan wouldn't say that.

She sipped water, probably needing fortification, then went on. "I was about ten when Doris and Burt went out to the local English pub one night. You might remember the one on Birch Street."

He nodded. "Darts and hard ales. I remember."

She gave him a quick smile. They had the same roots. Only, hers were laden with weeds instead of the pretty poppies little girls deserved.

"They'd put me to bed early that night and told me to stay there," she continued. "I knew they probably wouldn't come home until very late. What I didn't know was that the electricity had been turned off that day. They hadn't paid their electric bill, so when a bad storm hit that night I trembled every time there was thunder. And the erratic lightning really freaked me out. None of the lights in my room were working. I remember how black it was. And there were noises. Crazy, scary noises, shutters flapping against the house, wind howling, shrubs brushing against the outer walls sounding like devilish whispers. I ran downstairs, clicking as many light switches as I could find. Nothing worked. And then I remembered Burt kept a flashlight in a little storage closet under the stairs. S-somehow… s-somehow…as I climbed into that space, a gust of wind or something…slammed the door shut behind me. I was locked in that tiny dark space all night."

"Oh, man, Emma," Dylan said, taking her hand and giving it a squeeze. Her face was stone cold, as if reliving this memory had frozen her up inside. He could only imagine her terror that night. He had no clue what this had to do with her pregnancy, but he listened. Maybe she needed to get this off her chest. She could use him to unburden herself if that's what it took.

"It was the longest night of my life. I sobbed and sobbed most of the night, quietly, though, in case those devilish sounds materialized into something evil. My folks finally came home. It was almost dawn when they found me cowering in that closet. They told me everything was all right and that I'd be okay. Only, I wasn't okay. From then on, being in dark places has always screwed with my head."

"It's understandable that you get frightened. Those memories must be horrible for you."

Her lips tightened as she bobbed her head up and down.

He waited for more. A moment later, her sad eyes lifted to his. "Flash forward about sixteen years. It was the night of the blackout…my neighbor Eddie was having a big birthday bash on the Sunset Strip. It was one round of drinks after another. For the first time in my life, I indulged. In a big way. My friends kept my glass refilled until I was feeling no pain. My fuzzy head went on the blink, and unfortunately so did the lights. Before I knew what was happening, the entire club went black. I couldn't see a thing out the windows, either. Then I heard the rain. It wasn't a downpour, but it didn't have to be, just the steady pounding on the roof was enough. I freaked and began trembling uncontrollably. Luckily, I had Brooke on autodial, or I wouldn't have had the coordination to make the call. I couldn't reach her… She didn't answer."

Dylan leaned in, nodding his head. "Go on, Em. Then what did you do?"

Her eyes squeezed shut. This was hard on Emma but it was probably good for her to purge this memory. "When I couldn't reach your sister, I panicked and gave my phone to someone sitting on the floor next to me." She shook her head and took a deep breath. "My friend punched in your number."

"My number?" he repeated, and his forehead wrinkled as he scoured his memory for an inkling of recollection. Nothing came to mind.

"Yes… I…I thought Brooke might be with you."

His mind was a blank wall when it came to those days. "I don't remember."

Her eyes watered and she gave him half a smile, one of those unhappy smiles that tussled with his heart. "I was so scared."

"I'm sorry."

"Don't be. You came to rescue me. I just remember thinking *Dylan will come.* If he says he will come, he will come. He'll get me out of here. I couldn't wait to get out of that place."

He could've caught flies when his mouth dropped open and stayed that way. "What happened next?" And why didn't she tell him this before? She knew he was trying to piece together those lost hours before the blast.

"It's fuzzy, but I remember you finding me in the dark and carrying me out of there. You drove me home and… and…"

She gazed into his eyes then, and it hit him with dazzling clarity. He blinked rapidly several times. "You're not saying…"

She hadn't said anything yet. But a knot formed in the pit of his stomach. And he knew what she was going to say, not because he remembered it, but because she'd given him the full picture of her life leading up to that moment. And he was cast in the starring role.

"I wouldn't let you leave, Dylan." Her head down, she began shaking it. "I begged you to stay with me. I was scared out of my wits. The whole city was pitch-black and you knew I would freak out if you left me, so you agreed, and then…we, uh…"

"We made love?" He couldn't believe he was asking Emma, his little sister's friend, this question. Emma, the efficient one. The one always in control, the one who never took risks, never strayed from the straight-and-narrow path. Emma Rae Bloom. He'd bedded her?

Her eyes were filling with unshed tears. "It was my fault."

He winced. The entire script was now playing in his head. Emma had been intoxicated and scared and he'd come to her rescue and then seduced her. Crap.

He rubbed a finger over his eye. "I'm sure it wasn't."

"I wouldn't let you leave. I pleaded with you to stay with me. You kept saying something like *You've got it all wrong*, or *This is wrong*, but because of my fear and the alcohol I wouldn't listen. I just needed…you."

"I don't remember a thing, honey. I don't. So, you're sure…" Hell, what a creep he was, about to ask her if she was sure the baby was his. If it was anyone but Emma, he would ask that question. And demand proof. But Emma wouldn't lie. She wouldn't try to pull a fast one on him. Her story made sense. He wouldn't have left her to fend for herself that night. If she was in trouble, he would've gone to get her himself. But he thought he would've drawn the line at taking advantage of a frightened friend, tempting as she might have been. Damn it all.

Maybe his subconscious had known all along he'd been with Emma. Maybe that explained the reason behind his recent attraction to her. He'd always thought of her as off-limits, but after the accident, things between them seemed to change.

He kept his voice soft. "You're sure that you're pregnant?"

"I mean, I haven't seen a doctor yet, but the tests were all positive."

"How many did you take?"

She glanced away. "Seven."

"Ah, just to be sure."

"Yeah."

Dylan heaved a sigh. He realized his first words to her would have great impact, so he treaded carefully. But hell, he was stunned. And clueless about that night. He ran a hand through his hair and then mustered a smile. "Okay."

"Okay?"

"Yeah. I don't have any answers now, Emma. But you're not alone in this. I'm here. And we'll figure it out together."

He knew damn well he'd have to marry her. No child of his was going to grow up without a father and mother. He'd seen too much neglect and abuse over the years. Before Brooke came along and was adopted by his folks, they'd brought many frightened, insecure children into their family, cared for them and nurtured them until they could find a loving home. His child would have his name and all the privileges and love he could give. But now wasn't the time to propose marriage to Emma.

They were both in shock.

Dylan was trying to be charming, trying to be patient, but Emma could tell by the worry lines creasing his forehead he was at a loss. She was, too. But already, she was in love with her baby, Dylan's child, and would move heaven and earth to make things right.

She rose, steady on her feet, and Dylan bounced up from the sofa, his concerned gaze never wavering. "I need to use the restroom," she said.

"I'll walk you."

"No, I'm okay. I'm not dizzy anymore and I know where it is." Dylan's lips were pursed tight but he didn't argue as she walked away with steady measured steps and entered the bathroom.

She splashed water on her face, the cool, crisp feel of it perking her up. As her head came up from the sink, her reflection stared back at her in the mirror. The color had returned to her face. And her legs didn't feel like jelly anymore. Revealing a secret as big as this one was therapeutic, as if a light had been turned on and she could see again. She felt free, relieved and unburdened.

But that feeling lasted only a few seconds. As she exited the bathroom, Dylan was there, leaning against the wall with arms folded, his face barely masking his concern. He approached her and took her hand. "How are you feeling, Em?"

The slightest touch of his large hand on hers was enough to wake her sleeping endorphins. As they tried to spread cheer, all she could think about was pulling away from him. Pulling away from the caring way he said her name. Away from what she feared almost as much as being alone in the dark. Falling for him. Really, in the flesh, head-over-heels falling for him, leaving her broken and shattered.

She'd been unloved all of her life.

But to be unloved by Dylan would be the hardest of all.

"I'm fine. Much better actually."

"I want you to stay here tonight."

"Why?" She stared into the deep sea of his eyes. They weren't commanding exactly, but filled with expectation. Like the rest of him.

"You shouldn't be alone tonight."

"Isn't that how I got pregnant in the first place?"

It was a bad joke. Not a joke really, the truth, but Dylan didn't seem to take offense. His lips quirked a bit. "Oh, how I wish I knew."

"To be perfectly honest, I don't remember, either. My brain wasn't firing on all cylinders. I just have flashes here and there of how it was."

He nodded, staring at her as if he still couldn't believe they'd made love. As if the thought was foreign to him. He didn't say the words, but there was an apology on his expression. "Just for the record, and I do appreciate you *not* asking, but I'm sure it's your baby, Dylan. I haven't been sexually active in quite a while."

His tanned face became infused with color that wasn't there before. Dylan McKay blushing was a rare sight.

"I figured."

Her brows lifted at the quickness of his response. Had he just insulted her?

"I mean, you wouldn't lie to me, Emma," he explained. "I know you're telling the truth."

Better.

"I'm not staying here tonight, Dylan."

He'd walked her into the kitchen, where he handed her a glass of water. "You've been sick for days and you fainted just a few minutes ago. You need someone with you."

She sipped and took a moment to gather her thoughts. "You're not going to watch over me all night, Dylan."

"I didn't intend to. But there's nothing wrong with a friend checking in on a friend, is there?"

"That's what text messages are for."

He snorted, and it was sexy. How much trouble was she in?

"You're gonna cause me a sleepless night."

"Look, you can drop me off at home and then text me when you get back here. I promise to text you first thing in the morning."

"Whatever happened to phone calls?"

"Fine, I'll call you when I wake up."

"And what if you're sick again?"

"You'll come to my rescue. I have no doubt."

He rubbed his hand back and forth across the expanse of his jaw as he contemplated her words. "I wish you weren't so stubborn about this."

"I'm not stubborn, just practical. I think we need space right now…to think."

"That's my line, honey. And notice I didn't say it? Because right now, it's more important to make sure you get your health back."

"I've been taking care of myself for almost twenty-six years. I can manage, trust me."

He nodded slowly, giving her a stern fatherly look. God, she'd always hated when Dylan did that. He wasn't her guardian or big brother. "Fine, then. I'll drive you home."

Half an hour later, they pulled up to her building. Dylan insisted on coming into her apartment, his take on seeing her safely home. Her emotional well was dry and she didn't have it in her to argue the point.

"So this is where we, uh…conceived the baby?" His eyes dipped down to her belly and a searing heat cut through the denim of her dress as if she'd been physically touched. A tiny tremble rumbled through her system.

"Yes. This is it." She wouldn't say it was the scene of the crime. She couldn't label the new life growing inside as anything but wonderful. Whether or not Dylan or anyone else agreed. "In the bedroom, of course."

He shot another piercing look her way. "Right."

Dylan helped take her jacket off and then guided her to a seat on the sofa. She sat down without argument. He didn't sit, though. Instead, he walked around the room, scanning the picture frames on her bookshelf, looking at trinkets, the furniture and all the surroundings with a new and insightful eye. Then he turned to her. "Mind if I peek into your bedroom? See if it jars my memory?"

Oh, boy. This was awkward. But she understood the necessity. Things for Dylan would be so much easier if he could get those lost hours back. She nodded. "Just don't look in my lingerie drawers."

He laughed, his somber eyes finally twinkling.

He was gone only a minute before returning to her.

"Anything?" she asked.

He shook his head sadly. "No."

She understood his disappointment. All that she remembered from that night was a muscled body covering hers and the tender comfort his presence had given her. Afterward, she'd slipped into the tight cocoon of his arms and fallen into a drugged sleep. When she had woken up with the mother of all hangovers, Dylan was gone.

That next day, the power outage was old news in most parts of the city. The lights had come back on and everything had returned to normal. For most people. And the shocking death of Roy Benjamin on the set of beloved actor Dylan McKay's new film had usurped all the day's headlines.

Right now, she and Dylan were on even footing. Both were unsure of how that night had gone down. There was a chance Dylan would never get that time back. And her memory was fogged over and blurry at best. "I'm sorry."

"Don't be. It was a long shot."

His smile didn't budge the rest of his face. He turned his wrist and glanced at his watch, a gorgeous black-faced gold Movado. "It's ten thirty. What time do you go to bed?"

"Eleven."

He nodded and sat on the couch beside her.

"Let me guess. You're not leaving until I go to bed?"

"I'd like to stay."

Crapola. How many women would kill to have that offer from Dylan McKay?

"I'm just going to do some reading in bed before I turn in. You can leave now."

Dylan ran a hand down his face. "You're trying to get rid of me."

"Only because I don't need you to babysit me. I'm fine."

"Then I'll go," he said, standing up, leaving her gaze to follow the long length of his body as he straightened. "I'll text you at eleven and see how you're doing."

"My kind of guy," she teased.

His lips curved up. "You're not going to prevent me from checking on you."

She rose, too, and amazed herself at her own stability, considering she'd fainted just a few hours ago. "I'll call you in the morning. It's a promise."

"Thanks," he said, and she followed him to the door. When he turned to her, they were only a breath apart, him towering above her by six inches. The scent of raw power and lime emanated from his throat and lingered in her nostrils. His golden hair gleamed under the foyer light and his eyes, deadly and devastatingly blue, found hers. "Make an appointment with a doctor for next week. I'd like to go with you," he said.

It shouldn't have come as a surprise that he'd want to go with her, but Dylan escorting her to an obstetrician's office would be big news if word got out. And there would be repercussions. "Are you sure?"

"Absolutely," he said immediately. "I'll let you know my schedule."

He laced his hands with hers then and gave a little tug, bringing her closer. His beautiful mouth was only inches away. "I want you to move into my house, Emma. Think about it and we'll talk again tomorrow."

Without hesitation his head came forward and his lips met with hers. The kiss was brief, but amazing and glorious. A glimpse of what could be. A tease. A temptation.

And when she opened her eyes, he'd already turned away and was gone.

Yes, yes, yes would've been her answer. If only he'd asked for the right reasons.

But Dylan didn't want her. He wanted her baby.

And she wasn't about to live her life unloved.

Ever again.

Emma didn't pick up a book to read. Instead, she grabbed the phone and speed-dialed Brooke's number. She picked up on the first ring.

"Hi, Brooke. It's me, checking in."

"Emma, it's late. Are you okay?"

"Right now, I'm feeling fine. Did I wake you?"

"Gosh no. I'm dead on my feet, but wide-awake. I'm done prepping for tomorrow. Rocky and Wendy are doing their share and we're managing."

"That's great news. I've been thinking about you all day. How was the silent auction?"

"It went well. We had lots of bids and I'm guessing the charity made lots of money. I haven't tallied it up yet. That comes later tonight."

"Do it in the morning, Brooke. You sound beat."

"I am, but in a good way."

Emma's pangs of guilt resurfaced. Poor Brooke. The business side of things wasn't her forte. She had a creative streak a mile long and Pinterest could learn a few things from her when it came to party planning. But anything with numbers, and Brooke was at a complete loss.

"So, no snags for tomorrow?" Tomorrow was the celebrity golf tournament, the golf widow's luncheon and the formal Give a Dollar or a Thousand Dinner and raffle. All the celebrities golfing would attend the dinner. Their appearance made for heftier donations, but they came with a high price for their time. They were accustomed to and expected fabulous cuisine and service, so this task was even more daunting.

"Nope, not a one."

Emma breathed a sigh of relief. "Good."

"How are things with you?" Brooke questioned her in a softer tone that left no room for doubt what she was really getting at.

"You guilted Dylan into checking on me."

"Yeah, I did. I'm sorry, honey, but I'm worried about you. So, you spent time with him tonight?"

"Yes, and I…well…he knows my situation now."

"You told him!"

Her face scrunched up at her friend's enthusiasm. "Don't sound so happy. He's in as much shock as I am."

"But at least he knows the truth."

"Yeah, but nothing jarred his memory."

"That's not really the point. You can't worry about the past. At least you'll move forward toward the future."

Normally, she told Brooke everything, but tonight wasn't the night to tell her about Dylan's offer. She wasn't about to move into his mansion. And if Brooke knew, she'd probably side with her brother on this. Two McKays would be too hard to fight. "Yeah, I guess." She waited a beat. "I'm glad things went well tonight. And I know tomorrow will be amazing. You should hit the sack. That's what I'm going to do. Love you, Brooke."

"Love you, too. Sleep well."

Emma hung up the phone and undressed, slipping out of her street clothes and into her pajamas. She climbed into bed, shut off the table lamp and snuggled her face deep into her cushy pillow. Her body sank into the mattress and she sighed out loud. Nothing was better than a comfy bed after a rough day. But just as she closed her eyes, Dylan's image popped into her head.

She owed him a text.

Stretching her arm out, she fumbled for her phone on the nightstand, punched in his number and typed out her text.

I'm tucked in and feeling well. Good night.

Short and sweet. It'd been a long time since she'd had to answer to anyone. Derek Purdy, the man she now thought of as The Jerk, had cured her of that in her sophomore year of college. She hated even thinking of him anymore. He didn't deserve another second of her time.

But Dylan, on the other hand, would be in her life forever now.

He was no jerk, and from now on they would have to answer to each other.

For the baby's sake.

Five

"Rolling," the first assistant director called out as Dylan stood on his mark on the Stage One Studios back lot. The cast and crew of *Resurrection SEALs* became quiet. They were on the same dirt road where Roy had died and where Dylan had been hit with shrapnel. If being here didn't jog his memory, nothing would. Dylan tried to focus. He was a professional, and the crew had worked long hours this morning prepping this scene. The director called, "Action," and Dylan went into performance mode, delivering his lines. He stumbled once, mixing up the words, and looked to the script supervisor for his line.

Marcy offered it. "Whether or not you give me those papers, Joe, the colonel is going to hear about this."

They reshot the scene several times and Dylan went through the paces for coverage and tights on his face before his work was done. The director, Gabe Novotny, walked over and put a hand on his shoulder. "That first scene had to be hard on you. But you're through it now. How does it feel?"

"I can't lie. It's a little weird, Gabe. Mostly, it's knowing that Roy died right here, and now, here I am, doing my job, back to the status quo and moving forward without him."

"We're all feeling it, Dylan. But you managed the scene. And the next one will be a little easier, and then the next."

Dylan didn't have much choice. He was under contract, but a part of him wanted to bail on this project now, even though he'd done intense training, including daily ten-mile beach runs and weight lifting to become Josh O'Malley, Navy SEAL. "I'm hoping you're right. Still is strange to be here, though." He knew enough about survivor guilt to understand that the ache in the pit of his stomach wasn't going away anytime soon. He missed Roy, and if he'd been the one to get into the car that day as planned, instead of Roy, he'd be the one floating atop the high seas now with his ashes scattered all over the Pacific. "If we're done for now, I think I'll head back to my trailer."

"Actually, an officer from the LAPD is due in the production office any minute now. He's asked to speak to you and me, Marcy and the execs. Maury Allen was asked to be there, too, so it's something big if the police want the head of the studio there. You might remember the officer. He consulted with us early on in the film about two months ago."

"Oh, yeah. Detective Brice. He's a big Clippers fan. We talked basketball for a while."

"That's him. It's about Roy's death, Dylan." Gabe took his eyeglasses off and rubbed them clean on the tail of his shirt. "So I'm betting it's not a social call."

"All right."

Gabe glanced past the chaos of the crew taking down the rigging and spotted Marcy speaking with the girls from Hair and Makeup. "You about through, Marce?"

She slammed a folder closed, stood on her tiptoes and waved at him. "I'm coming."

Instead of golf-carting it, they walked to the offices together. When they entered the building, they were reintroduced to the detective, who was dressed in an austere gray suit. They all took a seat at a long table as if they were going to do a cold reading. But it wasn't play acting. Judging by Detective Brice's sullen expression, he didn't have good news.

"I'm here to ask a few more questions regarding the death of Roy Benjamin. After investigating the accident, it's been determined that the car in question had been tampered with before the stunt ever took place. We've already spoken with the stunt team supervisor and he's confirmed that they'd given the stunt the all clear. They went through a series of tests before Mr. Benjamin ever got in that car. There's a timeline factor that we're working with here. From the time the stunt team finished rigging the car until the actual shoot, there are thirty minutes unaccounted for."

"What are you saying exactly?" Maury asked, his brows gathered.

"Mr. Benjamin was to roll out of the car right before it blew up. But we believe someone sabotaged the rigging so that the car would blow up ahead of schedule."

"With Roy in it?" Dylan asked, barely recognizing the high pitch of his own voice.

Detective Brice nodded, his voice gruff. "That's right."

"So you think Roy was murdered?"

"That's what I'm here to investigate. Mr. McKay, do you have any recollection about that day, at all?"

He squeezed his eyes shut hating that he couldn't remember a damn thing. "No, none."

"Okay, well, if you do remember anything, give me a call." Detective Brice handed Dylan a business card that read Homicide Division. He stared at it, finding this whole thing bizarre, like something out of one of his movies. Who would want to murder Roy?

The officer proceeded to question Dylan about his relationship with Roy. How long had they been friends? How long had he worked as his stunt double? Any girlfriends? What was he like? Did he have any enemies? Dylan answered as honestly as he could, and when the detective moved on to the others, Dylan's mind wandered to some of the better times he'd had with Roy. They had a lot in common. Both liked to work out, both loved women, both enjoyed good whiskey.

By the time Maury, Gabe, Marcy and the other execs were through being questioned, they all began shaking their heads. They were as stunned as Dylan was. Then Gabe remembered one important thing. "Dylan was originally supposed to do that scene," he told the detective. "We changed the script a bit and decided the stunt was too risky for Dylan to handle."

Brice turned toward Dylan. "Is that so?"

"I don't remember, but that's what Gabe told me."

"I don't think it was changed on the call sheet for that day," Gabe offered.

"I'd like a copy of that, please," the detective said, and Gabe nodded.

Detective Brice was quiet for a while, writing things down in a notebook. "Okay. Well, until we get to the bottom of this, I'd suggest that all of you be wary of anything unusual around the studio and report any suspicious behavior. And, Mr. McKay, if that script change wasn't common knowledge, then there's a possibility that you could've been the target instead of Mr. Benjamin. Do you have any enemies?"

Dylan's head snapped up. He gazed into Detective Brice's serious eyes. "I get all kinds of fan mail. I have an assistant go through it. But she hasn't said anything about threats."

"Maybe you should ask her for details and start going through your mail for anything unusual. You might recognize something she doesn't."

"You don't really believe Dylan was the target?" Maury asked.

The detective shrugged. "It's better to take into account all the possibilities."

After the questioning, Dylan returned to finish his next scene, struggling with what he'd just learned. He couldn't believe someone was out to get him. He might have a few unhappy ex-girlfriends, but he was actually on good terms with most of them. He dug around his memory for anything else, anyone who might want to do him harm, and came up empty.

He left the studio unnerved and on the drive home made a call to his security team to beef up patrols around his house. Usually if he went out on studio appearances or interviews, he traveled with a bodyguard, so he was good there. And once he'd taken care of that business, he called Emma. She answered the call on the first ring. "Hello."

"Hi, it's me."

"Hi, Dylan."

"How're you feeling today?"

"Better. I went into the office today and did some work. It feels good to be back among the productive."

He smiled. "That's good. What if I told you I had a bad day and needed a friend? Would you have dinner with me tonight?"

Her silence at the other end of the phone made his heart race. It blew his mind how much he wanted her to agree.

"Would that be the honest truth?" she asked.

"It would."

Her relenting sigh carried to his ears. She wasn't happy

about the pressure he put on her and he was taking advantage of her good nature, but he really did need a friend tonight. He couldn't tell her about Detective Brice's visit on the set today, and even if he could, he wouldn't want to trouble her. Just seeing her tonight, knowing that she was carrying his child and something good had come out of that time he'd lost, would boost his spirits. "Then sure, I guess I could do that."

"Thanks." He released a pent-up breath. "I'll be there in half an hour to pick you up."

Emma faced Dylan across the tufted white leather booth at Roma's Restaurant in the city. Silly her, after he'd called, she'd waded through her closet and come up with the prettiest dress she could find: a soft sapphire-blue brushed cotton with lots of feminine folds and a draping halter neckline. She'd dressed for him and had been rewarded with hot, appreciative glances on the drive here.

Looking around the place, she noted that Roma's tables weren't covered with red-and-white-checked tablecloths, there were no plastic flower centerpieces and not a hint of sawdust was sprinkled on the creamy marble floors. Dylan was used to the best, and he'd come to think of these high-end places as the norm. But Emma wasn't used to eating pizza off expensive Italian dinnerware or having a violinist make the rounds from table to table, offering up a musical selection to soothe the soul.

"They make a mean eggplant parm here," Dylan said. "And the pizza is old-school, like back home."

"Eggplant sounds good," she said, folding the menu. "I'd like that."

Dylan nodded to the waiter. "Make that two, then, Tony, and two glasses of sparkling water."

After the waiter left, she picked up a wafer-like piece of

rosemary-and-garlic bread, almost hating to break up the fancy-schmancy geometric design in the basket.

"Feel free to order wine or whatever you want, Dylan. You don't have to drink water because of me."

God, tonight he looked as if he could really use a drink. He was a good actor, the best actually, but tonight he wasn't acting. His guard was down and she saw it in the pallor on his face, his sullen eyes and the twist of his otherwise beautiful mouth.

"Thanks," he said, giving her a nod. "Maybe I will order a glass of wine later."

"That bad a day?"

He glanced down at the pearly-white tablecloth. "Yeah, I guess. We had to resume shooting the scene in the location where Roy died. It was a hard day for everyone."

"For you especially, I would think."

He nodded. "It was just weird and sad."

"I'm sorry."

"Thanks. I guess there's nothing to be done about it. The show must go on," he said with a strained chuckle that barely moved his mouth.

A part of her wanted to reach out to him, to hold his hand or maybe fold him into an embrace. He looked a little lost right now. She knew the feeling and she was suddenly glad she'd accepted his dinner invitation.

"Enough about me," Dylan said. "How are you feeling?"

"I'm sitting here about ready to eat eggplant smothered in sauce and cheese and the thought of it doesn't turn my stomach, so I think I'm fine."

"No more morning sickness?"

"I didn't say that. I still get queasy, but it passes quickly and only seems to happen in the morning. Still, I'm not counting my chickens yet."

"Did you call the doctor?"

"Yes, the appointment is next Thursday at ten o'clock."

"Okay, good." He seemed pleased. He'd told her he wasn't filming on Thursday and she had been lucky enough to get an appointment with her ob-gyn that day.

"If you run into a bind or something, it won't be a problem. I can get myself there." She wanted to throw that out to him. She had other means, if he couldn't go that day. She was suddenly transported back in time to when she was a charity case, an unloved little young burden to those around her. She'd been a child then, scared of the future, but she wasn't now. Now she clung to her independence and needed it as much as she needed air to breathe. Single motherhood wasn't rare these days, lots of women did it and managed just fine. She wasn't looking to Dylan to be her savior.

"I won't run into a bind." His jaw was set as he spoke those firm words. He meant it. Dylan was a big enough star that schedules could be woven around his needs, and not the other way around. But still, she wasn't going to crumble if she did the mother thing alone.

"Brooke wants to go with me on an appointment later on," she said. "She wants to be a part of it, too."

"I'd like that. She'll be an amazing aunt."

Emma smiled. They both agreed on that. "She's been very supportive."

Dylan nodded. "What do you think of this Royce guy she's been dating? Is he the real deal?"

Ah, finally the conversation was moving away from her. She was glad for the distraction. "I haven't met him yet, but there's a bouquet of red roses on her desk at work that says he's an okay guy. She's seeing him tonight, as a matter of fact. She missed him like crazy while she was away."

Dylan made a grunting sound before he sipped the sparkling water the waiter had just delivered. "That always scares me."

"Why?"

He shrugged. "I want to see her happy. She's been disappointed before."

"Haven't we all," Emma blurted. And then squeezed her eyes shut but not before witnessing Dylan's brows lift inquisitively.

"I know."

She gave him a look that must have revealed her astonishment because his baby blues softened immediately. "Brooke told me about a guy in college you were seeing."

"When did she tell you that?" The witchy tone in her voice made her mentally cringe. She didn't mean to sound so darn defensive.

"A while back. I'm not prying into your life, Emma. I wouldn't put Brooke in that position, and if I want to know something about you, I'll ask you up front. But actually, my sister mentioned it a few years ago and I never forgot it because I thought you deserved better than a jerk who would verbally abuse you. I guess it always stuck with me. I sorta wanted to punch his lights out."

Emma pictured Dylan knocking Derek Purdy to the ground and grinned. "You've always been protective."

"There's nothing wrong with a friend looking out for a friend."

"I've always appreciated that." That was the truth. Dylan had never failed to be her champion when he was around. He had a thing for the underdog. It was quite commendable actually, but right now with her baby situation, she didn't want to be considered the underdog, or lacking in any way. "But it's old news now, Dylan. I've forgotten about him."

The meal was served and that part of the conversation ended. Emma dug in with tepid gusto, keeping in mind the capacity of her shrunken stomach and the queasiness that might rear its ugly head at any given moment, despite what she'd told Dylan. She didn't trust her gut not to act up. She was just getting used to the idea of eating a full meal and not paying the price afterward.

"It's delicious," she said. Steam rose up from the sizzling cheese and the garlicky scents made her mouth water.

"It's not too ostentatious for you?"

"The eggplant?"

His eyes twinkled with that you-know-what-I-mean look.

"The place."

"Let's see. I'm eating off handmade Intrada dinner plates while being serenaded by a sole violinist. The Waterford cut crystal and white rose centerpiece is a nice touch. Adds class to the joint. Nope, I'd say it's right on par with Vitellos back home."

He wiped his mouth with the cloth napkin. The gleam in his eyes became even brighter at her sarcasm. "How do you know all this stuff?"

"You're forgetting what I do for a living. It's my job to know about dinnerware and crystal and high-end table dressing."

"Right. I didn't put it together. You're good at your job. But you're not comfortable with all this, are you?"

"It's fine, Dylan. I have no complaints. If this is what it takes to cheer you up, then I'm all for it."

Dylan's smile faded a bit as he reached for her hand. "*You* are what's cheering me up. I enjoy being with you, Em. And I brought you here not to impress you, but because I knew you'd enjoy the food."

Her heartbeat sounded in her ears. She had no humorous comeback. "Oh."

She got a little more lost in his eyes. It was hard not to; those eyes could drown a lesser woman and she was certainly not immune. The clarity in them astounded her. Dylan knew what he was about, amnesia or not. There was no limit to his confidence, yet he wasn't arrogant or prissy. He was kinda perfect.

And that scared her more than anything.

"Maybe…uh, maybe you should have some wine now." She would if she could.

He shook his head, not breaking eye contact. "Not necessary."

"You're cured?"

He chuckled, the smile cracking his face wide-open. "For the moment, anyway." He squeezed her hand a little and a shot of adrenaline arrowed up her arm and spread like wildfire throughout her system. What was he doing to her? She'd come here to boost his spirits, not fall under his spell.

He glanced at her half-eaten plate of food. "Finish your meal, sweetheart." And he released her hand just like that, leaving a rich hum of delight in the wake of his touch. She filled up with deliriously happy hormones. "We'll talk about dessert when you're through," he added.

Dessert? She felt as though she'd already had a decadent helping of chocolate-espresso gelato with cherries on top.

The Dylan McKay Special.

And nothing was sweeter.

When they got back to her apartment, she made a feeble attempt to get inside with some semblance of grace and dignity. "Really, Dylan, you didn't have to walk me to my door," she said, her back to the front door and her hand on the knob.

His brows lifted and a lock of straight sun-streaked hair fell across his forehead. She was tempted to touch it, to ease it back into place and run her fingers through the rest.

"I never drop a lady off at the curb, Emma. I certainly wouldn't do that to you. You know that."

She did. But she couldn't invite Dylan in. She didn't

have willpower to spare right now. Yet she knew that's exactly what he wanted. "Well, now you've earned another gold star."

"I have many."

She imagined a black-and-white composition book filled with pages of gold stars. But she had to be kind in her not-too-subtle brush-off. "Thanks again for dinner. You must be tired after the day you've had. You should go home and turn in."

"I will soon enough. But you're not safely inside yet." His hand glided over hers to snare the key from her fingers. "Here, let me."

She nearly jumped from the contact and her hand opened. When he took the key, she moved away from the door and allowed him to insert it into the lock. With a twist, the door clicked open.

"Thanks again," she said breathlessly, again pressing her back to the door.

He leaned in so close she caught the slight scent of musky aftershave, a heady mixture that stirred all of her erotic senses. Oh, boy, she was in trouble.

She pressed her head against the door, backing away from him and staring at his lips that were coming way too close. "What are you doing?"

"I'm giving you a proper thank-you, sweetheart."

"The eggplant was thanks—"

And then his mouth came down on hers. Not roughly or aggressively, but not with tender persuasion, either. It was perfectly balanced, a kiss that could mean a dozen things that were not necessarily sexual. Yet as she raised her hands to push at his chest, he deepened the kiss, giving it more texture and taste, and the balance she relied on was starting to disappear. Her arms fell to her sides; there would be no shove-off-buddy move on her part. How could she think of ending something so amazing?

His hand came up beside her head, his palm flat against the door, and the darn thing moved, making her clumsily back up a step, then two. He followed her, of course, his lips still locked with hers, and the next thing she knew they were inside her dark apartment and breathing heavily. Dylan broke the kiss momentarily to guide her backward some more and then kick the door shut with his foot.

"Imagine that," he whispered. "We're inside your apartment."

"Uh-huh" was her brilliant comeback. She was too enthralled with his mouth, his tongue and the wonderful way he used them on her to think straight.

And then she felt his hand on her belly. Only someone who knew her intimately would notice the slight bulge above her waist. His fingers splayed out, encircling the whole of her stomach, and a throaty sound emanated from deep within his chest. "I've wanted to touch you here, Em. It's okay, isn't it?"

She nodded, not trusting her voice.

"I know it's not ideal, but, Emma, if there was ever a woman to carry my child, of all the women I know, all that I've been with, I'm glad it's you."

There was a compliment in there somewhere. Emma understood what he meant, but there were still issues, lots and lots of issues. She pulled away from him. "I'll turn on a light."

Before she was out of his reach, he was gripping her wrist and tugging her back to him. She landed smack against his chest and gazed up at his face, which was steeped in shadows. "Don't, Emma. You're safe with me. Don't be afraid."

She *was* afraid. Of where this was leading. "What do you want, Dylan?" she asked softly and heard the defeat in her voice. It was as if she couldn't compete, couldn't deny him, couldn't defend against him.

"Honestly, I don't know. You're good for me, Em. I like who I am when I'm with you. And I don't want to leave, not just yet."

Something almost desperate in his voice kept her rooted to the spot. Then he touched her, a light brush of his fingers feathering her face, a caress she had always dreamed about. And he kissed her again, tenderly and slowly, like a man treasuring a sacred prize. The prize, she knew, wasn't her, but the baby. She got that. She already felt the same way about the life growing inside her. She didn't blame the child for her bouts of sickness or regret the mere fact that the baby existed at all. Yet something was off. His kisses were new to her. His touch exciting and not familiar in the way she'd thought they'd be. They'd done this before, kissing and intimately touching when they conceived the baby, but she didn't remember...*him.*

"Dylan," she said softly, "we're friends."

"We could be more."

He nibbled on her lower lip. A blast of heat spiraled down to her belly and she closed her eyes, absorbing the pleasant torment while trying to contain the burning inferno that was building, building. Dylan's heat became her heat and she hardly noticed as they moved farther into her room, until Dylan was sitting on her sofa and she was being yanked down onto his lap.

His tongue danced with hers as he pressed her against the sofa cushions. His lips found her forehead, her cheeks, her chin, and then moved leisurely back to her waiting mouth. She ached for him and it was almost useless to try to fight the feeling. In her teenage imaginings, before his fame and fortune, Dylan had always been hers. She caved to those feelings now and moaned when his hand slipped under her dress and climbed her thigh, inching toward the part of her body that ached for him the most.

But Dylan bypassed that spot and moved his hand farther up to lay claim once again to her belly. He stroked her there gently and she caught a glimpse of the top of his head as he bestowed a loving kiss right above her navel over the spot where their baby resided.

She melted in that moment. Her eyes filled with tears. She bit her lower lip to keep from making a silly, revealing sound. But her heart was involved, now more than ever before. And it pained her in ways that she'd never dreamed possible.

"Dylan," she whispered.

He lifted his head and their gazes locked in the shadows. An unwavering gleam in his eyes spoke of the love he already had for his baby. He smiled. Dread pierced her stomach. She didn't have ammunition to fight Dylan when he was like this.

The next thing she knew, his hand was on her thigh again, moving up and down, rubbing away her apprehension and bringing on a new kind of tension. "You're soft, Emma. Everywhere."

Oh, God, but he wasn't. It was evident from the press of his groin to her hip. They were treading dangerous ground and she was too enthralled to put a stop to it.

He brought his mouth to hers again and again, his hand working magic over her throat, her shoulders, the steep slope of her breasts. His fingertips grazed her nipples and she jumped, sensitive and achy.

A groan rumbled from the depths of his chest and he moved more steadily over her, cupping her breast through the material of her dress, trailing hot moist kisses along her collarbones. Everything was on fire, burning, burning. The heat was combustible and then…and then…

The phone rang.

Her house line was ringing. It was used for emergencies, and only a handful of people had the number. The answering machine picked up and Brooke's voice was on the other end.

"It's me, Em. I'm looking for Dylan. Neither one of you are picking up your cell and it's sort of important. Is he there by any chance?"

Dylan immediately sat upright.

Emma gave him a nod and bounded up, adjusting her lopsided halter as she dashed to turn on a light and pick up the phone on the kitchen wall. "Hi," she said, breathless.

"Hi," Brooke said, drawing out the word. "Am I disturbing something?"

"No, no. We were just coming in from dinner. Dylan dropped me off. He's still here. Let me get him," she said. But there was no need. He was already behind her, his hands on her waist, planting a kiss on her shoulder as though they were a real couple, before he took the phone. "Hi, sis."

Emma walked out of the room to give him privacy, but her apartment had few walls and she could still see him and hear his voice. Her curiosity wouldn't allow her to turn away. "Renee?" He sighed heavily and after a few seconds said, "Okay, I'll take care of it." Then he ended the call.

Dylan squeezed his eyes shut and rubbed the back of his neck before turning to Emma. Their gazes locked and he moved toward her and grasped her hands. "I have to go. But I want you to promise you'll think about moving in with me. We could have a lot more nights like tonight. I want you with me, honey."

It was too much, too soon, and her head was still reeling from how close they'd come to making love. Inhaling a shaky breath, she shook her head. "I can't promise you that, Dylan. I'm not ready to make that kind of move."

He nodded and worry lines formed around his eyes. "Okay, but I'd like to see you again. Soon."

"Like a date?"

"Yeah," he said, his face brightening as if he was really warming to the idea. "I think we'll take one step at a time. Dating first. Can you manage that?"

She nodded. "I think so."

"Exclusively?"

Exclusive with Dylan McKay! She liked the sound of that. Not that she'd ever had a situation where she was dating two men at the same time. "Exclusively."

Seeming satisfied, he gave her a quick, chaste kiss goodbye and hurried away.

Leaving Emma to wonder about his ex Renee and what that phone call was all about.

Was *she* the exception to Dylan's rules of exclusivity?

Six

Dylan sat down at his desk as morning breezes blew in through the window, the fresh ocean air a jolt stronger than caffeine to rouse him out of his sleep haze. Each morning he'd scan his mind, hoping to get a glimpse of the time he'd lost, hoping his memory would be restored. It wasn't happening today.

He opened the drawer, pulled out his checkbook and wrote out a check for a larger sum of money than he'd normally sent Renee over this past year. The monthly checks weren't a fortune, but enough to help her get by and make sure her two children were fed, housed and clothed. She was in worse shape than a single mother. She had a lousy ex-husband who threatened to take her kids away from her on a regular basis and Renee needed to supplement her meager earnings as a waitress in order to provide for her family.

She seemed to be in a constant state of crisis.

Dylan had long ago forgiven Renee for breaking his

heart. But the fault wasn't just Renee's. He'd allowed himself to be persuaded to run away with her. He'd been crazy in love, young and impulsive, and so willing to do whatever Renee wanted to keep her happy. They'd been in a theatre production together in high school and had lofty notions of success. Later, at the age of nineteen, she'd convinced him to move to Los Angeles to pursue an acting career. He'd gone with her with eyes wide-open, understanding the risk, but when his success didn't come fast enough for her and Renee's so-called contacts in LA had dried up, her disappointment was hard to live with.

Then one day, he'd found her in the arms of another man, a director of a small theatre, an older man with a colossal ego who'd convinced her they were one step away from fame. That hadn't happened and she'd made one bad decision after another. While Dylan's career had finally launched through patience and perseverance, she'd given up on her dreams, becoming cynical and bitter, and wound up marrying someone who worked in the industry. Dylan had lost touch with her completely until last year when she'd reached out to his sister and asked if she could put her in touch with Dylan.

It was a pained conversation when they'd spoken, but Renee had touched something deep and tender in Dylan's heart as he remembered the young, vivacious girl she'd once been. She'd pleaded with him for forgiveness and he gave it willingly. She'd never once asked him for a handout, but after learning about her situation with an alcoholic, abusive ex-husband and hating the thought of her kids suffering, he'd started sending her checks.

"Knock, knock."

His head snapped up and he found Brooke dressed in a stretchy blue workout outfit standing at the threshold of his half-opened door. He gave her an immediate smile. "Hey, kiddo. Come in."

Once a week, he and Brooke exercised together in his gym on the second floor that overlooked the Pacific Ocean.

"Morning, bro. Ready for a workout?"

"Just about." He placed the check in an envelope and wrote out Renee's name on the front before sealing it. "You don't have to do this, Brooke. I can mail it."

"It's not a problem, Dylan. I know where Renee lives."

"It's half an hour out of town."

"Listen, I'm no fan of Renee's, but if she needs this pronto for her kids, then it's no big deal for me to put the check in her mailbox. This way, she'll have it earlier."

Dylan ran his hand along his chin. "Her daughter needs corrective eye surgery. She's in a panic about it."

"It's a good thing you're doing," Brooke said.

He didn't do it for accolades and no one besides his sister knew about this. Renee was part of his past, a one-time friend and lover. She needed help. Wouldn't he be a hypocrite to volunteer to help other charities and not help someone he knew personally who was in need? Why not give her a hand up?

"You have a big heart," his sister said.

"I can afford to."

"Yes, but she hurt you badly and I don't forgive as easily as you do."

"I didn't forgive her for a long time."

"But eventually you did. And she scarred you, Dylan. It was a betrayal of the worst kind."

"I'm hardly crying over it anymore."

But he'd lost his faith, and trust didn't come easily for him. He'd once believed in love, but not so much anymore. He hadn't come close to feeling anything like it since his last happy day with Renee. And then a thought rushed in and Emma's face appeared in his mind. He'd always liked Emma, and she was, after all, the mother of his child. Dating her was a means to an end. He was going to marry her and give the baby his name. At least he trusted her. As a friend.

Brooke took the check and plopped it into her wide canvas tote. "Let's go burn some calories."

An hour later, Brooke sipped water from a cold bottle, a workout towel hanging around her neck. "Inspiring as always," she said, glancing out the floor-to-ceiling windows at the low-lying clouds beginning to lift. It was going to be a blue-sky day.

Dylan set down his weights and sopped his face with his towel. "It's not half bad."

"You ready to talk to me about Emma?"

"Emma?" He sat down on a workout bench, stretched his legs out fully and downed half a bottle of water in one gulp. "What about Emma?"

She snapped her towel against his forearm. The painless rap and smirk on her lips had him grinning.

"Duh…" Brooke sat down next to him. "What's going on between you two?"

"Nosy, aren't you?"

"Concerned. I love you both."

Dylan flashed to the last night he'd been with Emma and the surprising, explosive way she'd responded to him. He'd taken liberties, but none that she hadn't wanted, and the feel of her skin, so soft and creamy smooth, the taste of her lips and plush fullness of her body against his, had him thinking of her many times since then. "I've asked her to move in with me, Brooke. She said no."

"You can't blame her for that," Brooke said. "She's struggling with all this, too. And you know her history. She's—"

"Stubborn?"

"*Independent* is a better word. And just because you're a celebrity doesn't mean every woman on the planet wants to live with you."

"I'm not asking every woman on the planet, Brooke. I'm asking the woman who's carrying my child."

"I know," she said more softly. "Give Emma some time, bro."

"I'm not pressuring her."

"Aren't you?"

"We're dating."

Brooke laughed. "Really? Like, in flowers and candy and malt shop hookups?"

His sister could be a pain in the ass sometimes. "Malt shop? I hadn't thought of that. Besides, little sis, isn't that what you're doing with Royce?"

Brooke's smile christened her flushed face. "Royce and I are much more sophisticated than that. We do art shows and book festivals and—"

"Intellectual stuff, huh?"

"Yeah, so far. We're still in the getting-to-know-each-other stage."

"Good, take it slow."

"Says the man who just asked a woman he'd never dated to move in with him."

"You're forgetting…that we—"

"Made a baby? Well, seeing as neither one of you recall much of that night, I say it's good you're starting out by dating. S…L…O…W and steady wins the race."

Dylan wasn't going to take it slow with Emma. No way. But Brooke didn't need to know that. She got defensive about Emma, and normally he loved that about his sister. She was loyal to her friends, but this one time, there was just too much at stake for Dylan to back off. He wouldn't give Emma a chance to run scared or go all independent feminist on him. He didn't want his child being raised in a disjointed home.

He had the means to provide a good life for both Emma and the baby. And the sooner she realized that, the better.

* * *

Emma tossed a kernel of popcorn into her mouth and leaned back in her maroon leather recliner seat, one of twenty in Dylan's private screening room. "I must admit, when you said you were taking me to the movies, I wondered how you would pull that off. I mean, it's not as if you can simply walk into a movie theater and not get noticed."

"Comes with the territory I'm afraid. Life has changed for me, but I'm not one of those people who complain about their fame. I knew what I was getting into when I started in this business. If I was lucky enough to succeed, then I wasn't going to cry about not having anonymity. I have a recognizable face, so I've had to alter a few things in my life."

"Like not being able to pop into a grocery store or travel unnoticed or window-shop?"

"Or take my date to a movie," Dylan added.

Emma laughed. "But you adapt very nicely."

"I'm glad you think so. So, what movie would you like to see? Chiller, thriller, Western, comedy, romance?"

"I'm at your mercy. You decide. You're the movie connoisseur."

Dylan picked an Oscar-nominated film about a boy's journey growing up and took the seat next to her. Wrapped chocolates, sour gummies and cashews were set out on a side table and a blue bottle of zillion-dollar water sat in the cupholder beside her chair.

"All set?"

She nodded. "Ready when you are."

Dylan hit a button on a remote control and the overhead lights dimmed as the screen lit up. Emma relaxed in her lounger and focused on the movie. They shared a bag of popcorn, and by the time they got to the bottom of the bag, her eyes had become a teary mess, a few escapees trickling down her cheeks from the poignancy of the film, its depiction of the heartfelt joy of family life, the struggles and cheerful moments and all the rest.

Picking up on her emotion, Dylan placed a tissue in her hand. She gave him a nod of thanks, wiped her watery eyes and focused back on the screen. It wasn't hormones that wrecked her heart this time. Whenever she witnessed a real family in action, the ups and downs and the way they all came together out of love and loyalty, she realized how very much she'd missed out on as a child. Though she was proud of the fact she hadn't let her childhood hinder her in any way. It had only made her more determined to seek a better life for herself, and now for her child.

Dylan reached over the lounger and took her hand. She glanced at their entwined fingers, his hand tanned and so very strong, hers smaller, more delicate, and she welcomed the comfort, the ease with which they could sit there together and watch a movie, holding hands.

The movie ended on a satisfying note and Dylan squeezed her hand, but didn't let her go. They remained in darkness but for the yellow floor lamps lighting a pathway around the room.

"Did you enjoy it?" he whispered.

"Very much."

"I didn't realize you're such a soft touch." His thumb rubbed over the skin of her hand in round, lazy sweeping circles.

"Only when it comes to movies."

"I find that hard to believe. You're soft…"

Her breath caught as she gazed into his heart-melting eyes.

"Everywhere."

Oh, boy.

He turned his body and leaned in, his mouth inches from hers. "I've been thinking about the other night. If we hadn't been interrupted, what would have happened?"

It wasn't really a question he expected her to answer. She thought of that night, too, so often. Wondering what if?

And then his lips were on hers, his mouth so exquisite as he patiently waited for her to respond, waited for her to give in. "Dylan."

"It's just a kiss, Em."

He made it seem so simple. "Not just a kiss," she insisted, yet she couldn't deny the temptation to kiss him back, to taste him and breathe in his delicious scent.

"This is what people do when they're dating," he whispered over her mouth.

"Is it?" Kissing Dylan wasn't anything ordinary. Not to her. It was the stuff of dreams.

"Yeah, it is," he said. "I want us to be more than friends, Em."

She wanted to ask why. Was it all about the baby, or had he somehow, after all these years, miraculously found her appealing and desirable? It was on the tip of her tongue to ask, but she chickened out. She didn't dare, because in her heart she already knew the truth.

He swept his hand around her neck and caressed the tender spot behind her ear. She closed her eyes to the pleasure and breathed deeply, soaking it in. His gentle touch and the power of his persuasion weren't anything to mess with. She could stay like this for hours, unhurried, just enjoying being the sole focus of his attention.

"I think we already are, Dylan. I'm having your baby. That puts us on a little higher level than friends."

"Maybe it's not enough," he rasped, and with a little tug, he inched her closer until their mouths were a breath apart. "Maybe we need to be more." And then he kissed her.

"What if that's not possible?"

He swept into her mouth again and deepened the kiss, his tongue working magic until her entire body grew warm and tingly. Her nipples pebbled and she gasped for sustaining breath.

"It's possible," he urged, rising from his seat and reaching for her hands. He seemed attuned to the exact moment when her body betrayed her. With both her hands in his, he gave a gentle yank and she came to her feet to face him in the soft glow of the floor lamps. "Let me show you."

Dylan was an expert at seduction; what he was doing to her now was solid proof. He took her face in his palms, looked deep into her eyes and then kissed her for long-drawn-out moments. Until her heart sped like a race car. Until her knees went weak. Until the junction of her thighs physically ached. It was too much and not enough. She was dizzy when he was through kissing her. Dizzy and wanting more.

"It's your choice, sweet Emma," he said, planting tiny kisses over her lips, his hands roaming over her body, taking liberties that she freely offered. She moaned a little when he touched her breasts and then gasped when he cupped her butt and pressed her firmly against his rigid, hard body so there was no doubt what he was about. He whispered softly into her ear, "We can take a walk on the beach to cool off, or walk into my bedroom upstairs and heat things up. You know what I want, but I'll abide by your decision, whatever it is."

She was out of breath. Her fuzzy mind told her to stall for time. As ardent as his kisses were, she couldn't wrap her head around him wanting to make love to her. It had once been her wildest dream. And yes, they'd done the deed already, but that wasn't really logged into her memory bank. Or his, either. "Is this what usually happens on your first dates?"

He laughed and took her into his arms, squeezing her tight as if she was a child asking an adorable question. "You know me. You know it's not what I do, Em."

Well, no. She'd never really quizzed him on his methods of seduction. How would she know how easily or often he took his dates to bed? He'd been in enough tabloids to wallpaper his entire mansion with the stories they'd concocted. And his sister defended him on every front. He'd even sued a few papers that had stepped over the line and had won his cases.

So, if she was to believe him now, then he was truly attracted to her. "I don't think I've ever seen your bedroom, Dylan."

He smiled then and nodded, and the next thing she knew, Dylan was lifting her in his strong arms and carrying her out of the screening room.

And up the stairs.

She roped one arm around his neck and laid her head against his broad shoulder as he marched to the double-door entry of his master suite. She felt featherlight in his arms, tucked safely into his embrace. He gave the door a nudge and pushed through, entering a massive room with an equally large bed. It faced wide windows that angled out with a magnificent view of the Pacific. Right now, only stars and a half-moon lit the night sky, but she heard the roar of the waves and smelled the brine of the sea coming through an opened terrace slider.

She wasn't sure about any of this, but lust and curiosity won over any rational sense inhabiting her brain at the moment. She'd done this before with Dylan, but now both were aware, both would remember. It was key. Monumental. Dylan would be in her life one way or another and she wanted this memory. Sane and rational or not, she simply didn't have the will to deny them both this night.

She did, after all, have secret dibs on him.

He lowered her down, her body flush against his until her feet hit the floor beside his bed. He let her go then, taking a step back to lock eyes with her and lifting his black polo shirt over his head. A rush of breath pushed from her lungs. His upper body was ripped and bronzed, his shoulders wide, the muscles in his arms bulging. He'd been working out hard for this Navy SEAL role and he had her vote. Hands down.

"We'll take this slow," he said.

Slow? She was on her first official date with him and about to get naked.

He reached for her and placed the palm of her hand flat against his concrete chest. His breath hitched and she lifted her lids to find the gleam in his eyes bright and hungry. Slowly, she moved her hand along the solid ridges that made up his six-pack and tiny coarse chest hairs tickled her fingers. He was amazing to touch, almost unreal. She'd never been with a man like Dylan before. It scared her, how absolutely perfect he was.

What was his flaw? Everyone had one, but she couldn't find it here, now.

He took her other hand, put it on him and encouraged her to explore. She did, running her hands over his shoulders, to his back and then returning to his torso. In her exploration, her fingers grazed his nipples and they grew taut from her touch. It was a turn-on, just seeing how she affected him.

He stood there, allowing her to know him, to feel his skin, absorb his heat and become familiar. She took her time, meeting his eyes once in a while, but mostly keeping a vigil on the beauty of his body.

He kissed her then, suckling her lips in a heady way that said he was ready to move forward. To take the next step.

"Should I undress the rest of the way?" he breathed over her mouth. "Or is it your turn?"

Fair is fair. She turned around and offered him her back. He didn't hesitate to unzip the long gold zipper on the little black dress she wore. The zipper hissed as it traveled all the way down to the small of her back. A shot of cooler air hit her as he pressed his hands to her shoulders and helped her shimmy out of her dress. Free of the fabric that pooled at her feet, he bestowed tiny kisses along her neck. Slowly, he turned her around and his eyes met hers once again, before drifting down her body over the slope of her ample breasts encased in her black lace bra, to her tummy that bulged slightly and the matching thong she wore. He rode his hands along her naked thighs and a tiny moan squeaked from her mouth.

"You are soft everywhere, sweetheart," he said, slipping his hand over her hip and edging up to her stomach. His palm against her growing belly, he stopped his exploration and bent on one knee to bestow a kiss there.

Her eyes slammed shut as Dylan worshipped their baby. It was a beautiful moment, so tender, so gentle, wiping away her fears. She couldn't fault him for anything. This situation was out of their control now. Maybe she'd been too hard on him, too rigid in her stance. He had a right to love their baby and want to share in the joy. She could give him that. She could try this dating thing, go in with an open mind and heart to see where it led.

He rose up then and stared directly into her eyes. "Our child will be beautiful like you, Emma. Inside and out."

Laying her hand flat against his cheek, scruff facial hair rough against her fingers, she whispered, "You're going to make a wonderful father, Dylan. I have no doubt."

Longing filled his eyes and he smiled. There was a moment that seemed to change everything; a newer intimacy and understanding passed between them in that moment.

And then Dylan reached for her again, pressing her fully against his hot, delicious body. Skin to skin, he kissed her for all she was worth. The next thing she knew, she was naked and they were on his bed and tangling in his sheets. Going slow was a thing of the past, and easily forgotten.

While one hand sifted through her long hair, his mouth created a dampened trail from her chin, along the base of her throat and farther down past her shoulders, until her breasts fairly ached for his touch. He came over her then and didn't disappoint, giving attention to one, then the other. Her back arched, the rosy nipples pointing up, hardened and sensitive, while white-hot heat scurried down past her belly, reaching her female core. A shudder ran through her, a beautiful sensual tremor as Dylan continued. She squirmed beneath him, the pleasure almost unbearable.

His mouth was masterful, his hands ingenious. When he moved, she moved and they were in sync, their bodies humming along together at a pace that suited her. She was in heaven, a bliss that she'd never encountered before. And it only got hotter when his hand slipped down past her navel, his fingertips teasing and taunting, edging closer to that one spot that would send her soaring.

She was damp and ready, and when he finally dipped into her soft folds, a tiny plea, a cry of pleasure, escaped her lips and she did, in fact, soar. The pressure, the light stroking growing firmer and more rhythmic worked her into a frenzied state. Dylan knew how to please. His kisses muffled her soft whimpers, his mouth devoured hers and his body radiated enough warmth to heat all of Moonlight Beach.

She reached a climax quickly. "Dylan, Dylan," she breathed, grasping his shoulders, clinging on, her heart pounding against her chest. He didn't let up until she shattered completely and was fully, wonderfully spent.

With glazed eyes, she watched him get up and remove his pants and briefs. Through the faint light streaming into the room she focused on the entire man, stark naked, virile and majorly turned on, and could only think, "Wow."

Before he climbed back onto the bed, he grabbed a golden packet from the nightstand, ripped it open and offered it to her as he lay down next to her. "For your protection."

There'd been someone before her. Probably Callista. And she was grateful for his concern, even though she was already pregnant with his child. She took it in her hands as he waited for her to slip it on him. The act was intimate, perhaps even more so than what had occurred just seconds ago.

She swallowed hard. When she was finished putting on the condom, Dylan wasted no time taking her back into his arms. "This all feels so new, sweet Emma."

"For me, too," she whispered, but there was no more room for small talk. Dylan was towering over her, using his thighs to move her legs apart. She was ready, watching him, his gorgeous face so determined, his body so in tune with hers, moving ever so slowly, nudging her core and finally, finally pushing forward, staking his claim.

She wound her arms around his neck and welcomed him. It was a glorious greeting, one that she'd always remember. Yet he took it slow, cautiously moving, giving of himself and making sure she was okay throughout.

He felt good inside her. As if she was home and where she belonged. As if she'd waited all of her life for this one moment. Safe. Secure. Happy.

But not loved.

She shoved those thoughts from her mind and concentrated on the amazing man making love to her. His blond hair was wild now, spiking up in sexy disarray. His chest heaving, his labored breaths fully accentuated his power and grace as he moved inside her. Muscles rippled and bunched. Skin sizzled and sensations ran rampant. Then those intent blue eyes locked on hers as he uttered her name and carried them both up, higher and higher.

Until the last thrust touched the deepest part of her.

She fell apart at the exact moment he did. In unison, they cried each other's names. He held on, allowing her to draw out the pleasure. And then he collapsed upon her, bracing his hands on each side of the bed to accept the brunt of his weight.

Looking at him now, she whispered, "Wow."

He grinned. The sexy man who'd just fulfilled her truest fantasy appeared to be quite satisfied. "Yeah, wow."

Rolling away from her, he landed on his back beside her. He took her hand and interlocked their fingers, staring out the window at the starry sky, listening to the pounding surf. She sensed him straining his mind, trying to recall that one night they'd shared before. "Anything?" she asked.

He gave her a quick noncommittal smile. "Everything."

She was taken by his sweet answer and the way he rolled over and kissed her. But he didn't remember anything from the blackout night. Nothing they did up until this point had triggered a memory.

"It doesn't matter if I remember or not. We've got this night and many more to come. We'll start out new, from here."

"I agree. It's a good plan." It was. She shouldn't dwell on the past any more than he should.

He laid his hand over her belly in a protective way. "New is good, Emma. Trust me."

She would have to trust him.

From now on.

"So everything looks good, Dr. Galindo?" Dylan asked, his face marked with concern. They were sitting in the office of Emma's ob-gyn.

"Yes, Mr. McKay, the baby is healthy and Emma's exam was right on point," the doctor said. She glanced at Emma and smiled. "All looks good. Be sure to continue to take your prenatal vitamins, and see me again in one month."

"Okay," Emma agreed. "I will."

"Do either of you have any further questions?"

"Just that," Emma began, "this isn't public knowledge, and we both expect our privacy to be respected."

Dr. Galindo gave Dylan a knowing look. "Of course. We honor every patient's privacy."

"Thank you. Where Dylan goes, news seems to follow."

The thirtysomething doctor smiled. Her eyes had repeatedly traveled to Dylan during the course of the consultation. Emma couldn't fault her. Dylan was A-list. He was hot and sought after and just about every woman from age ten to one hundred and ten ogled him. "Rest assured, your privacy will not be an issue with my office."

"I appreciate that." Dylan rose from his seat and shook the doctor's hand. "Thanks."

Emma noticed that his taut face had relaxed some as he led her out of the building and into his car. She, too, breathed a sigh of relief. "That went well."

"Yeah," he said. "The baby will be here in less than seven months. Hard to believe."

"For me, too. I'm grateful the baby is healthy. It was pretty cool hearing the heartbeat."

"It was awesome."

"I'll be big as a house soon."

"You'll look beautiful, Em," he said and started the engine.

"You're really okay with all of this, then?" she asked. He'd taken the news well and never once balked or hesitated when she'd revealed her pregnancy to him. It had been full steam ahead—they were having a baby together. Emma didn't quite understand his immediate acceptance, though she'd been grateful for it.

"I…am. I've always wanted to be a father. Just never found the right—"

He caught himself, but Emma knew what he was going to say. He'd never found the right woman to carry his child. Well, that decision had been taken out of his hands. She wasn't the right woman, but he was stuck with her. And she supposed that he was making the best of it.

He'd been attentive and had taken her on a date every night since that first one. One night they'd gone for ice cream at a local creamery, a place that Dylan's friend owned. They'd snuck in the back way and had taken a corner table, Dylan disguised in a Dodgers ball cap and sunglasses. The next night they'd gone to a concert at the Hollywood Bowl, Dylan scoring front row seats, and they'd gone in through a VIP entrance. Each time they went out, Dylan's bodyguards weren't far behind. It was kind of eerie knowing their every move was being watched, but as Dylan explained, it came with the territory.

She enjoyed her evenings with Dylan. And each night after their date, they'd wind up in bed together—sometimes in his gorgeous master suite and sometimes at her tiny apartment. They were growing closer each day, and getting to know one another on a different level. Dylan was kind and tender and as sexy as a man had a right to be. There were times when they were making love that she'd actually have to gasp for breath and remind herself this was really happening.

She had fallen in love with him. Truly and madly, and it had probably happened the night of their movie date. She'd always been halfway in love with him as a teen, but this was different. This was based on actually knowing him and spending time with him. It probably hadn't hurt that her orgasms were off the charts when they made love. Or that he was the father of her baby. Or that they shared a hometown history together.

But every morning, when she'd wake in his arms, he

would plant a bug in her ear. "Move in with me, Em. We could have all our nights and mornings like this."

It was a tempting offer, one that she debated for long moments, but ultimately always refused because, like it or not, she wasn't ready to give up her independence. To give Dylan her one last means of defense against heartbreak. He wanted to keep his baby safe and close at hand. She understood that, and it was a noble gesture, but what did that say about her relationship with him? It was what Dylan was *not saying* to her that fueled her resolve to stay out of harm's way.

"I don't understand why you don't want to, Em," he'd say. And she'd shrug her shoulders and shake her head. This was new to him, this constant rejection. He wasn't conceited or arrogant, but he'd been used to having women fall at his feet, she supposed, and he didn't understand her reluctance.

"I just can't, Dylan," would be her answer.

After the doctor's appointment, they went to lunch at a little private beach eatery and sat outside on benches facing the ocean. She had chicken salad and he had halibut in drawn butter. Afterward, Dylan dropped her off at the office. "Don't work too hard," he said, giving her a kiss.

"Never," she said, and he tossed his head back and laughed. He knew she was a workhorse, never settling until things were perfect and under control. He would tease her about that all the time. "You, either," she shot back.

"I won't. I'll be learning my lines for tomorrow's shoot. Which reminds me, the next two days will run long. We're having night shoots. I won't be home until after your bedtime. I'll miss you."

She smiled. "Me, too."

His eyes dipped to her belly. "Take care of the little bambino."

"Always," she said, placing her hand there protectively.

Touching her stomach and greeting the little one, warming to him or her and the idea of a baby, had become a habit.

She climbed out of the car, waved goodbye, and then he was off. She wouldn't see him for the next few days. Maybe that was a good thing. She watched him drive into the traffic stream before stepping into the office.

"Hey, how did the appointment go?" Brooke asked, gazing up from her desk.

"Wonderful. Everything is good."

Brooke grinned. "Great. I can't wait to find out if it's a boy or girl. I'm making up a shopping list and already have three my-auntie-is-the-best outfits picked out. Now, just gotta know if I'm buying blue or pink."

Brooke was definitely going to spoil the baby. "It'll be fun finding out."

"Yeah, but for now, I'm just happy knowing the baby's healthy."

Brooke rose from her desk and approached her. "Things are working out with Dylan, aren't they?" she asked. "I mean, you sound happy. You look happy and well. I know you've been dating, hot and heavy."

"Hot and heavy?" Emma's laughter sounded a little too high-pitched even to her ears and Brooke caught on immediately.

"Wow, so it's true. You and my brother are hooking up."

Well, yeah, she supposed they were. He'd asked her to move in with him several times, but never with any true sense of commitment. Was that what she was waiting for? Some hope, some sign that he wanted her, and not just because she was going to give birth to his child? Maybe what she wanted from Dylan was impossible for him to give. "Brooke, I have no name for what's happening between Dylan and me."

"At least something is happening." Excitement sparkled in Brooke's eyes.

"Maybe you should concentrate on your relationship with Royce," Emma countered, giving her BFF a wry smile.

"Oh, believe me, I do." Brooke giggled. "We're heading to hot and heavy, too."

"Wow, you two are moving fast."

Brooke sighed. "I know. It's crazy, but we're in tune with each other on every level."

"I'm happy for you."

"Thanks. Now, on to work issues. We've got the Henderson anniversary party on Friday night and then we've got Clinton's seventh birthday party in Beverly Hills all day Saturday. Which one do you want to confirm?"

"I'll take Clinton's party. I've made special arrangements for the petting zoo and the cartoon characters to show up and I've got the cake and food already set. I'll double-check it's a go, and you can make your confirmations for the anniversary gig."

"Okay, sounds good. It's going to be a busy weekend. Are you sure you're up for it?"

"I'm sure." Emma had been operating at 90 percent and feeling better every day. Dylan had been keeping her plenty busy at night, too, exhausting her in a good way. She'd been sleeping soundly and waking feeling sated and refreshed, but the thought of not seeing him for the next few nights suddenly cast a shadow of loneliness on her perspective.

How odd. Usually she valued her downtime and enjoyed being on her own.

"Oh, yeah," Brooke said, making a face. "I almost forgot to tell you, Maury Allen called today. Seems his event planner for Callista's big birthday bash had a family emergency and he can't continue the work. He wants us to take over. It's in two weeks."

"You told him no, didn't you?" Emma held her breath.

Brooke scrunched her face even more. "Well," she squeaked. "I couldn't do that. He used Dylan's name as a reference and made it seem like my brother recommended us to him. He's Dylan's boss and he said everything's pretty much done. All we have to do is show up and make things run smoothly."

"Brooke!"

"I know. But he took me by surprise and I didn't think I could worm out of it."

"Couldn't his planner get someone else from their company to step in?"

She shook her head. "They're all booked solid. And we're not. His secretary is overnighting the signed vendor contracts and the itinerary so we know what's planned."

Emma rolled her eyes. "That's just wonderful."

"Sorry." To Brooke's credit, she did seem genuinely apologetic. "You don't have to go. I'll get Wendy or Rocky to help out."

"Knowing Callista, it's going to be a giant production. You're going to need me."

Brooke ducked her head and looked sheepish. "I think you may be right."

Shoulders tight and arms crossed, Emma leaned against the wall and sent a disgruntled sigh out to the universe. "I guess I was destined to go to this thing."

"Destined? What do you mean?"

"Dylan asked me to go to Callista's party as his date. He said he wanted company in his misery, but I flat out refused. The woman barely gets my name right."

Brooke chuckled. "Just call her Callie, like I do. You know what they say about payback."

"I can't do that. She's our client now."

"Her father's our client."

"It's practically the same thing," Emma said. "She's got him wrapped around her diamond-ringed finger."

"True, but I wish I could be there when she…"

Brooke's expression was way too mischievous for Emma's curiosity. "What?"

"When she finds out you're carrying Dylan's child."

"Brooke! You're not going to say a thing. Promise me."

She glanced at Emma's belly bump and smiled. "I promise. But maybe I won't have to say anything. Maybe she'll find out on her own. Now, *that* would be worth the price of admission."

Emma couldn't suppress a smile. She grinned along with her friend. "You're wicked."

"Yes, and that's why you love me."

Seven

Emma dragged herself through the door on Saturday evening, her twenty-five-year-old bones aching. She was too tired to make it to her bedroom. She tossed her handbag onto the sofa, then plopped down next to it. The well-worn cushions welcomed her and she put her feet up on the coffee table. Stretching out, she closed her eyes.

Little Clinton's birthday party had done her in. It had gone fairly well for a seven-year-old's party, though there'd been a few potential disasters in the making. One of the goats in the petting zoo had escaped the pen and begun nibbling on the party decorations. The kids thought it hilarious, until the darn goat made a dash for the cupcake table and nearly downed the whole thing. Emma screamed for the zookeeper to do something, and he'd looked up oblivious to the goings-on from across the yard, giving her no choice but to navigate the stubborn animal back to the pen herself.

But that was an innocent mistake, unlike the guy dressed

in a furry purple character costume. Judging by the way he was walking, the guy must have been intoxicated. It was either that or balancing himself in the costume was too much for him. She'd kept her eyes peeled on him for the entire day and thankfully he didn't cause any trouble.

Then there was the incident at the taco bar. The kids took one bite of their tacos and their little mouths were set on fire from too much chipotle sauce added to the meat. Emma escorted those kids right over to the snow cone machine. Rainbow ice doused the flames and put smiles on their faces again. Disaster averted, but not before Emma scolded the cook. What had he been thinking?

Emma leaned forward and did slow head circles, first one way, then the other. The stretch and pull felt good, easing away a full day's worth of tension. Her cell phone rang and she had a mind not to answer it, but as she glanced at the screen name, she smiled and picked up. "Hi, Dylan."

"Hi," he said in that low, masculine tone that made her dizzy. "What are you doing?"

"Just putting my feet up. It's been a long day."

"Tired?"

"Yeah, pretty much. What are you doing?"

"Driving by your apartment."

"You are?" She bolted straight up, her heartbeat speeding.

"Yeah, I thought I'd take a chance and see if you were up to company. If you're too tired, I'll just keep on driving."

God, just the sound of his voice roused her out of exhaustion. It had been three days since she'd seen him. He'd been constantly on her mind. "I'm not too tired."

"You sure? You sound wiped out."

"I'm...not."

"I'll be right there."

A soft flow of warmth spread through her body. Her hormones were happy now. Beautifully, wonderfully happy.

Just minutes later, she opened the door and he walked

straight into her arms. He lifted her off the ground as he kissed her and moved her backward to the sofa, setting her down and taking a seat next to her. "I'm not staying. I just wanted to see you," he said, wrapping his arms around her shoulders.

"I'm glad. I, uh, I wanted to see you, too." It was always hard admitting how she was feeling toward Dylan. She wasn't playing hard to get. She was running scared, frightened that this big bubble of joy would pop at any moment.

"How was your day?"

"Chasing goats and kids and keeping parents happy, just a usual Saturday afternoon fun day."

Dylan smiled. "You love it."

"I do. I'm not complaining." It was what she was meant to do. She enjoyed every facet of event planning. Though it was a hassle at times and deadlines could be gruesome, the end result, a successful party, was her reward. She couldn't imagine having a nine-to-five job, although she thoroughly enjoyed keeping the books and managing the accounts, too.

Dylan grasped her hand and brought it to his knee. It was as natural as breathing for him to hold on to her this way. "I'm glad you're in business with my sister."

"Me, too. I think our talents complement each other. She's the creative one and I'm the practical one."

"You work hard. Don't take this the wrong way, but you look exhausted."

She sighed. "There's no fooling you."

"I'm quite perceptive." He smiled at her and his sea-blue eyes softened. "Turn around."

"What?"

"Turn your back to me and try to relax."

"Okay."

She angled away from him on the sofa and then his hand gently moved her hair off her shoulders. It fell in a tangle on her right side. Next, he placed both hands on her shoulder blades and began a firm but soothing massage. The tension was released immediately, and as he worked the kinks out and moved farther down her back, she closed her eyes. "Oh, that feels good," she cooed.

"That's the plan, sweetheart."

His hands on her body were a comforting, soothing presence lifting her spirits, a balm for her tired bones.

"Why don't we take this into the bedroom," he whispered, his breath tickling her ear. "Where you can stretch out and really relax."

She turned to face him.

"Just a massage, I promise. Deal?"

"Deal."

And then she was being lifted and carried toward her bedroom. Her independence had flown the coop the minute Dylan had shown up. But she loved his inner he-man and the way he took control of a situation. It was amazingly sexy.

She played with the curl of hair resting on his nape. "You don't have to make deals with me, Dylan."

"Don't tempt me. I know how tired you are and let's leave it at that."

She nodded.

A slender shaft of light from the courtyard illuminated her bedroom window. Dylan lowered her to a standing position by her bed and moved behind her. With one hand on either side of her back, he inched her blouse up and over her head, tossing it onto the nightstand. Then he helped to remove her slacks. Down to a white bra and panties, she kicked off her shoes and turned to face him.

There was a sharp rasp of breath as he looked at her. "This isn't going to be as easy as I thought," he muttered in a tortured tone. "Lie down. I'll be right back."

Emma pulled her sheets back and lowered down onto

her tummy, resting her head on her pillow. When Dylan returned, he held a bottle of raspberry vanilla essential oil. "This okay to use?"

She nodded and closed her eyes. She heard the sound of his hands slapping together as he warmed the oil and then felt the dip of the mattress as he sat beside her. "Ready?"

"Oh, yes."

He spread the oil onto her skin, his touch light and generous as he rubbed every inch of her back. The pleasing scents of raspberry and vanilla wafted to her nostrils in the most delicious way. Using his thumbs, Dylan pressed the small of her back in circular motions, his fingers resting on the slope of her behind. She tingled there and her breath caught noisily. This was quickly becoming more than a massage and almost more intimate than having sex with Dylan. He removed his fingers, using his thumbs to walk up her spine.

"Oh, so nice," she whispered.

"I'm glad you're enjoying this."

"Aren't you?"

"Too much."

She grinned and endorphins released merrily through her body.

He lifted his hands off her back and again she heard the smack of his hands as he warmed the oil. Next, he worked her legs, starting at her ankles, gliding his hands up and down, around and around, bringing new life to her tired limbs. First one calf, then the other, and then he was inching his hands up the backs of her thighs. He slowed his pace and stopped for a moment.

"Dylan?"

"I'm okay," he said, his voice quietly pained.

"This isn't supposed to make you tense."

"Too late for that, sweetheart. Just relax and enjoy."

But there was something too tempting, too genuine in

his voice for her to sit back and take this without giving something back. She shifted her position, landing on her back. One look at his gorgeous face, his gritted teeth and set jaw had her gaze moving down below his waist. She wasn't surprised to see the strain of material in his pants.

"I didn't come here for—"

"I know, and it makes it all the more sweet." She lifted her arms and reached for him. "Come here, Dylan." she said. "Let me do something for you."

"There's no need," he said, but it was too late. She grabbed him around the neck and pulled him down on top of her. He was careful where he landed and avoided plopping on her belly.

"I'm not tired anymore. In fact, I'm feeling pretty loose," she said softly. "And you deserve a massage, too."

Emma stood over the sizzling range top, flipping pancakes on a griddle, a pleasing hum running through her body. Last night's massages had turned into something pretty spectacular and now she was famished. She'd crept out of bed, leaving Dylan sleeping, to make him a nourishing breakfast. He'd sure earned it judging by the energy he'd exerted making love to her last night.

When his arms wrapped around her waist, she nearly jumped out of her skin. She hadn't heard him come up behind her. "Morning," he said, nibbling on her neck.

"I thought you were sleeping."

"I missed you."

God, he said all the right things. "Sweet."

"You're sweet to make us breakfast."

"Us?" She chuckled. "What makes you think this is for you?"

He tightened his hold on her and then reached around her body to turn the knob, shutting off the burner. "Dylan, what are you—"

He turned her around and kissed her complaint away. Then he gave her a heart-melting smile and tugged her away from the stove. He'd already put his clothes from yesterday back on. They looked amazingly unwrinkled and fresh, while she was wearing gray sweats and a pink tank sporting the Parties-To-Go logo in purple glitter, her hair in a messy ponytail.

Holding her hand, he led her to the living area. Her heart was beating fast now. What was he up to? He turned to her and the expression on his face was dead serious. "I've been thinking, Em. About us."

She gulped. Us?

"You and I, we're going to be parents soon and I guess I'm an old-fashioned guy when it comes to kids and all. I see a bright future ahead for us, the *three* of us. We'll be a family, a real honest-to-goodness family, and I think the baby deserves the very best start in life. That means having a mother and father raise the child together. I care very much for you, Emma. You know that. We're good together, if last night isn't proof enough." His smile was a little wobbly now and Emma's heart pounded even harder. He was going to press her to move in with him.

"I'm not going to ask you to move in with me anymore, Em."

"You're not?" She blinked. This was new.

He shook his head. "No. That's not the solution."

He gazed deep into her eyes. "I want you to marry me."

Emma's mouth opened and a sharp gasp escaped. "Oh."

"I'm asking you to be my wife, Emma. I've given this a lot of thought and I can only see good things in store for the three of us."

She dropped her hand from his and shuffled her feet. Inside, everything was stirring, a mad mix of emotions and thoughts flying through her head. "This is…um, unexpected."

"Really, Em? It's not so far-fetched to think that two people conceiving a child together would get married, is it?"

He made it seem so simple. He cared for her. And Lord knew, she cared even more for him. She loved him. Could they make it work, even though he didn't say the words a woman being proposed to was meant to hear? There was no claim of undying love, nothing about how he couldn't live without her and how his life would be empty without her in it. Yet Dylan had spoken honestly, giving her genuine reasons why this was a good idea.

But doubts immediately crept in. He was Dylan McKay, eligible bachelor extraordinaire, a highly sought-after movie star, a man whose life was obviously filled with temptations at every turn. Could she place her trust in him not to break her heart and soul? Could she marry a man who didn't outright love her?

"Em, you don't have to give me your answer right now. Take some time," he said, his voice laced with tenderness and understanding. "Give it some thought. I'm not going anywhere. I'll be right here."

A huge part of her wanted to say yes, but she couldn't make this decision on the spur of the moment. She was being given the moon, but was it greedy of her to want the sun and the stars, too?

"Dylan," she began softly, "I can't give you an answer right now. Everything is happening so fast."

"I know. I get it, Em. I don't want to add to your stress. Believe me, I only want what's best for you. But I wanted to get my feelings out in the open. I think it's the right move, but I won't pressure you. I'll wait until you've made your decision."

"Thank you. I appreciate that. So, um…where do we go from here?"

Dylan grinned. "You finish making me breakfast. I'm

starving and those pancakes look pretty appetizing. And tomorrow night, we'll have a dinner date at my house. Sound good?"

She nodded. So they'd resume dating, *with the option of marriage*.

So that was it. He'd proposed and now they were back to the status quo. The ball was in her court, as they say. How on earth would she be able to make this decision? Her foster parents' marriage had been a train wreck. They'd fought constantly and Emma often felt she was to blame. She'd cower under a blanket in the far corner of her bedroom and cover her ears to block out their vulgar arguments. She never wanted a child of hers to go through that kind of pain and torment. Would Emma and Dylan end up hating each other and fighting constantly, just as her folks had?

Just as important, could she possibly say no to Dylan and refuse his marriage proposal? Or even more frightening, could she allow herself to say yes to him without having his love?

"Sounds perfect," she said with a manufactured smile. Lying to Dylan and to…herself.

Monday morning Emma walked into her office, greeted Brooke, plopped into the chair behind her desk and began working. She was in the early planning stages of a Bar Mitzvah and had many calls to make. She worked diligently, struggling to keep her mind on business.

Later that morning, she met with vendors, a florist and photographer, and then returned to the office feeling somewhat accomplished. But all day long, she'd been distracted and had a difficult time focusing. She'd made a few mistakes along the way as well, giving the wrong dates to a vendor and then having to recalculate an estimate she'd given and call back a client with the bad news that she'd made an error. That never went over well and she'd wound up giving them a 10 percent discount to make up for it.

Brooke had cast furtive glances at her all day long and no matter how much she tried to behave like her normal self, Emma figured she hadn't fooled her friend. To add to her dismay, a gorgeous bouquet of pink Stargazer lilies had been delivered in a bubble crystal vase while she was gone. They sat on one corner of her desk now and flavored the air with a wonderful floral scent.

The note read: *Just Because. Dylan*

By late afternoon, Brooke approached, taking a seat on the edge of Emma's desk. "Hey, Em?"

Emma's lips twisted. She knew the drill, but refused to look up from her computer screen. "Hey, yourself."

"So what's wrong? You've been distracted all day."

"I can make an error once in a while, Brooke."

"I make errors all the time, but not you, Little Miss Organized. You don't make mistakes."

"Well, call me perfect, then."

"Emma?" Brooke put a motherly tone in her voice. "What's up? And don't tell me nothing. Did you and Dylan have a fight or something?"

Emma finally shifted her focus and looked into Brooke's concerned eyes. "No," she said emphatically. "We didn't fight. He asked me to marry him."

Brooke's face lit up. "Really?"

Emma ran both hands down her cheeks, pulling the skin taut. "Really."

"Oh, so you're bothered by his proposal?"

"It wasn't so much a proposal, but a sort of bargain, for the baby's sake. Not that I don't want what's best for the baby. I do, but I don't know. I'm...confused."

"Did he say he wanted to marry you?"

"Yes, of course he did."

"And did he say he wanted you, him and baby to be his family?"

"Yes. That's what he wants."

"He's very fond of you, Emma. He's always liked you."

"I know that."

"So how do you feel about him? And be honest."

Emma tugged on her long braid, twisting it around and around in her hand. Her mouth twitched and she blinked a few times. This was a hard thing for her to admit even to Brooke "I've fallen in love with him," she finally said.

Brooke didn't get excited about her admission and Emma was grateful for that. Instead, she took her hand and smiled. "I see the problem." Brooke knew her so well. "You're worried he may not return the feelings."

"Ever."

"Ever," Brooke repeated softly. "Well, all I can say is that Dylan is capable of great love. He accepted me from day one when I came to the McKay house to live. Here I was this little frightened girl with no family, and there was this older boy who seemed to have it all, a nice set of parents, and friends and a decent house to live in. I was afraid he'd hate me for imposing on his family, but he did just the opposite. He made me feel welcomed, and the first time he called me his little sister, I cried big sloppy tears and he hugged me hard and said something funny that made me laugh. From then on, I was okay with Dylan and he was okay with me.

"I can't tell you what to do, Emma. You're my friend and you deserve to be loved, but I know my brother will never intentionally hurt you. He's gonna love the baby you're carrying with all his heart. And I know you will, too. You'll have that in common and that's a bond that will carry you into the future. It's up to you, to figure out if that's enough." Brooke gave her hand a last squeeze, then stood up. "Are you okay?"

Emma nodded. "I'm much better. Thanks, Brooke. It helps."

A weight had been lifted from her shoulders. Brooke's rational, though slightly biased, opinion made sense to her. She had the moon in the palm of her hands, and maybe just maybe, the sun and the stars would come later on.

Late-afternoon runs always served to clear Dylan's mind, and today's jog along the shoreline did the trick. He wasn't running the ten miles he'd been doing before the accident, but he managed five miles today without too much problem.

As he climbed the steps that led to his house, he nodded to Dan, one of his bodyguards, who'd been on the beach running behind him and watching him diligently. That was another reason he hadn't resumed the longer runs. Dan wasn't up to it. Not too many people were. Dylan had been doing endurance runs for months during his training for this SEAL movie. His bodyguard was fit but hadn't been training as intensely as Dylan had.

He went inside and stopped in the kitchen, grabbed a bottle of water from the fridge and gulped it down in three big swallows. As he moved toward the staircase, he lifted his T-shirt over his head and used it to sop up beads of sweat raining down his chest. Emma was coming for dinner soon. He'd given Maisey time off today so that they'd have time alone. Yesterday, he'd jumped into the waters with both feet, spontaneously proposing to Emma, and he hoped he'd made an impression. He had a ring ready for her, one he'd been carrying around with him for days, but putting that ring on her finger would have to wait until she accepted his proposal.

When the doorbell rang, he blinked in surprise and strode to the front door. He'd given Emma the remote control to the garage door entryway and wondered why she didn't come through the back door as usual. Peeking through the peephole, his shoulders drooped when he saw Callista standing on the threshold. He made a mental note to change the code to his front gate.

Opening the door, he greeted her. "Hi, Callista, what are you doing here?" He put as much civility in his voice as he could muster.

"I came to check on you." She glanced at his bare chest and black running shorts, smiled and whizzed by him, entering his home. "Did I ever tell you how much I love this vertical garden? It's a masterpiece," she said, eyeing the lush wall of succulents spilling down from the tall ceiling in his foyer.

Dylan grimaced before facing her. She turned back around and waited for him to shut the door.

"No, I don't think you ever have." He closed the door.

"Well, I do. I love it."

He nodded and stood his ground.

"Aren't you going to ask me in?"

She was already in, but that was beside the point. He'd have to deal with her, explain that he wasn't interested in a relationship with her any longer and hope that they could still remain friends. She should've already gotten the hint, since he hadn't called her since the day of Roy's memorial service, but Callista wasn't easily put off. "Come in, please. After you." He gestured for her to lead the way.

She walked into the living room and leaned against one of the open double doors to the veranda. "It's a beautiful time of day, Dylan. I love the sea air. I've missed coming here."

He had nothing to say to that.

"It looks like you've been running."

"Yeah, I'm getting back into it. It feels good, clears my head."

"So, you're feeling better?"

"I'm doing well."

"That's good to hear. You look amazing."

"So do you, Callista. As always."

She was a beautiful woman, her honey-blond hair cut longer on one side than the other in a sleek style, her eyes a glistening blue, her body as slim as a supermodel's. She dressed impeccably, in the latest fashion, her clothes fitting her flamboyant personality. Unfortunately what she had on the outside didn't make up for her lack of humanity on the inside. She wasn't a bad person, just self-absorbed, and he couldn't lay all the blame at her feet. She'd been spoiled and indulged all of her life by her parents and her friends, and it had taken Dylan getting to know Emma as well as he did now to make the comparison and see which woman he wanted in his life.

"Are you okay, Dylan? I mean, really okay? Daddy told me about the possible threat to your life and I'm...I'm so worried about you."

"I'm fine. And they're not absolutely sure if it was an attempt on my life. But to put your mind at ease, I've added additional security around here and I travel with bodyguards all the time now. I'm sure your father told you to keep this private. There's an investigation going on."

"Yes, of course. On any given day there are hundreds of people at the studio, Dylan. How can they possibly find out who's responsible?"

"I don't know, Callista." At least he'd be finished shooting the movie in a few weeks and wouldn't have to go into the studio anymore. "All we can do is hope the investigation gives them some leads."

"Gosh, I hope so."

Dylan softened a little. Callista seemed genuinely concerned for him. He couldn't deny that they'd had a past relationship and that they still cared for each other's welfare. "Thanks. I appreciate it. I value your friendship."

She walked over to him, placed her palm on his cheek and locked her pretty doe eyes on his. "We're more than friends, Dylan. I'd hoped you'd remembered that." She brushed her lips to his and spoke softly over his mouth. "And it would make me very happy if you'd be my date for my birthday party."

Emma shut her mind off to all of her misgivings about Dylan and looked upon his proposal more openly now. Her conversation with Brooke had helped her see things in a new perspective. She was still debating about marrying him, but at least the roadblocks in her head were slowly being taken down. She'd realized this as she was baking him a chocolate marble cake today, just like the one she'd demolished on her birthday years ago. If they could have a good laugh over it, then the cake would serve its purpose. Smiling, she entered the gates of his home, noting a foreign sports car in his driveway she didn't recognize. Oh well, so much for having a quiet evening together. He had a visitor.

Emma parked her car in one of the empty garages on his property and carefully removed the cake holder, balancing it in one hand as she went up to the house and unlocked the back door with a hidden key. When she entered, she heard voices and debated about barging in, but as she moved into the kitchen, she recognized the seductive female voice.

Callista.

Emma set the cake down on the countertop and strode quietly toward the living room. She came to an abrupt stop when she saw Callista and Dylan tangled up in one another's arms at the far end of the room. She blinked several times, not believing what she was seeing. Her first thought was how wonderful they looked together, two stunning people living in the same high-profile world, a place where Emma didn't fit. They were the beautiful people, A-listers with friends who owned islands and airplanes and villas on the French Riviera. Seeing the two of them cuddled up good and tight, whispering to each other, brought it all to light. Emma didn't belong in Dylan's universe. Jealousy jabbed at her over the unfairness of it all.

But Dylan wasn't Callista's to ensnare. She wasn't the right woman for him.

Emma had had dibs on him since forever. Was she going to give him up without a fight? Shockingly, her answer was a flat-out no. She couldn't let Dylan get away. Jealousy aside, she wasn't going to hand her baby's father over to the wrong woman. Dylan had asked her, Emma Rae Bloom, to marry him, something he hadn't done since Renee had torn his heart to shreds. And now, Emma was beginning to see a life with him and their baby. So what was her problem? Why hadn't she jumped at his proposal last night? Why was she being so darn hardheaded?

To his credit, Dylan backed away from Callista instantly, wriggling out of her clutches before she could kiss him again. He didn't see Emma standing there, so there was no pretense for her sake. He really was rejecting the woman.

"I can't be your date, Callista," she heard him say.

Emma breathed a big sigh of relief.

"Why?" She approached him again, a question in her eyes. "I don't understand."

Emma gulped air loudly, deliberately. She'd heard enough. Both heads turned in her direction. Callista's mouth twisted in annoyance and Dylan, God love him, appeared truly relieved to see her. He put his arm out, reaching for Emma's hand, much to the other woman's horror, and Emma floated over to him and took it.

He smiled at her, and before he could say anything, Emma announced, "Dylan is my fiancé, Callista. I'm going to marry him."

Callista's mouth dropped open. Clearly stunned, she darted glances from Emma to Dylan and back again. And then her gaze shot like a laser beam down to Emma's slightly bulging belly. She was sharp, Emma had to give her that. "You're pregnant."

Dylan pulled her closer in, winding his arm around her waist in a show of support. "I'm sorry, Callista, but that's not an issue here. I was going to tell you about Emma and me."

"When, at my birthday party? The one she's supposed to plan and execute?"

Dylan's eyes never wavered. He was such a good actor. As far as she knew, Dylan had no knowledge of that latest development. "Under the circumstances, that's not going to happen now. I hope we can still be friendly, Callista. We've known each other a long time."

Callista ignored Emma once again, speaking to Dylan as if she wasn't standing there, in his embrace. "You can't be serious, Dylan. You're going to marry her?"

"Of course I'm serious. When have you known me not to be?"

"But…but…"

Emma stifled a giggle. She'd never seen Callista speechless before.

And finally, "You cheated on me with *her*!"

Dylan's brows gathered; his eyes grew dark and dangerous. "Don't go there, Callista. I never cheated on a woman in my life. We were on-again, off-again, and before my accident we were definitely off. Big-time off. And you know it."

Callista made a show of grabbing her purse and stomping away. Before exiting the room, she swiveled around and glared at Emma. "It'll never last. He's just doing this for the kid. Wait and see."

The front door slammed shut behind her.

Neither of them moved.

Seconds ticked by.

God, all of Emma's fears had come full circle in Callista's venomous declaration. Those three sentences revealed Emma's innermost doubts. A tremor ran through her. Could she do this? Could she really marry Dylan?

And then Dylan faced her, the darkness of his expression evaporating into something hopeful and sweet. His eyes gleamed and the way he held on to her as if she was precious to him, as if he was truly happy, convinced her to stay the course. She'd made up her mind and couldn't bear losing Dylan. If they had a chance at a future together, she was going to take it.

"You're really going to marry me? You weren't just saying that?" he asked.

"It wasn't the perfect way to tell you, but yes. I'm going to marry you."

His brilliant smile warmed all the cold places that threatened her happiness. "Good. Okay. Good. The sooner the better."

He kissed her then, and all of her doubts flittered away on the breeze. She would give herself up to him now. She wouldn't hold back. She was all in, and she would think only positive thoughts from now on.

After a long embrace, Dylan shook his head. "I'm sorry about that scene with Callista. I didn't know she was coming over."

"She was very upset, Dylan."

"She's dramatic and only upset because she didn't get her way. In her heart, she had to know we were over. But the truth is, I never cheated on her with you or anyone. It's important that you believe me."

"I do," she said. These past few weeks with Dylan had shown her what kind of a man he truly was. The tabloids liked to paint a less-than-rosy picture of celebrities, but

Emma didn't and wouldn't believe a word of it about Dylan McKay. She'd walked in on Dylan rebuffing Callista's advances and that alone was proof enough for her. She could place her faith in Dylan.

She had to.

He was going to be her husband.

Eight

Warm Pacific gusts lifted her wedding veil off her shoulders as she stood on the steps of Adam Chase's palatial oceanside home, waiting for her cue to walk down an aisle laden with red rose petals. They, too, blew in the breeze in sweeping patterns that colored the pathway in a natural special effect.

She looked out to the small cluster of friends and family in attendance, no more than thirty strong. Their secluded little wedding ceremony was about to begin. Dylan's mother was here, and Brooke, of course, was her maid of honor. She'd helped Emma into her ivory, Cinderella-style wedding dress. Wendy and Rocky were here, her part-timers who'd actually become dear friends. Dylan's agent and manager attended as well as his closest neighbors—Adam Chase, his wife, Mia, and their adorable baby, Rose, seated next to Jessica and her country superstar husband, Zane Williams.

It had been Adam's idea to hold the wedding here, the

reclusive architect offering a place for their secretive ceremony away from any paparazzi who might've gotten wind of their engagement. To their surprise, Callista hadn't spread any ugly gossip as yet and Dylan had insisted on marrying quickly. Parties-To-Go had immediately been fired from holding Callista's big birthday event, much to Brooke's glee. Ironically, Dylan's hectic work schedule only allowed them to get married on the very same day.

The music began, the traditional "Wedding March" played by a string quartet bringing tears to Emma's eyes. Her foster parents had declined the invitation to attend, claiming illness—aka too much alcohol—so Emma began her trek down the aisle on her own, the way she'd always done things.

She didn't mind, though, because waiting for her at the end of the white aisle, dressed in a stunning black tuxedo, his blond hair spiky, his blue eyes twinkling, was the man she'd always dreamed about marrying, Dylan McKay. As she held her bouquet of delicate snowflake-white lilies and baby red roses, beautiful emotions carried her toward him, each step a commitment to making their marriage work, to having the family she never thought she'd ever have.

The small group of guests stood as she flowed past them toward Dylan, her eyes straight ahead. When she reached him, he took her arm and led her to the minister and the flowered, latticed canopy that would be their altar. There, they spoke their vows of commitment and devotion.

For only a minute she was saddened that no words of actual love were spoken. Wasn't it odd, a union taking place where neither of the participants spoke of undying love and devotion?

But once they were declared man and wife, Dylan cupped her face and kissed her with enough passion to wipe out any feelings of sadness. From this day forward…

she would look only to the future. She'd promised. And so had he.

"Family and friends," the minister said, "I give you Mr. and Mrs. Dylan McKay."

As they turned to face their guests, applause broke out.

"Hello, Mrs. McKay," Dylan said, kissing her again.

"Dylan, I hardly believe this is real."

"It's real." It was the last thing he said to her before they were separated and the guests bombarded each of them with congratulations.

Brooke ran over to Emma and hugged her so tight, her veil tilted to one side of her head. Brooke stomped her feet up and down several times, her joy overflowing. "I can't believe you're my sister now! I mean we always were like sisters, but now you're truly family. This is the best. The very best. Oh, here, let me fix your veil. My duty as your maid of honor."

She refastened the veil just as Royce walked up. "Congratulations, Emma."

"Thank you, Royce. It's great to finally meet you."

"Same here. And on such a special day. I feel honored to be invited."

"I'm glad you're here. Brooke looks great, doesn't she?"

Royce glanced at his date. Brooke was wearing a red halter gown, tastefully decorated with sequins along the bodice. She'd promised she wouldn't wear black, and when they'd shopped and she'd tried this one on, both knew it was perfect for her. Her gorgeous long dark hair hung in tight curls down her back and complemented the dress. "Yes, she does."

"Have you met Dylan yet?"

"No," Royce said. "But I'm looking forward to it."

"He's scared," Brooke said, grinning. "Meeting my famous big brother isn't in his wheelhouse. Isn't that right, honey?"

"Well...uh...I must admit, he's such a big star, I'm a little intimidated."

"Don't be. Dylan's a good guy," Emma said. "He's harmless."

"That's good to hear."

"I keep telling him that, too," Brooke said. "But you, Emma, are the beautiful one. You look like the happiest bride in the world, and that dress...well, you destroy in it."

Emma laughed. "Thanks, I think."

"You do look very pretty, Emma," Royce said.

"And I agree." Dylan came from out of nowhere to take her hand. "You look gorgeous today, Em. My beautiful bride." He kissed her cheek and played with a curl hanging down from her upswept hair.

Brooke wasted no time introducing Dylan to her boyfriend. The two men talked for a few minutes and Brooke seemed immensely happy that they seemed to be getting along.

Just a few minutes later, Dylan's mother walked into their circle and took Emma aside. "I've always thought of you as my second daughter, Emma, you know that. You've been part of our family since the first day Brooke brought you over to our house, but I can't even begin to tell you how happy I am that you and Dylan are married." Katherine McKay hugged her tight, just as she had when Emma was a kid. Growing up, Emma was made to feel welcome and accepted, not by her own foster parents, but by the McKay family. "I know you're going to be a wonderful wife and mother to my first grandchild," Katherine continued, her gracious smile widening. "I am very excited about the baby, in case you can't tell. If you ever need help or advice, please promise you'll ask."

"I promise, Mrs. McKay."

"I'd be honored if you called me Mom."

Tears rushed into Emma eyes. The notion was so sweet and exactly what she needed to hear. "I will, from now on."

"That's good, honey." Katherine kissed her cheek and winked. "Now, I have to congratulate my son. He's made a wise choice."

After pictures were taken and the cocktail hour was observed, dinner was served on the veranda. A stone fireplace crackled and popped, adding ambience to an already elegant day. The wedding had been small, but with attention to detail. Leave it to Brooke to make all the last-minute arrangements. She was a dynamo, and Dylan spared no expense. It was a dream wedding as far as Emma was concerned.

As a disc jockey started setting up, Adam Chase, Dylan's best man, gave a toast. "To my neighbor and good friend Dylan," he said, holding up a flute of champagne. "May you enjoy the very same kind of happiness that I have found in Mia and my daughter, Rose. I'll admit it takes a very special young woman to get Dylan to the altar. He's avoided it for too many years, so to Emma, for making an honest man out of Dylan."

Laughter rippled through the crowd and cheers went up. Everyone but Emma sipped champagne. She opted for sparkling cider and enjoyed it down to the last drop. Dylan held her hand and nodded to Zane. To her surprise, the country crooner slid a chair over to the front of the veranda near the steps, took up his guitar and sat down. "If you all don't mind, I'd like to dedicate this song to my friend Dylan and his new bride, Emma. It's called 'This Stubborn Heart of Mine.' Dylan, feel free to dance this first dance with your wife. And no, this song wasn't written with you in mind, my friend, but if the shoe fits."

Another round of laughter hummed through the guests seated at their tables.

Dylan pulled Emma out onto the dance floor. "May I have this dance, sweetheart?"

And as Zane sang a sweet, soulful ballad, Dylan took her into his arms and twirled her around and around, his moves graceful and smooth. Emma was happier than she'd ever been, but still the notion of getting married to the most eligible bachelor on the planet at a beachfront mansion and having her own personal country superstar dedicate a song to her was surreal.

"You're quiet," Dylan said halfway through the dance.

"I'm...taking it all in. I'm not used to this much..."

"Attention?"

"Everything. It's...kind of perfect."

Dylan hugged her close as the song came to an end, whispering in her ear, "Kind of perfect? Just wait until tonight."

Emma snapped her head up, gazing into his incredibly seductive, amazingly clear blue eyes.

Maybe this marriage-to-Dylan thing would work out after all.

The light of a dozen candles twinkled all around Dylan's master bedroom, but nothing was brighter than the wedding ring he'd put on her finger today. The brilliance of the oval diamond surrounded by perfect smaller diamonds had stunned her into tears. The sweet scent of roses flavored the air, and her bouquet and flowers from the ceremony decorated the room as well, reminding her, as if she could forget, that Dylan was now her husband.

He'd succeeded in making her wedding day a fantasy come true. Now she faced him still wearing her wedding gown, feeling very much like Cinderella. Handsome in his tux, he gazed upon her, his mouth lifted in a smile. "Are you ready for the rest of our life?"

"Oh, yes."

He took her hands in his. "You were a beautiful bride

today, Emma, but now it's time to take this dress off and make you my wife."

Emma's body sang from his words and the anticipation of what the night would bring. "I'm ready."

She stood still as Dylan circled around her. He lifted the tiara from her head, the veil having long ago been removed. Cool air struck her back as he unfastened one tiny button after another. Her body warmed with each flick of his finger as he skimmed her skin. Once done, he spread the satiny material off her shoulders and kissed the back of her neck. A prickling feeling erupted there and followed the path of his hands as they moved the dress down her body. His gentle touch unleashed something wild in her, even as he took his time and took care with her dress. She stepped out of it and he gathered it up and set it over a chair. She stood before him in white lace panties, and as he approached her with fire in his eyes, he undid his bow tie, shed his white shirt and unbuckled his belt.

Pangs of impatient longing stormed her body. They'd gone the old-fashioned route and hadn't slept with each other since the day she'd agreed to become his wife. Now all that pent-up hunger was ready to explode and she couldn't remember ever feeling this way before. Not even on that first night, when she'd dragged Dylan on top of her during the blackout and they'd made reckless love. She knew the difference now. She understood why it seemed so different, answering a nagging question that had plagued her foggy memory. That time, she'd been desperate, eager to have a friend banish her fears. But this time, there was no desperation, only intense passion and true desire, and for her…love.

Dylan went down on his knees, caressed her rounded belly and placed a kiss there. His hands wound around to her butt. Holding her firm, he rested his head on her stomach, and after few reverent seconds, he rose and drew her close in his arms. "Welcome home, Emma," he whispered over her mouth. He lifted her up carefully and swung her around once. "This will have to take the place of carrying you over the threshold."

He laid her down on the bed.

"Thresholds are overrated," she whispered, reaching for him.

Dylan came to her then, climbing into the bed beside her. He leaned over and kissed her again and again until her head swam, her body ached and every nerve tingled. He cupped her breasts and made love to them with his mouth. Her hips swung up, her back bowing, the straining, pink peaks of her nipples sensitized and gloriously begging for more.

She wound her arms around his neck and caressed his shoulders, her palms flat against the breadth and strength of him, solid and sure and smooth. Her fingers played in the short blond spikes of hair, the military cut grown out some, and for the first time, she could say she possessed him as much as he possessed her.

"Ah," she cooed as his tongue licked at her and her entire body strained.

She had to touch more of him, to give as much as she was receiving.

She rolled him away and came up over him, kissing his lips and flattening her palms over his chest. His skin sizzled and she absorbed the heat, gloried in the rapid heartbeats nearly exploding from his chest. She kissed every part of it and a groan escaped his lips when she wandered down and hovered around his navel. His body pulsed, his breath caught. She wouldn't deny him what he wanted. She slipped her hand under his waistband and met with raw, powerful, hot silk.

"Emma," he rasped, almost in a plea.

She wound her hand around his full length and stroked

him, settling into a rhythm. Breath hissed from his mouth, as sensation after lusty sensation drove her on. She unzipped his trousers and he quickly removed his remaining garments. He lay naked before her. He was beautiful, broad where he should be broad, muscled in a jaw-dropping way and lean everywhere else. There wasn't bulk, but rugged, hard-won sculpture. She couldn't believe Dylan was her husband. How had she gotten so lucky?

She continued to caress his upper body as she dipped her head down and took him to a place that had both of them panting and hungry. Dylan's pleasured groans inspired her lusty assault. But then he grabbed her shoulders and backed her away. "Enough, sweetheart," he said. Yet his expression said anything but. His restraint was endearing and tender, even as both of them were nearly destroyed.

He rolled her under him and began the same kind of lusty assault, using his hand first and then his mouth. Pleas and moans slipped from her lips, over and over, until she reached the very edge of pleasure. Her release came fast and hard. It shattered her, split her in half and half again. It was powerful, explosive, the pinnacle of pleasure. When she came back to earth, Dylan's eyes were on her, watching her in awe. She couldn't pretend she wasn't immensely satisfied, nor would she want to. Dylan was an expert lover and she was attuned to him and his body.

She reached up to touch his face. He placed a kiss in the palm of her hand. She slipped her index finger into his mouth, and his hazy eyes widened, new energy erupting from him. No words had to be said. He growled and rose up over her. Within seconds, they were joined. She'd already gotten used to the feel of him inside her, the surge of power even as he took things slow, making sure she was comfortable. He couldn't possibly know how right this felt to her, how her body wrapped around his with possession and adoration. She had let go of her fears when she was in bed with him and gave of herself freely.

Dylan appreciated that—she witnessed it in his expression. She'd never tire of watching him make love to her, to see the complexities on his face, the hunger, the passion and raw desire. She watched him and he watched her and they moved in unison, his thrusts coming stronger now, filling her to the max, giving her another round of hot pleasure.

Dylan's guttural groan echoed in her ears. He reached as high as he could go. She, too, was there with him, arching up and taking that final earth-shattering climb. And then they exploded, sharing the precarious cliff and taking the fall together.

She gloried in the aftermath of his lovemaking and lay beside him, with no words, just feelings of total acceptance and tenderness and protection. If Dylan couldn't give her his love, at least she had that.

Dylan grasped her hand, lacing their fingers together. "My wife."

It was like a song to her ears. "My husband."

"After I finish this movie, I'd like to take you on a real honeymoon, Em. I have a place in Hawaii, or we can go to Europe. If the doctor says it's okay. If not, we can go somewhere locally. We'll find a hideout, maybe up north. A friend of mine has a cabin by a lake."

"Any of the above sounds wonderful."

"Really?"

"Really. I'm low maintenance, Dylan."

He turned onto his side to face her. Leaning on an elbow, he twirled a thick strand of her hair around his finger. "I love that about you, Em. You're easy."

"Hey!"

He laughed and the sound was beautiful and husky and

filled with joy. "I meant you're easy on the eyes, easy to get along with, easy…and fun."

"You think I'm fun?"

His eyes narrowed and his brows lifted in a villainous arch. "So fun," he said. He removed his hand from her hair and used his index finger to circle and tease the pink areola of her breast. Both nipples grew hard and pebbled. Gosh, she *was* so easy.

He bent and kissed both breasts and then sighed. "I should really let you get some sleep. You must be tired."

"Not all that much." Being in bed with him gave her energy and excited her as nothing else ever had. She ran her fingers through his mop of spiky, military-cut hair, grateful to have the freedom to do so—to touch him whenever she wanted. "Did you have something in mind?"

"You don't want to know what's on my mind." His mouth twitched, his smile wicked. But then he gathered her up in his arms and covered them both with the sheets. "Sleep, Emma. I'm not going to wear you out tonight."

"Darn."

He chuckled.

She rested her head on his chest and closed her eyes.

She'd have a lifetime of nights like this with Dylan.

She couldn't imagine anything better.

Cameras flashed like crazy as a dozen photographers on the red carpet of the premiere of Dylan's romantic comedy, *A New Light*, caught sight of him with Emma as they exited the limousine. Just one look at her and they started tossing out questions.

"Who's your date, Dylan?"

"You've been holding out on us!"

"Are you going to be a father? Is she your baby mama?"

Dylan hugged Emma closer, his arm tight around her waist. She looked gorgeous in an organza gown he'd had tailored just for her. Her belly bump couldn't be hidden any longer, but the Empire style of the dress and the floral colors showcased her skin tone and her pregnancy in a beautiful way. "Sorry, honey. This is my life."

"It's okay, Dylan," she said. "You warned me about this."

Selfishly, he'd wanted Emma by his side tonight. Hiding the news of his marriage and the upcoming birth of his baby was proving harder each day. He'd talked to his publicist and they'd both decided that tonight during the movie premiere would be the best time to introduce Emma as his new wife to the world. At least the media would get the scoop from him, and not have to speculate or make up lies to fill their pages.

So right there on the red carpet, with a crowd gathering and the media in his face, Dylan proudly announced, "I'd like to introduce my new bride, Emma McKay. We were married last week in a small ceremony on the beach. Emma and I have known each other since my days in Ohio. I'm happy to say we'll be parents by early next spring. She's an amazing woman and we're both thrilled to have a baby on the way."

"Is it a boy or a girl?" someone shouted.

"We don't know that yet."

"When did you get married?"

"Last Saturday."

"What is Emma's maiden name?"

"Bloom," Emma answered, and Dylan slid her an appreciative glance. She wasn't going to let him take all the heat. She'd have to learn to deal with the media and it might as well start now.

The reporters angled their microphones her way now. "How do you feel marrying the world's most eligible bachelor, Mrs. McKay?"

"I've never really thought of him that way. He's just

Dylan to me. His sister and I have been best friends since grade school."

"Are you going to—"

"Please," Dylan said, putting up a hand. "My publicist will issue a statement in the morning that will answer all of your questions. The movie is about to begin and my wife and I would like to enjoy the premiere together. Thank you."

With bodyguards in front and behind him, Dylan moved through the crowd keeping Emma right by his side. It wouldn't be long now. He'd make headlines and their secret marriage would be a thing of the past. He felt the loss in the pit of his stomach. He loved the anonymity, the intimacy of having Emma all to himself these past few days. Now the news would be out and their lives would change, once again. Lack of privacy was a penalty of fame and he accepted it graciously for himself, but there was Emma to consider now. And their baby.

"You handled yourself pretty damn well, Em," he whispered in her ear.

"I winged it."

"I like a woman who can think on her feet."

He took her hand and entered the iconic movie theatre. It was one of the last few truly historic theatres in Los Angeles, with its plush red velvet seats, sculpted walls and miles and miles of curtains. "Well, what do you think?"

Her pretty green eyes took all of it in. He wanted so badly for Emma to experience the same sort of awe that he did. Moviemaking was in his blood. He was producing more and planned to continue to direct other projects in the future.

"I've never seen anything like this, Dylan. I can picture this theatre back in the day. All those classic movies flashing on that big screen. The actors, directors and producers who've taken their seats here. It's all so…grand."

He smiled. She got it. Emma *was* an amazing woman. He hadn't lied to the press today. He was falling for her and it didn't scare him, or make him nervous. Brooke had said Renee had scarred him for life, but maybe it had taken a woman like Emma to make him realize he was completely healed.

He kissed her cheek then, and she glanced up at him. "What was that for?"

"Can't a man kiss his wife just because?"

She smiled and his heart warmed. He took her hand again. "C'mon, Mrs. McKay, there are bigwigs who would love to meet you. I guess we should get this over with before we take our seats."

"I'm down with that," she said. And he cracked up.

So far, marriage to Emma had been anything but dull.

Nine

"Honey, I'm home," Dylan called out as he entered his house on Monday afternoon. He'd always wanted to say that, but now that he had, his wife was nowhere to be found. He was home fairly early from the set, though. He took a look at his phone and saw that she'd texted him.

I'll be home a little late. Behind on work today. See you at 6ish.

Dylan was disappointed. Each day, he looked forward to coming home to Emma. He'd find her doing pregnancy exercises or poring over a book of baby names or helping Maisey make a healthy dinner for the two of them. Each day also brought him closer to fatherhood, something he discovered he could hardly wait for now. He and Emma had plans to design the nursery. It would be just another few weeks before they found out the sex of their baby.

"Emma's not here, Dylan," Maisey said, greeting him

in the hallway off the kitchen. "I've got dinner ready. It's in the oven, keeping warm. If you don't need me, I'll be heading home."

"Thanks, Maisey. Sure, go on home. I might as well take a run. Emma's going to be a little late."

"Have a good evening, then," Maisey said.

He waved goodbye and dashed up the stairs to change his clothes.

A few minutes later he was on the beach, the shoreline nearly empty as he began to jog. He started out at a good warm-up pace and did at least half a mile before he kicked it into higher gear. It was cloudy and cool, making the run more enjoyable. What had started out as a chore—a fitness program for his role as a Navy SEAL—had become a ritual lately, one he enjoyed. His runs helped him think, helped him work out his upcoming movie scenes and gave him a way to reflect on his life. He'd asked his bodyguards to keep their distance. They had trouble keeping up anyway and he loved the idea of solitude on the beach.

Once he got going, his mind clicked a mile a minute and he made mental tallies of his thoughts as they rushed by, one after the other. And as he ran, he thought back on the night of the blackout. If only he could remember his last day with Roy…

And then images popped into his mind. He was sitting in his house, drinking with his buddy Roy. He was laughing and they were talking about the upcoming stunt and then his phone rang. It was Emma. She was freaking out and slurring her words. She was drunk. She'd said there was a blackout in the city. Dylan's lights were still on. The power outage hadn't reached the beach. He still had full power. Emma was looking for Brooke to come pick her up. Dylan immediately told her to stay put, and he'd come get her.

Dylan slowed his pace, thinking back, happy to have

the memory return. To see Roy in his mind, who looked so much like him they could've been brothers. To remember their laughter and then…then he remembered Roy getting pissed at him. "Dylan, you're in no shape to drive. You've worked your way halfway through that bottle of Scotch. Give me your keys. I'll go get Emma."

The scene played out in his head. He'd been stubborn with Roy, but when he'd tried to rise to go get Emma, the room began to spin and he'd sat back down.

Holy crap.

He came to an abrupt halt on the beach, his feet digging into the sand. His limbs wouldn't hold him; they were like rubber now. He dropped to his knees, his face in his hands. He saw himself handing Roy the keys to his car.

Dylan's face crumpled. Tears burned behind his eyes.

Images that he'd prayed would return now haunted him. He'd let Roy pick up Emma that night, because his friend had been right—Dylan was in no shape to get Emma. Roy picked Emma up that night. Roy…made love to Emma. It was Roy all along.

And the next day on the set, right before Roy got into that car, they'd argued. About Emma. Roy told him what happened and said he'd let things get carried away with her that night. Dylan had gotten hot under the collar, accusing him of taking advantage of Emma. And minutes later, the car exploded, with Roy inside. A fire cloud went up and Dylan was hit with shrapnel.

Dylan dug his fingers into the sand to keep from collapsing entirely. His head was down as he rehashed his thoughts, trying to contradict what he knew in his heart to be true. A woman walked over to him, the only other jogger on the beach beside his bodyguard. "Are you okay?"

Dylan nodded. "I'm…okay," he told the woman. "J-just need a little break."

He warned Dan off. The woman wasn't a threat, but he

might never be okay again. His whole future had been destroyed. The baby Emma carried wasn't his. He was married, but his wife had lied to him. Was it all a ruse? Had she deceived him on purpose? How could she not know what man she was screwing?

The woman walked off slowly and Dylan waited until she was out of sight before he tried to rise. His legs barely held his weight. His entire body was numb from neck to toes. His head, unfortunately, was clear for the first time in weeks, and the clarity was enough to squeeze his gut into tight knots and suck the life out of him.

He walked along the beach, feeling broken, each step leading to his house slower, less deliberate. He was more broken than when Renee had dumped him.

More broken than at any other time in his life.

Emma tossed her purse down on the living room sofa and went in search of Dylan. His car was in the garage; he must be home. She couldn't wait to see him. They'd talked about planning the nursery and she'd brought home paint samples of blues and pinks, greens and lavenders. The sex of the baby would determine the color themes, and they'd find that out pretty soon. At least they could narrow down their options, if Dylan wasn't too tired tonight to help her make some selections.

Unless he had other things on his mind, like taking her to bed early. Lately, they'd been doing a lot of going to bed early and *not* sleeping.

She smiled as she walked the downstairs hallway, popping her head inside rooms in search of him. A delicious aroma led her to the kitchen. She opened the oven door and peered at the meal Maisey had left for them. The garlicky scent of chicken cacciatore wafted in the air.

She closed the oven door when she heard Dylan enter from the beach. He was dressed in a tight nylon tank and black running shorts. Her heart skipped a beat, he was so gorgeous.

"Hi," she said. "How was your run?"

Dylan didn't answer right away. He headed to the bar in the living room. She followed behind him, noting the lack of pep in his step. His shoulders slumped and he was extremely quiet. "Dylan, are you all right?"

Silence again. She waited as he poured himself a drink of some sort of expensive whiskey and gulped it down in one shot. "Did you have a bad day?"

He looked at her then, his face ashen, his cloudy blue eyes dim and lifeless. There was something so bleak in the way he looked at her. "You could say that. I got my memory back."

"Oh? Isn't that a good thing, Dylan? It's what you've been hoping for."

"Sit down, Emma," he said, his voice ice-cold. He pointed to the sofa and she sat. He poured another shot of alcohol and took a seat opposite her, as if...as if he needed to keep his distance. Her heart pounded now as a sense of dread threatened to overwhelm her. Something was very wrong.

"I remember it all, Emma. The night of the blackout, the call you made to me."

She nodded and blinked her eyes several times. Dylan's teeth were gnashing. He had a grip on his temper, but just barely. "I didn't come for you that night," he said, looking down at his whiskey glass. "It wasn't me. It was Roy."

"What do you mean it was Roy? You came for me. I called you looking for Brooke and you...you—"

He was shaking his head adamantly. "I was drinking with Roy that night. Roy didn't think I was sober enough to drive. He took my keys out of my hand and picked you up."

"No, he didn't." Emma's voice registered a higher pitch.

"Yes, he did."

"But…but…that would mean—" Emma bounced up from the sofa. This wasn't right. This wasn't the truth. Dylan had it wrong. It was all wrong. "Dylan, that can't be true. It can't be."

Dylan rose, too, his blue eyes hard and dark as midnight. "It is true. Are you denying it? Are you going to tell me you don't remember sleeping with Roy?"

"That's exactly what I'm saying. I didn't sleep with Roy. I wouldn't do that."

Dylan stood firm, poured whiskey down his gullet and swallowed. "But that's exactly what you did. You slept with Roy, and after he died, you told me the baby was mine."

"I…uh, oh no! I didn't. I mean, if I did, I didn't know it was him. I wouldn't do that, Dylan. I didn't lo—"

"Which is it, Emma?" Dylan asked, in a voice she didn't recognize. He sounded harsh and bitter. "You knew you were screwing Roy, or you didn't?"

Tears welled in her eyes, the truth slapping her hard in the face, but it was Dylan's mean-spirited words that hurt the most. How could she come to terms with what Dylan was implying? She thought she was making love to Dylan that night. Even in her drunken state, even as scared as she was, she would've never knowingly slept with Roy.

Yet he looked enough like Dylan to fool his fans. And he'd come for her in Dylan's car. Because of the blackout and her blurry head, it could have been Roy after all. But she never once thought he wasn't Dylan coming to her rescue.

But Dylan didn't believe that. And he probably never would.

Her memory sharpened to that night and all the things the man she thought was Dylan had said to dissuade her. *You've got this wrong. It's a mistake.* Those pleas made sense now, because she wasn't imploring Dylan to stay with her, it had been Roy all along. Roy who had held her tight and comforted her, Roy who had finally given in when she pressed him to make love to her. No wonder there were differences in Dylan's lovemaking since that first night. She couldn't put her finger on it before and blamed it on her drunken state. But now she knew why it had felt different making love to blackout Dylan versus the real deal.

The truth pounded her head. The truth hammered her heart. The truth made her stomach ache.

"I'm carrying Roy's baby," she said, her voice flat, monotone, as if saying it out loud would make it sink in. She trembled visibly, her arms going limp, her legs weakening. She wanted so badly to sit back down and pretend this wasn't happening. But she couldn't. She mustered her strength, though she bled inside for the life she might have had with Dylan. The bright future she'd only just come to believe in had been snuffed out forever.

She should've known her happiness wouldn't last. When had she really been happy? Only lately, working with Brooke and starting their business. "I can hardly believe this."

When she lifted her eyes, wondering if there was a way around this, a way to make this right, a way to preserve the goodness that had come from marrying Dylan, she met his hard, glowering stare. He blamed her for all this. He didn't believe her. He thought she'd betrayed him.

Like Renee.

Nothing was further from the truth, but it didn't matter. She saw it in the firm set of his jaw. Ice flowed in his veins now. He was convinced she had deceived him.

She faced facts. She wouldn't be Dylan's wife much longer. She'd file for an annulment and wouldn't take a dime of the prenup Dylan's lawyer insisted she sign. She didn't want his money. She had only hoped one day to earn his love.

"I'll pack my things and be gone in the morning, Dylan. Have your attorney contact me. I don't want anything from you. I'm sorry about this. More than you could ever know."

"Emma?"

"Don't worry about me, Dylan," she said, biting her lip, holding back tears. This news crushed her, but she didn't want his pity. She'd never wanted anyone's pity. "I'll land on my feet, as usual. We both know you only married me because of the baby and now that we know the b-baby isn't y-yours…" She couldn't finish her thought. She'd been robbed of the joy of carrying Dylan's child. She'd love her baby, but now her child would never know its father and never have the love of both parents.

Dylan was quiet for a long time, staring at her. His anger seemed to have disappeared, replaced by something in his eyes looking very much like pain. This wasn't easy for him, either, but she had no sympathy for him right now. She was in shock, devastated beyond anything she could ever imagine.

"I'll make sure the baby wants for nothing," he said.

She shook her head stubbornly. "Please, Dylan…don't. I really don't need anything from you. I'll manage on my own. Goodbye." She turned away and kept her head high as she made for the door.

"Emma, wait!"

She stopped, her tears flooding her face. She didn't pivot around. "W-what?"

"I'm…sorry for the way things turned out."

"I know. I am, too."

Then she dashed out of the room.

Dylan sat in his dressing trailer, on the studio lot, feeling uncomfortable in his customized honey wagon, staring at his lines for this evening's scenes and repeating the words over and over in his mind. Nothing stuck. It was as if he was reading hieroglyphics. He hadn't been able to concentrate since Emma had packed her bags and left home two days ago. Brooke had told him that Emma had returned to her apartment. She still had time left on her lease. And his ears still burned from his sister's brutal tongue-lashing that had followed. Brooke had defended Emma and basically called him a jerk for letting her leave that way.

He'd been hard on her. But how on earth could a woman make love to a man and not know who he was? The idea seemed ludicrous to him and yet Brooke had believed her without question and insisted that a man worthy of Emma should have, too. Which told him maybe they weren't meant to be together. Maybe the marriage had been a mistake all along.

Keep telling yourself that, pal.

He'd tried to convince himself he'd done the right thing in letting her go. He didn't love Emma. She was a friend, a bed partner and his wife for a little while longer, but he couldn't deny the reason he'd married her. The only reason he'd married her. He thought she'd been carrying his child and he'd wanted to provide for both of them.

Now the loss seemed monumental. He'd fallen in love with the baby he presumed was his and the notion of fatherhood. He'd begun to see his life differently. Having a family had always been a dream, something he'd wanted sometime in the future.

Now that future was obscure. He was more confused than ever.

He missed Emma. And not just in his bed, though that was pretty spectacular. He missed coming home to her at night, seeing her pretty green eyes and smiles when he walked through the door. He missed the infectious joy on her face when they'd talked about the baby and fixing up the nursery.

All of that was lost to him now.

Someone pounded on the trailer door. He rose from his black leather lounger and peered out the window. It was Jeff, one of his bodyguards. Opening the door, he took a look at the guy's face and the hand he held over his stomach. "Hey, Jeff. What's up? You're not looking too good."

Which was an understatement. His skin had turned a lovely shade of avocado. "Must've been something I ate. I'm sorry, Mr. McKay. I've put in for my replacement. He'll be here in an hour."

"Don't worry about it, Jeff. Go home. Do you think you can drive?"

He nodded and the slight movement turned him grass green. "I'll wait for Dan to get here."

"No, you won't. You can barely stand up. You go home and take care of yourself. There's plenty of security around here. I'll be fine and the replacement will be here soon. You said so yourself."

"I shouldn't."

"Go. That's an order."

Jeff finally nodded. Gripping his stomach, he walked off and then made a mad dash for the studio bathroom. Poor guy.

Dylan grabbed his script and took a seat again. He had to learn his lines or they'd all be here until after midnight. Sharpening his focus, he blocked out everything plaguing his mind and concentrated on the scene, reciting the words over and over and finally getting a grasp of them. He closed his eyes, as he always did, to get a mental picture of how the scene would play out—where his marks were and what movements he would make throughout.

The caustic scent of smoke wafted to his nostrils and he was instantly reminded of the day Roy died. The memory of the blast and the smoke that followed had now fully returned. It was so strong that every time he came upon a group of people smoking on their coffee breaks, he'd relive that moment.

He shook it off, determined to run through his lines one more time before rehearsal was called. But his throat began to burn and he coughed and coughed. That's when he noticed a cloud of gray haze coming toward him from the back end of the trailer. Seconds later he saw flames darting up from his bedroom. Right before his eyes, the fire jumped to the bed and wardrobe racks. Within moments, his entire bedroom was engulfed in flames. He ran for the trailer door and turned the knob. The door moved half an inch, but something was blocking it from opening from the outside. He pushed against it with his full weight. It wouldn't budge. Peering out the window, he looked around and shouted for help.

Flames lit the entire back end of the trailer, the heat sweltering, the smoke choking his lungs. Dylan darted quick glances around the trailer, looking for something sharp to break the small kitchen window. He grabbed his wardrobe chair and shoved the legs against the window above the sink with all his might. Once, twice and finally the window shattered. He broke out as much glass as possible with the chair and then dived headfirst, tucking and rolling his body the way Roy had taught him.

"Ow!" He met with gravel, landing hard, and instantly sucked fresh air into his lungs. The flames were blazing now and he struggled to his feet. He had to get away before the whole thing blew.

Members of the movie crew had now seen the fire and came running over. Two of them grabbed his arms and dragged him away from the trailer. In the distance, he heard sirens blasting.

"Are you okay?" one of the crew members asked.

"Dylan, talk to me." He recognized the assistant director's voice. "Say something."

"I'm...okay."

"Mr. McKay," another voice said, "we're getting you to safety. Hold on."

Once they were fifty feet from the trailers, a blanket was tossed onto the ground and he was laid down. Blood oozed out from scrapes on his body and his clothes were torn from the leap out the window. The stench of smoke and ash permeated the area. Within seconds, the studio medic arrived and assessed him. An oxygen mask was put over his mouth and soon a fresh swell of air flowed into his throat and down his lungs.

"Take slow, normal breaths," the medic said. "You got out in time. Looks like you're going to be fine."

Dylan tried to sit up but he was gently laid back down. "Not yet. You're not burned, but you do have abrasions on your arms and legs. You banged up your face pretty good, too. An ambulance is on the way."

He groaned. "Someone tried to kill me," he said.

"We figured. Those honey wagons don't just light themselves on fire. And we noticed how your door was blocked with a solid beam of wood from the Props Department. The police are on their way."

"I can't believe you didn't call me last night," Brooke was saying softly near his hospital bed. Concern over him was the only thing keeping her from unleashing her wrath.

Accompanied by a police escort, he'd been taken here for observation and to clean up his wounds last night after the fire, and decided not to call his sister until dawn. She didn't need to worry about him and lose sleep over this, but he had to call her before the story hit the morning news.

"There's a freaking police guard outside your room, Dylan. I had to practically strip down to my panties to get in here to see you."

"I bet that was fun," he said, winking the eye that wasn't bruised.

"Ha-ha. Well, at least you haven't lost your sense of humor. But this is serious, brother," Brooke said, her eyes misting up. "You're all bandaged and look like a train wreck. God, I don't want to lose you."

Brooke had a blunt way of putting things, but he knew what was in her heart. He took her hand and squeezed. "I don't want to be lost. They'll find whoever did this, Brooke. It has to be someone with access to the studio lot."

Brooke frowned. "That narrows it down to about a thousand or so."

"I'll be fine, Brooke. I'm going home with a police escort this afternoon."

Dylan flopped back against his pillow. A part of him was disappointed that Emma hadn't shown up here. Had Brooke told her? He couldn't ask, because then his well-meaning sister would give him another lecture. Emma would find out soon enough, if she looked at a newspaper, logged onto the internet or turned on a television set.

He'd already spoken to his manager, his agent and his publicist. They were taking care of business for him. He was set to be released from the hospital later today. Not that he wasn't grateful to the staff, but if one more person told him how lucky he'd been last night, he would scream. Someone was out to kill him. A crazed fan? Some lunatic who wanted fifteen minutes of fame? Or was it someone he knew? A tremor passed through him at the thought. Who hated him enough to want him dead?

He'd been questioned extensively by the police last night and he'd told the detectives everything that had happened that day. They'd been thorough in their questioning, and unfortunately, Dylan was still at a loss as to who might want to murder him.

"I called Emma and told her what happened to you,"

Brooke said, her chin tilted at a defiant angle. "She's your wife, Dylan, and has a right to know. At least she won't hear about it first on the morning news. She's pretty messed up right now."

"I didn't mean to cause her pain, Brooke." Yet that's exactly what he'd done. She was pregnant and his wife, and even though the baby wasn't his, he should've treated her better than he had. The fact that he wanted to see her, wanted her to come just so he could look into her pretty face and be comforted, made him question everything. "Please tell her that I'm all right and that she can talk to me anytime, but honestly, Brooke, until they figure out who's doing this it's best that you and Emma stay away from me."

Brooke opened her mouth to protest just as the nurse walked in. God, he'd never been so happy to have a medical procedure in his life. "Time to get your vitals and check on your bandages, Mr. McKay," the woman said. "If you don't mind stepping out of the room, please?" she asked of Brooke.

"Of course. I'll see you a little later, Dylan," she said, blowing him a kiss. "Be safe."

By five in the afternoon, Dylan was home. Both of his bodyguards were on the premises, keeping an eye out for anything unusual. His first order of business was to go through the past few months of fan mail. He'd had Rochelle skim the letters back when suspicions had first been raised about the cause of Roy's accident, but now that he was certain someone was out to get him he sat behind his office desk and read through each one. His cell phone rang and he sighed when he saw the caller's name pop up on the screen.

"Hello, Renee."

"Dylan, thank God you're all right. I heard about the fire at the studio." Renee sounded breathless.

"I'm fine. I got out safely."

"Oh, Dylan, I hope I'm wrong about this, but I think I know who's out to get you."

Dylan bolted upright in his seat. "Go on."

"My ex-husband is a maniac. I mean, Craig's gone off the deep end lately. He's been trying to get custody of my kids for months now. A few weeks ago, he stormed into the house, screaming at me. He found out about the money you've been sending to help us. Money he thinks is keeping him from getting his hands on the kids. Dylan, I don't know for sure he's behind it. As you might know, he… he…has a background in film and stunt work. He might be working at the studio. And I know he hates you."

"Why does he hate me? Aside from the money?"

"I guess he's always been jealous of you. He knows about our history, Dylan. And, well, he got it in his head that I'm still in love with you. That I compared him to you and he always came up short. I don't know… I guess I did. I've always regretted the way things ended between us. But I never thought he'd go to such extremes. Like I said, I'm not sure…but my gut is telling me it's him."

"Okay, Renee. Sit tight. I'll call the police. They'll want to question you. And, Renee, thanks."

"Of course, Dylan. I couldn't stand it if anything happened to you. Be careful."

"I will."

After hanging up with Renee, he called Detective Brice and relayed the information about Craig Lincoln. He gave him Renee's address and phone number and Brice thought it was a good lead. If her ex was involved, he wouldn't be hard to track down if he worked on the studio lot. Even if he'd used an alias, crews would recognize his face.

Dylan's heart raced. He hoped Renee was right and that Lincoln would be caught. A man like that could be dangerous to her and her kids, too, if he would resort to murder.

Dylan ran a hand down his face.

He needed a drink. As he headed toward the bar, one of his bodyguards entered the house and approached him. "Here you go, Mr. McKay." Dan handed him today's mail.

Dylan wasn't allowed outside to pick up his own mail. He was trapped in his house, a prisoner to the whims of a killer. The studio had shut down all production until the investigation concluded.

"Thanks." He poured himself a whiskey as Dan headed back outside.

He took his mail over to the kitchen table and sat down. Thumbing through ads and bills, he came across an unmarked letter. There was no postal stamp or address on the envelope. It simply read "McKay."

His gut constricted. His breathing stopped for an instant. There was something about this that didn't pass the smell test. He should turn the letter over to Detective Brice, but that could take hours.

It could be nothing or...

His hands shaking, he peeled the envelope open carefully and unfolded the short note.

"You took my family, now I'll take yours."

Dylan froze, staring at the threatening words. Momentary fear held him hostage. His mind raced in a dozen directions and came to a grinding halt. Emma.

His wife.

She could be in danger.

And Brooke, too.

His sister.

He had to get to them. "Dan! Jeff! Get in here, now!"

Ten

Emma sat at her desk at Parties-To-Go working on the numbers for an upcoming wedding. It was after five in the evening, but she'd rather be here than in her lonely apartment. She went through the motions robotically with none of her usual enthusiasm. Debbie Downer had nothing on her. She'd sent Wendy and Rocky home early. She needed to dive into her work with no distractions. She'd been on the receiving end of their sympathetic glances and worried expressions all afternoon. No one knew about her breakup with Dylan yet, aside from Brooke, but her employees were astute and of course had heard about the murder attempt on her husband's life. She was worried sick about Dylan, and missed him so much. She'd spent a good part of the night at the hospital waiting on word of Dylan. Once she knew he was doing well and they expected a full recovery, she'd breathed a sigh of relief and left the waiting room. She didn't want to bring him any bad memories by showing up. He didn't need a confrontation and he'd made himself clear about how he felt about her and their situation.

Resting a hand on her tummy, she closed her eyes and then…the baby kicked! It was more like a flutter, a butterfly taking flight, than an actual kick, but oh, her heart pinged with joy. This was amazing and so absolutely miraculous. A miracle that should be shared and treasured, and her mind went back to Dylan and how happy he'd been thinking he was going to be a father.

She couldn't dwell on what wasn't to be anymore. She was on her own, and her focus had to stay finely tuned to the child she carried.

From now on, she wouldn't be totally alone.

The back door jingled. She stopped to listen. Someone was trying to get inside. Her heart raced and she rose from her desk. She did a mental tally: the part-timers had been sent home, Brooke was on a special date with Royce. She heard more jingling and a couple of loud bangs as if someone was pressing their body against the door, struggling to get in. She glanced around, picked up a kid's baseball bat left over from a party and strode to the door just as it burst open.

"Brooke! You scared me to death."

"Sorry," her friend said. "The dang lock keeps sticking. We've got to get that fixed."

"I wasn't expecting anyone. Aren't you supposed to be with Royce tonight?"

Brooke shut the door and glimpsed the baseball bat in Emma's hand. That's when Emma noticed the hollow look on her friend's face. "What is it?" Bile rose in her throat. "Is it Dylan? Is he okay? Did something else happen to him?"

"Dylan's fine, honey. I've talked to him three times earlier today. He's been released from the hospital and had a police escort home. There's no damage to his lungs and his bruises are superficial. He told me he wanted to rest. Translation—stop bugging him. And I got the hint."

"Oh, thank God. But he's all alone there now. Are the police watching him?"

"He's got two bodyguards round-the-clock and you know about the added security he has around his house. He told me not to worry."

"How can you not? Someone tried to kill him."

"I know. Freaks me out." Brooke took the bat out of her hand. "Must've freaked you out, too."

"Yeah, well…this whole thing is so scary."

Brooke took a shaky breath. Her eyes were rimmed with red. She moved into the office and sat down. Emma did the same. "So why are you here? Shouldn't you be with Royce tonight?" she asked carefully.

"Royce and I are over."

Emma's brows lifted. She didn't expect this. "What do you mean, you're over?"

"I walked out on him, Em."

"Why?"

Brooke sighed. "When Royce said he had something special he wanted to give me, I thought, oh my goodness. A key to his place maybe, or a piece of jewelry, maybe even a ring. I let my imagination run wild. I mean, come on, he knows what I've been through this month with Dylan. And he actually used that. He told me he knew I was worried about my brother and that he'd probably have time on his hands, now that the studio shut down production, so—"

"He didn't!"

"Oh, yes, he did. He gave me three scripts for Dylan to look at. Scripts that were his pride and joy. He said he'd been working on them for two years and he knew Dylan would love them and want to produce and star in the movies once he read them."

"Oh, Brooke, I'm so sorry. You must've been..."

"Pissed and hurt and most of all shocked. That's the part that gets me. I was shocked and I shouldn't have been. I really thought he was the one guy I could count on, who didn't want to get close to me because of my brother. He's in finance, a Wall Street type. I didn't think there was a creative bone in his body. And I loved that about him. I mean...I really thought... Oh, I shouldn't feel sorry for myself. Not in front of you."

"Are you saying I have bigger problems than you?" Emma leaned in to give Brooke a goofy smile. "Is that what you're telling me?"

"No. Yes. You know what I mean."

"I do know. So, we're both hurting right now."

Brooke nodded. "But I'm not going to let that idiot ruin my life. I'm not going to fall to pieces."

"Promise?"

"I...uh...well, maybe a little crumble." Her voice shook.

Emma took Brooke's hand and they sat there for a few minutes, holding on to each other and trying not to cry.

"You know what?" Brooke said. "We should get out of here. They're showing a special screening of *The Notebook* at the Curtis Cinema down the street. If we're going to cry, it might as well be over our favorite chick flick. Let's go and then have a late dinner. Just like old times."

"I like the sound of that. No more moping."

"Pinkie swear?"

They locked their pinkie fingers, just as they did when they were kids. "Pinkie swear."

"We'll shut down our cell phones and have a night free of worries."

"Shouldn't you check in on Dylan?" Emma asked.

"I will, as soon as the movie ends. Deal?"

"It's a deal," Emma said, her spirits lifting for the first time in two days.

* * *

"Damn this traffic." Dylan sat shotgun as Dan navigated the streets leading to Emma's apartment, cutting in and out of the lineup of cars on Pacific Coast Highway whenever he could. "It would have to be the busiest time of day."

After Dylan had called Detective Brice about the threatening letter, he was ordered to stay put at home. That had lasted only half an hour. His nerves had been bouncing out of his skin and there was only so much pacing he could do. How could he sit around and wait when Emma's and Brooke's lives could be in danger? Neither of them were answering their phones and their part-time employees confirmed they didn't have an event tonight. He'd left countless messages at their homes and at the office, which had gone straight to voice mail. His texts hadn't been answered, either.

He'd moved fast then, ordering Dan to drive, while Jeff followed behind, both in black SUVs. The first stop was Emma's place. She should've been home from work by now. Dusk had settled in, a gray cloud cover shutting out the lingering light.

His unanswered voice mails put fear in his heart. Emma was in danger, he was sure of it. That creep Lincoln couldn't get at him after two failed attempts and now he was going after his unsuspecting pregnant wife.

Emma.

As soon as he'd read that damning note, his first thoughts were of her and the child she carried. *She* was his family now, along with the baby. That child was his best friend's baby, an innocent in all this, and someone who deserved to be loved. Dylan was ashamed of himself for turning away from Roy's baby. He hadn't been thinking clearly. He'd felt the same sense of deceit and betrayal from Emma as he had from Renee. It had all been too much; his hopes and dreams had been paralyzed and he'd lashed out at the injustice, but none of it was Emma's doing. He believed that now. Deep down he'd always known Emma wouldn't resort to that kind of devastating deceit.

Good God, had his heart been so hardened that he couldn't recognize true love when it slammed him in the face? Had it taken a threat to her life to make him realize what she meant to him?

He was in love with her.

And the very thought of Emma and the baby being hurt was too hard to imagine.

"Hurry, Dan. I can't let anything happen to her."

Once they finally reached Emma's apartment building, Dan parked on the street and Dylan threw open the car door.

"Wait!" Dan ordered. "You can't go running in there. It might be a trap."

Jeff raced over, blocking him from getting out of the car.

"Then what are we going to do?"

"The smart thing is to wait for the cops to arrive," Jeff said.

Dylan shook his head. "Think of another option."

His cell phone rang and he immediately picked up. "Dylan, it's me."

"Brooke, thank God. I've been trying to reach you. Are you okay?"

"I'm fine."

He got out of the car now, listening to the sweet sound of his sister's voice. "Where are you and is Emma with you?"

"Yes, I'm with Emma. But first tell me, are you okay? I panicked when I saw a dozen missed calls from you. Your texts said Emma and I were in danger?"

"Yeah, you might be. The creep who tried to kill me sent a note saying he was going after my family. You're sure Emma's fine?"

"Uh, well, she will be. We were at the movies and she started feeling weak. When I looked at her face, she had gone completely white. I didn't let her argue with me. I drove her straight to the emergency room. We're at Saint Joseph's."

Dylan stopped breathing. God, if she lost the baby, he'd never forgive himself. He loved the both of them with all of his heart. "What's wrong with her, Brooke? It isn't the baby, is it?"

"The baby's fine. Emma's been under a lot of stress lately. She hasn't been eating and, well, she's been upset and crying lately. She's dehydrated. Could've been really dangerous, but we caught it in time. They're pumping her full of fluids now and the doctor said she's going to be okay."

Dylan ran his hand down his face. "Okay." He heard the relief in his own voice. "I'll be there in a few minutes. And I'm calling Detective Brice to put a guard on her door. Don't leave the hospital under any circumstances."

"That won't be necessary." At the gruff-sounding voice, Dylan turned and found Detective Brice approaching, a frown on his face that would scare the devil. "You don't listen very well, do you, McKay? You almost blew our cover coming here."

"Brooke," Dylan said into the phone. "I'll call you back in a sec. Just stay with Emma." He hung up the phone, surprised to see Brice. "What do you mean?"

"We had the apartment under surveillance since this morning. Your sister's place, too, just as a precaution. Sure enough, we found Lincoln tonight, lurking in the bushes in the courtyard. He's in our custody now and he's not going to be able to harm anyone ever again."

The courtyard gates opened and Dylan faced the man who'd murdered Roy. Blood ran hot in his veins. Here was the man who'd tried to kill him twice, who was lying in wait to harm his pregnant wife. Lincoln was in handcuffs, two officers flanking him and three others following behind. All Dylan wanted to do was meet him on equal turf and beat the stuffing out of him. He took a step toward him and Brice got in his way, his hand firm on Dylan's chest. "McKay, don't be an idiot."

Lincoln's eyes bugged out of his skull when he saw Dylan. "You sonofabitch! You home wrecker! You don't deserve to live!" Lincoln was out of his mind, wrestling with the officers restraining him. "You think you can take my kids, my wife. Ruin my life! You hotshot, you'll live to regret this!"

Two of the other officers grabbed Lincoln, restraining his arms and maneuvering him into the squad car that had pulled up behind Jeff's SUV.

Dylan shook his head. "He killed Roy."

"He'll pay for that," Brice said. "And all the other crimes he's committed."

Dylan nodded. "Yeah."

"He's deranged, but something set him off. You said over the phone his ex-wife called you."

"Yeah, she was the one who figured it out after she saw the headlines today about the attempt on my life. I don't know too many details about her life, just that we were close once and that more recently she was near poverty, trying to raise her kids and keep her ex away from them. I've been sending her money to keep food on the table for her children. That was my crime. That's why he hates me."

"He's going away for a long time." Brice patted Dylan on the back. "It's over now, McKay. You can go on being a superhero, *on film*," he said, giving him a teasing smirk.

"There's only one person I want to think of me that way."

And unfortunately, it was the one person he'd hurt the most.

"Are we through here?" he asked.

"I'm going to need your statement," Brice said.

"Can I give it to you later tonight? I just found out my wife's in the hospital and I want to see her as soon as I can."

"Sorry to hear that." Brice puffed out a breath. "Okay. Sure. Go check on your wife. You both had some close calls lately. I hope she's going to be okay."

Dylan hoped so, too. "Thanks." Dylan shook the detective's hand. "I appreciate what you've done for my family. Your team did excellent work."

"It's all in a day's work. Sometimes things go sideways, but this one turned out in the best way possible. No one got hurt today. I'm proud of these guys."

Dylan left the detective to speak with his bodyguards. He dismissed them for the night, thanking them for their help, explaining that he wanted to see Emma on his own. He needed time alone to think things through on the drive over and he didn't want to show up at the hospital with an entourage. He'd had plenty of experience sneaking in and out of places—fame did that to a man, made him hunt for ways to go undetected. He borrowed Jeff's ball cap and his oversize gray sweat jacket as a disguise.

Dylan called Brooke back on the way to the hospital and told her the entire story. His little sister nearly broke down on the phone and he couldn't blame her. What had transpired was like something out of a bad B movie. But they were all safe, he assured her, and he told her to hang tight. He would be there shortly.

As the SUV's tires hit gravel on the way to the hospital, one thought continually nagged at him. How in hell was he going to make this up to Emma? He had no doubt he was responsible for her unhealthy state. She hadn't been eating well and she'd been terribly upset lately. All because he'd misjudged her and had the foolish notion that he couldn't love completely again.

At the hospital, he found Brooke sitting in a waiting room. She took one look at him, bolted up and flew into his arms, tears streaming down her face. "Dylan, my God… to think what could have happened to you. To Emma. I'm a freaking basket case."

"I know. I know." He brought her into his embrace and held on tight. Her face was pressed to his chest, her quiet sobs soaking his terrible disguise. "We're all going to be fine now, Brooke. The police have the guy in custody. He's not going to hurt anyone anymore."

"He murdered Roy."

"Yeah, he did." Dylan would have to live with that guilt the rest of his life. "How's Emma? I need to see her, Brooke. I need to tell her… I just have to see her."

Brooke pulled out of his arms, sniffled and gave him a somber look. How quickly she'd transformed into a mother hen. "Dylan, she's sleeping now. They gave her a sedative and she'll stay here for the night. She needs to rest and she especially needs no further drama in her life. Doctor's orders."

"I got that covered, sis."

"Are you sure? Because you can't mess with her, Dylan. She's not as strong as she looks. She's had a rough life. And she—"

"Brooke, I know what my *wife* needs."

Brooke's lips lifted in a smile and the defiance in her stern eyes faded. "And you're going to make sure she gets everything she deserves?"

"Yes. I've been a fool and I plan on rectifying that now. But I'm going to need your help. Are you willing to help me win my wife back?"

"Is it going to cost me her friendship?"

"No, it may even earn you a spot as godmother to the baby."

"Well, shoot. I've already got that in the bag."

"But you'll help me anyway because you love me?"

"Yeah, big brother. I'll help you. Because I love you *and* Emma."

Emma sat at her office desk and laid a hand on her belly, thanking God that her baby was thriving and growing as it should. The scare she'd had the night she went to the movies with Brooke couldn't happen again. She couldn't let her emotions get the best of her like that anymore. She was eating well now, drinking gallons of water a day, or so it seemed, and taking daily walks. All in all, she felt strong. Facing the future didn't frighten her as much as it once had. Emma adapted well and she was learning how the new life growing inside her only encouraged her own private strength.

"Look what just arrived for you," Brooke said, walking over with a vase full of fresh, snowy-white gardenias. "I love the way they smell."

"Your brother has a good memory." Emma admired the flowers Brooke set down on her desk. "Either that, or he's a good guesser. It's my favorite flower. You didn't tell him, did you?"

Brooke shook her head. "No. He must've remembered how you'd always ask Mom if you could pick a gardenia off the bush to put it in your hair. You'd wear it until the leaves turned yellow."

A fond memory. Emma smiled. "That's when the scent is sweetest."

Every day since her hospital stay, Dylan had done something thoughtful for her. The day she was released from the hospital, he'd sent her a basket of oils and lotions to pamper herself along with a gift certificate good for a dozen pregnancy massages with a message that simply read "I'm sorry."

Yesterday, he'd sent her an array of fresh fruit done up in the shape of a stork. It was really quite ingenious, with wings made of pineapple slices and cherries as eyes. Again, there was a note, which read "Forgive me."

And today, the flowers. She lifted the note card from its holder, her hand shaking. She wasn't over Dylan, not by a long shot.

He'd wanted to see her. To apologize in person, but she wasn't up to that yet. She needed time and strength and to make sure the baby was thriving again. She feared seeing Dylan would break her heart all over again. Luckily, because Brooke warned him off visiting her, he hadn't pressed her about it.

Brooke had already walked back to her desk. It wasn't like her *not* to nose around and ask what was going on. But then, Brooke's heart had been broken, too. She didn't believe in love anymore. Together, they were the walking wounded.

"I miss you," the note read.

Tears pooled in her eyes. The gifts were getting a bit much. Why was he torturing her like this? Didn't he know that she needed a clean break from him? That he owned her heart and soul and she was fighting like mad to take them back.

The capture of his stalker had made headlines and Dylan hadn't been back to work yet, according to Brooke. The investigation had shut down production at the studio for a few days. His adoring fans had been outraged at the murder attempt and the police thought it best for him to keep a low profile. Dylan had his hands full with news helicopters circling his home, reporters at his front gate and paparazzi trying to get glimpses of him. He'd hunkered down at his mansion on Moonlight Beach and had his publicist offer a statement, thanking the police for their diligence, thanking his fans for their support and asking for the press to abide by his privacy during this difficult time.

Emma, too, had been the source of news, especially since she'd been a target as well, and as Dylan's newly estranged bride, well...her life had become very public, very quickly. Emma refused to comment to the press and Dylan assigned Jeff to escort her to and from work each day to basically stand guard over her. It was weird having her own personal bodyguard, but she appreciated the gesture. No one had gotten near her, thanks to Jeff. Today, an equally juicy scandalous news story had broken and she hoped that she and Dylan were off the hook, at least for the time being.

This afternoon, she was working on a retirement party for a man who'd started his own business in foldable cartons back in the early 1950s. The exuberant senior citizen was finally retiring at the ripe young age of ninety-four, giving up the helm to his grandson. The party would be full of guests of all ages and she and Brooke worked tirelessly to throw an event that would encompass every one of the three generations attending.

Brooke turned away from her computer screen for a second. "Are you still on board for our meeting with the manager of Zane's on the Beach tonight?"

"Yep, I'll be there."

"Okay, he'll make time for us at around eight and we can go over the details for the party. I'll meet you there, though. I have to run a few errands after work."

"Sure. Jeff and I will meet you." Emma lifted her lips in a smile.

Brooke rolled her eyes. "It's for your own sanity, you know. Dylan's used to having a swarm of reporters dogging him, but you're not."

"The reporters have backed off. Dylan's probably getting the brunt of it."

"He can handle it. The press loves him. Especially now. Since his murder attempt they're treading carefully and trying to give him the space he needs."

"For his sake, I hope so," Emma replied. She'd lived in his world for a short time. There was never a time when people weren't gawking at him, sneaking peeks or flat out trying to approach him.

"Me, too," Brooke said. "Love that guy. I'll be forever grateful he wasn't hurt by that creep. I only wish…"

"What do you wish?"

"Nothing," she said, dipping her head sheepishly. "I've got to go." Brooke tossed her handbag over her shoulder and then bent to give Emma a kiss on the cheek. "See you later, Em."

Emma closed up shop at precisely five o'clock, exited by the back door and found Jeff waiting for her by her car. He stood erect in his nondescript black suit, waiting. When he spotted her, she put her head down, stifling a frown. "I'm going home to have dinner. And then I've got an appointment."

"Okay. I'll follow you home. What time are you going out again?"

"Seven thirty. And I want you to eat something before you come back. Promise?"

He nodded and a silly smile erupted on his face. She was mother henning him to death, but in some weird way she thought he actually liked her fretting over him. If she was a better liar, she'd tell him she was calling it a night and going to bed early, but with her luck, she'd get caught in the lie and then feel bad about it for weeks. So, the truth had to be served.

Once she got home and Jeff was on his way, she created a healthy chicken salad with vegetable greens, cranberries and diced apples. She took her food over to the sofa, plopped her feet in front of the television screen and turned on the news until a report came on about Dylan's would-be killer. She hit the off button instantly, shaking her head. She knew all she wanted to know about Craig Lincoln, Renee's homicidal ex-husband, thank you very much. Her stomach lurched, but she fought the sensation and ate her salad like a good mother-to-be.

After dinner, she walked into her bedroom, took off her clothes and stepped into the shower. Until the warm spray hit her tired bones, she didn't realize how very weary she was. For the past few weeks, she felt as if her emotions were on a wacky elevator ride going up and down, never really knowing where she was going or when it would finally stop. She lathered up with raspberry vanilla shower gel and lost herself in thought, allowing the soothing waters to take effect.

After her shower, she threw her arms through the sleeves of a black-and-white dress that belted loosely above her waist. There was no hiding her pregnancy any longer; her baby was sprouting and making its presence known. A cropped white sweater and low cherry heels completed her semiprofessional look. Next, she applied light makeup, eyeliner, meadow-green shadow and a little rosy lip gloss. The last thing she cared about right now was how she looked, but this was an important meeting.

She stepped out of her apartment at precisely seven thirty and there was Jeff, waiting for her. How long had he been standing guard outside her apartment? Gosh, she didn't really want to know.

"Hi again," she said.

Jeff stood at attention, his gaze dipping to her dress, and a glimmer of approval entered his eyes. Something warmed inside of her that she thought had been frozen out. She told him where she was headed.

"I know the place" was all he said.

She arrived at the restaurant a little before eight. She

didn't see Brooke's car in the parking lot so she waited until eight sharp and there was still no sign of Brooke.

She got out of her car, and Jeff did the same. It was dark now, except for the full moon and the parking lot lights. The roar of the ocean reminded her of Dylan and the time she'd spent living as his wife and she sighed. Fleeting sadness dashed through her but she had no time for self-pity. She had a client to meet.

Jeff did a thorough scan of the grounds as he approached her. "I'm meeting my partner here," she said, "but since it's already eight, I'd better go inside to start the meeting."

"I'll walk you inside."

"Is that necessary?"

He smiled. "It'll make me feel better."

She smiled at his comment. He'd taken a page from her mother-hen book. "Okay."

When they reached the front door, he opened it for her. "After you."

"Thank you." She stepped inside the restaurant and her heart seized up at the sight before her eyes. Hundreds of lit votive candles illuminated the empty space. "Oh, no. We must've gotten the date wrong. Looks like someone is setting up for a party," she said to Jeff.

When he didn't answer, she turned around. Jeff was gone. Vanished into thin air.

Her heart pumped harder now and she was ready to scurry away, when a figure walked out of the darkness into the candlelight—a man wearing a dark tuxedo with lush blond hair and incredible melt-your-soul blue eyes.

"Hello, Emma. You look beautiful."

Her hand was up at her throat. She didn't know how it got there. "Dylan?"

He smiled, eyes twinkling, and walked over to her. She nibbled on her lip, trying to make sense of all this, and when he took her hand and held on to it, as if for dear life, she was beginning to see, beginning to hope that she knew what all this meant.

"I've been a fool," he said.

Oh, God, yes. Not the fool part, but that, too. He was here for her. "Why do you say that?"

"Come," he said, pivoting around and guiding her with their hands still clasped to a table set for two overlooking Moonlight Beach. Roses and gardenias at the center of the table released an amazing sweet aroma. A chilled bottle of sparkling water sat in a champagne bucket, along with two flutes. The crystal glassware and fine bone china reflected the candlelight, added sparkle and a heavenly aura to the room. Right now, that's exactly how she felt: out of this world.

"As you might've guessed, there is no appointment for you to keep tonight. Just dinner with me."

She blinked and blinked and blinked. "You arranged all this?"

He nodded, but his smile seemed shaky and unsure, not the usual confident Dylan smile. "I know the owner."

Zane Williams. Of course. He'd attended their fateful wedding. "And I wanted to do something for you that was as special as you are, Emma."

"I'm not that special," she whispered.

"To me, you are. To me, you're everything I've ever wanted and it's taken me nearly losing you to that maniac to figure it out. When I thought you were in danger, I panicked and my thick head finally cleared. I was willing to do anything to keep you safe."

"Jeff told me you were ready to risk your life for me."

"Jeff, huh? Well, it's true. The thought of you getting hurt made me realize that my life, all of my success, everything I have now, would mean nothing if you weren't right there beside me. You and the baby. God, I've been so selfish, Emma. I only thought of what I'd lost when I found out you were carrying Roy's baby. But I never stopped to realize what I'd be gaining. Until I almost lost you."

"I was never in any real danger."

"Not that night, no. But if Renee hadn't called to warn me, things might've turned out differently. He threatened your life. He probably wouldn't have stopped until... I can't think about it."

"Well, I'm thankful to Renee for putting the pieces together."

Dylan nodded. "I owe her for that. And the best way to repay her isn't by sending her money. A friend of mine has a job waiting for her, as a personal secretary. She's going back to work and she's happy about it. The job pays well and she'll be able to hold her head up high again and support her family."

"Dylan, that's wonderful. You're giving her a second chance."

He nodded. "I hope so."

"You're a good man, Dylan."

"Good enough for you to give me a second chance?"

"Maybe," she said softly. "After the attempt on your life, I came to the hospital and made Brooke promise not to tell you. I wanted to see you so badly, but I didn't want my being there to upset you, so I stayed outside your room until I found out you were going to be okay."

"I wanted to see you. I'd hoped you would come."

"I didn't think it would be wise."

"Emma. I'm sorry for how I've behaved. I'm sorry about everything. I should've stopped you from walking out on me. I let you leave my house pregnant and alone to face an unknown future. I hope you can forgive me for being obtuse and selfish."

"I think I already have, Dylan. I couldn't hold a grudge when your life was in danger. And I've made mistakes, too. I shouldn't have lost my head and gotten so drunk that night that I didn't realize what was happening. I told you the baby was yours. It was only natural for you to be disappointed to find out the truth. I'm sorry you were hurt. Truly."

"Apology accepted. Now it's time for us to put those mistakes in the past and look to the future." Dylan went down on one knee then, and her out-of-this-world experience got *real*, really quickly. "Emma, I want to do this right this time. I love you with all of my heart. I love the child you're carrying, my best friend's baby, and it's my hope that we raise the baby together and—"

"Wait!" She put up her hand and the hope on Dylan's face waned. It wasn't that she hadn't heard him the first time or that she wanted him to stop, but she'd waited a long time for those words. They were worth repeating. "Can you say that again?"

"The I-love-you-with-my-whole-heart part?"

"That's the one."

"I do, Emma, I love you," he declared. "I didn't think I'd ever let myself love again. After Renee, it was just easier to have casual relationships with women. No risk, no injury. I guess it was a way of protecting myself from ever feeling that kind of pain again. I'm not making excuses, but for me, falling in love wasn't an option, mentally and emotionally. I wanted no part of it. Everything changed, though, when you became part of my life. Suddenly, everything I've ever wanted was right in front of me. It took a blackout and a baby to make me see it. It was a strange journey to be on, but I can't imagine my life without you and the baby in it. You're my family, and I see a wonderful future ahead for us. So, sweetheart, will you please come back home…to me? Be my wife, mother of our child. I propose for us to stay married and love each other until the end of time. Could you do that?"

Tears of joy streamed down her face. Dylan's proposal

was everything she'd ever wanted. She loved him beyond belief. How could she look at that man, see the truth in his humble blue eyes and not love him? "I can. I will. I love you, Dylan. And I want a life with you. That's all I've ever wanted."

On bended knee, he caressed her growing belly and placed a sweet kiss there. The outpouring of his love was evident in the reverent way he spoke about the baby, spoke of his love for her. She believed in his love now, believed in their future.

Then he rose to his full height, his gaze clouded with tears. "I love you, Emma. And our child. The best I can do is promise to share my life with you and try to make every day happy for our family. Is that enough?"

"More than enough," she whispered.

She was drawn into the circle of his arms and he bent his head to claim her mouth in a deep, lingering kiss. By the time he was through, her mind was spinning and only one fulfilling, delicious thought entered her head.

She'd finally claimed *dibs* on Dylan McKay. And quite fantastically, he'd also claimed dibs on her.

And that would be no darn secret anymore.

* * * * *

LET'S TALK
Romance

For exclusive extracts, competitions
and special offers, find us online:

f facebook.com/millsandboon

📷 @millsandboonuk

🐦 @millsandboon

Or get in touch on 0844 844 1351*

For all the latest titles coming soon, visit
millsandboon.co.uk/nextmonth